THE WAKE

GILBERT MORRIS

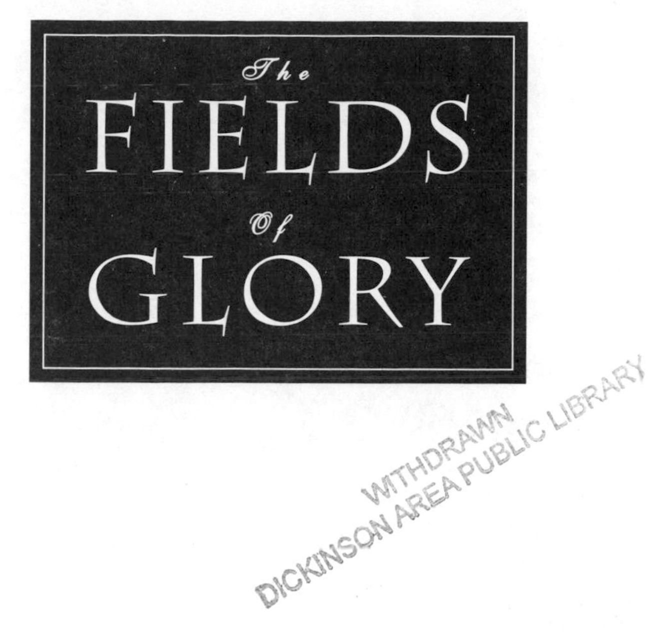

TYNDALE HOUSE PUBLISHERS, INC.
Wheaton, Illinois

Scripture quotations are taken from the *Holy Bible,* King James Version.

Library of Congress Cataloging-in-Publication Data

Morris, Gilbert.
The fields of glory / Gilbert Morris.
p. cm.—(The Wakefield dynasty ; 4)
ISBN 0-8423-6229-0 (sc : alk. paper)
1. Great Britain—History—Puritan Revolution, 1642–1660—Fiction.
2. Great Britain—History—Charles II, 16601685—Fiction. 3. Family—England—History—17th century—Fiction. I. Title. II. Series: Morris, Gilbert. Wakefield dynasty ; 4.
PS3563.08742F54 1996
813′.54—dc20 95-20576

Printed in the United States of America

99 98 97 96
5 4 3 2 1

To my niece Ginger Leach—

You're all grown up now, with a family of your own,

but I have fine memories of a beautiful, blonde baby girl

sitting on my lap and pulling my tie. You did grow up nicely!

And your uncle is proud of you!

CONTENTS

PART FOUR: THE CALLING—1670–1672

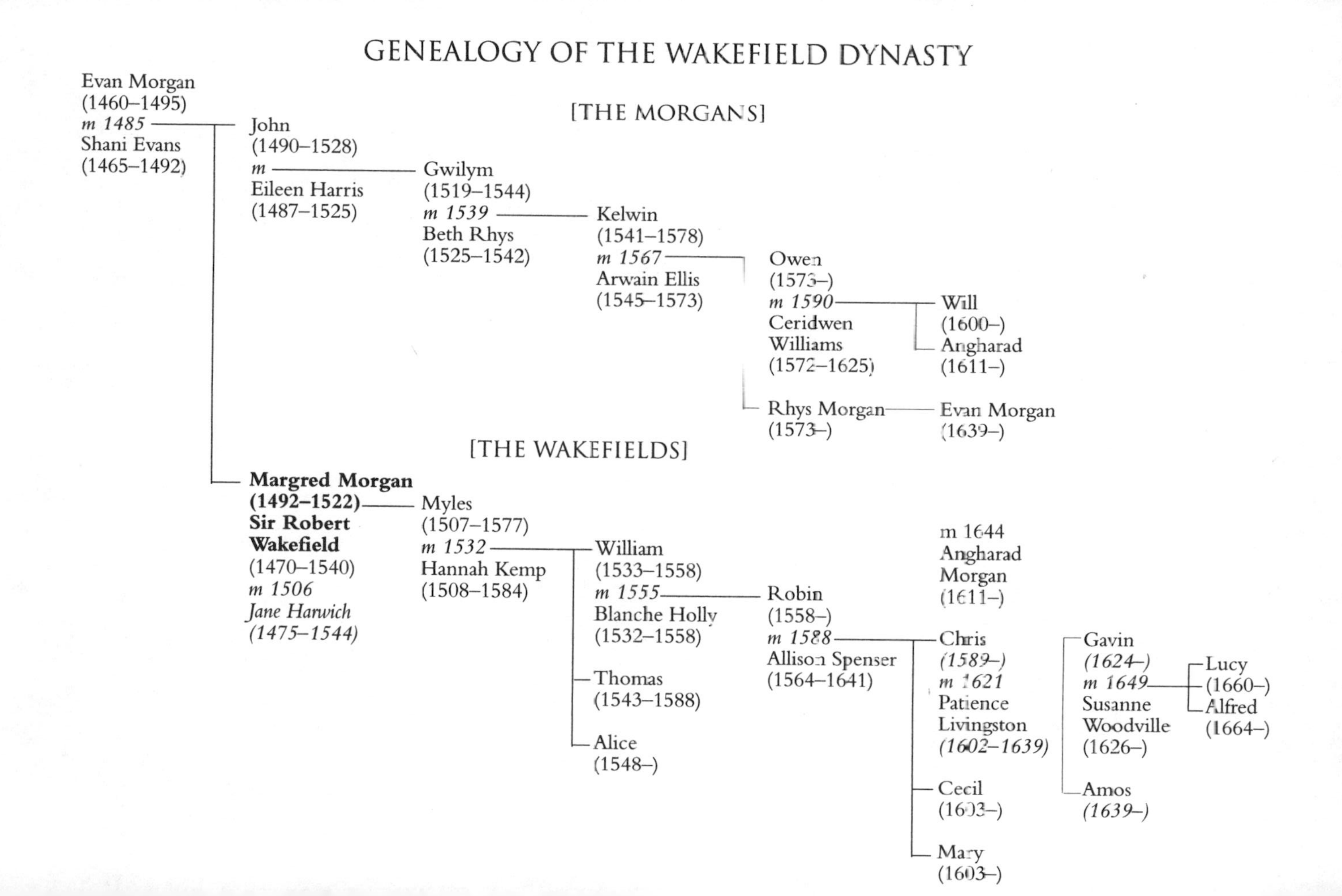
GENEALOGY OF THE WAKEFIELD DYNASTY
[THE MORGANS]
Evan Morgan
(1460–1495)
m 1485
Shani Evans
(1465–1492)
John
(1490–1528)
m
Eileen Harris
(1487–1525)
Gwilym
(1519–1544)
m 1539
Beth Rhys
(1525–1542)
Kelwin
(1541–1578)
m 1567
Arwain Ellis
(1545–1573)
Owen
(1573–)
m 1590
Ceridwen
Williams
(1572–1625)
Will
(1600–)
Angharad
(1611–)
Rhys Morgan
(1573–)
Evan Morgan
(1639–)
[THE WAKEFIELDS]
Margred Morgan
(1492–1522)
Sir Robert
Wakefield
(1470–1540)
m 1506
Jane Harwich
(1475–1544)
Myles
(1507–1577)
m 1532
Hannah Kemp
(1508–1584)
William
(1533–1558)
m 1555
Blanche Holly
(1532–1558)
Thomas
(1543–1588)
Alice
(1548–)
Robin
(1558–)
m 1588
Allison Spenser
(1564–1641)
m 1644
Angharad
Morgan
(1611–)
Chris
(1589–)
m 1621
Patience
Livingston
(1602–1639)
Cecil
(1603–)
Mary
(1603–)
Gavin
(1624–)
m 1649
Susanne
Woodville
(1626–)
Amos
(1639–)
Lucy
(1660–)
Alfred
(1664–)

1645 Part ONE 1659

Commonwealth

One

A Woman of Spirit

1645

Sudden wariness ran along Leah Grayson's nerves when she heard the sound of horses. Moving to the window, she peered out cautiously. At the sight of two heavily armed soldiers dismounting, her lips set grimly and she moved to bar the door. She had heard the sound of cannon rolling the previous day and knew that the battle was raging all around her home. Several bands of horsemen had passed earlier but none of them had stopped.

Why can't they leave us alone? Leah thought, anger rising as the voices grew louder. Her aunt and uncle had warned her about staying, speaking in dire tones about her being at the mercy of enemy soldiers. Even so, she had refused to leave the animals. Poverty had seared her too often in her young life. To lose the stock was more than she could bear.

"If any of Prince Rupert's men come, you will be in grave danger," her uncle had urged. "No woman is safe with them!"

"Let them lift a hand against me," she had replied, her eyes narrowing, "and they will find themselves on the wrong side of a pitchfork! God gave us this home and these animals, and I will not abandon them out of fear!"

The door shook and a loud voice shouted with a curse, "Open up!"

Apparently she was going to have the opportunity to test her brash words.

Surreptitiously Leah backed against the wall, her hands forming fists. *Father God,* she prayed, *give me wisdom . . . and courage!* She slipped from the room and hurried into the kitchen. As the front door shook beneath mighty blows, she glanced around, then went toward the table. Just as her hand closed around the handle of a butcher knife, she heard the front door burst open.

Quickly she moved to the doorway only to see a large man, sword in hand, enter her home. Behind him followed another man. Both wore the uniform of Rupert's crack cavalry.

"Well, what's this?" The larger of the two was a bulky man with a red face, most of which was covered by a thick auburn beard. His hair hung down his back in long ringlets—a style often affected by the Cavaliers—and his eyes were cruel. Turning to the other soldier he grinned. "Looks like we've got a prisoner, Matthew."

The other man was much smaller, with sharp foxy features. He advanced toward Leah, his slate blue eyes glittering. "Come now, missy, let's have what's in the house."

"There's no money, sir," Leah answered, her voice quiet but steady. "We are poor people."

"Don't lie to me, girl!" The soldier named Matthew moved like a striking snake, his hand shooting out to grasp the girl's arm. Leah forced herself to remain still, keeping the knife concealed in the folds of her skirt.

She would not use it unless they gave her no choice.

The man who held her peered at her through narrowed eyes. "We know you've hidden the silver. Don't take us for fools. Look around, Charles. You know these pigs."

"Right!" The larger man set his sword down and began to rummage through the small cottage, scattering the meager belongings roughly. He moved to the other room, tore it to pieces, then came out growling, "Nothing but rags and trash, Matthew."

"She's buried it then." Matthew fixed his eyes on Leah's face. "Look, girl, we're going to have what you've got, so give it up, eh? No sense making it hard on yourself."

Leah's face was pale but she answered him calmly. "I have already told you, sir, we have nothing."

Disgust swept Matthew's face and he reached out to grasp Leah's chin, forcing her head up. She met his eyes without flinching as he cursed her roundly, demanding that she reveal the hidden goods.

Charles peered into a pot that was sitting over a small fire. Wrinkling his nose, he said angrily, "Swill! Fit for pigs!" He moved across to where his companion was holding the young woman, and a sly expression came to his blunt features. He winked at his cohort. "Well, if she won't give us anything else, I guess she'll have to furnish us with a little entertainment, won't she?"

"Now there's an idea." Matthew grinned, moving his hand from Leah's face to her arm. Then he froze, his mouth falling open as he gaped at Leah, who had suddenly brought the knife up and was pressing the point against his throat. "What the—!" he sputtered, then clamped his mouth shut when Leah pressed the knife a bit deeper.

Charles made as if to grasp her arm, but she shot him a warning glance. "Unless you are ready to watch your friend die," she said, her voice cold, "you'll back away to the wall."

He looked uncertainly at Matthew, who squawked, "Do it, you fool! Before she slits me!"

Leah watched the soldier slowly move away until his back was against the wall. She met Matthew's eyes—and he felt a chill at the steel he saw reflected in the woman's gaze. "If you believe nothing else I've said," she told the man, her gaze never wavering from his, "believe this: I will use this knife in any way I must to protect myself." She increased the pressure slightly for emphasis, noting with satisfaction the way the man's eyes widened. *"Any* way. Now let me go."

The man slowly released her arm.

God, now what do I do? she prayed, feeling a bit desperate. Stopping their assault had been one thing, but how was she going to force these men to leave her home without any further trouble?

Suddenly another voice came from the doorway.

"Do you need any help here, miss?"

Startled, Leah turned her head in the direction of the voice, being careful to keep the knife in place. But as she did so, Charles took advantage of the distraction and lunged for his sword.

"Watch out!" Leah screamed to the newcomer, a tall young man who was dressed in the armor of Cromwell's outfit. Fortunately, he balanced a sword easily in his large hand. He was fully as tall as the larger of the two soldiers and there was something dangerous in the way he moved to meet the now-armed Charles.

"Lay down your weapon and we're quits," the young soldier said evenly. "If you don't, I'll be forced to cut you down."

At once Charles readied his sword, a rough grin on his loose lips. "We'll see who cuts who!" He moved forward, sword outstretched, and when he was close, cried out and swung it in a practiced motion—but it never touched his opponent, for the sword of the other whirled in a blurring motion and caught him squarely on the temple. Charles dropped soundless to the ground, the whites of his eyes showing, blood dripping from the cut in the side of his head.

The soldier turned to Leah, taking in the way she held Matthew captive. A smile crossed his face and an admiring look came into his eyes. "Well, you seem to have this one under control," he said.

Leah flushed and she could not keep a smile from curving her lips in response. "Actually, I would greatly appreciate you taking care of him for me," she said. "I find I tire of his company, yet I fear he will not leave of his own volition."

"Well, sir," the man said, pinning Matthew with his gaze. "What say you? Will you come along quietly to join the rest of Cromwell's prisoners, or shall I let the fair lady finish you off?"

Matthew's only reply was an enraged choking sound, for the pressure of Leah's knife effectively prevented him from speaking.

"Fine. I'm glad you surrender so willingly," the tall soldier said, his smile growing broader. "Now, if you'd be so kind as to hold out your hands?"

Matthew did so, and the young man pulled a piece of rawhide from his pocket, then pulled the scoundrel's hands behind his back and tied them securely. Only then did Leah lower the knife.

"Well met, my lady," the soldier said, grasping Matthew's arm and pushing him toward the still-unconscious Charles. He bound the motionless man's hands as well, then shoved Matthew to the floor beside his accomplice.

His prisoners secured, he turned and came toward her. "My name is John Bunyan. I'm in General Cromwell's army." He had a pleasant face and there was concern in his blue eyes as he asked, "Are you all right? They didn't harm you?"

"No, sir, by God's grace they did not."

Bunyan saw that while she was not an exceptionally pretty young woman, her features were even and she had a trim figure. She had mild brown eyes, and a wealth of chestnut hair had escaped from beneath her cap. There was a gentleness in her lips, and the smooth planes of her face lent a grace to her expression. She was not tall, and as she stood looking up at him, he thought there was something almost childlike about her. Still, the manner in which she had faced those men was anything but childish. He had no doubt she was a grown woman.

"Now then, I'm glad I came along," he said, nodding. "The rest of my squad are no more than half a mile away. I came to your house seeking something to drink—"

"Oh, we have a fine well! Let me draw you some fresh water!" Leah flew to the well and Bunyan followed her. As he drank the sweet, cool water, she related how her aunt and uncle had fled. "They entreated me to go with them, but I couldn't leave Lucy and Alice."

"Lucy and Alice?" Bunyan asked. "Are those your cousins?"

She laughed suddenly, two dimples appearing in her cheeks. "Oh no—that's the cow and the new calf! I couldn't leave them for the soldiers to butcher!"

He smiled in return, enjoying the sound of her laughter. "That's very good of you, and I'm sure Lucy and Alice are most grateful." Bunyan sat down on the well curb, listening as the young woman spoke. He was tired and the water was refreshing—and he had not spoken with a young woman for some time. He found her quite appealing and would have liked to stay longer, but he knew he could not. Shrugging the weariness from his broad shoulders, he said, "I must get these two to camp. Thank you for the water."

Leah looked up at him, her eyes warm. "And thank you for your help, sir. I was at a loss as to what I was to do next. I doubt I could have held those men at bay much longer without someone coming to a bad end. I am grateful that was not necessary. Indeed, I wish I could repay you." A thought came to her and she asked, "Perhaps you could stay for a meal? My uncle and aunt are hiding no more than a mile from here. I'll be going to get them right away, now that the war's over."

"Why, that's kind of you," Bunyan said and she saw sincere pleasure in his eyes. "I have to get back to the others, but I think we'll be in camp for a time. If I can get leave, I'll come and try your cooking. So long, of course, as you don't cook Lucy or Alice." He smiled down at her.

Leah returned his smile. "God must have sent you, Mr. Bunyan."

Surprised, Bunyan stared at her eager face. "Why, I don't know about that. I'm not a Christian man."

But Leah nodded, her eyes warm with assurance. "That matters not, for God uses all men as *he* chooses. And he surely sent you here to help me. Praise his name!"

Bunyan was attracted by Leah's simple faith. She had a winsome air, and he determined to get to know her better. "I accept your invitation, miss. I'll be back as soon as I am able." He loaded Charles's unconscious form on one horse, tied him down, then mounted the other horse and led the sullen Matthew down the road. When he glanced back, he saw the young woman standing and watching. She waved at him and as he returned the gesture, a smile creased his face.

Yes, indeed, that's a fine, courageous young woman! I'll be interested to find out if she can cook!

It had been three weeks since Prince Rupert's forces had been driven from the field of battle at Naseby. For Lieutenant Gavin Wakefield, the time had been blessedly peaceful. On this particular morning, he had mounted his horse and gone in search of his friend, John Bunyan. A strapping young man of seventeen, Bunyan was blessed with a ruddy face and a pair of bright blue eyes and was well known among the men for his cheerful disposition.

But the lieutenant's friendship with the young soldier stemmed from a far deeper reason: Bunyan had saved Gavin's life in an earlier battle. So it was, in the campaigns that followed, that

Wakefield had made it a point to keep an eye out for his new friend.

As he rode, Gavin's ash blonde hair blew gently in the breeze, and his blue-gray eyes searched the encampment. It wasn't long before he found Bunyan at the makeshift forge, where the younger man was busy mending a broken sword guard.

As Gavin swung down from the saddle, he said cheerfully, "Well now, John, how's your courtship going?"

John, whose ruddy face was made even more so by the heat of the forge, gave his friend a reproachful look. "Now, Lieutenant, I'd not call it that." He looked down and gave the glowing metal a few skilled taps, then plunged it into a tub of water. As it hissed, he turned back to Gavin, his face more sober than usual. "I've not got anything to offer a woman, so I can't go courting one, now can I?"

Gavin leaned against the towering elm tree that provided shade for Bunyan. The troop had been allowed to rest up, and he had enjoyed the leisure. Cromwell had left for London after the battle and discipline had relaxed. Now, as Gavin watched Bunyan's tall form, he realized he hadn't the least idea what a man of Bunyan's class thought of courtship. Being from a wealthy family, Wakefield knew only the ways of his own class. He lifted his eyes, and as Bunyan worked delicately on the metal guard, he asked, "What will you do when you go back to Elstow, John?"

"Go back to what I know, sir."

Gavin watched him silently, considering his next words carefully. "If you'd like, I can ask my father if we can use you at Wakefield. Lots of work there."

Bunyan looked up and smiled. "Now that's kind of you, sir. But my father is expecting me to help him."

"And what about a wife? Wouldn't you like to start a family of your own?"

"Like it or not, sir, I don't have anything to offer a woman. I'll certainly not ask someone I care for to share in my poverty."

Gavin nodded. Well he understood such reasoning. And yet . . . Bunyan seemed more than slightly interested in the young woman he'd been seeing. *Ah, well, it's none of your business,* Gavin told himself and went on to speak of other things.

Over the next two weeks, Bunyan visited Leah five times. He found himself looking forward more and more to their time together. Her home, or rather her uncle's home, was only four miles from the camp, so Bunyan often arrived as the sun was just touching the eastern hills. Generally he was met by Leah's uncle, a fine old man named Henry Jacobs. While Jacobs didn't much care for soldiers, he'd gotten to know Bunyan; the younger man's humor and character had won him over so that the two had become good friends. John had put his tinker's skills to good use for Jacobs, too. He had repaired anything that needed it. This only endeared him all the more to Leah and her uncle.

One Saturday Bunyan worked at the military camp until late afternoon, then asked permission to be relieved until morning. His sergeant grinned at him. "Tell the young woman hello for me, Bunyan. And bring me back one of her cakes like last time."

"I'll do that, Sergeant," he replied, a grin on his own face. He'd discovered long ago that his commanding officer had a weakness for home cooking. So he had made good use of Leah's talents, thus ensuring himself a positive response when he requested time off.

He made his way to the Jacobs' cottage, and after a fine supper, he accompanied Leah as she went to feed the stock. He helped her at her task, then led her to sit beneath an ancient oak where they rested in companionable silence and watched the stars.

Finally Bunyan turned to study Leah's face. "I'll be leaving next week," he said hesitantly.

"Leaving?" Leah turned to face him at once. "The army is moving out?"

"No, some of our troop has been discharged. I'll be going back to Elstow."

"Oh." Leah looked down at her hands for a moment, then whispered, "I'll—I'll miss you, John."

"Will you now?" His voice was teasing, though tender.

She looked up to meet his eyes reproachfully. "You know I will!"

The silver light of the moon bathed her face, making her look very young and almost pretty. She wore her best dress, and as he looked at her, John found himself speaking the thought that had been growing in him for many days.

"Leah, I don't have any money. Just my pay from the army. But I'm a good worker. Everybody says that."

Leah was silent, waiting for him to go on, but he looked away as if suddenly embarrassed. She reached out to lay her hand on his—it was the first time she had touched him so. He looked at her in surprise and she said softly, "You're the kindest man I've ever known, John."

Her words brought a light into Bunyan's eyes and he closed his hand around hers. "Leah . . . have you ever thought of me as a man you might marry?"

Leah nodded, then whispered, "Yes, I have."

John's heart seemed to sing and he pulled her into his arms. She was small and fragile, and her lips were soft and sweet as he kissed her. "I care for you very much," he said, drawing back. "We'll be poor, but you'll never know meanness from me. I will be a good and faithful husband to you."

"Oh, John!" Leah clung to him happily. She knew she was safe with this big man. "We'll have each other, and we'll have God!" She drew back and there were tears in her eyes as she said, "God sent you to me. That I know!"

John drew her close, and as she nestled against his side, he was filled with wonder that this woman—this wondrous treasure—was to be his. He leaned his cheek against her soft hair and whispered, "Yes, beloved, I know it, too. Come now, let's go tell your people."

Two

AMOS MEETS A TINKER

1650

Amos Wakefield hated being ten years old! He was permitted to do little that he wanted and forced to do a great many things that he hated. The latter included studying Latin and going to bed early, while the former included hunting with his hawk, which he had named Hook after the needle-sharp talons that the peregrine used to kill his prey.

One bright February morning, sick to death of conjugating meaningless Latin verbs—*amo, amas, amat*—he left his room and stealthily made his way down the stairs. He was nearly caught by one of the maids but managed to duck behind the full suit of armor that had belonged to a distant ancestor. When the maid passed by, Amos quickly left the house and made his way to the mews, where the birds were kept.

The mews, to Amos, was the second most important building on the grounds—the most important being the stables, where his horse, Destrin, was kept. The mews faced south and had very small windows that were covered with horn to protect the hawks from drafts. Amos knew every inch of the place, from the little fireplace at one end to the small room where the grooms met to clean the tack on wet nights after foxhunting.

Moving along quickly, the boy ignored the gear, which included a cauldron, a bench with all sorts of small knives, and shelves with pots on them. Coming to the bench that held the hoods and jesses, he studied them carefully. There was quite an assortment: old cracked hoods that had been made before Amos was born, tiny hoods for merlins, and small hoods for hawks. All were in Wakefield colors: white leather with green baize at the sides, surrounded by blue-gray heron feathers.

Amos picked up a hood, then turned to the birds. He ignored the two little merlins and the old tiercel goshawk. He slipped the gauntlet onto his hand, then reached forward. Hook at once lifted his wings and came to perch on the leather. His grip was so fierce that Amos could feel the mighty talons digging into his arm. A shiver went through him. *I wonder what it's like to be a bird or a mouse and feel those talons digging into you.*

He felt a moment's pity for the hawk's victims, but that was quickly overshadowed by his anticipation of the hunt. He made sure the hawk was secure on his arm, then left the mews. Thirty minutes later Amos was in a large open field west of the castle. He searched the skies for prey and soon saw a goose making its way south. Quickly the boy undid the hawk's leash and the swivel from the jesses. Hook at once roused, and Amos scratched his feet and softly teased his breast feathers upward.

"Come now, let me see what a royal bird can do," he whispered fondly. Then he cried, "So-ho!" and threw his arm upward to give the raptor a better takeoff. Hook's mighty pinions beat the air, driving him upward until he was a mere dot in the sky. He passed the goose in his ascent, then wheeled. As always when a hawk readied to take his prey, Amos's heart seemed to beat like a drum! He watched as the peregrine dove and hit the goose, sending feathers flying. The force of the blow killed the larger bird instantly, and Hook circled, giving a shrill cry as the body of his prey fell to the earth.

Amos ran through the briars, barely noticing when he received a wicked scratch across his cheek. When he arrived at the body of the goose, Hook had just ripped out a beakful of feathers.

"Good!" Amos cried out. He quickly reached down and despite Hook's reluctance, replaced the hood and took the bird on his arm. "I'd like to give you that goose for breakfast," he explained as he made his way back to the field, "but if you stuffed yourself, you'd have no reason to attack anything else, would you now?"

The eager boy stalked the woods for an hour, watching with pleasure as Hook took a pigeon and a woodcock. The sun was rising higher when Amos finally turned regretfully toward home.

"Back to that old Latin, Hook!" he complained. He stroked the hawk's silken feathers, adding, "I wish *I* was a hawk. *You* never have to study anything but killing, do you?"

He hurried down the pathway to the castle and was relieved to see that no one was in the mews to note his arrival. Quickly he moved inside and went straight to Hook's perch. He removed the bird's hood and, when the hawk stepped to the perch attached his leash.

"This doesn't look like studying Latin to me."

Startled, Amos wheeled and saw his father standing in the shadows. "Oh—Father!" He swallowed hard. "I—I didn't see you."

"No, you were too busy with Hook."

Amos was not exactly *afraid* of his father but there were times—like now, when he'd been disobedient or willful—when something akin to fear came over him. His mind raced as he tried to think up some sort of excuse that might get him past the crisis, but nothing came. Putting his hands behind his back, he twisted them and waited for his father to speak.

"I'm disappointed in you, Son."

Amos looked up quickly, noting his father's wedge-shaped face was sad. Christopher Wakefield was sixty now and time had worn him down. His auburn hair was streaked with gray and there were lines around the eyes and broad mouth that spoke of enduring hardship. But Chris's eyes were the same as in his youth: dark blue and luminous. They were a perfect reflection of the eyes of the boy who stood pinned by his father's gaze.

As he met his father's eyes, Amos knew he could not lie. "I disobeyed you, Father," he said, holding his head up high.

"Yes, you did."

"You—you can use the cane on me if you like."

Christopher's lips were set in a stern line, but Amos's unexpected offer caused them to turn up at the corners. Wakefield dearly loved his younger son and often saw his own youth in the lad. He studied the sturdy figure, the dark red hair with the slight curl—so like his own at that age—and the pugnacious chin. He knew his son had inherited more than just his physical likeness, for Christopher had been a rebellious young man as well.

He studied Amos's serious face for a moment, then asked, "Would caning you stop you from disobeying me?"

"No, sir, I suppose not."

Christopher laughed aloud at the admission. "Well, then I won't do it."

Relief washed over the boy's face, but Chris was glad to see there was still regret in his son's young eyes as he looked up at him. "I am sorry, Father. I promise I'll do twice as much work on that old Latin as a punishment!"

"Just what I was about to suggest." Christopher moved over and touched the peregrine's fierce head. "Did he fly well, Son?"

"Oh yes, sir!"

Christopher listened as the boy, his features glowing with excitement and pleasure, described the hunt. As much as he enjoyed his son's animated recounting, he found himself overwhelmed with a sense of fatigue and went to sit down on a three-legged stool. Though he had mentioned it to no one—not

Angharad or the doctor—Christopher knew all was not well. His heart had been behaving strangely for the past six months. At rare times a pain would strike him in the chest—as if a sword were being driven in up to the hilt. More often, as was happening at that moment, he had a strange *hollow* feeling inside his chest, as though he had suddenly grown very fragile. He always sat still until the feeling passed, bringing in its wake a sick, gray emptiness, which washed over him now as he sat listening to Amos.

Christopher was careful not to let the pain or discomfort show on his face; he did not want to worry his family. Finally Amos ended his tale and Christopher smiled at him fondly. "I'll have to go hunting with you soon. We haven't done that for a long time."

"Tomorrow?"

"If I can, and if you do your Latin."

"Father, tell me about the king," Amos said abruptly.

A shadow crossed Christopher's face, and he sat silently for a long moment. He could well understand the boy's interest, for nothing had ever happened in England like the execution of King Charles I. Kings had died in battle, had even been murdered by assassins, but never had one been slain as a criminal!

"I marked the calendar," Christopher said slowly, looking directly into his son's eyes. "On January 30, 1649, England executed her king."

Amos stared at his father's face, noting how sad he seemed. "But he was a—a man of blood. That's what they all say."

"Charles was not a perfect man, Son, but which of us is? But he was not a criminal, either. And now . . . now who is the man of blood?"

It was a question that would rack England for years. Cromwell and parliament had come to believe that only the king's death could restore the stricken land; others, men such as Christopher Wakefield, were convinced that Charles's death would never bring peace to England.

"Did he die well, sir?"

At first the question startled Christopher; then he realized he himself had instilled into both his sons the importance of facing death with courage. He hesitated to answer—but it was important for Amos to know the truth of the matter.

"Yes, he died well," he said. "He walked out to the scaffold without a sign of fear. I am told he wore two warm shirts, saying that he did not want to tremble from the cold lest men think he was afraid."

"That was bold, sir!"

"Yes, indeed, it was. The king's attendant let it be known that when he was awakened to meet his death, he said, 'This is my second marriage day. I would be as trim today as may be, for before tonight I hope to be espoused to my blessed Jesus.'" Christopher shook his head, adding, "I must believe that he knew God, Amos. He did many foolish things but deep down he felt that God had chosen him to be king of England."

One of the hawks loosed a raucous cry and man and boy turned to look at him. Amos said abruptly, "When Hook killed the goose this morning, I wondered what it was like to die."

"We all wonder that at times," Christopher answered. "To my mind, the dying is the hard thing. I don't fear to meet my Savior, but dying is something a man can't practice. Yet we must all do it. 'It is appointed to man once to die, but after this the judgment.' Even knowing this truth, the flesh shrinks from the act of dying." He looked across at the boy. "Wakefield men and women all have died well, Son. When your turn comes, I am sure you will meet it with courage."

Amos stared at his father. "Yes, sir, I'll try."

Christopher knew a burst of pride in this son of his and he smiled as he continued speaking. "On the day of the execution, the weather was cold. But the king didn't seem to notice. With his silver beard and hair, and his straight carriage and calm features, he looked every inch a king. And when he spoke, his stammer was gone! That was a miracle, for he always had a stammer."

"What did he say?"

"He said that he desired the liberty and freedom of the people—but he also said that such things mean men must have government. He was right about that, Son! We will see hard times in learning that lesson."

"What else did he say, Father?"

"Why, he said that he forgave those who had brought him to death and that he was putting aside a corruptible crown for one that was incorruptible."

The scene flashed before Christopher's eyes, and he shut them as he said, "He took a small white cap from his chaplain and put his hair under it. Then he raised his hands and eyes to heaven and prayed."

"Did the people pray with him?"

"Many of them did. I did. Finally he slipped off his cloak, knelt, and laid his head down on the block. The executioner made sure his hair was not in the way, and the king said, 'Wait for my sign.' Then a deep silence fell over the crowd. The king stretched out his hand—and it was done!"

A pained expression appeared on Christopher's face and he whispered, "The marshal picked up the head and held it high. He said, 'This is the head of a traitor!' But when the axman struck, a groan went over the crowd. It was a terrible thing!"

Amos had always been against the king, for he greatly admired Oliver Cromwell. But seeing the grief on his father's face, he said, "I feel sorry for the king."

Christopher rose and put his hand on the boy's shoulder. "I hope you'll always feel compassion for those who suffer loss, Amos. It's the mark of a *real* man. Any man with a strong arm can hack another man who is weaker to bits, but to know grief for those who suffer, that is the mark God seeks!"

"Yes, sir!" Amos whispered, not really understanding, but glad that his father was pleased with him.

Christopher smiled, glad that he'd been able to speak with this young son of his in such a fashion. "Now, to your Latin, you rascal. Off with you!" As the boy ran out of the mews, Christopher felt a stab of pain in his chest and a gasp escaped his lips. He stood there enduring the pain, sweat beading on his forehead, and the thought came to him: *Whatever I want to pass along to Amos, I must do it quickly.*

"Well, a birthday, is it?" Will Morgan smiled at Amos, who had come to the stable. "How old is it you are? I've forgotten."

"Eleven." Amos nodded, but grinned at his uncle. "You haven't forgotten, Uncle Will. You never do."

Will Morgan, the older brother of Angharad Morgan, was fifty years old, but his hair was still coal black and his Welsh accent unchanged from the day he'd come to Wakefield. He'd been a servant to Sir Robin Wakefield; a friend and tutor to Robin's grandson, Gavin; and now was passing his earthy wisdom along to the newest generation. Reaching into his pocket, he pulled out a package and handed it to the boy. "Happy birthday, Amos."

Amos ripped the paper away and stared down at the fine steel knife that lay in his hand. "It's the one I wanted!" he exclaimed, his eyes big.

"Well, no point in giving a fellow a knife he *doesn't* want, is there now?" Will accepted the boy's fervent thanks, then said, "Now, saddle that pony of yours. Mr. Gavin is taking you with him to Elstow, I hear."

"Yes, and after that we're going to London!"

"Well, I'll tell him to keep an eye on you." Will grinned. "I don't want you falling off your horse like you did last week."

"It wasn't my fault!" Amos protested, but Will laughed and left the stable. He ambled across the ground and entered the house, going to find his sister, who was dressing his niece. He watched her affectionately, then said, "Amos is going to pop, I think. Never saw a boy so excited."

Angharad Wakefield had married late, but at the age of thirty-nine she had a rich Welsh beauty that many ladies of the court would have given much to possess. Her luxurious black hair hung down her back in waves and she had regained her figure after Hope's birth.

Christopher's two sons, Gavin and Amos, were thrilled with their new sister. And with their new mother as well. Though they missed their own mother at times, both had come to think of Angharad in the fondest terms. Indeed, within a year of their father's remarriage, both Gavin and Amos had gladly named Angharad "Mother," for the love this new family shared was deep and strong.

Now Angharad's eyes sparkled gaily as she smiled at her brother and said, "Gavin said the boy just wore him down. He wouldn't take no for an answer."

"Be good for them to be together." Will nodded. "The boy needs to spend time with men." He paused, then asked, "How's Christopher?"

A shadow passed over Angharad's face. "Not too well. He's not sleeping and sometimes he has pain—though he never admits it to me."

Will watched the emotions play across his sister's face and his heart was moved for her. They had been through much together and understood one another well, so she was little surprised when he murmured, "You're worried about him."

"Aye." The simple answer was typical; Angharad was not a great talker. Her Welsh nature was reflected in her quietness, in an almost mystic nature that seemed tuned to the inner world of the Spirit. Now, as she held her small daughter to her breast, her eyes filled with an emotion she could not hide.

Will knew she was struggling—and that she preferred not to speak of it. And so he sat there, talking with her of other things for some time. Finally he rose, his dark eyes somber as he studied his sister. "I'm thinking Christopher is in need of a touch from the good Lord, Angharad. We will agree on a healing touch, yes?"

She smiled at him, her confidence in her God shining from her eyes. "Yes, and God will answer!"

"Tell me again how Mr. Bunyan saved your life, Gavin."

Gavin laughed and shook his head. "That I will not! You know the story by heart, Amos."

The two were riding down High Street and Gavin pointed toward a cottage set almost on the edge of the street. "There's the Bunyan house. Come along now and mind your manners."

Amos gave his elder brother an irritated look. "My manners are as good as yours!"

"Are they now? Well, we'll see."

Gavin had received word that Bunyan's wife had had her baby, and he had decided to stop on the way to London to congratulate the couple. He had seen Bunyan only once since coming home from the army and so was glad for this opportunity to visit with his friend.

The two brothers pulled up their horses in front of the whitewashed cottage and dismounted. Tying the reins securely to the post, they went to the door. Amos knocked and the door opened almost at once. A trim young woman stood there, her face framed in chestnut curls, mild questioning in her brown eyes. She smiled at them. "Hello, may I help you?"

"Mrs. Bunyan? I'm Gavin Wakefield and this is my brother, Amos."

Leah Bunyan's eyes widened and a slight flush washed over her cheeks. Gavin wagered she had not expected a pair of wandering aristocrats to suddenly appear on her doorstep. But to her credit, she hesitated only for a moment, then opened the door wide. "Mr. Wakefield, what a pleasure! John's spoken of you so often. Come in, please."

As the pair entered, Leah said, "I'll get John. He's out in the back, mending a wagon." She disappeared, only to return with Bunyan following her, his eyes lit up with surprised pleasure.

"Why, Mr. Wakefield, I'm glad to see you, sir!"

Gavin shook Bunyan's hand and introduced Amos. "We're on our way to London, but I had to stop and offer our congratulations, John."

"That's kind of you," Bunyan said, smiling. Turning to Leah, he said, "Well, Wife, bring the little one."

Leah moved to a small cradle, picked up the bundled baby, then came to stand before the two. Gavin reached out and pulled the blanket away from the face. "Why, it's a fair one!" He smiled. "What name did you give him?"

Bunyan smiled. "Mary," he said.

"Oh, a girl, is it? Well, Mary. Let's hope she grows up to be as pretty as her mother!" He turned to Amos and said with a twinkle in his eyes, "What do you think of this baby?"

The boy peered at the baby's face and struggled to find something to say that would not offend the parents. The child looked red and wrinkled and ugly, so he finally gave up and fibbed. "Very pretty," he mumbled.

Leah fixed tea and Amos listened as the two men talked of their time in the army. He studied the baby, who woke up and cried for a time, and wondered if he'd been as homely when he was little.

Finally the two men walked outside and Leah turned to Amos, asking him questions about his home and himself. He was bashful, but she was so interested that he found himself telling her about his horses and hawks. While he spoke he found himself watching the baby's face intently. Something about her troubled him, though he couldn't say what it was.

Leah saw the boy staring at her daughter but said nothing. Finally the two men came back and soon Gavin said, "We must be off to London." The two made their farewells and soon were on the road.

Gavin was silent and there was a troubled look on his face. After a time, Amos asked, "What's the matter? Is something wrong?"

"I'm concerned about my friend John," Gavin said slowly. "He's struggling with God." Seeing the puzzled look on his young brother's face, he added, "He doesn't know the Lord, Amos. He's fearful for his soul."

"Why doesn't he just get baptized and become a church member?"

Gavin gave Amos a sharp look and his voice was tight. "Do you think that's all there is to knowing God, Amos? I'm surprised at you."

Amos felt the rebuke and said no more, but when they put up at an inn for the night, Gavin brought the issue up again.

"Knowing God," he said as they were preparing for bed, "means that a person turns from his sins, asks God to forgive him, and trusts in Jesus as his savior. John Bunyan won't give up his sins."

Amos's forehead creased in a confused frown. "What kind of sins?"

"Nothing really vile," Gavin answered. "He's got a bad habit of cursing and he gambles some. But it doesn't matter *what* sins a man has. The question is, will he give them up no matter what they happen to be?"

The two got into bed and Amos pulled the heavy comforter up to his chin as his brother continued.

"There's another thing that grieves me about John. It's about the baby, Mary."

Amos yawned, then looked at his brother curiously. "What's wrong with her, Gavin? Is she sick?"

"No, Amos. She's blind."

Amos felt a shocked sadness at this news and turned his face into his pillow. Gavin seemed so pained, so concerned, that Amos wasn't sure what to say, so he said nothing. Silence fell on the room and Amos was nearly asleep when Gavin said sadly, "A heavy burden rests on John Bunyan and his good wife in caring for their baby. I'm afraid it's made John doubt God's mercies."

Three

Bunyan Has Bad Dreams

Since his marriage, John Bunyan had gone on with his daily work as a tinker, traveling about the district, calling at big houses and making repairs from his horse-drawn cart. At times he hammered away in the lean-to shed attached to his little thatched cottage. And yet, as occupied as he was with working on pots and pans, certain unwelcome thoughts echoed incessantly in his head. Ever since he had faced death while serving in Cromwell's army, a terror had come to lurk deep within Bunyan's spirit.

He said nothing of this to Leah; he did not want to disturb the happy tone of his married life. Though his wife had brought with her no dowry, she had brought a treasure into the tinker's life, a legacy that had been both a blessing and a curse: her godly spirit and two books on religion. The blessing was the daily life with a woman who sought to serve and follow Christ; the curse was that her two small books warned in graphic terms of the doom of sinners. One book, *The Practice of Piety,* was unbelievably gruesome in its depiction of the condition of the damned. While these descriptions disturbed Bunyan greatly, he and Leah continued to explore the passages illustrating the miseries of a man who was about to die but had not been reconciled to God and Christ.

The other book, *The Plain Man's Pathway to Heaven,* dealt with subjects such as sin, salvation, and especially damnation. Bunyan found this work easier to read because the arguments put forward were not as vitriolic as those in the other. Even so, the message was clear: to die without God is to be consigned to a horrific eternity.

John and Leah would sit and read these two books for hours. Because Bunyan kept his fears and inner torment to himself, Leah had no idea how distressed he was. She urged him to go to church, which he did, but he found no comfort there, continuing to see himself as a vile sinner.

Then, when Bunyan's daughter Mary was almost two years old, the nightmares began. John had never dreamed much, yet now there came to him such terrifying and frightening dreams that before long he dreaded to go to bed at night. Sometimes he tossed so frantically that Leah, frightened, awakened him, begging to know what was the matter. Bunyan, however, did not tell her the nature of the nightmares. He simply insisted they were bad dreams.

He began to find himself doing and saying strange things. For quite some time he had rung the five bells in the church tower. He enjoyed this activity both because of his occupation as a tinker and because he felt the joyful sound of the bells was a kind of symbol of peace with God. Suddenly, for some inexplicable reason, he came to believe that his bell ringing would send him to hell. He well knew that there had been a man, another bell ringer, who had been struck dead by lightning in a church in the north of the county while ringing a bell. Though his mind did not believe such would happen to him, his spirit was plagued by an unreasoning fear.

One day he stood looking up at the bell tower, preparing to go in, when he was overwhelmed by terror. *I can't go in and ring the bells!* he thought and his hands began to tremble. As he looked up, the tower seemed to topple over, almost as though he were in another nightmare. He turned and fled. Later, when Leah asked him why he had stopped ringing the bells, he simply said, "Oh, it grows tiresome." Yet the idea of heavenly joybells remained for him a symbol of peace with God and he could not think of them without longing to know that peace.

Sometime after this, he became so convicted about his swearing that he tried valiantly to quit. He was aware that his swearing was not as bad as that of many others, yet he too freely took the name of God in vain. Though Leah was convinced John needed to cut his swearing out of his life, she had no idea of the terrible conflict going on within her husband, because he concealed it well. Indeed, she would have been sorely distressed had she known how often at night he would awaken, feeling as though he were sinking into a bottomless pit.

So, on they lived, Leah delighted with her daughter, grieved by the little girl's blindness, yet drawn even closer to the Lord and the child because of it; John hard at work, keeping up the appearance of calm on the surface, yet swept within his heart and spirit by turbulent storms of fear and uncertainty.

One day Bunyan took the afternoon off, saying, "I think I'll take a walk along the village green, Leah. I'll be back in time for supper."

She came to him and put her hands on his shoulders. She was proud of this man of hers, and marriage had given her a warm, placid spirit and a touch of beauty. She stroked John's cheek and said, "All right, John. When you come back we'll take Mary out for a walk."

"Fine. I'll look forward to that."

Leaving the cottage, Bunyan hurried to the green and there found some of his friends in a game of tipcat. He watched the rather simple game for a while, noting the skill of those who tipped the "cat," which was nothing more than a piece of wood hit with a specially shaped stick. One man in particular was especially adept at the game, tipping the cat expertly with the stick, tossing it into the air and keeping it aloft with sharp, hard blows.

John's friends welcomed him and he played the game with them for some half an hour. It was a brisk September day. The wind was growing cool and Bunyan knew that winter lurked just over the hills. His ruddy face glowed with pleasure and for a time he put away his fear of hell and damnation and simply enjoyed himself.

Finally, he reached down with the stick and tipped the cat with his usual ease and then, just as he was about to strike the stick a second time, a voice seemed to dart from heaven into his soul: *Wilt thou leave thy sins and go to heaven, or have thy sins and go to hell?*

Bunyan froze. The block of wood fell to the ground unnoticed and his mind seemed to be paralyzed. Ignoring the voices of his friends, which urged him to try again, Bunyan looked up toward heaven—and there he thought he saw the Lord Jesus Christ looking down. It was not a visual thing, he knew that plainly, but somehow an image of the Savior's face—stern and unyielding—formed in his heart and in his mind.

Bunyan began to tremble, and then the Lord Jesus spoke, his voice harsh as he repeated, *Wilt thou leave thy sins and go to heaven, or have thy sins and go to hell?*

John never knew how he got home. So stunned was he by what had happened that he paid no heed as he walked past the houses on the way back to his own little cottage. Over and over again the words echoed in his mind: *Wilt thou leave thy sins and go to heaven, or have thy sins and go to hell?*

By the time he reached the cottage his trembling had increased until he shook almost violently. He entered the large room that served as kitchen, dining room, and family room, and fell into a chair.

Startled, Leah turned from the fireplace to scan her husband's ashen face. "What is it, John?" she cried in alarm. Quickly she came to him, took his chin, and lifted his head. His ruddy face was pale and his lips were trembling. "What is it?" she cried. "Are you ill?"

Bunyan whispered, "I'm damned to hell, Leah! There's no hope for a man like me!"

Leah stared at him, aware at last that here was a man under a heavy burden. She took his hands and sat down beside him. "If you are condemned, John," she said quietly, "there is hope. The Lord Jesus died for sinners. If you be a sinner, then it was for you he died."

Bunyan sat, trying to listen, but fear seemed to cloak his mind in confusion. This was no nightmare, he knew, this was *real;* he stood under the condemnation of God.

Later, after John had gone to his shop to try to work a bit, Leah pulled off her apron, put on her warm coat, and left the cottage. She carried Mary in her arms and found her way to the small church at Elstow. Pastor John Gifford, who was in his office, rose at once as she entered.

"Why, Mrs. Bunyan," he said, surprised, for though she was a regular attendant in services, she had never come before to his office. "It's good to see you," he began and then, looking carefully at her, saw that she was troubled. "What is it? Is someone ill?"

"No, Pastor Gifford, it's John," Leah said. "He's fallen under the terrible burden of his sin."

John Gifford was a short, muscular man with dark blue eyes and willful black hair. He was a fine preacher, although in his youth he had been rather wild. He had endured the wars and now had come as pastor of the church and the people had welcomed him gladly.

"Sit down, Mrs. Bunyan," he said quickly. She did so, holding the child in her arms, and Gifford listened carefully as Leah related the scene that had taken place in her kitchen. When she finally ended and sat staring at him hopefully, he said, "I must admit I'm a little surprised. I had thought that John knew the Lord. He seemed such a good man."

"So I thought, as well," Leah said, her lips trembling. "But, oh, if you could have seen his face, Pastor Gifford! Not a drop of color in it. And his hands were trembling. He's frightened to death."

Gifford leaned forward, his eyes bright. "That's a good sign," he assured Leah quickly. "It proves God is speaking to him, and the Holy Spirit is bringing him under conviction for his sin."

"Will you talk to him, Pastor Gifford?"

"Certainly! Certainly!" Gifford swept from his chair, picking up his Bible from his desk and turning to smile at Leah. "If you'll allow me to accompany you home, perhaps now would be a good time. I don't like to put these things off."

"Oh yes!" Leah rose at once, and the two of them left the church.

When they arrived at the cottage, Bunyan looked up with surprise at the pastor. "Why, Pastor Gifford," he said, and then he halted, his eyes going to Leah.

"John, I want you to talk to Pastor Gifford," she said, meeting his gaze calmly. "I'll go in the bedroom with Mary so the two of you can be alone."

As soon as she disappeared with the child, Gifford said, "Mr. Bunyan, your good wife has told me that you are having a difficult time. I'd like to help you with it, if you'd let me."

Still shaken by his experience on the green, Bunyan looked at the pastor and drew in a steadying breath. He liked and respected John Gifford more than he'd ever liked any minister. After a moment, he nodded and said in a troubled voice, "I need help, Pastor Gifford, badly."

The two men sat down, and for over an hour Gifford wrestled with the problem. It became evident that Bunyan suffered under a rather common delusion: that he was not chosen by God to be one of the saints. Bunyan wanted God, this he openly confessed, but he said, "The Bible plainly says, does it not, Pastor, 'The elect are chosen by God'? Well, how am I to know if I am one of the elect?"

Gifford had wrestled with this before, both in his own life and in dealing with others. "It's a difficult thing to understand, John," he said gently. "There are certain passages that seem to indicate none of us have any choice, that God himself decides who will be saved. I don't understand this fully, nor, I think, does any man." He leaned forward, his dark eyes intent on the rawboned tinker. "But I urge upon you one Scripture: 'Whosoever will may come.' *Whosoever,*" he urged. "That means everyone, wouldn't you say, John?"

With this and many other words and Scriptures, the pastor spoke fervently. However, something in Bunyan blocked a response.

Finally he looked away, his expression bleak and hopeless. "I suppose I'm just stupid, Pastor Gifford. But I do ask you to pray for me."

Gifford rose, disappointment heavy in his heart. Shaking his head, he cautioned Bunyan, "John, the one that's keeping you from Christ is wearing your hat. Your obstacle is none other than John Bunyan himself. I urge it upon you. The Scripture says, 'Come unto me, all ye that labor and are heavy laden, and I will give you rest.' Think on that Scripture. Put it in your mind when you go to bed tonight. Perhaps God will speak to you. I pray so."

After Gifford left, John called Leah from the bedroom. She came to him, her eyes studying his face. "Have you received any help, dear?"

John sat down at the trestle table, locked his fingers before him, and stared at them. "I'm a lost man, and unless God, in his mercy, speaks to me, there is no hope."

Their supper was unusually quiet that night, and Bunyan said finally, "I think I'll go to bed early."

Leah nodded in understanding, so the two sat down together and she read a passage of Scripture from their worn Bible. Bunyan listened listlessly. He felt drained of all energy, all strength, as though he could barely keep himself awake. He struggled to listen and take in the words of the Scripture, but he felt as though he were in a dense fog. When his wife had finished reading, he arose and went to the bedroom.

When Leah had gotten Mary into bed, she came into the room and saw that her husband was asleep. *I hope he doesn't have any of those awful nightmares,* she thought as she slipped into the bed beside him.

"Wake up! Wake up, John Bunyan!"

Bunyan stirred in his sleep. The sudden voice was harsh and implacable. Opening his eyes he saw a tall, angular shape in front of him. A hazy mist seemed to fill the room, and he could not tell whether he was asleep or awake. He could not even turn his head to see if Leah lay beside him. His strength seemed to be gone and he could only manage to mutter, "Who . . . who are you?"

"Hategood is my name. I think you know me well."

Bunyan stared at the shrouded figure and was repelled by the creature's grotesque face, which was twisted with hatred.

"What do you want with me?" Bunyan whispered.

Hategood stepped closer. There was a frightful odor about him that made Bunyan want to shrink back. He tried to move, but suddenly he was bound in place by iron chains. Terror rose in his heart and he cried out, "What do you want with me?"

"I've come to show you something."

"Show me what?"

"I've come to show you a dark room, John Bunyan."

With that, the room began to spin wildly. Then John felt a cold hand on his forehead turning his head until he was staring at what seemed to be a man confined in a small room. Hategood whispered, "You see that man? Look at him! You know him, don't you?" The specter seemed to laugh deep in his chest. "You see yourself as you are, Bunyan. Look! Do you hear that? Cursing! Cursing the God you claim you want to love and serve!"

Bunyan struggled against the cold hand that still held his head, forcing him to look at the figure. "No!" he cried. "No! That's not what I want to be! That's what I hate most of all."

Hategood's grip tightened. "Ah, but that's what you are, that nasty little fellow you keep captive deep in that poisonous heart!" Again the scratchy laugh. "Oh, you keep close watch, don't you? Pretending to be a saint. Going to church." Again the grip tightened. "That oh-so-godly image is not you! There!" He pointed, forcing Bunyan's head forward again. "You keep that dirty, filthy-mouthed beast under lock and key, but deep inside you know. You know that is who you are, Bunyan . . . who you really *are!"*

"No! I'm not like that! I'm not! It's a lie!" Hategood didn't even pause to acknowledge John's frantic denial but continued to speak, accusing the desperate man of lust and envy, forcing him to watch the spectral figure of himself. "Admit it," Hategood wheedled gleefully. "This wretched man, this wicked creature with no redemptive qualities . . . that's *the real John Bunyan!"*

Finally, Bunyan began to weep. "Yes! That's what I am! That's what I'm like! I live in a dirty, dark room and no matter how I clean it up, it gets dirty again!"

As soon as he made this confession, the room was plunged into darkness, but then it began to clear up. Bunyan lay back in his bed, exhausted and fearful. "I must be dreaming. This can't be real!"

Suddenly another man stood before him, this one quite different from the first. The figure stood before him, a smile on his face, looking quite pleasant and reasonable.

"My name is Mr. Easy Way," he said. Noting that there was no threat in his voice, Bunyan sighed with relief. The creature ignored him and continued, "Mr. Easy Way! That's my name. I've come to make things much easier for you, John Bunyan."

"What do you mean?"

"Well, I can see you're disturbed by my colleague, Mr. Hategood. But there's no need." The visitor's rather mild-mannered comportment was almost soothing after Hategood. Still, Bunyan was not at ease. The man wore a smile that did not reach his eyes. Easy Way watched him almost sympathetically as he went on. "You're no worse than others. All men live in dirty rooms, you know. But dirty rooms can be whitewashed. They can be made to look quite nice. All you have to do is take the easy way."

Bunyan stared at the visitor and managed to ask with a constricted throat, "Take—take the easy way?"

"Quite right! You'll do it sooner or later, you know. Everyone does."

Bunyan felt a sweeping sense of relief. This visitor was not so threatening, but even as his mind raced over what he had heard, another ghostly form entered, dressed all in black. He held a hangman's noose in his hand and said in an iron tone, "My name is Implacable."

"What's—what's that in your hand?"

"Why, this in my hand is your certain death." The sinister figure walked over and slipped the noose over Bunyan's head. He began tightening it. "You stand condemned. Does he not, Mr. Hategood?"

The first figure appeared again, somehow there but not there as he materialized in a swirling form of vapor. "As vile a sinner in his heart as ever walked the face of the earth!"

"You've offered him a reasonable way, have you not, Mr. Easy Way?"

The face of Easy Way seemed to dissolve, "I have, sir. He only needs to give up and paint his sins white."

"Now," Implacable said, "will you, on pain of death, sell Christ?"

Bunyan drew in a sharp breath, his heart hammering. This very thought had come to him over and over, though he knew not whence. Time and again, when he'd been working at his pots and pans, it had slipped into his mind: *Sell Christ! Sell Christ!*

Now he heard it from what seemed to be the open tomb of his own hopes. He began to cry out, screaming, "No, I won't! No, I won't!" It seemed that all three began pulling at the rope binding him, screaming, "Sell Christ! Sell Christ!"

And then he heard another voice, a voice filled with concern, calling his name. . . .

"John! John! Wake up! You're having a nightmare!"

Bunyan's eyes flew open, and he lay there, terror washing over him, his heart pounding so that he thought it would burst from his chest. A soft hand touched his cheek and he started, but when he looked, the face he saw in the light of the moon was his wife's. Blessed relief swept over him as he looked about. He was in his own bed. Leah was by his side, her face filled with fear. He was wringing wet with sweat and as she stroked his face and felt his tears, she cried out, "Oh, John, what are you to do? What are you to do?"

John Bunyan lay silently, knowing he could not live under such terrible pressure. Finally, he groaned, "I'll go see Mr. Gifford tomorrow. Whatever he tells me to do, I'll do it. I can't go on like this."

John Bunyan's struggle was not solved overnight. He went almost every day to speak with Pastor Gifford, who encouraged him greatly, but still the tinker could not shake himself free from his fears. All the pastor's wise words and quoted verses only served to make him feel more a failure, more imprisoned by his worthlessness.

Finally one day he was walking toward town when he heard some ladies talking. He glanced about and saw them sitting out on the front doorstep of a house. He took cursory notice of them—he knew them well and was aware they were godly women—then made to move on, until one woman made a remark about how God had worked in her life. Bunyan halted at once. He was so hungry for the truth that he went to the two women and asked them what they knew of God. Immediately the ladies realized that here was a man who longed for and needed God.

One of the women became especially interested in helping the troubled young tinker. She spent many hours talking with him and one day said, "John, you've tried a thousand times to change and improve yourself, haven't you?"

"Why, yes, a man must try."

"But you've always failed, haven't you?" When he lowered his head and admitted ruefully that he had, she said simply, "You're a failure, but Jesus is not. In much of the Bible it is written, I think, that *he* is the savior, not we ourselves. Consider the dying thief, John. What could he do?"

"Why . . . nothing," Bunyan replied.

"Nothing but look to the dying Son of God. And that is what you must do, sir. Indeed, what we all must do."

Those simple words from a simple woman struck deeply, so much so that Bunyan could not seem to get away from them.

Finally, weeks later, burdened by a depression so heavy that he feared it would crush him, John was walking home from church. His mind was on the sermon, which had been full of the love of God. He looked up and thought he saw the rays of the sun, and it seemed to him they were trying to avoid his head. He looked down and thought the cobblestones were trying to avoid touching his feet, and the nearby houses were leaning backward, away from him—to Bunyan's mind, all of creation abhorred him because he had deserted his Savior, the Lord Jesus Christ. But even as he looked, he heard a whisper so faint he had to strain to hear it. It came from deep down within him and it offered him the first ray of hope he had known in many many months: *"This sin is not unto death."*

Stunned, yet strangely encouraged, John Bunyan clung to the truth. He went through the next few days searching the Scriptures. He found a verse that said, "My grace is sufficient for thee," and was so lifted that he made it his anchor, saying it to himself over and over again.

At last, at long last, the end of the torment came very simply.

Bunyan was sick to death of himself, tired of his sins, weary of life. One night after Leah and Mary were asleep, he rose and went to the window. The weight of his sins pressed down upon him, and as he looked out at the moon shining down with silver rays on the small town of Bedford, he said in desperation, "Lord Jesus, be merciful to me, a sinner!"

He had prayed this prayer in one form or another a hundred times—but he knew at once that *this* time something had happened! His heart seemed to be flooded with peace and he realized that God had come in! He stood there, tears running down his cheeks, the assurance of God's love flowing over him. Falling to his knees, John Bunyan began to thank God fervently. Finally he stood up and went to wake his wife.

She looked at him, confused at first; then her eyes widened at the joy she saw on his face. Before she could say a word, he cried out in a glad voice, "Leah, you have a new husband and Mary has a new father!"

Relief swept over her as she took his hands and tears of gratitude to God ran down her face as she smiled at her husband and said, "John, oh, my dear John, you've found the Lord Jesus!"

His eyes met hers, and he nodded—and she thought her heart would burst with the elation she felt. Her husband's face, which had for so long been drawn and fearful, now shone with happiness and purpose.

"Yes," he agreed, smiling broadly, "At last, I have found my Savior. And now the one thing I want to do is serve him every day the rest of my life!"

Four

"Take Me with You, Sir!"

Will Morgan walked into the small room where his sister was sitting at a mahogany table and staring down at a sheet of paper. "Hello, Angharad," he said, stopping to look down at her. "You wanted to see me?"

Angharad looked up, a troubled light in her brown eyes. "Yes, Will. Sit down." She waited until he seated himself on a joint stool, then said, "I have a letter here from Rhys."

"Uncle Rhys? I'm surprised to hear it. He doesn't write much."

"No, and I can barely make out some of it, the writing is so bad." Angharad picked up the sheet of paper and stared at it. "One thing is clear, though. It's about Evan."

Will's eyebrows arched and he angled a look at his sister. Evan, the son of their father's brother, Rhys, was well known from his earliest childhood for his outrageous antics. When Will and Angharad had lived in Wales, they had been very close to their uncle. He had, in fact, been a second father to them. As such, they had seen and heard a great deal about Evan and his latest difficulty.

Angharad met her brother's knowing gaze. "Uncle Rhys says that Evan's in danger of winding up in a bad way."

Will shrugged. "Well, we knew that was coming for the lad, didn't we?"

Angharad shook her head. "It's worse than usual, I think. Here, read the letter."

Will took the parchment, squinted at the scratchy writing, and finally looked up. "Aye, this is not good. What are you thinking?"

"I think we ought to talk to Christopher. Evan needs to get away from Wales. Rhys is too old to look out for him. Besides there's nothing for the lad there anyway. It's a wonder he hasn't starved to death."

"Like we almost did," Will said quietly. "In truth, I'd like to see the young fellow come." He hesitated, then spoke what they both knew. "Of course, he'd be bound to bring trouble in his wake."

"Devil fly off!" Angharad said with some irritation. "When was a young Morgan anything *but* trouble?" And then she smiled at him. "You were no saint, sir, when you were his age. Indeed, I remember a few times when we thought you were headed straight for the gallows."

Will returned her smile. "Aye, it's God's mercy I didn't wind up with a rope around my neck." He glanced at the letter again, his brow furrowed in thought, then he nodded. "We can always use a strong young fellow around here. Talk to Christopher. I'll stand for Evan's good behavior—or break his neck!"

Angharad came over to stand beside her brother. She put her hand on his shoulder, saying, "I don't think it'll come to that. He's a godless young man according to Rhys, but there's hope. I'll talk to Christopher right away."

Later that day she mentioned the matter to her husband as they sat in the large bedroom they shared. She showed him the letter and watched quietly as he read.

Chris gave her a quick look. "You're troubled about the lad, are you, Angharad?"

"Yes, he's bound for trouble in Wales. I'd like to do something to help him."

"Send him money, perhaps?"

"No, that wouldn't answer," she said quickly. She moved over to sit beside him, entwining her fingers with his. "I'm always asking something of you, aren't I?"

Chris smiled, gazing at his wife with admiration and affection. He admired the smooth lines of her cheek, noting that she still was a young woman. Though he felt pangs of guilt at times for tying her to an old man such as himself in marriage, he was thankful God had brought them together. Now his smile deepened as he met her sweet gaze.

"Ask me anything, my darling wife," he said. "That's the way to get it." He put his arm around her and leaned close, gently kissing her cheek. Her skin was smooth beyond description and he leaned his forehead against hers. "I feel like a young man inside," he said with a laugh. "Do you know that every time I look into a mirror I ask, 'Who is that old man?' Inside I'm still seventeen years old, I think."

"You'll never grow old." Angharad smiled, squeezing his hand.

His eyes met hers and husband and wife both smiled, moved, as always, by the deep love they felt for each other. Chris brought her hand to his lips and kissed it tenderly, then leaned back. "Would you like to send for the lad? Is that it?"

"Would you mind too much, Chris?" she asked. "I know it will be a trouble and a responsibility—"

"Not at all, my dear! It will be good for you to have more of your family here. Send for him at once. He'll need money, I suppose, to make the trip, so send that along as well."

"That's sweet of you, dear," she said. "I'll send the money right away. Will says that you're not to worry about Evan. He's a Morgan through and through, which means he has some wild ways—" she grinned and her eyes twinkled merrily—"but Will has promised to break the boy's skull if he doesn't behave himself."

Chris hugged her again. "It's always good to have young people around. How old is Evan now?"

"He's seventeen," she said with a rueful expression, "and if he looks anything like he did when he was younger, we'll have to lock some of the good-looking young servant girls up. He was a heartbreaker even as a small boy." Her eyes grew roguish and she reached up to tug at her husband's hair playfully. "Just like you, I should imagine!"

He laughed and caught her wrist, then pulled her into his arms. She snuggled against him, resting her cheek on his broad chest, listening to the beat of his heart. What a wonder was this man God had given her!

After a moment she said, "It'll be good for Amos to have another young man around. Of course, Evan may not be the best example for our boy, but we'll have to see. If God can save me and you, then 'tis a certainty he can save the likes of Evan Morgan."

"And furthermore, if you ever show your face inside this town again," Judge Watson said, his voice rising with indignation and fury, "I'll not only put you *in* jail, I'll put you *under* the jail!"

Evan Morgan stood before the magistrate, staring at him without expression. A well-built young man, Morgan was blessed with wild, thick midnight-black hair, and eyes of such a dark blue they seemed almost black as well. His broad shoulders bespoke strength; his handsome face, high cheek bones, and wide, sensuous mouth all gave hint to a certain devilishness of character. Despite the torn and dirty appearance of his clothes—a souvenir of his stay in the local jail—there was a graceful, even noble, air about the young man as he considered the judge's words. There was a bright light in his dark eyes as he answered, "Indeed, sir, and I thank you for your hospitality. Though it's glad I'll be, not to have to stay in your stinking jail any longer!"

The magistrate shook his head and turned to Rhys Morgan, who stood beside his son. "Mr. Morgan, I respect you greatly, but I must warn you that your son is not welcome in my town any longer. Legally I could put him in prison right now, but as you have agreed that he will leave our town, I'm releasing him into your custody."

Rhys nodded, speaking in a deep, steady voice, "It's thanking you, I am, sir. And you have my word the boy will be no more trouble to you."

"See to it then!" Judge Watson said and waved the two aside.

Rhys took firm hold of his son's arm and leaned toward him. "Come along, Evan," he whispered, then led the tall lad out of the courtroom. When they were outside, the elder Morgan looked up at the sun, which was almost hidden by a sullen bank of clouds that threatened rain. He drew a deep breath and shook his head, and when he spoke, his voice was filled with weariness. "Well, you won't go to prison anyway. God be thanked for that!"

Evan glanced back at the courtroom, a mulish expression on his face. "There's people in this town who've done worse than I have, Da."

"That's no excuse for misbehavior, boy." The father's retort came quickly. "That some are worse than you! Fah!" The weight of his eighty-three years rested heavily on Rhys Morgan. In some ways, he was still a fine figure of a man. His mane of silver hair gave him a somewhat debonair appearance, and the lines on his face added character rather than years. Still, since he had lost his wife he had known little happiness and this tall son of his had been the cause of more anxiety than he cared to admit. He was tired. And, though he'd told no one, increasingly ill. Much of the strength he'd relied on all his life seemed to have seeped away, leaving him weaker, more frail, with every passing day.

He shook his head regretfully. "Do you feel no shame, Evan?" he asked quietly as they walked. "Isn't there *anything* in you that tells you you've done wrong?"

For one moment, Evan dropped his head. He had done wrong; he knew it. But he'd not be likely to admit such a thing to anyone . . . even his father. He shook his head stubbornly. "No point in talking about it, I suppose, Da. It's too late, after all. I'm being kicked out of Wales. So at least my behavior won't trouble you anymore."

The two walked down the street and Rhys tried to find some way to make Evan realize the seriousness of his offense. The young man had fallen in love with the daughter of one of the leading citizens. Though the father had warned him off, Evan had refused to obey. The girl's brother, a burly, powerful man, had watched the unfolding events with increasing fury until he finally came after the young Morgan and the two had engaged in a bloody fistfight. Although battered himself, Evan had won. Or he thought he had, until the girl's father had charges of assault brought against him and had him thrown in jail.

As he walked and listened to his father's words, Evan pressed his lips together in a thin line. He knew he had grieved his family, and he regretted it. Even so, despite his fury at the injustice of being thrown into jail for defending himself against an attacker, Evan had learned a valuable truth during his imprisonment: He detested being in jail. True to his heritage as a Morgan, he was a man of the out-of-doors; he loved to roam the hills and valleys around his cottage and would have liked nothing better than to spend his time working outside. But times were hard in Wales and there was little work to be had anywhere, least of all in their small town. Evan knew himself well enough to understand that he had allowed frustration and boredom to build until he had turned his endless energies and imagination to less than beneficial endeavors—thus ending up in trouble at almost every turn. *I suppose it was only a matter of time before I made the acquaintance of the local jail,* he thought ruefully.

Evan pictured the confines of the small cell, remembering how he had been able to see the sky and the woods but was unable to enjoy them. After just a few days he'd feared he would lose his mind. More often than he cared to admit he had been tempted to batter his head against the stone walls until he knocked himself senseless. At least then he would not have to think about where he was—or where he couldn't be! When his father had come at last with the announcement that his relatives had invited Evan to come and live with them in England, the young man had been vocal in his opposition. But actually the news was a relief.

The two reached the house, and at once Evan said, "I'll be leaving in the morning, Da. I'll get my things together. Not that I have much to take."

"It's sorry I am to see you go, boy." The elder Morgan turned from his son with sadness heavy in his heart. Regret washed over him and he feared he would fall beneath the weight of his sorrow. If only things were different—but time was running to an end for Rhys Morgan. The increasing weakness in his body told him all too often that he would not be getting better; certainly he could not live much longer. And well he knew that he was Evan's only stabilizing influence. *I'll not let the boy stay home and watch me die. Better to send him off to others in the family who might be able to make something of his rebellious self.*

The next morning when Rhys said good-bye, he put his hand on Evan's shoulder. "It's not likely we'll meet again, Son," he said evenly. "Not in this world, at least."

Evan looked startled. "Why, I'll be coming back for a visit, Da."

"Come soon, or you'll not find me here. Oh, I'm not complaining. I've had a full life, 'specially when your mother was alive. But now that she's gone, there's not much here for me." He looked into his son's eyes. "My prayer is that you'll find Jesus,

Evan. You've got a wild streak in you, but then, we Morgans have all had it." He smiled briefly. "I had a touch of it myself before it was beaten out of me. Still, I'd hate to see you go the way of so many wild young men."

Evan stood silent. He wanted to argue with his father, but the evidence supporting what the man was saying was too strong. His father was losing ground rapidly. *I'll probably never see him again!* They had not been particularly close, but now that the time had come for him to leave, Evan found himself struggling with a sudden heaviness settling deep within him. He shook his head, wanting to say so much, yet unable to find the words. Finally he whispered, "Good bye, Da." Impulsively he threw his arms around his father and held him tightly. He knew the uncharacteristic gesture had surprised his father almost as much as it had surprised himself. He felt the fragility of his father's form, and when he released him and turned to leave, his eyes stung with tears.

"Good bye, Da," he repeated huskily and moved rapidly away.

Rhys Morgan watched his son as he disappeared into the distance, then turned and entered the house, praying, *God, be with him. He needs you more than he knows!*

Evan did not hurry, for he suspected that a great deal of hard work waited for him at Wakefield. It was the middle of April in the year of 1656. He had brought enough food to last him several days. He had little money, but that had never worried Evan. He was quite accustomed to such circumstances. As he passed through the valleys of Wales, spring seemed to be more beautiful than ever before. Evan loved the countryside and now he felt a deep pleasure at the greenness of the grass, the tiny golden leaves that were beginning to appear on the trees, and the white, fluffy clouds overhead being pushed along by warm breezes. Indeed, it was a glorious world.

He slept where he could find a place, sometimes in barns, sometimes in homes when he was invited. Once, a cheerful widow welcomed him. She was hardly over thirty and had three young children. She fed Evan well—so well that he stayed for three days and helped her with the work that had piled up. But he knew he could not tarry long, and soon he went on down the way.

The morning he left the widow, he walked at a fast rate, pausing at noon at a farmhouse to buy a loaf of fresh-baked bread and six large potatoes from the family, then proceeding on his journey.

When he arrived at a sparkling brook at about four o'clock that afternoon, the rippling water, warm sun, and refreshing breeze all coaxed him to try his hand at a little fishing. He had brought hooks and lines with him, and soon had trimmed a sapling with his knife and fashioned a suitable fishing pole. Baiting his hook with a bit of meat, he tossed the line into the water and was rewarded almost at once when a small fish took the bait. With a sense of satisfaction he pulled it in and cut it up for bait.

He moved down the stream, intent on his endeavors, enjoying as always the challenge of coaxing fish from their hiding places. Patiently he waited, then he got a solid strike that bent his slender sapling double. His heart pounded with the thrill of the catch, beating so hard it seemed it would burst out of his breast.

"Must you always go crazy when you catch a fish?" he said aloud, but his eyes were bright with pleasure as he landed the fish. "Oh ho! You're three pounds if you're an ounce, my fine fellow," he said, grinning. "I can't eat you all, fish, but I'll do my best." He fished for another thirty minutes, catching only a fish about half the size of the first. At last he took his catch back to where he had made a camp. With a quick ease born of experience, he cleaned the fish, then set them aside while he built a fire, which he rimmed with rocks. That done, he pulled a small pan from his pack and set it on the rocks. Soon the grease was frying in the skillet, and he cut up the fish, savoring the scent of the cooking meat as he laid it in the hot pan.

As he worked, a sound attracted his attention. He looked up quickly, but saw nothing. Years spent in the wilderness had refined his hearing so that it was almost as acute as an animal's, but after a moment he decided he'd heard little more than the rustling of some small animal. He fried one of the fish, along with one of the potatoes, then sat back and forked the first steaming morsel into his mouth, chewing happily, inordinately pleased with such a fine supper.

After he had eaten, he set the rest of the fish aside for breakfast, then rolled up in his blanket, lay his head on his pack, and stared up into the skies. The stars spangled the purple background, twinkling and shining, and he wondered how many there were. "The Bible says the good Lord knows your names," he muttered. "That's a lot of names to know. . . ."

Finally he grew sleepy, and rolling onto his side, he drifted almost instantly into slumber.

Sometime later, he came awake as quickly as a startled cat. His eyes flew open, and though he did not move, he cautiously scanned all within his field of vision. The moon was bright, the silver beams flooding the small area and enabling him to see clearly. He could hear the brook bubbling nearby and lay very still, listening.

There! There it is again! The sound was muffled but discernible nonetheless. His muscles began to tense; he could tell that someone had come from his left, just out of his line of sight. Slowly, imperceptibly, he moved his hand down to the knife in his belt and pulled it out.

When the sound occurred again, this time louder, he sprang out of the blankets with a shout. Looking about, he spotted a form that seemed to be readying to run away. "Hold there!" he cried and launched himself into a headlong dive. He nearly missed, but he managed to bump into the intruder, knocking him to the ground. The person scrambled frantically to his knees, trying to scurry away, and Evan reached out with his left hand to grab an ankle. "Hold it right where you are, or I'll slit your throat!" he shouted.

A muffled cry came to him, but he ignored it. Quickly he jerked the thief down, threw himself on top of the thrashing form, and straddled the intruder's body. He reached out to grab the coat roughly, then held the knife high, letting the moonlight glint on the blade. "Stop fighting," he commanded, "or I'll slit your gullet where you lie!"

"Please, don't hurt me!"

Evan blinked in astonishment and lowered the knife; this was not the rough voice of a man. He became aware that the form beneath him was small, almost childlike. He came to his feet, still holding the front of the person's jacket. He pulled the small form up and turned the face to the moonlight. His eyes widened. This was no burglar. Or, if it was, it was a very small and feminine one.

He put the knife back into its sheath, then reached out and pulled the cap from the intruder's head. A cascade of curls fell down around the white face, and he saw that he was holding a young girl.

"What are you doing out here, girl?" he demanded. "You're awfully young to be living the life of a thief."

The girl could not move; she was held fast by Evan's hand. She looked up at him, her eyes wide and filled with a mixture of fear and frustration. "I was hungry," she whispered, and Evan heard the shame in her voice. "I meant no harm to you."

Perplexed and troubled, Evan looked around. He was out in the middle of nowhere! Where had this girl come from? With a scowl, he studied her smudged face again. "What's your name, lass?" he asked roughly.

"Jenny. Jenny Clairmont."

Her voice was thin, giving him no hint as to her age. "How old are you?"

"Thirteen," came the listless reply.

"Thirteen years old and out in the middle of this woods all by yourself?" He looked around again; surely someone was with the girl! But he saw only woods and darkness around them. With an impatient sigh, he asked, "Where do you come from, girl?"

She only shook her head in silence.

"Tell me where you come from!" he demanded. "You must have a home somewhere?"

"I—I don't have a home," she whispered.

Something about the girl's tone of voice gave Evan pause. He loosed his grip but watched her warily. "You don't have a home?"

"No, sir. I've—I've never had a home."

"What then, did they find you under a berry bush?" Evan demanded. He saw that she was trembling—indeed, she looked as though she might faint. Realization struck him, and he scanned her face intently. "So you're hungry, are you? Well, we can fix *that,* at least. Sit down there, and I'll cook you a bite to eat."

The girl sat down, hugging her knees and watching him with large, expressive eyes. Evan stirred the fire up, added fuel to it until it was burning briskly, then cut up another potato and several pieces of the fish and fried them. When he was through, he put the food on the single wooden trencher he had brought for his own use, added a thick slice of the bread, and handed it to the still silent girl. "There!" he said. "Get yourself on the outside of that. Then we'll talk."

Leaning back, Evan watched the girl as she ate. He could tell she tried not to appear gluttonous, but it was clear she was almost literally starving. She tore at the fish, chewing it rapidly and swallowing, even though it was still hot. Evan frowned again. "Here now, lass, you'll burn yourself. Slow down. There's no hurry," he cautioned her. "I'm not going to take it away from you."

She met his gaze, then nodded and tried to eat more slowly. He rose and walked to the creek, scooping up some water in his tin cup. Coming back, he handed it to her.

Again her eyes met his and he wondered at the bleakness he saw reflected there as she whispered, "Thank you, sir."

Finally, she had eaten her fill. She licked her lips tentatively and stared down at her lap as though deep in thought. *Troubling thought, too,* Evan decided as he watched the expressions play across her face. She startled him a bit when she suddenly looked up and their eyes met. A sharp pang of some emotion swept over him. *Was ever a young girl so sad?*

She dropped her eyes. "I'll wash the dish and cup."

"No need of that," Evan said, noting the ragged appearance of her clothing and the thinness of her arms and legs. "But," he said, "you *can* pay for your supper with a bit of information. What are you doing out here all by yourself?"

Jenny stared across at him, the thinness of her cheeks making her eyes seem enormous. "I run away," she said finally.

"Run away? From who?"

"I won't tell you." There was a stubbornness in her lips and in the rigid way she held her back. "He—beat me. I wouldn't do what he said, so he beat me," she whispered. "He was always after me. Yelling. Telling me I had to do it. I couldn't stand it no more. So I run away!"

The pained tone in the girl's voice told Evan more clearly than any assurance that she was speaking the truth. "Who beat you?" he asked gently, pushing down the rage that anyone would use this slight girl so. "And what did he want you to do?"

She was reluctant to speak at first, but eventually Evan's kindness and quiet voice pulled the story from her. He discovered she had been an orphan all her life. Her first memories were of a workhouse of sorts, and then, when she'd grown too old at ten years of age to stay there, she had been farmed out to a family. Forced to work from before dawn to long after dark, she had been misused and half-starved. Then the brutal husband had received an offer for her from an older neighbor, a man who, according to Jenny, watched her with "the meanest, hungriest eyes" she'd ever seen. "He wanted to buy me," she said. "But I knew it wasn't to work. He wanted to . . . to use me." Her eyes filled with tears. "I told Mr. Owens I'd rather die. He said that was all right with him. That's when he started beating me."

Pity for the girl and anger toward the villainous man who had so misused her swept over Evan. There were many young girls like her, he knew. He wanted to help her somehow, but he could not think of a single thing to do.

They sat in silence for a time, until she finally looked up at him, curiosity in her big eyes. "Where are you from, sir?" she asked timidly.

"Well, I'm from Wales, but I've been kicked out for being too much of a rascal. So now I'm going to England to live with relatives in a place called Wakefield."

"Is it—is it a nice place?" The wistfulness in the girl's face caught at him. As she continued to ask about Wakefield, he told her what little he knew.

The creek murmured softly and far off an owl cried. Evan said finally, "I'll take you to the next town. Perhaps we can find someplace for you there."

Jenny studied Evan Morgan's face for a moment. Despite her young years, experience had taught her to read faces for character. Sadly, she was best acquainted with the signs of those who were cruel and treacherous and would hurt her—but a few times she had seen kindness, and that was what she saw now in the face of the young man who sat across the fire from her.

If she stayed in the area, she knew that sooner or later she would be caught and sent back to those who claimed to own her—and a great fear seized her. Once again she focused on Evan's face, noting the gentleness in his eyes, the patience in his silence—and felt the stirring of hope. "Please," she whispered hesitantly, "take me with you, sir."

Evan's jaw dropped and he stared at her. "Take you with me?" he asked. "Why, I can't do that, girl!"

"I'll work! I only want to be let alone," she pleaded. "Take me with you, and I won't be any trouble. I promise!"

Evan was stunned by her request. "I can't do that, Jenny," he said. "If it was my home I go to, it would be different, but I'll be going as a servant myself. If I come there with a little girl in tow, they might send me on my way."

Jenny bit her lip and felt the tears gather in her eyes. She was tired and weary and very frightened. She said no more but sat there, a pathetic figure.

Evan felt absolutely terrible. Rotten and selfish. His heart was always moved by the sight of wounded creatures from the woods . . . how could he show any less sympathy to this one who was no mere woodland creature but a living being filled with grief and fear. Clearing his throat, he said gruffly, "Here, I've got a blanket. Get some sleep. We'll think of something and I'll help you if I can."

Jenny did not answer but rolled up in the blanket. At once she fell into an exhausted sleep. Evan, however, was not so fortunate. He sat, deep into the night, staring at the girl's pale face as it was reflected in the firelight and pondering weighty thoughts.

Jenny came awake slowly, drawn from her deep slumber by the fragrance of fresh fish being cooked over the fire. She sat up at once and saw Evan holding the small frying pan. He smiled at her.

"Did you sleep?"

"Yes, sir, I did."

Evan poked the fish with his knife, turned it over, and looked at her. "Well, hop to and clean up, then have some breakfast." He paused for a moment, then smiled again. "You'll need all the strength you can get. It's a long walk to England, you know."

Jenny's eyes widened, and Evan was struck by the enchanting picture she made. Her strawberry blonde hair formed a soft frame to her sweet face. Her eyes, which were an extraordinary shade of green, shone with sudden hope. "To England? Then I'm going with you? Really, Mr. Evan?"

"Really," he said. Evan had struggled with the thing all night and taking her with him was the only right solution he could devise. He'd finally set aside his concerns with, *Well, I'm taking her with me, and if they don't like it—why, I'll find another place!*

Now he handed her a piece of fish. "Maybe you'll be a good influence on me. I'm a wicked young man, you know."

Jenny looked at his face, at the open smile and the bright eyes. She took the fish and her voice quivered a little with relief. "Mr. Evan," she whispered, "you're *not* a wicked young man. I just know you're not! Why, I think you're the goodest, kindest man I've ever met."

Evan looked at her and shrugged his shoulders. "There are plenty of good folk who wouldn't agree with you," he muttered. Then he cast off his frown and grinned at her. "Devil fly off! It's too grand a day to let ourselves get gloomy. Let's eat us a good breakfast and be off for Wakefield!"

Angharad and Will stared, nonplussed, at the young man now standing on the threshold of Wakefield. Though he looked somewhat as they had expected—a younger version of their Uncle

Rhys, tall and strongly built—he had one thing neither of his relatives had expected: a companion.

The knock they'd been waiting for had come first thing that morning, and they'd opened the door eagerly to find the lad standing before them, a slightly defiant air about him as he announced, "I'm Evan Morgan, and this is Jenny Clairmont."

Angharad and Will had looked at each in shock. It was Angharad who asked cautiously, "And where, Evan, did you get this young lady?"

His gaze never wavered. "She and I are friends," he answered firmly. "I met her on the road, but after our travels, I can tell you she's trustworthy. And she needs a place to stay." At Will's raised eyebrow, a slight flush crept over Evan's cheeks as he went on, "She's a hard worker, young and strong. I hate to come asking favors, but I'm afraid I'll have to."

Angharad looked again at the girl where she stood silently beside Evan, and her heart went out to her. Dressed in nothing but rags, she was as thin as a sparrow; her cheeks were hollow from lack of food. "Well," Angharad said thoughtfully, then she nodded. "Jenny, you come along with me. I think we can find you something . . . warmer to wear. Will, you take Evan and show him his place."

"I can stay?" Jenny whispered, her eyes wide with disbelief.

Angharad went over and put her arm around the thin young shoulders. She smiled into the winsome face peering up at her, then whispered conspiratorially, "As big as this place is, I don't see why we couldn't find a place for one small girl."

Jenny's eyes filled with tears at the kindness in this woman's face. "I'll work hard," she whispered. "I'll do *anything* for you!"

Angharad laughed. "You can certainly sit with our little girl. She'd be pleased as can be at the companionship. Come along, I'll introduce you to Hope. After we get you cleaned up, that is."

As soon as the two had left, Will turned to his young cousin, studying him carefully. Evan bore the scrutiny in silence—a fact Will noted with pleasure. He nodded slowly. "Well, Evan Morgan, you've the look of old Wales about you." He reached out to clap the younger man on the shoulder. "It's good to see you, my boy."

Evan's only response was to say in a grim voice, "I might as well tell you, I just got out of jail. You won't get any good recommendations from anybody at home. Not on me, that is."

"Well, this is your home now," Will said quickly. "And what you were in Wales doesn't matter so much as what you are now. This is Wakefield, boy. We'll not be judging your past here. As for your present, well, it's up to you what we think of that. Come along now. I'll show you around the place."

Evan paused for a moment, as though struggling with himself, then he took a deep breath and nodded. Will led the young man around, watching his expressions and reactions as they surveyed the buildings and grounds. What he saw pleased him.

He's a goodly young fellow. Got a smell of brimstone about him, of course, so he'll be hard to handle at first. But he's got a good heart, picking up that little girl like that. Shows compassion. And character. And those are a good start on becoming a man.

Five

A Trip to Bedford

"I don't know if you've heard, Evan," Gavin said, "but Mrs. Bunyan's been very ill."

Evan Morgan looked up from the piece of leather he was shaping into a bridle. "Yes, your father told me of it, Mr. Gavin," he said. "Hope it's not serious."

Gavin shook his head, doubt in his eyes. "She hasn't been doing well and I'm worried about her. She's a fine young woman, but evidently she's not too strong—" He broke off as he noted what Evan was holding. "What's that you're making?"

"A new bridle for the mare."

In the year since he had come to Wakefield, Evan had become an expert worker in leather. He had, in fact, completely reoutfitted all of the horses with saddles and bridles. He had become a true asset to the place and Gavin had said as much to Angharad and Will: "If you have any more relatives like that young fellow, send for them." Now, as he admired the young man's work, he thought again what a valuable addition Evan was to Wakefield, and to the family. He smiled. "It's a beauty, Evan. As are all the others. But I'd like you to take a break from this for a bit."

Evan looked at him curiously. "You need me to do something?"

"I want you to ride over to the Bunyans' home and take some things that Mother's been putting together. Mostly clothes and food." Gavin stroked his jaw thoughtfully and shook his head. "Ever since John started preaching, I've been a little bit worried about him."

Evan looked up from the leather that he was stroking. "I heard he was arrested a few months ago."

"Yes, the law's getting stricter on itinerant preachers. You'd think we'd have gotten rid of all that oppression with a monarchy, but there still are those who want to have a monopoly on God."

"It's against the law to preach?" Evan asked with surprise.

"Only if you are an independent," Gavin replied. "The parliament and the army are so mixed up in their thinking, it's dangerous to cross them. From what I hear, Bunyan's become quite a fiery young preacher. Just the kind of man those who want a strong national church would like to stop."

"Well, I'm not a Christian man myself," Evan admitted, his dark eyes thoughtful. He rubbed his hand across his unruly black hair in a futile attempt to smooth it down, then added, "But if I thought God wanted me to preach, then I'd do it, and the devil take anyone who said anything different!"

A smile crossed Gavin Wakefield's face. He'd learned to like this young man, and he saw in him great promise—as well as a streak of rebelliousness that could lead him into trouble. "I fear John Bunyan feels much the same way, and you might as well tell the wind to stop blowing as to tell him to stop preaching."

"Good for him!" Evan nodded.

"I want you to take Jenny with you. She can help Mrs. Bunyan with the children."

"Right, you. When shall I go?"

"Leave this afternoon. Just get there before dark."

"How long shall I stay?"

"I think you might be of some help to John in his business.

You've shown you're a bit of a tinker yourself, the way you're always patching things together." Gavin smiled. "Just feel your way, Evan. I'd like you to be of help to the man. After all, he did save my life. It's the least I can do for him."

"Aye, sir. Shall I take the carriage?"

"Yes. My mother's accumulated quite a bit of plunder for you to take to them."

Evan tossed the bridle on the table, stood up, and stretched. He had grown during the year and put on weight. His chest had deepened and his face had grown somewhat fuller. "I'll get Jenny ready," he said. "She's a handful, that one."

Gavin nodded. "She's been a great deal of help to Angharad with Hope. As a matter of fact, I think Hope might throw a fit when she finds out that Jenny's gone. But Mrs. Bunyan's need is greater." He half turned, then stopped. Wheeling back he said, "Tell John I'll be there when I can and that my prayers are with him." He turned and left the stable.

Going at once to his mother, he informed her of what he had done, adding, "Can you spare Jenny for a time?"

Angharad looked down the corridor to where Jenny was playing some sort of game with Hope. "*I* can spare her, but you know how Hope is. She cries if Jenny isn't there every minute." She smiled. "I'm in the way of being jealous. She's quite a little mother, Jenny is. But send them on. Hope will be fine, and I'm worried about Mrs. Bunyan."

Elizabeth Mills stopped long enough to look into the mirror before she left her small bedroom. She touched her cap, pushing her blonde hair underneath it more firmly, and then turned and moved into the sitting room. "I'm ready to go, Mother. I don't know how long I'll be gone."

Sarah Mills, Elizabeth's mother, was sitting in a chair reading her Bible. She looked up at her daughter and a troubled light came into her eyes. "You're spending far too much time at the Bunyans' house. It doesn't look right."

It was an old argument between the two, one that Elizabeth did not want to take up again. At seventeen, Elizabeth was tall and full-figured. Her blue eyes were quick and alert; her manners were much the same. She had a winsome way about her and a maturity that went far beyond her age. "Mother," she said now, patiently though firmly, "we've talked about this so many times. It's a Christian charity, taking care of the children for Mr. and Mrs. Bunyan. Since Mrs. Bunyan's been ill, it's been very hard on them."

"I realize that," Sarah replied sharply, "but for a young girl to spend so much time away from her own home—well, it just might not *look* right."

Elizabeth smiled, went over to her mother, and kissed her. "It *is* right, Mother, to God at least. If tongues wag, why, there is nothing you can do about that, is there?"

"The Bible says to avoid the very appearance of evil."

"What evil?" Elizabeth said sharply. "I go and help Mrs. Bunyan cook. I help with the children when she's too ill to do it. Where's the evil in that?"

Her mother pursed her lips, silent but unconvinced. A thought had been building in her mind for several months. When Leah Bunyan had begun failing, Sarah had noticed that her daughter was the first to go to the aid of the couple. Indeed, this was commendable. But there was another factor of which Sarah Mills dared not speak. She knew this daughter of hers hardly at all, for they were so different. Yet she had wondered more than once if Elizabeth had formed an . . . infatuation for John Bunyan. There was no proof of such, yet Elizabeth never missed an opportunity to hear the man preach. True enough, she was not alone. Bunyan had proven to be a fine speaker and many were interested in his words.

Still, Sarah was not altogether happy with the situation.

Elizabeth looked at her mother and sighed. "I'll be back after I get the children fed and their clothes washed. Don't worry about me, Mother."

She left the house and made her way down the narrow streets of Bedford. As she passed the church, she thought what a tragedy it had been for the entire village when John Gifford had died three years earlier. She had had great respect for the minister, for he had been responsible for leading her into the ways of the Lord. And he had introduced her to John Bunyan.

She had been but a young girl of fourteen then, but Bunyan's preaching had been a great factor in her spiritual life. She had been greatly moved by his simple words and his knowledge of Scripture. During the formative years of her life she had developed a deep respect for Bunyan.

She pressed her lips together, painfully aware that some thought her interest was more than spiritual. One of her friends had even cautioned her, "Elizabeth, take care. John Bunyan is an attractive man. I know he's a preacher, but you wouldn't be the first young woman to fall in love with her minister."

Elizabeth had angrily rejected that suggestion. "I admire him. He's a fine preacher of the gospel, and it's silly to think that I have any other feelings for him."

Now, as she made her way down the street, she examined her heart yet again. She was a very devout young woman with a hunger after God, but there was a broad realistic vein in her character as well. No one could grow up in a small farming community and be unaware of the facts of life. She was aware that becoming a woman had brought changes, not only physically but emotionally. At times, she had thoughts of what it would be like to be married, to love a man. It was, perhaps, natural enough that she would wonder about the physical side of love, although such things were usually not mentioned in the presence of young women.

She had no sisters to talk with, and her friends were as ignorant as she of these matters. Nevertheless, as she walked along, she wondered if she would ever know what it meant to be loved by a man. Caring and demonstrative, Elizabeth was aware that she was wont to touch people from time to time, though only in tenderness and compassion. Nevertheless she fought against the tendency constantly, for it seemed to be a weakness to her.

Arriving at the Bunyan house, she knocked at the door. On hearing a voice bid her enter, she went in and found John Bunyan with the children.

"Hello, Mr. Bunyan. I've come to help your wife a little."

John Bunyan was surrounded, it seemed, by children. Mary, aged nine, was moving around the kitchen, feeling her way, washing dishes. Little Elizabeth, age six, and John, age four, hung on Bunyan, who was holding the baby, Thomas, on his lap. He looked up with a grateful smile, exclaiming, "Mistress Elizabeth! Come in!" He watched with a laugh as the three children ran at once to greet her, pulling at her. Mary reached up and pulled the girl's head down for a kiss. "Well," he said warmly, "we see who is the most popular around here."

Elizabeth hugged all the children, then came over and said, "Let me have Thomas." She took the baby and cuddled him in her arms, then kissed his cheek. "What a fat old thing you are!" she said. "Look at those cheeks and those chins!"

Bunyan watched carefully as the young woman made much of the children. Finally he sighed. "I meant to clean the house up, but I just haven't had time. And I've got to go out to a meeting tonight, Mistress Elizabeth."

"I'll see to that, sir. Now I'll go in and see Mrs. Bunyan. You get ready and I'll fix you something to eat before you go."

Carrying the baby, Elizabeth entered the bedroom and found Leah Bunyan lying in bed. *She looks worse,* she thought with dismay. *She doesn't have any color at all.* However, she let none of her concern show in her face. Going to the bed, she stroked Leah Bunyan's hands, which were clasped outside the coverlet. "Well, now," she said cheerfully, "I've come to keep you company for a while, you and the children."

Leah Bunyan had lost her youthful appearance. Though only twenty-eight, she looked ten years older. Her babies had come hard for her, and now her face was thin, her cheeks and eyes sunken. She smiled feebly and put out a thin hand, which Elizabeth took. "God bless you, Elizabeth. I don't know what the children or I would have done without you."

Elizabeth never liked to be thanked for her good deeds.She hugged the baby, laughing at the way he was chortling and kicking, then turned her attention again to the frail woman in the bed. "How have you felt, Mrs. Bunyan?"

"I can't complain," Leah replied quietly.

"You never do." Elizabeth was very fond of the older woman. She set the baby down beside Leah. "I'm going to make you some soup, and I'm going to pour it down you until you eat it all, so don't argue with me, you hear?"

She released the thin hand, went back into the kitchen, and began working rapidly. Somehow she managed to entertain the children, fix a large pot of fresh soup—which sent savory aromas throughout the cottage—build a fire under the iron pot outside, and begin washing some of the clothes.She was an energetic young woman who could never be happy unless she was busy. Finally she called out, "All right, children. Come and let's have our dinner." There was a scramble for the stools, and Bunyan came to sit at the head of the table.

"You'd better eat quickly, Mr. Bunyan," Elizabeth said to him, smiling, "before these hungry children eat it up from you."

Bunyan bowed his head and said a quick blessing; then Elizabeth dipped the rich soup into the dishes. Bunyan tasted it and his eyebrows went up. "This is delicious," he said. "I don't know why I can't make soup like this. Mine always tastes like pond water."

"That's because you don't wash the pot before you use it," Mary said. She was a bright girl, quick in her ways. Her blindness almost had ceased to be a handicap, at least for her, but Elizabeth did not miss the tender, sad glance the father gave his little girl.

Elizabeth took a bowl of soup in to Leah and cajoled her into eating some of it. Afterward she said firmly, "You rest now. I'll take care of the children while Mr. Bunyan's gone."

She went back into the room, and Bunyan left shortly thereafter. The children, as always, begged her for stories and after the work was done, she sat down and began to tell them a story that she made up out of her fertile imagination.

The sun was going down, throwing shadows over the landscape as Evan and Jenny approached the small village of Bedford. Evan had been to the Bunyan house more than once during the year he had been at Wakefield, but Jenny had never met the Bunyans.

As they rode along, Evan cast a sideways glance at the young girl, thinking how different she looked from the raggedy girl he had seen that night in the woods.

Only a year has passed, but what a difference that year's made, he thought. She was talking in an animated fashion, her eyes fixed on the little village ahead, so he could observe her freely. She was wearing a simple green dress that fit her neatly and revealed the budding young figure that bespoke the passage from child to woman. Her hair seemed more red than blonde in the fading light and the crimson sun seemed to make it gleam as it hung down her back. At fourteen, Jenny had formed the habit, unlike most young women, of letting her hair hang down and the beauty of its strawberry blonde color attracted the eyes of many.

She turned to him suddenly, saw him watching her, and smiled. "What are you looking at me for, Evan?" she demanded.

"Just thinking what a starved little rat you were when you came out of the night back in Wales." He grinned, noting with pleasure that her face had filled out nicely. Her lips were full and her eyes were extremely large, shaded by heavy lashes. "I hate to say it," he added, "for fear it'll make you proud, but you've turned out pretty well. I would never have believed it from the way you looked that night."

Jenny flushed and snapped at him, "A little kindness, is it? It wouldn't hurt you to say something nice once in a while."

Instantly, Evan regretted teasing her. "In truth, Jenny, I was just going to say how pretty you look in that green dress. It matches your eyes exactly. I always like to see a woman who can pick her clothes to match her eyes."

Jenny's anger left immediately when he called her a woman. Though she tended to cling to her childhood, hesitant to leave that part of life, she was on the brink of that mystery called womanhood. Carefully, she looked at him again and smiled, a dimple touching her right cheek. "Now, that's the way I like to hear you talk." They were almost to the village now but she gave him one parting shot. "It's the first of your sweet talk I've heard," she said. "Though I've heard enough *about* it from all the girls you're chasing around after."

"I am *not* chasing around after girls," Evan said haughtily.

"Yes, you are. Or they're chasing you, which is worse."

This was true. In Wales, Evan's dark good looks and cheerful ways had made him the object of many a young woman's fancy. He had found the same was true in England. "Well," he laughed, "I'll have to get myself a big stick to beat them off. Look," he interrupted himself, "there's the Bunyan cottage. Come along."

Elizabeth was in the middle of a story when a knock sounded at the door. Putting the baby in Mary's arms, she walked across the room, opened the door, and found a young man and a still younger girl standing there. "Yes?" she asked. "Have you come to see Mr. Bunyan?"

Evan Morgan, always a man to notice beauty when he saw it, found more than a little in the young woman who faced him. At once, his manner became brighter and more alert.

Jenny glanced at him swiftly, knowing exactly what was going on in his mind. *Every time he sees a pretty woman, he acts like a silly goose,* she thought in disgust.

"My name is Evan Morgan. Mr. Gavin Wakefield is my employer. Is Mr. Bunyan in?"

"Why, no, he's gone to preach, but come in, won't you?" Elizabeth stepped aside and the two entered. "Mrs. Bunyan is probably not able to see you right now. I think she's asleep."

"That's all right," Evan said quickly. "We brought some things from Lady Wakefield for Bunyan and his family."

"I'm Elizabeth Mills. I'm taking care of the children while Mr. Bunyan's gone to preach."

"Well, we've brought you some help, Mistress Mills. This is Mistress Jenny Clairmont. Mr. Gavin thought she might be some help with the children until Mrs. Bunyan is improved."

Elizabeth turned a smile on Jenny, admiring the girl's fresh, young beauty. "That will be a help indeed, Mistress Clairmont. Come in and I'll introduce you to the children."

Jenny and Evan were quickly given the names of the children, and Mary came at once to put her hand out. "I like to touch hands," she confessed, holding Evan's broad hand in hers. She felt it with both hands carefully. "You have good, strong hands, Mr. Morgan. You work, don't you?" Then she turned to Jenny, took her hand, and said, "You work, too, but your hands are nice and soft."

Jenny slipped her arm around the girl. "Yes, I work, but you and I can play, too. There's not so much difference is our ages, is there? How old are you, Mary?" She listened as the girl chattered on, yet aware all the time that Evan was having a conversation with the beautiful young woman. She found herself listening with half her mind to Mary, while the other half focused on Evan's exchange.

"I'm sorry Mr. Bunyan's not here," Elizabeth said. "Have you heard him preach?"

"No, I've not had that pleasure, Mistress Mills," Evan said, "but Mr. Gavin tells me that he is a fine preacher."

Elizabeth nodded. "Oh, I wish you could hear him. I'd plan to go myself, but somebody has to take care of the children."

Instantly Evan replied, "Why, that's easily taken care of." He nodded toward Jenny. "Jenny, Mistress Mills wishes to go hear Mr. Bunyan preach. I can escort her if you'll take care of the children. Would you mind?"

Jenny well knew that this was Evan's way of getting the young woman off by herself. However, there was nothing for it. She met his gaze, a cynical expression in her green eyes. "Yes, I'll take care of them."

Evan didn't even seem to notice the sarcasm in her tone. He merely smiled at Elizabeth. "There, Mistress Mills," he said, nodding with satisfaction. "All taken care of. Is it far? We can go in the carriage."

"There they are," Elizabeth said. She had enjoyed her ride with the young man, but was aware that he was very interested in women. Though she had little experience with men, she found herself amused at Evan's obvious methods.

As they pulled up in an open field where a group of people had gathered, Elizabeth glanced around. "I don't think the service has started yet."

Evan looked about. "I've never heard anyone preach outside of a church."

"Well . . . there's some trouble," Elizabeth said carefully. "Some of the churches are closed to our people."

Evan jumped down and hurried around the rig before Elizabeth could move. He held his hand out and, when she placed hers in it, held it for just a moment longer than was absolutely necessary. "I've enjoyed our talk, Mistress Elizabeth."

Elizabeth looked up into his dark eyes. *He's the handsomest thing I've ever seen—and does he ever know it!* With a smile she pulled her hand back. "It's good to be able to talk about the things of the Lord with you."

Evan looked a bit subdued at this, for their conversation had indeed tended toward the Scripture. When he had tried to speak of other things more interesting to him, he somehow found himself again confronted with a young woman who apparently thought of nothing but the Bible and singing and preaching.

And of John Bunyan.

As they moved forward toward the small crowd, Evan asked abruptly, "You admire Mr. Bunyan a great deal, don't you, Mistress Elizabeth?"

He noted that a quick flush came to Elizabeth's cheek, as though he had discovered some secret. "Everyone admires Mr. Bunyan," she said evenly. "He's become quite a notable speaker. I believe he's just getting ready to start."

The two stopped to see that Bunyan had indeed just begun his message. His quick eyes caught the two latecomers. He recognized Evan Morgan instantly from his previous visits and remembered how he had tried more than once to talk to the young man about the things of the Lord. But Evan apparently had no interest in that subject. He lifted his eyebrows slightly. How interesting that the young man should show up at a meeting.

Lifting his voice, Bunyan began to preach. He was a simple speaker with a modest manner, although his voice was strong and powerful. He preached on the Scripture "Christ the hope of glory," and using simple illustrations to which all of the common people gathered around him could relate, he made the Scripture come alive.

Evan found himself listening carefully to the preacher, caught by the vivid use of simple things to illustrate truth. He had not found ministers interesting back in Wales, but something about Bunyan's openness and obvious good-heartedness attracted him. Now as he heard the Scripture interwoven with homey illustrations, he found himself thinking, *Well, now, if I ever did pay heed to a preacher, it would be one like John Bunyan.*

The service did not last long and soon Bunyan dismissed his listeners with a quick prayer. As the crowd began to disperse, he walked over to Elizabeth and Evan, nodding at the young man.

"Well, Evan, good to see you."

Morgan took the preacher's strong hand at once. "Mr. Gavin asked me to come see about your good wife and also to bring a few things."

"He brought many good things for the children," Elizabeth said. Her eyes were shining as she exclaimed, "That was a wonderful sermon, sir. It made me think of the glory of God in Christ Jesus."

Bunyan looked at this tall young woman and nodded his thanks. "It's a poor preacher I am, but I have a good subject—the Lord Jesus." He turned to Evan. "And how is Mr. Gavin's father?"

"Not too well, not too well at all," Evan said.

"Too bad, too bad." Bunyan shook his head. "One of the great men of our times, to my thinking."

"We have a carriage to ride home in," Elizabeth said quickly. "You won't have to walk, Mr. Bunyan."

"Yes, come along, Mr. Bunyan," Evan said. The three went to climb into the carriage. All the way back to the Bunyan household, Evan listened as the two beside him spoke of the things of God. By the time they reached the house, he felt left out and somewhat irritated.

Later, Evan went outside with Jenny to help her draw water. Taking advantage of their privacy, he said grumpily, "Too bad such a fine-looking young woman is so caught up with religion."

Jenny shot him a glowering look. "It wouldn't do you any harm to have some religion of your own!" she snapped.

"Well, devil fly off!" Evan exclaimed, irritated further by her sharpness. "A woman's made to be used by a man, Jenny Clairmont. That's what men and women are born to, having each other. I can tell you, Mistress Elizabeth Mills is caught up with more than just religion. She has eyes for that preacher."

"Don't be a fool, Evan! Not everyone spends every second thinking about—" She broke off.

"About what?"

"About men and women falling in love."

Evan stared at the girl, amused. "It wouldn't do you any harm to think about love a little, girl. I hate to see a beauty like yours wasted."

Jenny felt the anger leaving her. She could never be angry long with Evan. She owed him too much. Her feelings about him had become more difficult to explain to herself, especially over the past few months. "You're just jealous," she said calmly. "You think every woman ought to be looking at you, Evan. You're vain as a peacock!"

He laughed, then reached out and put his hands on her head, ruffling the thick crown of strawberry colored hair. "That's what you think of the old man, is it? Well, when you grow up, you'll see things are a little bit different." He was surprised when she slapped his hand away, picked up the bucket of water, and stomped toward the house, her face filled with indignation.

"*Now* what did I do wrong?" he asked, but she paid him no heed, her back stiff as she left him. Evan followed her back into the house, wondering if he would ever understand this fiery young woman who had found him in the woods of Wales.

Six

A Time to Weep

On September 3, 1658, Oliver Cromwell, Lord Protector, met his death.

He had led his country through a time such as it had never known before. The English Puritans under his leadership had valiantly sought to repress vice in England. A law had been passed making adultery punishable by death. Drunkenness was under attack and many ale houses were closed. Even swearing was penalized on a graduated scale: A duke paid thirty shillings for his first offense; a baron, twenty; a squire, ten. Common persons could volubly relieve their frustration at a penalty of only three shillings.

The country had passed through hard and difficult days. The feast days of the church were replaced by monthly fast days. Christmas aroused the hostility of the Puritans. Soldiers were sent round London on Christmas Day, without warrants, to seize meat cooking in kitchens and ovens.

The Jewish laws of the Old Testament were mild compared with some judgments of Cromwell's England. Maypoles were cut down. Walking abroad on the Sabbath, except to go to church, was punishable. It was even proposed to forbid people sitting on their doorsteps or standing and leaning against their doorposts on the Sabbath. Bearbaiting and cockfighting were stopped. The bears were shot and the necks of the cocks were wrung. All forms of athletics and sports, including horse racing, were banned.

Nevertheless, Oliver Cromwell was not so bluenosed or harsh a Puritan as many believed him to be. He treated all men with dignity and held a tenderness toward young people. His unabashed passion for England was both intimate and emotional. Oliver Cromwell was ever ready to share his power through a parliament—if that parliament would establish and uphold the laws and taxes that he felt were necessary.

Although a very passionate man, Cromwell was often beset by doubts. He was certain that God had chosen him to lead his people out of a figurative Egypt. Yet he was sometimes torn by the political expediencies he was forced to choose to obtain his—and God's—goals. When he drew his last breath, it was as a broken man, partly because of the death of his favorite daughter and partly because of the knowledge that the England for which he had so fervently fought would never stand. The England he loved had never lost its taste for a monarch.

When Christopher Wakefield received the news of his friend's death, he was deeply grieved. One afternoon as he sat gazing out the window, Christopher called Gavin into his study. Snow was beginning to fly. The autumn sky was gray and featureless. The trees, which had been glorious with greenery during the summer, now lifted bare arms toward a leaden heaven. The branches swayed in the wind as snow began to collect on them.

"I've had a word from our friends in Bedford, Gavin," he said.

Gavin sat down and studied his father carefully with some concern. *He doesn't look well,* he thought. *I wish he'd go to Spain for warmer weather . . . but Father will never leave Wakefield.* Aloud he asked, "Yes, what is it, Father?"

"Mrs. Bunyan," Christopher answered slowly. He held up a single page. "This just came. Mrs. Bunyan is dying, I think."

"I'm very sorry to hear that. I suppose we've all known that she couldn't live very long."

"He's a good friend of yours, this John Bunyan," Christopher said carefully. "I suppose you'll want to send someone to help."

"Yes, I think we should," Gavin agreed. "John is all alone now." Several times over the past year Gavin had sent Jenny and Evan to help. Bunyan had needed help, for he had been kept busy with his preaching, and the two had been glad enough to go. Gavin continued thoughtfully, "I think Evan's been interested in a young woman there, according to what I get out of Jenny. But evidently this lady is not too interested in him."

Christopher gave Gavin a quick flash of a grin. "Then she's the only young woman who's not! You're going to have to speak to him. He must learn to stop acting like some kind of French popinjay!"

Gavin could not restrain his smile. "He reminds me of myself, sir—and you! I guess the Morgans are just as hard to handle as the Wakefields!"

Christopher nodded. "I suppose we could blame our waywardness on that Welsh blood, but that probably wouldn't be fair."

At that moment Angharad entered the room, followed by Hope, who was protesting something quite loudly. "Be quiet!" Angharad declared. "You sound like a yowling tomcat!"

Hope quieted somewhat and Angharad turned to Gavin. "I have the things ready to send. Will you go, Gavin, if Mrs. Bunyan dies?"

"Yes, of course. Perhaps I ought to go now, but I feel that I'm needed here."

Angharad shook her head sadly. "Jenny's told me a great deal about the Bunyans. She's very fond of them. And Evan, of course, is fond of that young woman."

"I'll warn Jenny to keep an eye on him. She already treats him as if she were the adult and he the child."

"She's not a child anymore," Angharad insisted. "She's fifteen, and old beyond her years. I sometimes think she's got more sense in her little toe than Evan has in his whole body."

"Seems that's true," Christopher agreed. "So, Gavin, get them on their way."

As soon as Gavin left the room, Christopher smiled at Angharad. "Gavin was just remarking that young Evan Morgan is just as much a romantic as he himself was. And he even had the gall to say that I was cut from much the same cloth! I've never been guilty of such behavior as those two scoundrels!"

Angharad sat down close beside him and put her arms around him. Pulling his face to hers, she kissed him lightly. "There's an old liar you are! You were as romantic as any man can be, and still are!"

Christopher pulled her even closer. *She should have married a younger man,* he reflected a little sadly. Christopher had said such things before but Angharad always grew very angry with him when he did. So he said nothing, allowing himself to enjoy the moment of warmth and nearness.

For once, Hope was sitting quietly, and Christopher studied her. *Now she's a true Wakefield,* he thought. It gave him a strange feeling to think that he might never live to see this child grow up. That was the penalty of having a child at an older age. Christopher knew his health was growing worse. He never spoke of it to Angharad, but he could tell from the look in her eyes at times that she knew.

Christopher and Angharad stayed seated close together, talking, with Hope at their feet. "I'm proud of Gavin and Amos," Christopher said. "They've come a long way, haven't they?"

"Yes. And we'll see them come farther in our time," Angharad said firmly.

Elizabeth had been sitting beside Leah for over an hour. From time to time she would look up from her sewing to note the still, pale face. Once she rose, put her sewing down, and mopped the dying woman's brow with a damp cloth. There was no response, even when Elizabeth spoke softly to her. So she seated herself again and quietly resumed her sewing—and her vigil.

Elizabeth had spent part of every day with Leah. Evan Morgan had once again brought Jenny Clairmont, and she had taken over the children. *Thank God for that girl!* Elizabeth thought fervently. *I don't see how we could have made it without her help.* From thinking of Jenny, her thoughts drifted immediately to Evan. Her mouth tightened with disgust.

Evan had proved to be an aggravation. From the first time he had met Elizabeth, he had found every conceivable excuse to make the trip from Wakefield to Bedford. Always there was some reason, such as bringing some gift from Wakefield to the household or bringing Jenny for the children. He had been sly about his admiration for Elizabeth, pretending that he considered her a friend whom he admired and nothing more. Yet, as inexperienced as she was, there was an essential maleness in Evan Morgan that she recognized.

It was on his third visit that he had attempted to kiss her. When Elizabeth had rebuked him, he had laughed, his dark eyes gleaming with rich humor. "You'll grow to like it one day!" he had teased. "Better get used to it!"

Elizabeth had done all she could to discourage him, but he was a man obviously accustomed to success with women—she had learned that much from Jenny. Even so, she knew he was not a man who would do for her.

As she sat beside Leah, she began to wonder at her certainty regarding Evan's unsuitability. *He's as handsome as a man could be,* she told herself. *I know he has no money—but that wouldn't matter to me.*

She reflected again on the time he had put his arms around her and actually touched his lips to hers. It was a moment she had often thought about, but only with irritation. *I wonder if there's something wrong with me?* Nevertheless, she felt no great or lasting concern. Evan Morgan was a man who needed to have the approval of women, but she felt no great need to add her name to his list of devotees.

The door slammed in the adjoining large room. Casting a single worried glance at Leah, Elizabeth put down her sewing and left the bedroom.

"How is she?" John had come into the house, a white mantle of snow on his shoulders.

"I'm afraid she's no better," Elizabeth said quietly. "Let me take your coat." She shook off the snow onto the hearth, then hung the heavy cloak up on a peg. "Will you eat now, or—"

"No. I'll see Leah first." Bunyan went into the bedroom, his step heavy.

Elizabeth busied herself preparing dinner. After a long time he returned into the great room, his face showing a terrible strain. "Sit down, Mr. Bunyan," she said softly. "You must eat something. You haven't had a single bite all day."

"I'm not hungry," he said automatically. Despite the words, he sat down at the table and Elizabeth placed a bit of beef before him. He sawed a bite off with his knife, stabbed it, and lifted it to his lips. He ate from instinct, not from hunger. His mind was on the woman in the bedroom.

"Here, Mr. Bunyan," Elizabeth said. "Take some ale." She poured the amber liquid into a tankard and handed it to him. He took it, his expression as blank as when he chewed, and drank it obediently.

"Jenny and Evan took the children out to play," Elizabeth said as she took the empty tankard.

Bunyan's face lightened. "I don't know what we would have done without them."

Elizabeth's face glowed at the use of the word "we." She sat down across from him, folded her hands, and began to speak gently of the practical considerations of Leah's illness.

Bunyan listened for a while, his eyes downcast, his expression drawn. Finally he looked up at her and a strange expression crossed his face. Then he did something he had never done before: Reaching across the table, he placed his hand over hers. His hands were big and strong, roughened by his tinker's work, and one of them completely covered both of Elizabeth's folded hands. A warm light flickered in his large blue eyes. "I must tell you just how greatly I am in your debt, Elizabeth," he said. "Throughout these last months, at times, I have—" He paused, trying to frame the words, then seemed to lose his train of thought. "Well, if it hadn't been for you," he continued with some difficulty, "I might have given up."

Elizabeth was conscious of the warmth of his hand upon hers. She did not move. "I'm glad that I could be of help."

He studied her serene features, then slowly pulled his hand away from hers.

Soon they heard the sound of the children's voices and then the room was filled as Jenny and Evan herded them back inside.

Once everyone was seated, Elizabeth served the meal she had prepared. As they ate, Evan asked, "What do you think will be the effect of Cromwell's death on you preachers, Mr. Bunyan?"

"Not good, Evan."

"I've heard some talk of bringing Charles back to be king," Evan said conversationally. "People aren't satisfied with the way things are going."

"Cromwell made a mistake in naming his son Richard to succeed him," Bunyan said wearily. "He's not an able man."

Evan smiled. "No, guess not. They call him 'Tumble-Down Dick.' He's not much, I'm afraid. What would happen if Charles came back?"

Bunyan put his knife down, stared at his plate for a moment, then looked at Evan, his face serious. "It would be a hard time for those of us who sided with Cromwell. Those loyal to the king would come back from France, where they've been in exile, breathing fire and looking for revenge."

"And the first place they'd find it," Elizabeth said, "would be with those who are preaching the gospel."

Evan turned to her quickly. "Is that so? I didn't know you were a student of politics."

"That I am not," she murmured, her cheeks reddening slightly. "But everyone knows that the parliament is making it hard on independent preachers. If Charles and those who supported him returned, it would be much worse."

"Elizabeth is right." Bunyan nodded. "And I should not be surprised at all to see it happen."

They finished the meal and Bunyan went to sit with his wife. While Jenny occupied herself with the children, Evan managed to engage Elizabeth in conversation.

"Mrs. Bunyan's not going to live long, I fear," he said.

"No, unless the Lord performs a miracle, she cannot live."

Evan looked around to make certain that they could not be heard and lowered his voice. "That would leave Mr. Bunyan a widower. How would that strike you, Elizabeth?"

Elizabeth was startled. It was the plainest he had spoken to her for some time; she had forbidden him long ago to speak of such things. But now he sat there unrepentant and watched her with intense eyes.

"Evan, I forbid you to say such things," she replied sternly.

"It's our Christian duty to help Pastor Bunyan and his family in their hour of need. That's what I am doing and I'll hear no more about it!"

In that instant, seeing the fire in her eyes and the stiffness in her posture, Evan realized exactly how serious Elizabeth's attraction was toward John Bunyan. Evan watched her carefully as she rose and left the table, two red spots high on her cheekbones, but he said nothing further.

Later that night, however, when Elizabeth had left and Bunyan had gone to bed, he spoke of it to Jenny. "I'm worried about Elizabeth. She's in love with John Bunyan."

Jenny looked up. In the last year, she had grown into full womanhood and her freshness and striking beauty had brought her many admirers from the areas around Wakefield. She had paid no heed to any of them, despite the fact that some of them were considered highly eligible suitors. Now she stared at Evan, folded her hands, and said merely, "It's none of our business."

Evan gave her a curious glance; he could never quite reconcile the fact in his mind that this glorious young woman was the same skinny little girl that he had brought with him from Wales. He had watched her blossom and now was struck again by what a beautiful young woman she had become. Leaning forward, he clasped his hands together and studied her. "You don't think much of me, do you, Jenny?" he asked. "You think I'm nothing but a flirt who spends his time chasing after every skirt I see."

Jenny had not expected this question from Evan—certainly not in as sincere a tone as it was posed—and she gave him a startled glance. "I think," she replied with some difficulty, "that you're too interested in young ladies. Oh, they've given you cause to be that way, I well know that! But you're too interested by far."

"A man has to look around. How would he know the right woman unless he's seen several of the other kind?" Evan quipped, lapsing into his usual careless manner.

"That's foolish talk," Jenny retorted. "You know better. In any case, I've told you from the start that Elizabeth would never look at you. She's not one of your silly little girls that fall down every time you roll your eyes."

Evan's wide, generous mouth turned upward in a grin. "What if I rolled my eyes at you, Jenny?" he teased. "Would you fall down?" She gave him a scathing look, and he let out an exaggerated sigh. "No, you wouldn't. You know me too well." He studied her for a few moments and then asked abruptly, "What about you? Young Brian Satterfield is more than intrigued with you. He's a comfortably set-up fellow. He'll have plenty of money if his father ever has the grace to die and leave it to him. He's been trotting around behind you like some sorrowful hound dog for the last six months. Will you have him?"

"No."

"No? That's sprightly said! What's wrong with him?"

"There's nothing wrong with him," Jenny answered calmly. "I just don't love him, that's all."

"Ah, I fear you've been listening to too many ballads! 'All for Love!' they cry. Truly, I believe you'd be an actress if Cromwell hadn't forbidden theatres! I'm sure that if the king returns we'll have acting again—and you'll be front and center stage, won't you! 'All for Love,' indeed. Life just isn't like all that, Jenny. Not really."

She shrugged. "I don't know what you mean by 'all that,' Evan. But I believe in love. Don't you?" she asked suddenly, her fine eyes searching his face with a trace of anxiety.

"Why . . . uh . . . I suppose I do," Evan stammered, "but I think we mean different things by it."

"I don't know what there is to *mean,*" Jenny insisted. "When you love someone, you love them! It's that simple."

Evan laughed, shaking his head. They talked for some time and Evan found himself well entertained. Jenny was quite intelligent—a fact Evan had discovered soon after he brought her to Wakefield. She had a phenomenal memory and had learned to read with astonishing quickness. It wasn't long before she'd read every book that Angharad had given her. Her mind was far quicker than his own, Evan admitted to himself, but he did not begrudge her this. Indeed, he enjoyed her company.

Now he sat, enjoying the wit that flashed brightly from her and the intelligent, thoughtful way she conversed with him. "Recite one of those poems that you've memorized, Jenny," he ordered her, leaning back lazily. "And make it one about love."

She gave him a sharp look and saw that he was smiling affably, even somewhat wistfully. She nodded. "All right, I will." She began to recite and as the words of the poem filled the room, Evan listened carefully.

Come live with me and be my love
And we will all the pleasures prove
That valleys, groves, hills, and fields,
Woods, or steepy mountain yields.

And we will sit upon the rocks,
Seeing the shepherds feed their flocks,
By shallow rivers to whose falls
Melodious birds sing madrigals.

And I will make thee beds of roses
And a thousand fragrant posies,
A cap of flowers, and a kirtle
Embroidered all with leaves of myrtle;

A gown made of the finest wool
Which from our pretty lambs we pull;
Fair lined slippers for the cold,
With buckles of the purest gold;

A belt of straw and ivy buds,
With coral clasps and amber studs:
And if these pleasures may thee move,
Come live with me, and be my love.

The shepherds' swains shall dance and sing
For thy delight each May morning:
If these delights thy mind may move,
Then live with me and be my love.

Evan stared at Jenny with wonder in his eyes. The young voice had a fullness and depth that he had seldom heard, and her expression as she recited was intent. "Why, that's fairly done!" he exclaimed. "Was that one of Mr. Shakespeare's poems?"

"No, it's by one of his friends. A man called Christopher Marlowe."

"What's it all about . . . 'belts of straw' and 'lined slippers'?"

She dimpled at him, caught up in the beauty of the words she'd just quoted. "Oh, I don't really know, Evan, but isn't it just lovely!"

Evan laughed. "Well, the man who gets you will have to be a poet, that's clear!"

Jenny flushed. "Don't make fun of me, Evan!"

"Why, I'm not! Truly. I like a beautiful young lady quoting poems about love." Evan applauded her sincerely, but he could see in her eyes that she felt he was mocking her. Quickly he added, "You are a fine girl, Jenny. You're beautiful and smart. Some man's going to get quite a treasure one day when he gets you for his wife." He stretched, yawned, and went to climb the ladder upstairs, where he slept with the boys.

Jenny sat alone, watching the fire die and feeling the room grow cold. *I wonder,* she thought dully, *if he'll ever see me as a woman and not as a starving little girl that came to him out of the woods?*

Hearing a small sound, Elizabeth looked up quickly. She rose at once and bent over Leah Bunyan. "Are you awake, Leah?" she whispered. "Can you hear me?"

The thin, drawn face twitched slightly and then Leah opened her eyes. There was awareness and knowledge in them as Leah whispered weakly, "Elizabeth—"

"Shall I go get John?" she asked urgently.

Leah's pale face settled into lines of calmness and her eyes, which had been filled with pain and uncertainty for the past twenty-four hours, became clear. When she spoke, her voice had grown stronger, firmer. "No, not . . . just yet. I have something . . . to say to you first."

Elizabeth saw that the woman's life was slowly running out and she felt desperately that she should run now and get the family. But the dying woman reached out to take her hand. "What is it, Leah? Can I get you something?"

She shook her head slightly. "I will be leaving here soon. The Lord has told me that. But . . . there is something . . . I must say . . . to you."

"To *me?*"

"Yes." Leah's grip tightened and she looked directly into the eyes of the young woman by her deathbed. "You have been a blessing to me . . . and to the children," she murmured. Her voice was firm, though faint, and Elizabeth saw she was free of delirium. Leah went on for a few moments, thanking Elizabeth for the kindness and care she had shown the Bunyan family. "You have been . . . a mother to my little ones."

"I love them as if they were my own," Elizabeth said quietly as tears gathered in her gentle blue eyes.

A strange expression crossed Leah Bunyan's face and she studied the younger woman. "Elizabeth. Please . . . listen. . . ."

"Yes? What is it, Leah?"

"The Lord has spoken to me concerning my children. I could not die easily unless I knew that they would . . . be loved and cared for. John loves them, but he is only a man . . . though the best man I've ever known. . . ."

She faltered and her eyes closed with weariness. Elizabeth grew alarmed as Leah drew several short, labored breaths—as though she were reaching deeply for air and strength.

Then her eyes opened again and she said urgently, squeezing Elizabeth's hand, "You . . . must be a mother . . . to my children. Will you do that, my dear?"

Somewhat bewildered at the request, Elizabeth responded, "I will love them, Leah, and—and do my best. I promise you!"

"You have been faithful. I pray that God . . . will let you know . . . what it means to be a mother . . . and a wife." Elizabeth blinked rapidly, trying to understand the meaning of the dying woman's words. Then Leah said weakly, "Get . . . my husband . . . and little ones."

Elizabeth hurried from the room. John was sitting in the great room, holding the baby, Thomas, in his lap. The other children had gone to sleep. It was after midnight and they were all exhausted.

"Mr. Bunyan!" Elizabeth whispered. "Quick! Go to your wife!"

At once he stood, immediate understanding in his eyes. "Hurry! Let's wake the children!" Between them they got the children awake and hurried them into their mother's bedroom.

Elizabeth never forgot the next few minutes. Leah was conscious long enough to kiss each of the children and to hold her baby in her arms. Then, after blessing them, she reached up to John. "You have been the best husband earth could provide, but I go . . . to the . . . heavenly Bridegroom." She sighed deeply and closed her eyes, and both John and Elizabeth thought she was gone.

But she opened her eyes and looked at John, then her gaze shifted to Elizabeth. "You . . . will love and care f-for my little ones. The two of you. God will honor you." She closed her eyes, a smile on her lips, and her frail body went limp.

Elizabeth felt as though her heart had come up into her throat. Tears burned her eyes and she fought them back, turning to leave the room silently. John and the children gathered round Leah's bedside and the family said their last farewell to the wife and mother who had slipped away.

Seven

A Time to Embrace

John Bunyan entered the cottage and frowned wearily at the disarray that met his eyes. He had not known how hard it would be to keep a house and manage four small children. Leah had been gone only a little more than a month, yet it seemed to him an eternity. The days since her death had passed interminably—each one a struggle, what with making arrangements for the day and trying to cook, see that the children were clothed, and carry on his business. In addition to this, whenever he could find someone to help, he would go to minister in various places throughout the county.

Now, dirty and tired, he was returning from a full day's work. He stared at the dark fireplace—the wood was burned down to gray, forlorn chunks—and shivered at the coldness of the room. The children, he supposed, were in bed. Tiptoeing over to the bedroom, he opened the door quietly and saw that all four of them were piled up in the big marriage bed that he had shared with Leah all their married life. They made four small humps under the piles of covers, only their heads showing.

Silently he moved to stand over them, tracing their features by the light of the single candle that burned steadily in its holder. Mary, he saw, was sucking her thumb.

Poor little thing, he thought painfully. *She tries so hard to take her mother's place—and she's so tiny.* He wanted to pick her up and hold her, but he knew that she needed to sleep. Turning quietly, he left the room.

He built up the fire until it was a blaze that comforted him somewhat, then made himself a pot of tea. He knew that Mrs. Smith, from next door, would be coming back soon. She had been wonderful with the children since Leah's death, but the woman had three small ones of her own and a heavy workload to bear in her own household.

The kettle began to hiss, and to prevent it from breaking into a shrill whistle, John hurried to take it off the coals. He poured the hot water into his cup and the aroma of tea made his mouth water, making him realize suddenly that he was hungry. He rose up to search the cupboard and found nothing at all to eat save a bone with a few morsels of beef clinging to it. That and half a loaf of bread would have to do. Sitting down, he ate slowly, chewing thoroughly and washing the cheerless meal down with two cups of tea.

He leaned back in his chair, bone weary. His mind was dazed and clouded with fatigue. *I can't go on much longer like this!* he thought with discouragement. He had known it would be hard, but this was beyond difficult—it was deadening. Sitting before the fire, watching the cheerful yellow flames rise and send bright sparks dancing up the chimney, he half-closed his eyes and stretched, trying to soak in the heat.

Memories of his early days with Leah danced in his mind. How happy they had been! Theirs had not been a wild, breathless passion as some ballads and storybooks would have it. He and Leah had loved each other quietly, surely. They had been joined together and had become one.

John Bunyan did not regret never knowing a great, sweeping stirring of his emotions. He had loved Leah dearly. She had been a faithful and loving wife. The last few years had been hard because of her sickness, but he had not begrudged one moment of the effort and the strain it took to keep her as happy and free from worry as he possibly could.

"Thank God I was faithful to that!" he muttered, staring into the flames, somewhat comforted. Still, he longed for companionship. He sorely missed the warmth of a woman's spirit and the solace of her love.

Some men were made for marriage; John Bunyan was such a man.

A tap at the door interrupted his reverie. He arose and opened it, saying, "Mrs. Smith—," and then broke off in surprise.

Elizabeth stood there, holding the handles of a steaming pot in her hands. The vapor from the pot rose gently in the night's cold. "Mr. Bunyan!" she said, mirroring his surprise. "I didn't think you'd be home tonight."

At her startled words he recalled that long, long ago that morning he had told Mrs. Smith that he would likely be away all night. He had entreated her to take care of the children as best she could.

"I'm—I'm so tired, I'd forgotten—," he stammered in some confusion, then stepped aside, shaking his head wearily. "Never mind. Please come in, Elizabeth."

When she was inside, he hastened to explain. "I finished the job much sooner than I thought, so I hurried home. But I thought Mrs. Smith would be here."

"Her youngest boy has the measles," Elizabeth said. "We didn't want to expose your children, so she sent for me."

Bunyan's shoulders drooped. "I'm sorry to be such a burden," he groaned.

"How could you be that?" Elizabeth replied matter-of-factly. "Here, I've brought some broth. You must be hungry."

"There's no food in the pantry," Bunyan said with frustration. "I thought there was plenty! I can't keep up with anything!"

"I know," she said soothingly. "Now sit down." She put the pot on the fire, then went to the cupboard and found a clean bowl. She filled it with the steaming broth and firmly placed the bowl and a spoon in front of him. "Please go ahead and eat. Did you have any lunch today?"

Bunyan smelled the rich broth gratefully. "Hm? I don't know. Oh yes, I had . . . something." He began to eat hungrily, savoring every mouthful of the broth with relish. Staring at the empty bowl, he muttered, "Did the children have any supper?" Then he looked up to smile ruefully at Elizabeth. "Well, of course they did! You took care of that, too, didn't you?"

"Oh yes," she replied. She had made two more cups of tea while he ate and now she sat down at the table with him. As they enjoyed the hot, strong liquid, she told him what the children had done that day.

As she recounted an amusing story of the baby, a small voice in her mind observed, *Just like old married people, sipping a late cup of tea and talking about the children.* The thought sent a warm and somehow unsettling current of emotion racing through her, and she broke off midsentence.

Noticing her consternation, John searched her face curiously. "What is it, Elizabeth? Is something wrong?"

"Oh no, nothing's wrong," she replied hastily. "I—I must be going home. It's late. I'll come back in the morning to take care of the children. Will you be going to work?"

"Yes—no—yes—" With an effort, Bunyan stopped his stumbling words. His elbows on the table, he clasped his big, rawboned hands together and touched them to his forehead briefly, then looked back up at Elizabeth.

The strain was showing on his face, she could see. His countenance was usually cheerful and open; now his face was drawn and his eyes darkened by suffering. "I . . . I—just don't know—what to do anymore, Elizabeth," he wearily whispered.

Elizabeth Mills was a devout—and sheltered—young woman. She was old enough to be courted, but she had never shown any interest in the young men of the neighborhood. There was only one man who interested her: John Bunyan. For some time she had been aware that her interest in him was—unusual. And she had thought many times of the last words that Leah Bunyan had spoken to her. She had fasted and prayed and at times she had felt nothing but a grim despair. At other times a strange exultation would course through her, though she could never quite formulate the reason for it. A steady woman, filled with life and a desire to serve God, Elizabeth was also hungry for affection.

The two sat in silence for long moments until Elizabeth found herself beginning to tremble. She had stayed up almost all the previous night, feeling that God was speaking to her. But there was a cloud of confusion in her mind that she knew was not of God, so she had struggled to clear her soul and listen with her spirit. Somehow, in her struggles, she had decided that the thoughts and longings that sometimes filled her were of God and that she did not have to be afraid.

Looking down at her hands, she realized she was squeezing them so tightly together that they were white. Forcing herself to relax, she lifted her eyes. "Mr. Bunyan? . . . John?" she asked hesitantly.

Caught by the timbre of Elizabeth's voice and her use of his first name, he looked up. He saw that her face was pale and her lips trembled slightly. The expression in her eyes made him wonder what was coming. "What is it, Elizabeth?" he asked quietly.

"I—I want to . . . say something to you."

She was grave and somehow fearful, and John began to dread hearing whatever she was struggling to tell him. *She's going to say she can't come anymore,* he thought with despair. *That it's not right for a young, unmarried woman to be alone so much with a man, even though the children are here. People might begin to talk. . . .* These thoughts brought a bleakness to his heart and mind and he realized just how much he had come to trust in this tall, clear-eyed young woman. Bracing himself, he set his jaw and nodded. "I think I know what you're going to say, Elizabeth."

"No, I think not," Elizabeth breathed. She wanted desperately to get up and leave the room, the house, to escape. She was about to put herself at the mercy of a man that she greatly respected—no, revered—and she was too afraid to speak.

Across the table from her, Bunyan cocked his head to one side, then leaned forward to study her countenance closely. He said nothing for a moment, his mind searching for the reason she should be having such difficulty framing the words to speak to him. *Is she . . . is she going to be married? But why would she be afraid to tell me that?* Aloud he said, "Don't be afraid, Elizabeth. Whatever it is won't change what you've done for me and for the children. And for Leah. It won't change how grateful we are to you and how thankful we are to have you. Come now, tell me."

Elizabeth swallowed hard, then formed the words, her voice trembling. "John, you need a wife. And . . . and I believe—" She broke off and raised her hand to her lips. It was no use. She could go no further.

Bunyan stared at her in amazement. Of all the things that she might have said, this was the last that he had expected to hear. His mind seemed to simply stop functioning. Then he saw that she was trembling and her breathing was uneven, like a frightened doe's. He rose and hurried around the table to pull her to her feet.

Holding her hands, his gaze burned into her. "Elizabeth! Tell me! What is it?"

She grasped his rough hands in a desperate attempt to steady herself as she spoke. With an effort she made herself meet his eyes. "I . . . am very young and have no—no knowledge of men," she stammered. "But I have learned to love your children. They have no mother . . . and . . ." Still he waited in silence, his eyes searching her face as she spoke. She took a deep breath before going on. "I have prayed much about this and I must say what I believe God has put on my heart."

"Whatever God bids us, we must do," Bunyan agreed. "Though we may at times mistake the voice of the Lord, it is better to make an honest mistake than to ignore the prompting of the Holy Ghost." Strange emotions were beginning to sweep him as he stood holding Elizabeth's soft hands. Long had he admired her sweetness and quiet dignity, but now, as they stood so near, her hands nestled in his, he grew deeply aware of her beauty and grace.

"You need a wife, John," Elizabeth repeated tremulously. "And I . . . I believe that God is telling me that I am the woman he has chosen for you."

Blood hammered in John's ears so loudly that for a moment he thought he could not have heard her right.

Elizabeth mistook his silence. "You . . . you think me a fool," she faltered. "And no doubt I am!"

Pulling her hands free, she turned away from him and dropped her head. Hot tears scalded her eyes and she fully meant to run out of the room—but found she could not move.

Then his hands were on her shoulders, turning her around. He gazed down into her face, his eyes warm and somber. "You are not like any young woman I have ever known," he said quietly. He made a tall, angular shape by the light of the flickering flames. His face was strong, though now it was drawn with care. She met his eyes, and even as he looked at her, his face softened and his eyes brightened. "We will pray," he said. "But I tell you now, I do not think it can be—"

"You do not love me," she said quickly. "That is as it should be. You had a faithful wife and your love is for her. But I could be a mother to your children, John." She met his uncertain gaze squarely now. "That is what Leah said before she died. She entreated me to be a mother to her children. It gave her great comfort to know that I would try."

Bunyan nodded slowly. "Yes, perhaps that is what she meant when she spoke those final words about us taking care of the children."

"I would not expect to receive the love you gave to her," Elizabeth said in a low voice. "But I must tell you that I have a great admiration for you and I promise you I would be a good wife." She hesitated and dropped her eyes. "It shames me that I would say this . . . to ask a man to marry me—"

Again Bunyan took her hands. Then he did something he had never done in all of his life: He lifted her hands and kissed them. When she blushed with confusion, he smiled. "You would not have done so if you had not felt that God was in it. You are a godly woman, Elizabeth Mills! I have never doubted that."

The room grew quiet. She was aware of the strength of his hands and a peace settled over her.

After a time, Bunyan said, "Come, let us pray and seek God's will. Whatever he directs, we will follow. But I tell you this, Elizabeth, you would be throwing yourself away. You ought to have a man of youth and prospects; I have neither."

"Oh yes, you have prospects!" Elizabeth said eagerly. "You are a fine preacher of the gospel and God is blessing your work. I feel in my spirit, John, that he will do great things through you!" She clasped his hands tightly for a moment, then pulled one free to reach up and touch his cheek. "You have wondrous prospects, John Bunyan, of being faithful to God." A beautiful smile lit her face, and she whispered, "And I will be your helpmeet."

END OF PART ONE

1660 **Part TWO** 1665

Restoration

Eight

JENNY IN LONDON

The hour was very late when John Evelyn sat down at the table beside his bed, dipped his quill in ink, and then began to write:

May 29, 1660

This day His Majesty Charles II came to London after a sad and long exile and calamitous suffering, both of the King and Church, being 17 years. This was also his birthday, and with a triumph of above 200,000 horse and foot, brandishing their swords and shouting with inexpressible joy; the ways strewed with flowers, the bells ringing, the streets hung with tapestry, fountains running with wine; the Mayor, Aldermen, and all the Companies in their liveries, chains of gold and banners; Lords and Nobles clad in cloth of silver, gold, and velvet; the windows and balconies all set with ladies; trumpets, music, and myriads of people flocking, even so far as Rochester, so as they were seven hours in passing the City, even from two in the afternoon 'til nine at night.

I stood in the Strand and beheld it, and blessed God.

Evelyn paused to recall the almost miraculous events that had brought Charles II back as king. Primarily Evelyn's thoughts were of General Monk, head of the army, who had exercised the necessary muscle to bring the exiled king back to England. Aided by Chancellor Hyde, who had shared his master's exile, the king had drafted the Declaration of Breda. In this document Charles promised to leave the settling of all difficult problems to future parliaments. Upon receiving this declaration, parliament had sent Charles a large sum of money and dispatched the fleet, which once was so hostile to the king, to conduct him back to his native shores.

Evelyn reread his entry, then said aloud, "Now every man crowds to welcome the king home to his own. I never heard such cheering or witnessed such weeping and uncontrolled emotion." Drawing his hand across his brow, he muttered, "I feel as if our country has been delivered from a nightmare. Now we can go on to a golden age."

Across the city, in another room, another man sat writing in a secret journal. Samuel Pepys, the son of a London tailor, had been an eyewitness to the execution of Charles I. He was with the fleet when they brought Charles II back from exile and was slated to become secretary of the admiralty.

The marks that he painstakingly made on the paper before him could not have been translated by any reader, for they were in a secret code. He wanted to write down the absolute truth, but he well knew the penalty for doing so. Therefore, he had devised a complex, secret manner of writing that no other man save himself could read.

Had another been able to decipher the man's words, this is what he would have read:

> His Majesty had saturnine features set off by a black periwig, and a powerful athletic frame. We weighed anchor at Ancre and came with a fresh gale and most happy weather as we set sail for England. All the afternoon the king walked here

and there, up and down. Quite contrary to what I thought him to have been, he was active and stirring.

The boat that we took from the ship was small. In it was a dog that the king loved, which proceeded to relieve himself, which made us laugh and made me think that a King, and all that belongs to him, are but just as others are.

When we landed at Dover, infinite the crowd of people and the gallantry of the horsemen, citizens, and noblemen of all sorts.

December 1660

Jenny had not expected that she would make the trip to London and so was elated when Susanne Wakefield came to her. "I need you to go to London with me. Start packing my dresses and everything I'll need, at once!"

"Yes, Mrs. Wakefield," Jenny said with excitement.

It had seemed natural for Jenny to serve as Susanne's personal maid. Gavin's wife, to be sure, was an easy mistress: kind and requiring little. Jenny had grown quite fond of her, as she had of Gavin. Now as she ran up the stairs and began pulling the necessary clothing together for the trip, she found herself wondering what life would be like in England with the king once again sitting on the throne.

Passing before a mirror, Jenny was caught by her own reflection and studied herself critically. She was accustomed to hearing admiring remarks about her appearance; at the age of sixteen she was well into full-fledged womanhood. She ran her hand over her red-blonde hair, which hung down to her waist.

The Puritan women had kept their hair carefully bound and under caps. Many still did, even under the Merry Monarch King

Charles. Jenny, however, loved the freedom of leaving her hair unbound. Besides, she knew that it was pleasing to the eye. Peering at her reflection, she scrutinized her widely spaced eyes. Today they were a deep green, but she knew they sometimes were a light blue-green, much the same color as the seas from a southern ocean. At other times they seemed to grow darker green with only a slight bluish tinge. The fact that all of Jenny's emotions and expressions shone from her eyes bothered her at times, but she didn't mind at the moment, for what she saw there was excitement.

Her dress was simple enough, as befitted a servant. It was maroon and of a modest cut, yet it could not help but outline her trim waist and generous curves.

Abruptly she laughed at herself, her eyes crinkling at the corners. "Well, if you're done admiring yourself, Jenny Clairmont," she admonished the reflection in the mirror, "you can get about your work now!"

An efficient young woman, Jenny soon had her mistress's clothing and toiletries packed and ready. Hurrying downstairs, she encountered Angharad. "I have Miss Susanne's things ready. Will you be going, Lady Wakefield?"

"No, I'll stay here with Sir Christopher." Angharad smiled at the pretty young girl. "I see you're excited about the trip. I'm glad. You've had a rather boring life here, I'm afraid, caring for Sir Christopher and the rest of us."

"Oh no, Lady Wakefield!" Jenny protested. She loved this woman, who had shown her unending kindness. "I'm excited, but I wish that Sir Christopher was well enough to go."

A shadow crossed Angharad's features. "I'm afraid he is not strong enough." Jenny's distress was evident in her eyes, and Angharad reflected that the girl had a sensitivity far beyond the normal for most young, pretty women. "It's hurting I am only a little," Angharad said to comfort her, the old Welsh patterns of speech creating a lilt to her words and voice. She patted Jenny's shoulder. "You go along now and be certain you keep an eye on Amos! I'll want a full report on his behavior when you get back. And on Evan's, too!" With mock despair she added, "Two handsome young men like that! I'm hating to see them turned loose on London Town!"

Jenny flashed her bright smile, the dimple in one cheek popping into place. "There's nothing I can do with them. You'd best tell Mr. Gavin to keep them on a short leash!"

"I'll do that," Angharad agreed and went on to Christopher's study.

She found Gavin with his father in the study, the two of them absorbed in a chess game. "Well, devil throw smoke!" she exclaimed. "Are you two ever going to give up that silly game?" Angharad had no patience with chess; it required a type of mathematical mind that she lacked. Christopher had tried to teach her, but she had soon given up, saying, "Nothing but numbers and thinking! I'll have none of it!"

"Nor do you need to. You're far better with dreams and romantic notions," Christopher had replied with a laugh.

Now her husband looked up from the chessboard, a smile on his lips. "I must convince this young rascal that I'm still the best chess player in England!" he told her in mock indignation. Reaching over the black-and-white squares, he moved a piece with a flourish. "Checkmate! Now that's three games in a row, Gavin! Be off with you. I'm bored with such paltry competition!"

Gavin shook his head ruefully. He was a few months shy of thirty-seven and he looked a great deal like his father, except that his hair was ash blonde instead of the dark auburn of most of the Wakefield men. His straight nose had been broken, which gave him a rather tough appearance. He rose, carrying his right shoulder slightly higher than the left, and came to stand beside his stepmother.

"Angharad," he muttered darkly, "this husband of yours is impossible. I don't see how you've put up with him." He put his arm around her and gave her an affectionate squeeze. "I'll bring you back a present from London." He scowled at his father. "But none for you! The truth is, I lose on purpose just to make you feel good!"

Christopher laughed delightedly. Today was one of his good days and he looked almost hearty. The color in his cheeks only made the blue of his deep-set eyes seem even darker and one could still see, despite his illness, remnants of the strength that had been great in his youth. "Off with you, boy! And mind you keep an eye on Amos!"

"Oh, I'll keep him on a tight bit, sir!" Gavin assured his father. A thought occurred to him, and his blue-gray eyes lit with humor. "I had an idea about the lad—something that might make him behave a little better."

"And what is that?" Angharad demanded.

"Well, we put hoods on the hawks and falcons until we're ready to fly them," Gavin said solemnly. "What I propose is that we make the same kind of hood for Amos so that he can't see anything 'til we pull it off! That way he won't be dashing off at full gallop after the poor country girls and the minister's daughters! What do you think of the idea?"

Christopher grinned broadly. "I approve wholeheartedly! Capital idea! Have Will make a leather hood for that boy before you leave!"

"Perhaps Will had better make two," Angharad muttered, "one for Evan as well. He and Amos have become two of a kind, much too free—and too spoiled by half—by their good looks!"

Gavin went over to put his hand on his father's shoulder. "Don't worry, I'll watch over them as best I can, Father." He glanced back at Angharad. "They may be fifteen years younger than I, but they'll not overcome me. I'm old, but I'm crafty."

"Good, you," Angharad said with satisfaction. "I've told Jenny that I'll hear everything about everyone when you return."

Gavin squeezed his father's shoulder affectionately, kissed his stepmother, and left them alone.

Angharad watched him go, a fond look in her eyes. "What a fine man he is! So like you, Chris."

"He's like his mother, too," Christopher told her warmly. "She had so many fine qualities."

Angharad sat beside him and they spoke for a long time. Their conversation, as was common with happily married couples, was punctuated by long, comfortable silences. Finally Angharad said, "I've been wondering what will come now that we Roundheads are out of favor."

"So have I." Christopher's brow furrowed with thought. "Charles has surprised me. I had feared he would come back crying for blood and revenge for his father, but that hasn't happened."

"He must be a kind man, do you think?"

"Not so much kind as . . . well, *indifferent*. At least that's what I hear from my friend John Evelyn. He says that Charles simply wore himself out in debaucheries while he was in France. All the bad habits those Frenchmen have!" He shrugged. "He's had countless mistresses, and half a dozen illegitimate children are trailing in his wake. But I will give him credit that he seems to lack bitterness regarding his father's execution. That's more than I can say about many of the Royalists who are returning to England's shores."

"Perhaps the king will be able to do something to free men like John Bunyan who are imprisoned for preaching," Angharad said hopefully.

"I think he would be so inclined," Christopher ventured, nodding thoughtfully. "But he may not be able."

Angharad stared at him. "He's the king. Can't he do as he pleases?"

"No, not even a king may do that. Especially after the death of his father. England has seen one king executed. Now anyone who sits on the throne has to be aware that he could well become another victim." Christopher leaned a little closer to her. He could smell the faintest touch of a flower scent in her hair. "I got a letter from another friend of mine, Angharad. He's in government." He motioned to the table. "Would you mind fetching it for me? It's over there."

Angharad hurried to get the letter and sat down again close beside him. As she handed him the letter he explained, "It's from Samuel Pepys. You met him once, I think. He's a fine man, bound to rise high in the government. I did him a good turn once and now he keeps me informed about the new monarchy. Listen to what he has to say.

"The letter is dated October 13, 1660. He writes, 'I went out to Charing Cross to see Major-General Harrison hanged, drawn, and quartered; which was done there. He looked as cheerful as any man could do in that condition. He was presently cut down and his head and heart shown to the people, at which there were great shouts of joy. It is said that he was sure to come shortly at the right hand of Christ to judge them that now had judged him; and that his wife do expect his coming again. Thus it was my chance to see the king beheaded at White Hall and to see the first blood shed in revenge for the king at Charing Cross.'" Christopher paused, shaking his head. "'The first blood shed in revenge for the king.' I daresay that's a bad omen, Angharad. I pray that more will not follow," he finished in a low voice.

Instantly she asked, "Is it safe for the children to go to London?"

"London or Wakefield, it doesn't matter. If the bloodhounds bay hard enough and the parliament listens, we may see many who stood by Oliver Cromwell suffer for that decision." Again he leaned close to his wife and covered her hand with his. "Hard times may be coming, I'm afraid."

Angharad took his hand and laid it on her smooth cheek. She smiled up at him, and her confidence and peace made her eyes glow. "Through God we shall do valiantly," she said. Christopher smiled. His wife's abiding faith always rose above every doubt and extremity, and he thanked God that he had been given such a woman.

"I'm sure your parents wouldn't like it."

Amos Wakefield winked at Evan Morgan, who immediately returned the wink. Amos glanced at Jenny, who had uttered the caution as they rode along the streets of London in a carriage.

"What they don't know won't hurt them," Amos said.

"Right, you." Evan nodded vigorously. "Nothing wrong with a bit of playacting. That's one disservice Cromwell did with his government, to close all the theatres down."

Jenny's chin lifted. "You don't talk like that around Mr. Gavin or Sir Christopher. You'd be afraid to. And Angharad and Will would cut your ears off—all four of them—if they thought you two were going to a play!"

Amos threw up his hands in exaggerated despair. "Faith, Jenny, you're nothing but a bluenosed Puritan! You've got to come out of that shell of yours! This is not the Protectorate! It's the reign of King Charles II, the Merry Monarch!"

"I know how 'merry' he is," Jenny sniffed. "What has he ever done, besides father a bunch of illegitimate children and stash a mistress in every bedroom he passed?"

Evan's eyes widened in astonishment at Jenny's blunt speech. "Well—well—I didn't suppose you knew about such things as that!" he blustered. "You've been listening to gossip, have you?"

"I speak no more than everyone knows," Jenny retorted. "The king is a lecher and an adulterer."

Amos had had his fill of this conversation about his monarch. "All right, we'll take you back to the inn if you're set against the play. But I'm going to the theatre! I hear tell they even have a woman as an actor!"

Jenny snapped, "A woman, indeed! I can imagine what kind of baggage she must be. Exposing herself, flaunting about on a stage."

"That's as may be," Evan commented lightly, "but I never found it to my liking to watch men playing women's roles. I've seen a play or two where the so-called ladies needed a shave badly! No, give me a woman in a woman's role every time!"

"Oh yes, you do know much about a woman's role," Jenny said disdainfully.

"Oh, look!" Evan said quickly. "There's the theatre. Make up your mind, Jenny. Are you going or shall we send you back?"

"I'm going," she declared. She turned to Amos and went on darkly, "I told Angharad I'd report everything you do. So you're not getting away from me! Nor you, Evan Morgan!"

The two men laughed. When the carriage stopped, they hurried out to assist her down. *They're a handsome pair, no doubt,* Jenny admitted to herself.

Amos, at six feet tall, with dark auburn curly hair and dark blue-gray eyes, made a striking figure of a man, strong and sure of himself. She shifted her gaze to Evan, who was only one inch shorter than Amos but quite different in appearance. He had dark, smooth features and gleaming black hair, which he wore long. His smoldering black eyes were set in a tapering face, which was made striking indeed by his wide mouth and high cheekbones. The look about him was one common to the Welsh, she supposed—an almost mystic quality in the expression and the eyes. This quality was pronounced in Angharad, and sometimes Evan reminded Jenny very much of his relative.

"This playhouse is the Red Bull," Amos pronounced, waving expressively. "The play is something called *Romeo and Juliet*. I can't recall who wrote it, but it's the first time it's ever been performed."

Jenny walked between the two tall young men, feeling out of place and rather uncomfortable. Nevertheless, she was fascinated by the activity that surrounded them. The people crowding into the playhouse were dressed in various forms of finery, and suddenly she felt rather dowdy in her plain gray dress and dark green cloak.

The theatre had a high ceiling; the chandeliers, lit by what seemed to be thousands of candles, threw an amber light over the audience as they took their seats. Amos, Jenny, and Evan had no sooner found seats than a man sitting behind them exclaimed, "Look! There's the Queen Mother!"

At once the three of them looked around to see Queen Henrietta Maria, widow of Charles I and mother of the king, enter the playhouse. Then another excited hiss came to their ears: "There! There's the king and the queen!"

As the royal pair were escorted to one of the balconies, Jenny examined them carefully. The queen wore a white lace waistcoat and a crimson petticoat. The king's attire was even more ornate than his queen's. He wore white hose, and the garters that rested just below both knees glittered with diamonds. His shoes were white leather and had golden buckles, also studded with jewels. His silver breeches were puffed and his short full blouse was a deep shade of crimson. The cloak he wore over this finery was adorned with bows of dark maroon and a fur trim dyed the same rich hue; this contrasted with the lining, which was of glimmering white silk. On the left sleeve of the cloak was the emblem of royalty: a red cross on a white shield. The king's hair was longer than many women's and fell well past his shoulders in waves of raven black. He had sparkling eyes and a sensuous mouth, Jenny saw.

Soon Jenny's attention was drawn to the stage as the drama began and slowly unfolded. The young woman found herself caught up in the play, moved as she had never been before. Though many of the expressions were somewhat formal, Jenny's quick ear and sharp mind enabled her to follow the events and action easily. The story of the young, ill-fated couple and their doomed love thrilled her. Tensely she leaned forward, oblivious to her two companions and the rest of the audience, absorbed in the action that took place on the stage, sharing the experience as though she were living it herself.

Evan was interested in the play, but he was equally fascinated by Jenny's reaction. *Why, she's inside this story!* he reflected with surprise. Her body strained forward, her eyes fixed intently on the actors, her lips slightly parted as she listened to each word and watched each gesture. *Looks as if we won't have to beg her to come to another play,* he thought with amusement.

When the play ended, Evan startled Jenny when he remarked, "Well, Jenny, it was pretty awful, hm? I wager you'll never come to another play, will you?" He winked broadly at Amos, who had also watched Jenny's fascination with amusement.

Jenny drew a deep breath. "I never saw anything like this," she murmured, ignoring their teasing. "That poor Juliet!" Her eyes were misty as she went on, "It's so sad—and poor Romeo! Such a handsome young man!"

"Both of them probably as godless as people can be," Amos remarked cheerfully. He had attended several plays and felt he knew a bit about acting. Still, he was pleased Jenny had enjoyed the play. "Come along, we'll go down and meet the actors."

Jenny stared at Amos with amazement. "You know them?"

"Oh no," he said carelessly. "But actors are always happy to meet important people. Like us. So come on."

Jenny never forgot that night. She was introduced to the young man who had played Romeo, and was somewhat surprised to find him older than he appeared on stage. But it was her meeting with the young Juliet, whose true name was Nell Gwyn, that thrilled her the most.

Nell was the most exquisitely beautiful creature Jenny had ever seen. With her smooth, beautiful complexion, a crown of auburn curls, and her full red lips, she seemed made as a woman to entice men. Her dress was low cut, and the smooth skin of her bosom gleamed in the candlelight.

"Why, you shouldn't bring beautiful young women such as this to me, Mr. Wakefield!" the actress said playfully to Amos. "Don't you know, sir, that an actress must always be the most beautiful woman in the room?" Her expressive eyes twinkled as she turned to Jenny. "Did you like the play, Mistress Clairmont?"

"Oh yes, Mistress Gwyn!" Jenny breathed. "It's the first play I've ever seen, and it was wonderful!"

Nell Gwyn's eyebrows shot up. "The first play you've ever seen! Oh, how your education has been neglected, child!" She was favorably impressed with the two handsome young men accompanying Jenny—especially with Amos Wakefield, as his father was a titled lord. "I insist that all of you come out to supper with us!" she said.

It did not take great persuasion, and the three accompanied the actress and several of her fellow thespians to an ornate private dining room in the heart of London.

Nell Gwyn was a charming young woman and she paid special attention to Jenny. "Will you be in London long, Mistress Clairmont?" she inquired.

"I think maybe for two weeks," Jenny answered eagerly.

"Wonderful! We must see each other often!" Nell looked across the table at Amos Wakefield, who was talking animatedly to other members of the company. Then she turned back to study Jenny carefully and remarked, "You would make an excellent actress."

Jenny blinked with amazement. "An . . . actress? But—but—!" The proposal shocked her, but she could not deny that the idea intrigued her very much. "Thank you, Mistress Gwyn, but I don't know anything about acting," she said doubtfully.

Nell's eyes gleamed with humor. "With beauty like yours, my dear, all you need do is stand on the stage. Some will think whatever you do is acting; others probably won't care whether you act or not, just as long as they get to watch you. But I suppose your family would object to this. Most families do."

"Oh, I have no family," Jenny said too quickly.

"But Mr. Wakefield there—" she nodded carelessly toward Amos—"I thought perhaps he was your relation."

"Oh no! I'm a servant in his father's house, to Sir Christopher Wakefield and his lady."

The actress found this interesting and questioned Jenny closely about her history.

When dinner was over and everyone was getting ready to leave, Nell said, "Come and see me, my dear. I'll give orders to see that you are admitted. Here is my address."

On the way back to their inn, Jenny said little. Evan and Amos were boisterous, filled with the excitement of the drama—and of having had dinner with the most famous actress in London—so they didn't notice Jenny's silence.

When the three were parting to go to their rooms, Amos asked Jenny curiously, "What were you and Nell Gwyn talking about?"

"Oh, just about the theatre," she answered vaguely.

"Well, she certainly knows about that! There isn't another actress in London who can compete with her. Rumor has it that the king himself is not immune to her charms."

Startled by Amos's words, Jenny didn't respond. She just nodded a good-night and, careful to walk softly as she passed Gavin and Susanne's door, went into her room. She tried to settle down but found that she could not sleep. She kept hearing Nell Gwyn's intriguing words, *"You would make an excellent actress."*

The truth was that Jenny Clairmont was an incurable romantic. Her life at Wakefield had been placid and she was grateful for it, but this visit to London had opened her eyes to a world she had never imagined. She could not sleep for thinking of the drama that she had seen—and lived.

Finally she whispered, "Juliet was so sad, but I could play that role." Indeed, Jenny had a vivid imagination, and though she had never acted in a play or in any sort of production, something inside her told her that she had the same qualities she had seen in those people on the stage, the ability to make people respond to her.

"You're going to do *what?"* Evan Morgan stared at Jenny as if she had announced that she was going to sprout wings and fly to the moon.

Jenny had braced herself for this explosion. They had spent a full three weeks in London and Jenny had spent time with Nell Gwyn almost every day. When Susanne inquired one morning as to how Jenny was occupying her free time, Jenny responded with a bright smile that she had found a friend with whom she could study and discuss classic writers. While it bothered her a little to stretch the truth so far, she consoled herself with the fact that she and Nell truly did discuss writers . . . well, playwrights.

Unbeknownst to her master and mistress, Jenny had seen a play every night, though not always a different play. Amos and Evan had laughed and teased her unmercifully for her change of heart. But they helped her slip out, often telling Susanne that they were showing the young maid the night sights of London and promising to watch out for her. While this announcement was met with some skepticism by Gavin and his wife, they did not openly question the truth of what was being said.

And so it was that Evan and Amos faithfully escorted Jenny each night to the theatre, both grateful that they truly enjoyed the plays—and didn't mind seeing them two or three times.

At last the time had come for them to leave London and return home—and Jenny had shocked Evan almost speechless when she had calmly announced, "I'm not going back to Wakefield. I'm going to stay here and be a maid to Mistress Gwyn."

"You can't do that!" Evan argued. "I won't allow it! It's insane!"

"You never cared what I did one way or another!" Anger flared hot and quick in Jenny's heart. Though she would never admit it, it had hurt that Evan had paid so little attention to her. She had longed to spend time with him, but he was too busy with his own interests. He had spent most of his time out-of-doors, working, hunting, and traveling for Sir Christopher. While a part of her understood that was as it should be, another part of her was filled with hurt and resentment at being so unimportant to him.

She could see from his expression that he was astonished by her vehemence, so she made an effort to speak more reasonably. "Come now, Evan. You don't really care anything about me. I owe you a great deal for helping me and I will pay you back one day. But that is the extent of our obligations to one another."

Evan stared at her, thunderstruck, and he groped for words. "There's no question of paying back," he finally said curtly, his expression troubled. "Jenny," he said desperately, "you don't know what these acting people are like. They have no more morals than . . . than *foxes!*"

Jenny knew there was truth in Evan's statement, but she had been over this in her own mind—and she had decided. "Mistress Gwyn's going to teach me how to act," she said defiantly. "She says that I may be a great actress!"

"But—an actress!" Evan said scornfully. "That's no better than being a streetwalker!"

If Evan had put forth a month's effort to find the wrong thing to say, he would never have arrived at a better choice of words. And as soon as he spoke, he knew it. As fire flashed in Jenny's eyes, he scrambled to repair the damage. "Jenny, I didn't mean—"

"I know what you meant!" Jenny replied stiffly. His careless words had driven any doubts from her mind. She was not certain that she was doing the right thing, but she would not give this . . . this *skirt chaser* the pleasure of seeing her back down. He had finalized her decision more effectively than Nell Gwyn ever could have done. Jenny lifted her eyes and stared at him, her face pale. "I'm going to show you that I can be an actress *and* a good woman! You will see, Evan Morgan!"

And that was the end of it.

Evan argued; Amos joined in. Gavin and Susanne, who had at last been informed of recent events by a most chagrined Amos, had long conferences with Jenny.

Nothing worked.

As they left London, Gavin said sadly, "Somehow we've made an awful mistake with that girl. We must find a way to get her away from London. I'll have Angharad come and see her," he said hopefully. "Jenny loves Angharad and trusts her."

"It won't do any good," Evan said shortly. "I'm sorry, Mr. Gavin, but that girl is as stubborn as the tides." He sat back in the carriage seat and crossed his arms, his eyes smoldering with a mixture of anger and doubt and a strange sense of emptiness.

It wasn't until much later, as they neared Wakefield, that Evan Morgan began to understand that he had lost something precious on this trip to London.

Nine

UNDER ARREST

Francis Wingate entered his study and sat down at the table. He looked around at the books that lined the wall, picked up the bottle of wine on his desk, then poured a small tumblerful. He sipped it slowly, staring into space, a meditative light in his eyes.

Wingate was thirty-two years old and had missed this study greatly. He had been exiled as a result of his Royalist activities and his faithfulness to King Charles I. With the arrival of the new king, he had been restored to his rightful place and now, as he sat in the walnut-sheathed study, he thought of those years of exile with resentment.

There were many, he knew, who had returned to England after prison and exile thirsty for blood. He, himself, was not a man of vengeance; he desired only to get on with what was left of his life. "There's no time for revenge," he murmured contemplatively.

He was quick and sharp-edged, but there was a basic fairness in him. This everyone admitted.

A knock sounded at the door. Wingate called out, "Come in!" The door opened and Wingate said cordially, "Ah, come in, sir. It grows colder?"

Enoch Lyndall, Wingate's father-in-law, entered and removed his cloak. "Yes, it does. I think we might have snow."

"Here, have some of this port. It will keep the chill off," Wingate urged. He poured a generous amount of the wine and handed it to his visitor. "Have you seen Foster?"

"Yes, I saw him as I came in."

"Good. I wanted to go to Dover to look at that new breed of cattle. I think they'll upgrade our stock." He looked up as another man entered the room. "Come in, William. Join us—have some wine."

William Foster was married to Wingate's sister. He was a large man with a loose expression that sometimes grew crafty, particularly when his own comfort or safety were being considered. He was a justice of the peace and a champion of the orthodox—so much so that a few of the Puritan persuasion who had already been feeling the weight of his hand were beginning to call him "A Right Judas."

"That's fine wine," Foster said, sipping appreciatively. He had settled comfortably into a chair.

"I'll have a couple of bottles sent over to you," Wingate offered. "And to you, too, sir," he said to his father-in-law.

Abruptly Dr. Lyndall said, "Francis, I want to speak to you about these independents. Especially about this fellow Bunyan."

Foster nodded emphatically. "That fellow's got to go."

Wingate sat back and studied his two visitors cautiously. "We've talked about him," he said evenly. "I see no particular harm in him."

"Have you read the latest law?" Dr. Lyndall demanded.

"I've read it," Foster put in.

"What's the force of it?" Wingate asked.

Lyndall answered with unnecessary vehemence. "It puts a stop, once and for all, to these Puritan 'Divines'! These self-appointed apostles of goodness!"

Foster continued languidly, "It'll be called the Conventicle Act.

What it will do is forbid any meeting of more than five people for religious purposes."

Wingate said wryly, "Hm, I see. It gives the appearance of liberty—without the substance."

"Yes." Foster nodded. "Five Puritans can't do much."

Lyndall surveyed the other two men critically. "Of course, they'll not keep this law, these independent preachers."

Wingate was distressed. He would much have preferred not to have conflicts with the independents. "No," he sighed, "they won't. What will be the penalty, do you think?"

Foster replied smugly, "The copy I saw said: 'Fine, transportation, or imprisonment for any exercise of religion in other manner than is allowed by the practice of England.'"

Shocked by the severity of this decree, Wingate burst out, "By the Lord! *That's* potent enough!"

Lyndall stared at him with narrowed eyes. "You can say such, Francis, after living in exile for a third of your life? By the merciful God above, it's too lenient by far! I'd prefer to see them hang!"

Carelessly Foster said, "But it won't come to that." He sipped his wine and a sly look came into his eyes. "These preachers may be religious fanatics, but some of them do possess a certain measure of business sense. They may not be afraid of much, but they'll not be eager to suffer what that law will put on them."

Wingate mulled over the matter in his mind. "I hear there will be other restrictions passed that all ministers will be required to employ *The Book of Common Prayer.*"

"That's as it should be," Foster said emphatically. "These Puritans have no sense! Imagine trying to drag God even into politics and commerce."

Wingate was quiet. He had been through difficult times, and memories of the cold cheerlessness of his exile rose in his mind. He studied Foster and Lyndall, knowing that there was a harshness in both men that did not bode well for the independent preachers of Bedford—and the rest of the country.

Sadness welled up in Wingate; he would have much preferred the way of peace. Still, he was a magistrate and would carry out the laws of his country. It was his responsibility.

Elizabeth Bunyan moved carefully as she crossed the room. She was large with child and something about the way she carried herself gave the impression to her husband that she was caring for something infinitely more precious than silver or gold.

John had been dismayed for her sake to discover that his young wife had become pregnant during the harsh winter months. "It's difficult enough to bear a child, but in the winter . . . !" he'd said with concern. "It will be very hard on you—and mayhap on the babe."

Her answer had been immediate and firm. "Every child is in God's timing, John. We will receive this one as a gift from the good Lord."

Outside, the November wind was whistling around the eaves. The apple tree beside the house seemed to claw at the structure, almost as a spectral ghost seeking entrance. There was a mournful sound in the keening of the wind that depressed Bunyan. He shook it off, however, and rose to cross the room. Stooping down, he picked up the iron pot for which Elizabeth was reaching.

"Here, let me get that."

Elizabeth looked up at him, her face a picture of the serenity that seemed to fill many women when they were bearing a child. She was happy. Though times had been hard financially for their family, Elizabeth had never known such joy as she had experienced with John Bunyan.

"You pamper me too much." She smiled and reached out to smooth his hair back from his forehead.

He stood still for a moment, the pot held in one hand, then reached out with the other to draw her close in an embrace. He could almost feel the life within her stirring. As with all his other children, there was a glory in knowing that God had entrusted him to be a father. "I don't pamper you nearly enough," he countered. He leaned over to kiss her and she put her arms up around his neck and held him tightly. For a moment they were caught up only in each other and their love.

Elizabeth drew her head back and her blue eyes brightened with pinpoints of light. "I didn't know I'd get a husband who was such a romantic man! Imagine, kissing me like that when I'm as big as an old cow!"

Bunyan shook his head and stroked her silky cheek gently. "A man would have to be made of stone not to be romantic about a beautiful creature like you."

"Oh, now I'm going to get sweet talk!" Elizabeth teased. "And the next thing, you'll be writing me another of those love poems!"

"I hope you didn't keep those things," John grumped.

Elizabeth's eyes widened with surprise. "Why, of course I kept them!" she admonished him. "And when I get enough of them, I'm going to publish them in a book! You aren't the only one in this family who'll have a book then!"

She referred to several pamphlets that John Bunyan had published over the past few years, all of which were doctrinal arguments—quite different indeed from the richly ornamented poetry that he wrote to her.

Bunyan grinned. "I hate to think what would happen if our church members saw their pastor's love poetry! They would likely kick me out on my ear!"

"Not so," Elizabeth said firmly. "They love you too much. You have made a fine pastor, John. I'm so proud of you."

Her words disturbed Bunyan somewhat. He reached out to set

the pot he held onto the table, then turned back to her. "I'm concerned about these new laws. I've already been arrested twice, and Judge Wingate tells me if I'm arrested one more time, he'll be forced to take more serious action."

Judge Wingate, Bunyan knew, had been far more lenient than the judge's father-in-law, Dr. Lyndall, would have been. But Bunyan also knew that Wingate was under heavy pressure to put a stop to the independent preachers of the area. Two of Bunyan's friends had recently been arrested and were in Bedford Jail awaiting their hearing.

The wind howled again outside, and John walked over to the single window to stare out. "It's very cold," he murmured. "There can't be many people who will attend the meeting. Perhaps none at all."

Elizabeth came to stand beside him. She put her arm around his waist and the two stood there silently, their eyes on the bleak scene outside but their thoughts upon each other.

They had been married almost two years and in that time Elizabeth had come to know John Bunyan as well as she knew herself. There was a childlike quality in this big husband of hers, so much so that at times he seemed to be one of the little ones whom she had come to love so dearly. She knew there was also a rocklike solidness deep within this man she had married. He was often lighthearted and witty, with a strain of quirky humor that was so strong it was an essence of his character. Now, as she thought of the danger he faced of being arrested—again—and put in jail, a chill seemed to settle into a cold lump in her heart. She had given herself to John so utterly and completely that the thought of not having him by her side caused an almost physical pain.

"Perhaps you shouldn't go, John," she whispered tremulously.

He looked down at her, aware of her fear. She was beautiful to him. He well knew how utterly she trusted in him. He studied her face, admiring the calm and classic features—saddened at the fear and beginnings of pain that lurked behind the quiet blue eyes.

"I'd much rather stay here with you and the children," John said slowly, "but I must go." He hesitated, trying to put his thoughts in order. "I don't know why God called a poor, unfit man like me to preach his glorious gospel, but I know that he has. That means I am responsible to those who otherwise might not hear." He turned back to stare out the window again, watching as the wind picked up a piece of paper and sent it scudding along the street. The force of the wind lifted it high and he watched as it twisted in a small whirlwind, high in the air, and then fell, fluttering, in a pile of dead brown leaves.

"What if one person were at that meeting today," he said softly, "and the only time he would ever hear of the Cross and the one who died for him was when he heard me today? Suppose I didn't go and that person turned and went away . . . and never heard another word about Jesus?" His tone grew solemn, almost fearful. "On Judgment Day I wonder if that person would point his finger at me and cry out, 'I'm damned because John Bunyan wanted to stay home in his warm cottage with his wife! Now I must spend eternity in hell because he didn't bring me the Good News!'"

A deep silence fell on the room. Elizabeth clung to her husband, knowing that arguments and pleading would be useless. She had known before she married him that his preaching meant everything to him. He saw it as a mandate from God. Regardless of how kind he was to her or how loving he was to his children, she well knew that his commission from God was so strong that he could never deny it.

Elizabeth forced herself to smile. "All right, John, you sit down and eat. I must sew up that rent in your coat. That wind will likely reach right down into it with icy fingers."

Thirty minutes later John Bunyan stood at the door. He turned and kissed her just as the children came trooping in. They had been next door at the Smiths' and now they clambered all around and over their father, holding on to his coat and begging him to stay. "It's going to snow," Mary said. "We can build a snowman! Please don't go!"

Bunyan bent over to kiss her on the cheek. "I'll build that snowman as soon as we get snow! I'll be back by the time that happens, little one!" He spoke to each one of the children, then looked over their heads at Elizabeth. "Good bye, wife," he said lightly. "And I'll be having a good supper when I get home."

"Yes, dear." Elizabeth smiled. She watched him as he left, a tall form making soldierly strides as he walked away—and she felt a sudden chill in her spirit. "Come, children," she said uneasily. "You must have your lessons now."

As they gathered about her she began to read to them, all the while trying to quell a sense of foreboding somewhere deep in her consciousness. She did not hear a voice, per se, but something—someone?—seemed to be trying to warn her of what was to come.

Titus Henry, the farmer on whose land the service was to be held, appeared to be very nervous. He was a good man who loved God, but now Bunyan saw that he was upset, perhaps even frightened.

"Mr. Bunyan," he said with agitation. "I think we should postpone the meeting."

"Postpone the meeting? Why should we do that?" John had come to Lower Samsell, some thirteen miles south of Bedford, and now stood outside the Henry farmhouse, which was surrounded by elm trees. There was a hawthorn in the adjacent field and Bunyan had often preached in its generous shade. But this was November—it was too cold to subject oneself to the out-of-doors—so the service was to be held inside the barn.

Henry wove his fingers together and squeezed them powerfully, looking down at them. When he lifted his eyes, they were troubled and his voice was urgent. "Mr. Bunyan, I have word that Judge Wingate has written a warrant for your arrest." He looked toward the barn nervously. "There are two strangers here. I don't know them. It's my thinking that they might be the agents of the magistrate."

Bunyan said firmly, "We must be obedient to God, Titus. This is your home, your place, and if you call the meeting off, there is nothing I can do. But once we start fearing for ourselves, I think that our cause is lost."

The two men stood outside, the wind rising in a threatening whine as though warning them of snow just over the low-lying hills. The air turned colder, reddening the faces of both men and numbing their lips a little. Titus Henry shrugged. "It's not me they'll be arresting, sir. You must make the decision."

"Then come along. We will have our meeting."

The two men made their way to the barn and stepped inside. Lanterns had been lit so that the faces of those who stood waiting for the service to begin were illuminated in a soft light. Bunyan knew almost all who stood there, if not by name, at least by the familiarity of their faces. He saw two men wearing heavy coats and gloves who stood apart from the others. He knew exactly why they were there, but he ignored them.

A time of prayer ensued. As he prayed John Bunyan closed his mind to the two strangers who stood silent and watchful and he spoke to God. Then the small group sang several hymns. When those were ended and Bunyan took his Bible and stepped forward, he saw the eyes of the tallest of the two strangers begin to glitter. As he began to read the Scripture, the tall man stepped forward and said in a loud voice, "John Bunyan, you are prohibited from preaching!"

Bunyan regarded him calmly, holding his Bible steadily in his big hands. "Only God can do that, sir."

The smaller man, thickset with a round, red face and light blue eyes, stepped beside his companion. "We have a warrant for your arrest if you persist! You are breaking the laws of King Charles II and of parliament!"

"We ought to obey God rather than men," Bunyan said simply. He continued reading the Scripture—and at once the two men came and bracketed themselves on each side of him.

"Will you resist arrest? Must we use force?" the tall man demanded.

"No, I will not resist you." Bunyan closed his Bible and his arms were seized.

"We then arrest you, John Bunyan, in the name of the king," the shorter man said.

As Bunyan left with the two men, he turned to Titus Henry, who watched with helpless sadness. "Mr. Henry, will you see that my wife is informed of what has occurred? Tell her that I shall not be long."

The tall man's grip tightened on Bunyan's arm and he laughed. It was a distinctly unpleasant sound. "You won't be home until you agree to stop preaching," he growled. "Come along now. We'll have no trouble with you!"

Bunyan moved along between these two strangers, who would deposit him as quickly as they could in Bedford Jail.

The rank, stinking straw that composed his prison bed had gotten down John Bunyan's neck. As he stood in the courtroom, he twisted his shoulders, trying to ease the itch.

The courtroom contained a long bench that ran along the back wall under a wide window. To the left was a door leading to the outside; another door leading to the rest of the building was located behind the judge's bench. The courtroom was small and could hold only twenty-five or thirty persons.

Bunyan had been here before when he had been arrested and before that when he had testified for neighbors in several minor cases.

Francis Wingate was sitting on a raised platform, and there was a settled determination in his face as he commanded, "The prisoner will stand there." When Bunyan was brought to stand before him, he went on sternly, "This hearing will consider certain charges brought by the state against John Bunyan: preaching without a license, as well as suspicion of conspiracy and rebellion against the King's Peace. I will hear the evidence of the arresting constable."

Thomas Cobb, the constable, was a tall, lean man with a cadaverous face. "Yes, sir," he said smartly, then turned to look at Bunyan. "I arrested the prisoner. He was preaching at Lower Samsell, just as Dr. Lyndall said he was—"

Instantly Wingate interrupted, "You will answer the questions as they are asked! Now, Constable, when you made the arrest, did the prisoner or any of his hearers have anything in particular with them?"

"Well . . . like, what is it you mean, sir?"

"Did you see any arms? Were they bearing weapons? Anything of that nature?"

Cobb thought the matter over. He was a slow-thinking man and finally said, "Well, no more dangerous than any other Baptists. All they had was Bibles."

A twitter went over the room at that and Wingate's eyes, as they rested on the prisoner, were severe. "Mr. Bunyan," he said firmly, "there is much unrest in England and there is a law against such gatherings. Now you may defend yourself. What did you there?

Why do you not content yourself with your calling as a tinker? Why did you break the law?"

"My Lord Justice, I mend pots to make a living, but I preach that souls might be won and that hearts might be made whole."

"Are there other witnesses against this man?" Wingate demanded.

Dr. Lyndall stood up, his face red, his eyes harsh. "Yes! I will accuse him! He will not come to hear the Word of God from authorized ministers but consorts with men like himself who resist authority. He is a rebel!"

Bunyan responded calmly. "I have come to speak to the justice, sir, not to you."

"He has no defense, my lord," Lyndall insisted. "He has no warrant! He has not taken the oath!" He shook his fist vehemently at Bunyan. "The law clearly condemns him to prison!"

Bunyan stood quietly, his tall form sturdy and strong. He gazed steadily at the vicar and said calmly, "Dr. Lyndall, I will answer any sober questions."

"Answer, then, why you preach when you have not the authority!"

Bunyan smiled, his broad mouth relaxed. "Has not Peter said, 'As every man hath received the gift, even so, let him minister the same'?"

Lyndall smiled triumphantly. "Yes, Mr. Bunyan, you have the gift—the gift of disturbing the peace!" He waved his arms toward the audience, his voice rising. "I say let the coppersmiths and tinkers mend their pots and leave off mutilating the Word of God!"

The hearing continued and soon Bunyan was forced to take his stand. He looked at Justice Wingate and said calmly, "God has ordained that I should preach. You and I are both under God's commission, you to be a justice and I to be a minister."

Wingate scowled. "I do not recognize yours, sir. You have no license to preach."

"My calling is from God." His voice rose and the cadence of it was strong as it filled the room. "You cannot change that, Justice Wingate! This body you can imprison, but God's decrees are not so easily destroyed!"

Wingate was angered by the certainty in John Bunyan's voice. "I will take you at your word. If you will not keep the laws of man, the law's man will keep you close. Once more, will you tend to your mending of pots and leave off preaching?"

A silence fell over the room and then Bunyan's voice rang out, "I will obey God rather than men."

Wingate shouted, "Then I will break the back of your meetings! I sentence you to be held in Bedford Jail until such time as you learn to keep the law! You will be tried, sir, for your rebellion! Constable, take him out and lock him up!"

Bunyan dropped his head for one moment, then lifted it again slowly. "Sir, might I have one word with my family before I go?"

"They may visit you in jail," Wingate said curtly. "Take the prisoner out."

Bunyan turned and his eyes met Elizabeth's; she had remained silent and pale throughout the hearing. He tried to smile but his lips seemed frozen. He saw that her face was stricken and that she struggled to keep back the tears.

There was no time to speak to her, for he was hurried out of the courtroom by Cobb and taken at once to the prison. Watching her husband's departure, Elizabeth decided to go directly to the prison to see if she might visit him immediately.

She left the courthouse and moved down Silver Street until she reached Jail Lane. Along this lane prisoners would hang out bags or purses from the second story of the jail, begging for alms. Elizabeth didn't even notice such things, though, for her thoughts were focused elsewhere. Passing through a small courtyard, she was admitted by Cobb, the jailer, and he led her to a small room where her husband stood waiting for her.

"John!" she whispered and hurried to him.

Bunyan took her in his arms and felt her tremble. He wanted to give her words of comfort, but the best he could manage was to murmur, "There, there, sweetheart. . . ."

It was poor comfort, indeed, but he himself had been somewhat taken aback by the severity of Judge Wingate. The judge had always been friendly and Bunyan had heard that the man was not vicious. Apparently the pressure Judge Wingate was enduring from his superiors had finally brought about a change in the man.

The husband and wife stood holding one another tightly. Finally John lifted Elizabeth's chin and tried to smile. "So we will see what God can do," he said gently.

Elizabeth had thought much of what she would do if her husband were arrested. But now that the harsh reality of it was upon her, she found that despair threatened to overcome her. With an effort she pulled herself together, not wanting to cause John any more grief than he knew already. Forcing herself to smile, she said with as much brightness as she could muster, "You won't stay here long. There will be a trial, won't there?"

"Oh yes, there'll be a trial," Bunyan answered. "And we will pray that God will vindicate us." Remorse suddenly washed over him and made him weak. "Oh, Elizabeth," he groaned, "I can bear the thought of prison, but how can I bear the thought of you, alone, with the children—and bearing a child!"

Elizabeth replied quietly and felt the beginnings of strength even as she spoke the words, "God is faithful. We know this, John. We will believe him to deliver you."

The two sat down and began to discuss practical things: how the children could be cared for until he should be set free, finances, the household, Elizabeth's well-being and that of the child she bore.

Bunyan spoke and listened to his wife's quiet replies, but within his heart he was crying out to God. *God, I have promised to preach your Word! But I ask you, for the sake of my family—for this woman and the little ones—deliver me! Let this cup pass from me!*

Yet even this desperate prayer, though it came from the deepest part of his being, did not bring Bunyan a sense of the presence of God.

Presently Cobb appeared and grunted, "Time's up, Mrs. Bunyan!"

John kissed Elizabeth, then followed Cobb to the cell. It was not a single small cell; this was a common prison and all the prisoners were kept in one room. Bunyan walked over to the wall, sat down on the straw, and lowered his head. Closing his eyes, he shut out the sights, but he could not shut out the foul odors and hopeless sounds that permeated the air about him.

As he sat there, alone and desolate, shivering in the cold, he knew that he was in God's crucible and that there would come a cleansing fire that would try his very soul. Over and over again he cried out from his heart, *God, give me strength to be faithful to you!*

Ten

"I Will Preach the Gospel Though I Hang for It!"

Angharad found Evan sitting in his room, staring out a window at the winter scene. "Evan, what are you doing up here?" Her voice had a scolding note and she came over to look down at him rather accusingly. "You haven't said ten words in the last two weeks. Are you feeling worse?"

"It's only just resting a little I am." Evan looked up at her, his eyes dull. Angharad had had enough of his subdued quiet and determined to make him tell her what disturbed him so.

Settling into a chair opposite him, she studied his face carefully. He returned her gaze steadily for a long moment, then grunted, "Well? You have something to say?"

"That I do," she replied firmly. "It's no good for a man to wall himself up. Turned into an old stone, you have! You need to talk."

"I have nothing to talk about." Evan had always been light-hearted, his countenance full of life. Now his voice was a weary monotone, his face heavy.

Angharad asked shrewdly, "It's Jenny, is it?"

"Not saying a word about her, I was."

"No, you haven't said anything about Jenny," she countered.

"Nor have you said anything at all. For days now. And it's tired of your sullen silence I am!" Suddenly Angharad heard her voice, scolding and pushy. She sighed regretfully and softened her tone. "Forgive me, Evan dear. It's not cruel I'm wantin' to be. But faith, at times you're just like a small child. Don't you think I can see your grief? Your hurt?"

Evan sat up straighter and smiled wearily. "I suppose you're right, Cousin. I guess I took Jenny so much for granted. . . . She thought so, anyway."

"Right she was," Angharad sighed. "Jenny's a woman grown since two years and yet you insisted on treating her like a little girl."

Evan knew his cousin was right. Indeed, he had thought of little else since Jenny had announced her decision to remain in London. He had a feeling of foreboding, as though no good would come of her choice—and as though it were somehow his fault.

He had just returned from hours of solitary wandering in the forest surrounding Wakefield, wondering desperately how he could persuade Jenny to come back. More than once he had considered going to Angharad or Christopher to talk with them about the girl but had never quite worked up the courage to admit to them just how bad he felt—and how much he missed Jenny.

"She's headed down the wrong road," Evan said grimly. "Wait, you'll see. I know these actors and actresses."

"Yes? They are bad people? And this makes Jenny bad?" Angharad demanded. "She's who she is: herself."

Evan took heart at her stout words, but he still felt burdened for Jenny. "She's gone and there's nothing I can do about it. It's just that—well, somehow, Jenny was like a sister to me. Ever since I found her in the forest that night I've felt—responsible, you might say."

Angharad knew that the young man was hurting. She had seen in Jenny's eyes her affection for him and had known that, like many young men, Evan was a careless, thoughtless young fellow. Now he seemed to have matured—by way of sadness and loss. Gently she said, "Saying nothing wrong about you I am. Most of us have to learn by falling down, brushing ourselves off, and getting up again. There's a nasty fall you've had, but God will see us through it."

She sat with him for some time, speaking quietly or merely sitting in companionable silence. At length she rose. "I must go and speak to Gavin. He—"

"Oh, is he back from Portsmouth?" Evan asked.

"Yes, and when I told him about John Bunyan, I thought he was going to lose his religion!" Angharad asserted.

"Angry, was he?"

"You should have heard what he said about the parliament, and especially the choice words concerning His Highness King Charles II!"

"Good," Evan said with satisfaction. "I could say worse, for certain. The fools! Here we've had a war to gain freedom and now the first thing they want to do is clap people in jail for worshiping God! Devil throw smoke, it's not too late to fight another war!"

Angharad laughed, the sound coming from deep in her chest. She had a pleasing, hearty laugh, like a healthy, happy man's laugh. She pulled Evan to his feet and hugged him until he gasped. "You will have them for it!" she exclaimed. "Just another rebel, like all the rest of the Morgans!" Then she released him and continued solemnly, "Still, you must learn to trust God, Cousin. I know you want to rush out and rescue Jenny, but she's taken up with this acting, with the glamour of it, the attention she gets, the noisy excitement. I'm sure she's sought after by many men."

Evan looked at her sharply and she smiled. "But worry you not, Evan. Jenny has a sound head on her shoulders."

"She'll need it," he grumbled. He reached out, took Angharad's hand, and lifted it to his lips to kiss it. "Thank you, Angharad. It's good to know that both of us care."

Angharad left him alone and went to find Gavin, who was already preparing to leave again. "Are you going now?" she asked with surprise. "Already?"

"Yes." He nodded, his lips a thin, white line cutting across his face. "I hope I can keep a civil tongue in my head, but I doubt it."

"Keep a civil tongue, indeed! You have a wife now and a child coming. In prison you'll do them no good!"

With an impatient gesture Gavin flung his coat about his shoulders and narrowed his eyes. "Prison? Why should *I* be going to prison?"

Angharad shot back, "Because those who are now ruling over England have the bit in their teeth! They've been waiting their turn and it's here! Now you watch. It will be a hard time for the Wakefields. Many haven't forgotten that your father was a close friend of Oliver Cromwell's, that he served him faithfully in the war. As did you! Be wise, Gavin." Her voice dropped to a soft and menacing tone. "If they put you in jail, I'll have the bones hot from their body."

Gavin laughed and put his arms around his stepmother. "There's an old rebel you are!" he said, mimicking her Welsh speech. "I've already said good-bye to Susanne and Father. I'll be back tomorrow at the latest. But now I must hurry to Bunyan."

"I've had Will pack food for Mrs. Bunyan and the children," Angharad told him. "Tell them that we're all praying for them here."

"I will. Good bye, Angharad."

"God go with you."

Gavin entered the prison and was struck forcibly by terrible odors. The smell almost gagged him and he wondered how the prisoners could stand it. *I suppose they get accustomed to it in time,* he thought dismally.

"This way, sir," Cobb said. "The prisoners be down on the first floor."

But the first floor, Gavin Wakefield discovered, might as well have been called the dungeon. The lower part of the jail was half-buried in the ground, with only the last few feet near the ceiling above ground level. The dim light that filtered through the grimy windows gave no warmth, serving only to illuminate the desolate condition of the prisoners. It was a large room holding about thirty men. Some of them stood, walking back and forth in what small space was available, not unlike caged animals. Some were propped listlessly on the floor, their backs to the filthy walls. Others were lying on the rotting straw that served as a cover for the dirt floor. A few of these clutched pieces of blankets.

"Bunyan! A visitor for you!" Cobb called out, waving toward a corner of the room.

Gavin saw John Bunyan sitting on a wooden bench propped close to the wall. He hurried toward his friend, his hand out. "John—" He broke off, unable to finish his greeting so shocked was he by how haggard Bunyan looked.

Seeing Wakefield react to the squalor of the prison, Bunyan summoned up a smile. "It's not as bad as some, you know, Mr. Gavin. Here. Will you sit beside me?"

Gavin had come to bring the imprisoned man comfort and solace, but it occurred to him that he had little to give. As he sat on the splintered bench beside Bunyan, he dropped his eyes. "I—I heard about your troubles—earlier. But I couldn't come until now. What is your status, exactly?"

Bunyan shrugged. He was wearing a heavy coat, but still the dank, cold chill of the jail seemed to seep into his bones. "Awaiting trial," was all he said.

"And when will that be?"

"Likely another month, I fear."

Gavin's head came up, the horror in his eyes poorly veiled. "I've been to see the magistrate to offer to make bond for you. But he refused. Rather small of him, I thought. It's not as if you're going to run away."

"Mr. Wingate has little choice in the matter, I think. The winds are blowing hard against me and other independents like me. I don't think those in London would allow him to set any of us free."

For half an hour Gavin and Bunyan talked. Gavin looked toward the door and for the first time his face lit up. "Look! It's Elizabeth, and she's brought Mary with her."

Gavin rose as Elizabeth Bunyan crossed the crowded floor, Mary at her side. In spite of the unfamiliarity of the awful surroundings, Mary did not clutch at Elizabeth. Instead she held her stepmother's arm lightly, making her way unerringly past the men sitting or standing around.

"Elizabeth! You shouldn't have come out in this weather!" John scolded.

She smiled and lifted her face to his kiss. "Mary's brought you something she's cooked herself. Look, it's fresh lamb, fixed just the way you like it!"

Bunyan reached down to lift Mary into his arms and kiss her. "So, my own cook has brought me her specialty. I'll warrant it's delectable."

"Oh, it is!" Mary said eagerly, her blank eyes fixed on her father. "Here, let me cut it up for you!"

Bunyan sat down and pulled Elizabeth close to his side. Mary began to cut up the lamb, talking excitedly all the while in her high, childish treble. Gavin caught Elizabeth's eye. "I just came to offer what comfort I could, Mrs. Bunyan." The strain had left clear signs on Elizabeth's normally smooth features, and Gavin noted the cautious way she moved and the protective hand that rested on her swollen belly. His eyes reflected his sympathy. "How is it with you, madam?"

She hesitated slightly, but spoke positively. "Fine, Mr. Wakefield. It was so good of you to come. Thank you."

"I have some things that my stepmother sent," he said. "I'll take you back home when you're through here."

Bunyan ate hungrily and said under his breath, "It's so unfair, Mr. Gavin. I have my family to bring food to me, but some of these poor fellows have no one. I usually try to share what I have." He looked down at Mary. "That would be all right with you, my dear?" He smiled as she nodded, and pulled her onto his lap. "Now, tell me what you've been doing."

"No, Father, you tell me a story." Her face turned upward and her hands clutched the lapels of his coat. "I miss that more than anything else! Your stories at night. Tell me one now."

"Why, Mr. Wakefield doesn't want to hear stories—"

"Indeed, but I do," Gavin demurred. "You go right on, John."

He stood close to them so Elizabeth could keep her seat on the rickety bench and lean back against the clammy wall. Her eyes closed and the corners of her mouth turned slightly upward as her husband began to tell Mary his story.

"Well, I have been thinking of a story. I may write it down someday," Bunyan told Mary quietly, "when I get it all straight in my head."

"What's it about?" Mary implored.

"Oh, it's about a man whose name was . . . um . . . let's see—Christian."

"That was his name?" Mary asked. "Christian?"

"Yes. And this man had a huge burden on his back. And he started out—"

"What was the burden, Father?" Mary demanded.

"Why, it was the burden of his sin," Bunyan replied easily. "You know about sin. We've talked about that. So this man Christian began to weep and to cry. And one day he met a man named Evangelist. And Evangelist asked Christian, 'Why are you weeping? Flee from the wrath to come!'"

Bunyan, feeling stronger after the good meal, set Mary aside and rose to act out his story. Gavin watched the girl's face fixed in the direction of her father's voice, her expression rapt.

"'This is the City of Destruction,' Evangelist said. 'It will be destroyed! You must flee to the Celestial City!'"

"I know!" Mary cried. "I know, Father! That's heaven, isn't it?"

"Yes, it is. But, you see, this pilgrim had all his sins on his back. And no one goes to that city until the burden is off his back." Bunyan continued his story for a while, then finally said, "That's enough for now, Mary dear."

"But, Father, did Christian ever get rid of his burden?" Mary asked insistently.

"Yes, he did."

"Tell me about it! Please!"

Bunyan smiled indulgently. "Well, Christian found himself on a road called Salvation. He ran down the road, staggering with that load on his back. Then he came to a certain place and he looked up—and what do you think he saw?"

"I don't know! What was it?"

"He saw a cross. And at the bottom, a tomb. And do you know what? As soon as he saw that cross, that big, heavy burden fell off his back, and it began to tumble, and it rolled and rolled and rolled, right to the mouth of the tomb! And it fell in! And Christian never saw it again. And that is the end of the story."

"Oh, I like that story!" Mary cried with delight. "Tell it to me again!"

"Oh no, not now, Mary dear." Bunyan smiled. "But perhaps later I'll tell you more about Christian."

"Do you promise?"

"Yes, I promise I will. But now you must take your mother home. It's too cold in here for her."

"All right, Father."

Bunyan stood up and helped Elizabeth rise, then kissed her and Mary. Turning to Gavin, he shook hands firmly. "Thank you, Mr. Gavin, for coming and for all the help you've been to me and my family."

"It's little enough," Gavin said, "but I'll do the best I can."

John watched as they left, then sank back onto his bench. After a brief pause, he reached for the remainder of his meat and began to share it with some of the needier prisoners. He had seen them watching him eat and watching him and his family and friends, their eyes too large for their wan faces, their pain slightly dulled by hope of a few morsels of his food.

"I wish," he told them, "I could do like Jesus with the bread and fishes and make enough to feed everyone until they were full. But, alas, my faith's too small for that."

As he distributed the meat, he was certain to give each man a cheerful and hearty word of encouragement. Yet the whole while, his mind was on his wife and unborn child—and on the fact that soon he would have to make the most critical decision of his life.

"Come along, sir. The magistrate wants to speak to you."

Bunyan looked up with surprise at Cobb but asked no questions. It had been several days since the visit from his wife and friend, but their encouragement still upheld him. He followed the jailer out of the common room to a small, private room and found Justice Wingate waiting for him.

"Yes, sir? You wanted to see me?" Bunyan asked.

Wingate appeared to be nervous. "I wanted to have a private word with you, Bunyan."

"Yes? What is it?"

"I have thought about your case many times. I want to make one more appeal to you." He waved his hands at the stubborn light that came into the tinker's blue eyes. "Bunyan, you must agree, from this moment forth, to cease your preaching! Not for my sake—faith, not even for your sake—but for your family's sake!"

"Justice, we've been over all this!"

"Things are very different now," Wingate said in a low voice.

"How so, sir?"

For the first time since he had entered the room, Wingate met Bunyan's eyes without turning away. "The name of the judge sitting on your hearing is Kelynge! Of all the judges in this land, Kelynge is the last man who should hear your case!" He took a deep breath and twisted his hands with some agitation. "I must confess, I wanted to defeat you. But this judge can hang you!"

John stared at the man, stunned. "But—but that's not possible!"

"I tell you it's not only possible, it's very likely if you don't submit!" Wingate retorted. Then he went on reluctantly, "And there is something else I must tell you. It's your wife, Bunyan. She's having a difficult time."

"The child has come?"

"No, not yet. But very close." Wingate leaned forward and said urgently, "Listen to me, Mr. Bunyan. Please open your mind and listen to me most carefully." He took a deep breath and his sharp eyes bore into Bunyan's. "Right now, if you will promise to leave off preaching, I will let you go. You can go be with your wife. It will make things very difficult for me, but right now—at this time—I do still have that authority. I will bear the responsibility."

Bunyan was silent. The longing he felt to go, to be with Elizabeth and his children, was so strong that he did not trust himself to say a word.

Wingate pressed him. "If you stand before that judge tomorrow and if you persist in your stubborn course . . . John Bunyan, you are lost!"

"I must go to Elizabeth!" The words seemed to be forcibly wrenched from Bunyan's lips.

"You may and you shall," Wingate said in a low, intense voice. "But right now—" he motioned to the empty room—"there is no one to hear. And so I ask you this, John Bunyan, not as your magistrate. I ask you this as a man, a husband, and a father. Give me your promise now that you will not preach, regardless of what you intend to do later."

Every bit of John Bunyan's body and mind strained to agree with this man and thus be able to leave. His throat actually burned from the effort of keeping from shouting, "Yes!" But somewhere in his spirit was a quiet knowledge that the moment he turned from his duty, in even so small a manner as this, he would indeed be lost. He took a deep breath, then said quietly and firmly, "I am sorry, Justice Wingate."

Wingate dropped his head in a moment of helplessness, then rose from his seat. "I have done all I could," he said evenly.

Bunyan went back to the common room, led by Cobb. The jailer said, "Your trial's in the morning, hey? I'm sorry to hear your judge will be Kelynge. He's a hangin' judge, they say. I'm that sorry for you." His sallow face broke into a broad grin as he opened the cell door and ushered the silent prisoner inside.

"This court, the Quarter Sessions of Bedford, meets under the royal authority of Charles II, monarch of England. Let the prisoner stand here."

Sir John Kelynge was a huge man, stern of disposition and massive of chin. He had the manner of a bulldog. Only recently had he been released from an eighteen-year sentence to parliamentary jail, put there by Cromwell's orders. He had determined to make any and all persons who had had any part in the Commonwealth—the "rebellion" as he called it—pay dearly for their actions.

"Read the charges."

Wingate rose and read to the court in an emotionless tone. "John Bunyan, of the town of Bedford, laborer, hath devilishly and perniciously abstained from coming to the Church to hear divine services, and is a common upholder of unlawful meetings and conventicles, to the great disturbance and distraction of the good servants of this kingdom, contrary to the laws of our Sovereign Lord the King."

"What say you to this, John Bunyan?" Kelynge demanded.

"As to the first part, I am a frequenter of the house of God, and by grace, a member of the body of Christ."

"Do you go to church? Not to your *meetings!* I mean to the parish church?"

"I do not."

"And why not?"

"I do not find that commanded in the Word of God."

Kelynge stared at him angrily. "We are commanded to pray!"

"Oh yes," John Bunyan agreed easily. "But not by *The Book of Common Prayer.*"

"How else can we pray?"

Bunyan looked up at the burly judge. "As the apostle said, 'I will pray with the spirit and with understanding.'"

Kelynge snapped, "The Scripture says, 'Teach us to pray,' I think."

"Yes, that is true, my lord. The Scriptures say, 'The spirit also helpeth our infirmities, for we know not what we should pray for as we ought. But the Spirit itself maketh intercession for us.'" His voice rose with passion. "It is the Spirit that teaches us to pray, not the *Book of Common Prayer.*"

"What do you have against the *Book of Common Prayer?*"

"It is not commanded in the Scriptures," Bunyan said patiently.

"Neither is it commanded in the Scriptures that you should go to Bedford or Elstow—and yet it is lawful that you should go to either, is it not?"

"That, sir, is a civil thing and not material. I must go wherever God's Spirit leads me."

Kelynge leaned forward and clasped his hands together tightly. "Now we are at the heart of the thing. The law says that you must not hold a meeting for the purposes of worship unless you are so authorized."

Bunyan did not flinch. "But, my lord, the Scripture definitely tells us that we are to meet together. Can I disobey God?"

Disgust distorted Kelynge's face. He had sent many to prison—and many more out of the land—for challenging him thus. "Bunyan, I will not trifle with you. You are a lawbreaker. Where is your authority for preaching?"

Bunyan again quoted the Scriptures. "'As every man hath received the gift, even so minister the same one to another, as good stewards.'"

"Is not that plain to you?" Kelynge rumbled. "'As every man hath received the gift . . .' You, Bunyan, are a tinker! That is your gift! Minister that gift and you are free of this court!"

Whispers and murmurs went around the courtroom. Cobb whispered to another bailiff in amazement, "That's the first time Judge Kelynge ever offered to let anyone out of jail! Bunyan better snap at it!"

But John Bunyan never hesitated. "You do not comprehend the Scriptures. The last part of the verse says, 'Let him speak as the oracles of God.'"

Kelynge threw up his hands. "I am done with you! Do you confess the indictment? That is, did you meet illegally in conventicle?"

A silence fell over the courtroom. Bunyan did not waver, but seemed to be carefully considering his words. His voice, when it came, was even and slow. "This I confess: We have had many meetings together, both to pray to God and to exhort one another, and we have had the sweet, comforting presence of the Lord. Blessed be his name! I am guilty in this!"

Judge Kelynge leaned back in his chair, his eyes hard as agates. "Then hear your judgment, John Bunyan. You must be back again to prison and there lie for three months following. At the end of that time, if you do not submit and leave your preaching, you must be banished from the realm!"

Bunyan bit his lip. "That is strict, my lord—"

Kelynge interrupted, "I have not finished! If after that time you preach again and are found in England or her colonies, your neck must be stretched for it!"

Suddenly John Bunyan was fearless and his gaze was as stern as if he were the judge pronouncing a judgment on the man before him. "I hear your judgment and I am at a point with you! Judge Kelynge, hear me! And all of England! If you turn me loose out of the prison tomorrow, I will preach the gospel, though I hang for it!"

Bunyan sat in the jail, silent and alone. He knew he could expect no mercy from the court. Now his thoughts were centered on Elizabeth.

He looked up as Cobb entered with a visitor. It was Gavin Wakefield.

The two men shook hands. "I'm sorry to see you here like this, John." There was a hesitancy in Gavin's voice, and instantly Bunyan knew something was wrong.

"What is it, Mr. Gavin? Is it Elizabeth?" he demanded.

Gavin Wakefield nodded slowly. "I have bad news, John."

Bunyan grabbed the front of Gavin's cloak. "Is she . . . is she dead?" he cried.

"No, no, it's not that." He put his hands on his friend's shoulders and looked at him with grief and pity in his eyes. "I hate to be the one to tell you, John, but the child has come . . . a little girl . . . and she did not live."

Bunyan slumped down on his customary bench and Gavin sat beside him. "Elizabeth will be all right, the doctor says. She grieves, of course, but she will have other children."

The pain, fear, and grief finally overwhelmed Bunyan. Tears came into his eyes. "She's so young, Mr. Gavin, to bear all of this! It's bad enough, me being in jail, and likely to be here for some time! But now to lose her baby!"

"I cannot tell you what to do, John," Gavin said hesitantly, "but is there no way under heaven—only for now, perhaps—that you can come out of this place? It isn't too late! I'm sure that if you . . . would give your word to give up preaching, at least for now—"

Gavin's words broke off as John looked at him, anguish etching deep lines of pain upon his honest, kind face. "Everyone wants me to stop preaching. You want me to stop, Judge Wingate wants me to stop, Judge Kelynge wants me to stop . . . faith, *I* want to stop! But there is one voice that sounds louder than all of these."

Gavin was sure that he knew the answer, but he asked, "And whose voice is that?"

"The Good Lord Almighty, who redeemed me from the pits of hell and put his spirit within me. He has not told me to stop." Bunyan's eyes flamed with blue fire. "And until God says, 'Stop,' I will preach until the moss grows up to my lips!"

Eleven

EVAN ATTENDS TWO PERFORMANCES

August 1661

The theatre was packed as Evan managed to squeeze his way inside. He had come to London at the behest of Gavin, escorting Elizabeth Bunyan for the purpose of presenting a plea to the judges for her husband. The two of them had arrived in a carriage and, it being late, Evan had seen to it that Mrs. Bunyan had a comfortable room. The assizes would begin early the next morning and Evan had promised to see that Elizabeth was there on time.

But he was restless and determined to see Jenny. He had inquiried about the troupe Nell Gwyn was connected with and found that they were appearing at the Hampton Theatre. He found his way there, managed to wedge himself onto one of the crowded benches, and looked around curiously.

The audience was composed primarily of two classes: the wealthy, who sat close to the front—some of them, at times, even on the stage—and the middle class of people. All of the audience, however, seemed to be equally noisy. The performance had not started, and the babbling of the crowd made a din that made Evan want to shut his ears.

He sat there, his eyes running over the building, noting the high, arched ceiling and the balconies that overhung the stage running along the sides, then studying the fantastic attire of some of the spectators. The men, especially, wore clothes of garish hues and looked like strutting peacocks. Almost all of them wore wigs, as did the women.

Evan sighed, uncomfortably aware of the restlessness that had brought him here. Jenny had been in London for almost a year. He had seen her only once during that time and had received only two letters, which he had found difficult to answer. Their worlds were so far apart that he hardly knew what to say to her. Looking around now, he muttered, "She wouldn't be interested in cows or country matters, not living in this kind of world." Even as these thoughts ran through his mind, the play began. He leaned forward and, for the next hour, watched intently.

The play itself he disliked. It was a drama concerning an unfaithful wife and a stupid husband. The jokes were all directed at the dim-witted fellow who was married to the flighty wife. Evan knew this was quite the fashion in drama now, to make light of marriage and of the sanctity of the home. Most of the plays glorified immorality and extolled the old and faulty philosophy of "Eat, drink, and be merry" as a fine way of life. Morgan certainly was no Puritan and had been outspoken about Cromwell's decision to shut down the stage, but he did not like this fashion of discrediting marriage. As the play unfolded, he felt the stirrings of disgust at what he saw. Marriage, faithfulness, loyalty, all of these gave way to licentiousness, immorality, and self-gratification.

Still, though the play did not entertain Evan, the sight of Jenny made up for it. She had only a small part as far as the speeches were concerned, as a friend of the heroine, Nell Gwyn. When she first came on the stage, Evan stared at her, unable to believe that this was *his* Jenny. She wore a beautiful dress of pale green with trimmings of white and her hair was done in a most attractive fashion. Even under the flickering lights of the stage, her beauty shone forth freshly and Evan sat there feasting his eyes on her.

At one point the man sitting next to him made a crude remark about Jenny, typical of many he had already heard regarding Nell. Anger flared in Evan and he turned, almost grabbing the impudent fellow by the throat. Then he forced himself to be calm. *That's the kind of reprobate she's working for,* he thought in disgust. *I wonder if she knows what they say about her?*

After the play was over, the actors and actresses came forward, taking bows. Evan waited until they finally disappeared behind the set, then he made his way backstage, where he was stopped by a burly man who evidently served to protect the actors from their public.

"What is it you want?" he demanded, putting his hand on Evan's chest.

Evan looked down at the hand and was tempted once again to put the fellow on the ground. He swallowed and said in a mild tone, "I'm a friend of Mistress Jenny Clairmont. I think she'd like to see me. My name is Evan Morgan."

"You wait right here. I'll see if Mistress Clairmont will see you."

Evan stood there in the semidarkness of the backstage, waiting for the man to come back. When he did return, he merely grunted and jerked his head for Evan to pass. Moving in the direction of the gesture, he found Jenny coming out of a door. Her face was lit up with a smile and she came to him at once, putting out her hands.

"Evan!" she cried. "I'm so glad to see you."

Evan took her hands and held them, saying, "Jenny—" He could say no more for a moment, for the pleasure of seeing her swept over him. Finally, he nodded. "You did very well in the play."

Jenny flushed and shook her head. "I'm learning a little, Nell says. I'll never be the actress she is."

Evan looked around. "Is there some place we can talk?"

Jenny thought for a moment, then said, "Let me change and we'll go to a coffeehouse. It's just down the street."

An hour later the two of them were sitting in a secluded part of a coffeehouse. Jenny had been hungry and was eating a chop; Evan was drinking some of the thick, black coffee. Jenny talked between bites, demanding to know all that was happening back at Wakefield and listening as Evan did his best to fill in the gaps. Finally, she finished and the two sat there for some time. Her eyes were enormous and luminous, reflecting the soft lights of the whale-oil lamps. Her skin had a faint translucent quality that was set off by the simple dress she now wore.

She seemed more beautiful than ever to Evan.

"I miss it all so much at times," Jenny said quietly. "I stay very busy, but there are times when I'm alone and I think about all the servants, my friends, about Angharad, Mr. Gavin . . . and about you, Evan."

"Do you?" Evan was pleased and leaned forward. "I wish you were back. I miss our times together."

Jenny said quietly, "You didn't pay much attention when I was there."

"I know it," Evan confessed, shaking his head ruefully. "I didn't realize how much you meant to me until you left." He hesitated, then said what he'd really come to London to say. "Will you ever come back?"

The coffeehouse was humming with small talk from the other patrons. The corner where they sat was close and intimate; the air was filled with the rich smells of food and coffee. No one could hear them and yet Jenny lowered her voice when she responded. "I don't think so. There's really nothing for me there, Evan. Here

I can make a good living. Nell says I have talent and she's going to get me a better part in her next play."

Evan looked down, disappointed. "It's not a good way to live, Jenny. Men talk about you. They think actresses are low and cheap." He saw her grow tense and added at once, "*I* know that you're not. But do you know what they say about you, those men out in the audience?"

Jenny flushed and her hands fluttered nervously at her throat, "Yes, I know." She hesitated, then said almost bitterly, "They come up and say things directly to me. I don't like it and I don't listen to it, but they come anyway."

"You don't have to do this."

"What would I do then? Come back and be a servant?"

"Would that be so bad?"

Jenny looked directly at him. "I'm just like everyone else, I suppose. I liked the life I had when I was at Wakefield, but now it's different. People admire me. Oh, I know, some for the wrong reason," she added quickly. "But I have fine clothes. Here in London there are so many things happening. It's exciting. And there's the chance that . . . that I could be a great actress. I can't leave all of that just to go back and help Mistress Susanne dress, can I?"

"I suppose not. I didn't really think you would."

Jenny saw the unhappiness in his face. Impulsively she reached across the table and covered his hand with her own. "I'm sorry that we can't be together more. Had you ever thought of coming to London?"

Evan looked at her in shock and laughed shortly. "What would I do here? No, I'll stay where I am."

Shortly after that he took her back to the small house she was sharing with one of the other actresses. When they reached the front door, he paused.

"I'll leave you here," he said, and there was note of finality in his voice that troubled Jenny. She wanted him to stay longer, to keep talking with her. He was different from the men she usually encountered. With them, she had to keep her guard up constantly. But this was Evan, the one who had saved her when she was a shivering, skinny, homeless waif. He had handed her life and, though he had been thoughtless in recent years, she knew there was a basic goodness in him.

"Will you be in London long?" she asked timidly.

"No. Mrs. Bunyan wants to get back to her family as soon as the assizes are over."

"Does Mr. Bunyan have any chance to get free?"

"I don't know. The judges could turn him loose, but Mr. Gavin says there's lots of feelings against the independent preachers, so I don't think there's much of a chance of that."

Jenny saw he was preparing to say good-bye. She put out her hand and he took it instantly. "Evan, it's been so wonderful just seeing you," she whispered.

He was halted by the touch of her warm hand. He looked down into her face, trying to find some way to tell her what was happening inside him, but he had said all he knew to say. He leaned over, kissed her cheek, and said huskily, "Good bye, sweet Jenny."

And then he was gone. She stared after him, overwhelmed by a sudden sense of sadness—as though something good and clean and wonderful was leaving her. Tears sprang to her eyes and slipped down her cheeks.

She was losing him and did not know how to prevent it.

Elizabeth had come to London with high hopes. It was common practice that, at the coronation of a king, selected prisoners would be released. The coronation of Charles II had followed that tradition and yet, though hundreds had been released, John

Bunyan still remained a prisoner in Bedford jail. So Elizabeth determined to present her husband's case as best she could. She was grateful for Evan's presence, which had cheered her greatly. Now, as they entered into the large room, however, her heart seemed to sink. The judges were all lined up behind a long table and they looked most formidable. The room was filled with those who had come to present their petitions. She held on to hers so tightly that her fingers began to ache.

"Look! There's Judge Hale," Evan said quickly.

Elizabeth turned to see the judge he was indicating. She had seen him once before. He was a kindly man in his late fifties who had promised to do the best he could for her. Now, however, he seemed to avoid her eyes as he moved through the courtroom and took his seat.

"I fear Judge Hale isn't happy to see me, Evan," she whispered. "He wouldn't look me in the eye. That's a bad sign."

Evan had seen the action and felt the same, but he said as cheerfully as he could, "Don't despair, Elizabeth; we'll do whatever we can."

They sat there for two hours and finally Elizabeth's turn came. She was taken into the Swan Chamber where two judges and many justices and gentry of the country were in company. With a trembling voice she addressed Judge Hale, "My lord, I make bold to come once again to Your Lordship to know what may be done with my husband."

Hale hesitated, then shook his head. "I could do thee no good, I am afraid, Mrs. Bunyan. The court has taken for a conviction that which your husband spoke at the sessions and unless that can be undone, I can do thee no good."

Elizabeth lifted her head high and said, "My lord, he is kept unlawfully in prison. They clapped him up before there was any proclamation against the meetings. The indictment also is false.

They never asked him if he were guilty or no. Neither did he confess the indictment."

Judge Twisdon, who knew something of the case, said loudly, "My lord, he was lawfully convicted."

Ordinarily Elizabeth would have been intimidated, but her courage rose within her. "It is false," she said. "When they asked him, 'Do you confess the indictment?' he only said that he had been at several meetings where there was preaching of the Word and prayer."

Judge Twisdon answered very angrily, saying, "Your husband is a breaker of the peace and is convicted by the law!"

Another judge, named Chester, was known to be hotly opposed to any independent preaching. "He was lawfully convicted. It is recorded, woman! It is recorded!" While Elizabeth continued to speak, he shouted, "It is recorded! It is recorded!"

Elizabeth said bluntly, "If it be, it is false."

Justice Chester snarled, "He is a pestilent fellow. There is not such a fellow in the country!"

Twisdon leaned forward. "Will your husband leave preaching? If he will do so, then send for him!"

"My lord," Elizabeth said, "he dare not leave preaching so long as he can speak."

Twisdon leaned back. "You see! Why should we talk anymore about such a fellow? He is a breaker of the peace."

Elizabeth saw that she was being shoved aside and said desperately, "My lord, I have four small children that cannot help themselves, of which one is blind, and we have nothing to live upon but the charity of good people."

Justice Hale was moved by her statement. "Do you have four children? You're but a young woman to have so many."

"My lord," Elizabeth said in a pleading tone, "I am but stepmother to them, having been married to my husband not yet two years. Indeed, I was with child when my husband was first taken, but being young and unaccustomed to such things, I fell into labor and so continued for eight days and my child died."

Hale looked very soberly at her. "Alas, poor woman, I grieve for you."

Twisdon broke in. "She makes poverty her cloak. Let the fellow stop preaching and answer his calling."

"What is his calling?" one of the judges asked.

"He is a tinker, my lord," Hale said.

Elizabeth felt an anger rising in her. She saw the way the trial was going. "Yes, he is a tinker and a poor man; therefore he is despised and cannot have justice."

Hale answered very mildly, saying, "I tell you, Mrs. Bunyan, thou must apply thyself to the king, sue out his pardon or get a writ of error."

But when Judge Chester heard this counsel, he grew angry. "My lord, this man will preach and do what he wants. He is a pestilent breaker of the peace."

"He preaches nothing but the Word of God," Elizabeth said instantly.

"He preach the Word of God?" Twisdon's words were dripping with disdain. "He runs up and down and does much harm."

"No, my lord," Elizabeth protested. "It is not so. God hath owned him and done much good by him."

Twisdon shouted, "God, indeed! John Bunyan's doctrine is of the devil. My lord, do not mind her, but send her away."

Hale saw that the pressure was tremendous. He looked down at the implacable faces of the other judges and finally turned to Elizabeth regretfully. "I am sorry, Mrs. Bunyan, but I can do thee no good. You must apply yourself to the king, sue out his pardon—or get a writ of error."

Elizabeth tried to speak but Twisdon cut her off. "Enough! Enough! You have heard the decision of the court."

Heavily Elizabeth turned away and walked slowly out of the

courtroom. She was joined by Evan, who could find little comfort to give. The two of them walked out into the street and Elizabeth said at once, "We must go back. I will have to tell John."

"Is there nothing more to do?" Evan asked quietly.

"It's all in God's hands now. Come, let us get out of this city, for I hate it."

As soon as Elizabeth entered the common cell, Bunyan knew that she had no good news. Her shoulders were slumped and there was a listlessness on her face. *The judges have refused our petition,* he thought. At once he stepped forward to meet her. He took her in his arms and kissed her, then said, "Sit down, Elizabeth. You look very tired."

She stood still and her lips began to tremble. "I failed," she whispered. "They wouldn't listen to me, John."

Bunyan saw that she was grieving and on the verge of breaking down. He put his arm around her, led her to the bench beside the wall, and when he had seated her, sat down beside her. Taking both her hands, he held them firmly and said cheerfully, "Well, now, we had to try, didn't we? Don't be so disturbed, my dear."

But she had been drained by the trip to London. She had gone with at least some hope that she would be heard, that the nightmare would come to an end. All the way home, she had thought of the hearing and searched vainly for something she might have said that would have changed the outcome. But there had been nothing and now, as she sat in the dank cell, a shiver went through her. Despite herself, tears ran down her cheeks. She could say nothing for a time and the two sat there quietly.

Finally Bunyan said, "Mary's been in to see me every day. She's such a comfort. Only a child and yet already she has wisdom beyond her years."

"Did she bring you plenty of food?"

"Oh yes. The neighbors have been good. I haven't lacked for that. Tell me about the trip. I know it's painful for you, but I want to hear all about what the judges said."

Elizabeth began to speak and Bunyan listened as she detailed the hearing. He was not greatly surprised at the outcome. He himself had had little hope that the judges would set him free. He knew that Elizabeth was keenly disappointed and when she had finished her tale, he said cheerfully, "Well now, God has not forgotten us, has he?"

"No, of course not," Elizabeth said. A thought came to her and she held it in her mind. Finally she said, "Even Judge Twisdon—evil man that he is—said that you could come out of this place any time you choose."

Bunyan stared at Elizabeth. "And what were his terms?"

She lowered her eyes, feeling a flush come over her cheeks. "I think you know, John," she whispered.

He put his arm around her and held her close. "He wants me to stop preaching, doesn't he?"

"Yes." She lifted her head and looked around the foul jail, her nose wrinkling with the terrible odors. It was cold—it was always dank in the cell—and she could not bear the thought of leaving her husband here. "I am weak, John. I know what you want to do is right, but I miss you so much. And the children . . . they're lost without you."

Her words cut him deeply. He looked up at the single window, which admitted a bar of golden sunlight. He thought about the green fields, the leaves of the trees that would be putting on glorious fall color soon. He thought of the pleasure he took in the out-of-doors, the animals, the streams, the roads that wound over the county. How much he would give simply to walk out and pick up his life where it had been! There was an actual pain in his heart as he thought of what lay before him. With all of his strength, something within him cried out to surrender.

And yet . . . he could not. His voice was broken and husky as he said, "Elizabeth, I would give almost anything to leave this place." He groaned and put his head in his hands, leaning forward. "If you but knew how much I miss you, just your touch, the sound of your voice . . . and the children, how I long to be with them!"

Immediately Elizabeth knew she had made a mistake. She had known before she spoke that Bunyan would never leave. Regret washed over her as she slipped her arm about his stooped shoulders. When she spoke, her voice was filled with tears of remorse.

"John, I am sorry. Fear not, my dear. I will be faithful to my promise to do my best. You must be faithful to your promise to God!"

Twelve

Home Is the Sailor

Charles II, after coming to the throne, tried valiantly to suspend the persecution of the independent preachers of England. In May of 1663 he attempted to eliminate the Act of Uniformity but the reestablished bishops frustrated his effort. In December of that year he issued his own Declaration of Indulgence, which was an attempt to relieve dissenters from laws that sent them to jail, but this also failed.

As a matter of truth, Charles II had need of a declaration of indulgence in his personal life. Life at court had become one flagrant scandal. Charles took mistresses as casually as other noblemen took snuff. Barbara Villers, one of his principal mistresses, he named the countess of Castlemaine, and another, Louise De Kerouaille, he made duchess of Portsmouth. He did find time away from his mistresses to marry Catherine of Braganza—for her dowry of eight hundred thousand pounds. The cruelty that lay deep down in Charles was revealed in his treatment of Catherine. He forced her to accept Barbara Villers as her lady in waiting. This so disturbed the devout Portuguese princess that she fell into deep depression.

The people, however, were lenient. When they learned that he had taken Nell Gwyn as a mistress, she was lustily cheered in the streets. There seemed to be no one to challenge the king's notorious life of lust and self-indulgence. Indeed, immoral behavior was embraced by many and spread throughout the kingdom. Some said this was welcomed as relief from the tyranny of the Puritans. The Commonwealth had punished adultery by death; Charles treated chastity and faithfulness with ridicule.

One personality of force had risen in the restoration: Shaftsbury had fought on the Roundhead side, working with Cromwell. It took him some time to rise, but he became the most powerful representative of the banished dominion. He guided the realm well, standing by the city of London as the city stood by him.

Clarington continued as first minister, a wise, venerable statesman. He often stood as a lone voice against the immorality of the king and the court. It was he who at times kept the kingdom from plunging into the very depths of degradation. Charles was an indolent monarch, unwilling to fight for his beliefs, so it was left to his ministers to do what they could.

During all this time, John Bunyan and many others like him languished in foul cells across the land. Most of these prisoners could have had their freedom by simply speaking a promise: never to preach the gospel outside the religious forms prescribed by the Crown. To a man they chose imprisonment rather than surrender the calling of God on their lives.

There were other concerns through the country as well. The rivalry on the seas between England and Holland had become intense. These nations fought over fisheries and engaged in trade wars. The strength of the Dutch on the sea had revived, making them powerful adversaries for the English fleets. Dutch ships were sent around the world. The commerce of the East Indies flowed to Amsterdam; herrings caught off Scottish coasts produced rich revenues for Holland. The Dutch East India Company—the powerful mercantile empire that financed many of the king's pet projects—grew stronger daily. And since the Portuguese governor of Bombay would not yield Catherine's dowry, the English had no base in India. This meant that while England shipped little, heavily laden Dutch ships rounded the Cape of Good Hope several times a year and Dutch traders prospered, their colonies growing tremendously.

Parliament was pressured by desperate merchants to halt Holland's growing monopoly on commerce. Even the king was aroused to action. The duke of York, the king's brother, had always had a hunger for military glory and this seemed to provide the means. A great sum, over two and a half million pounds, was devoted to the war. More than a hundred new ships were built and armed with heavy cannons. Former Cavalier and Cromwellian officers joined hands and received divisions of the fleet. In 1664, incidents began to occur between the two navies and finally, stirred to a national pride, the king decided on a full-scale war against the Dutch, his former allies.

England might have been thinking mostly of the profits that a war against the Dutch might bring, but to the children of Christopher Wakefield, glory and fashions were much more fascinating! Hope Wakefield's birthday came at the time when her brother Amos was preparing to leave for the war. Hope had been angling for months to have a ball to celebrate her birthday and finally Angharad and Christopher had surrendered.

Hope had developed into a beautiful young woman. At seventeen, she was tall, well formed, and blessed with the luxurious black hair that made her mother so attractive. She had driven Angharad almost out of her mind in selecting a dress, and the treasure had at last arrived from London in all of its glory!

Angharad managed to keep the young woman still long enough to trim the hem. Finally she said in exasperation, "Hope, will you *please* be still! You're driving me crazy."

"I can't help it, Mother. I'm so excited!" Hope had large, well-shaped brown eyes that gleamed with animation. She pulled away from her mother, ignoring her cry of frustration, and stood before the mirror, studying the dress. It was light blue with a high-waisted bodice. The neck had a low décolletage but was cut higher in the back. She fingered the bodice, which had a turned-down, narrow lace edging in front, then let her hands run over the sleeves, which ended in turned-back cuffs that also were finished in lace.

Angharad got to her feet and stared at her daughter. "That dress is cut too low."

Instantly Hope argued. "It is not, Mother! It's the way everyone wears them in London."

"If they want to dress like harlots in London, that's their affair," Angharad said. "But my daughter's not going to go parading herself around half naked!"

The argument went on for some time. Finally Christopher, attracted by the rising voices, wandered in. Miraculously, he had gotten over the ill health that had plagued him. Now, at the age of seventy-five, he was stronger than he had been several years earlier. One of his greatest joys in the past years had been this daughter of his old age. Now he smiled faintly as the two women in his life continued their warfare.

Hope at last turned to him and put her hands on his chest, "Father, Mother won't be reasonable. Explain to her that I can't go to my own ball dressed like a peasant."

Christopher turned and said blandly, "Angharad, Hope can't go to her own ball dressed like a peasant."

Angharad threw up her hands. "I give up! If she wanted the moon, Christopher Wakefield, you'd give it to her." She gave her husband a disgusted look. "I'll let *you* be responsible for her then," she sniffed and walked out of the room, her back stiff.

Christopher waited until she was gone, then turned to his

daughter. "Your mother's right, my dear. That dress is too—daring."

She came to him and at once reached up and patted his cheek. She was not at all concerned by his statement. She had learned early how to handle her beloved father. She was totally confident of his approval.

"We'll talk about it later." She nodded. "It *is* a beautiful dress, isn't it, Father?"

"Yes, it is. Cost enough to feed the town for a month," he grunted. He was inordinately proud of Hope, of her beauty, wit, and charm, and he begrudged her nothing. "Ought to be good bait for some young fellow," he said with a straight face. "Might even catch an earl's older son if you play your cards right."

"Father! Don't talk so foolish."

"It's not foolish for a father to talk about his daughter's husband, is it? Here you are, an old maid of nearly eighteen and no husband yet! Utterly disgraceful, if you ask me."

Hope reached up and slapped his cheek lightly. "You're awful," she said. "And I most certainly am *not* an old maid!"

"I know several young women your age who are married already," he teased. "I think I'd better raise the price of your dowry a bit."

Hope's face lit up in a grin and she giggled. "You know better than that! As a matter of fact, I've been thinking about this dowry business."

Christopher raised his eyebrows. "What about it?"

"Whoever gets me," she said saucily, "will be getting such a bargain, I think *you* ought to demand a dowry from *him.*"

Her father laughed outright at her audacity. "You'd do it, too, wouldn't you?" He came over and put his arm around her, squeezed her, then turned to leave. "All the same, I don't think we'll give up on a husband for you. How about young Thomas Brighton?"

"He's not handsome enough."

"There's always Taylor."

"Hmmm, he's handsome enough but he doesn't have any money." She grinned at him puckishly. "I want someone who is tall, very rich, and *very* handsome." She ran over and threw her arms around him. "Someone like you!"

"You mercenary wench!" Christopher cried. He pushed her away but could not keep the smile from his lips. "I don't know what's to become of you. We'll just have to pray you find a man who can keep you in line!"

She ignored this entirely, slipping her arm through his. "May I go with Amos when he goes to his ship?"

"No. You wouldn't have any way to get back."

"I can get back by myself," she insisted. "I think it would be nice if I saw him off. He would like it."

Christopher hesitated. "Well . . . I'll talk to your mother about it."

Hope was sure that meant yes. She pulled his head down, kissed his cheek, then said, "I want you to buy a new suit for my ball. That old thing you wear is nothing but rags." She began to instruct him on what colors and style to purchase and on which tailors to use. Finally he raised his hands in surrender and escaped, leaving her calling instructions after him.

He encountered Amos in the study, examining the large globe. "I'm afraid Hope has volunteered to escort you to Portsmouth."

Amos looked up and smiled. At the age of twenty-five, he had filled out and there was an air of authority about him. He had always loved the sea and had made several voyages in the past few years. Now, at his urgent pleading, Christopher had agreed to furnish a ship to send against the Dutch. The lad was full of naval things, so that everything he spoke of was cannons, sails, rudders, navigation, and so on.

Amos put his finger on the globe, gave it a small spin, then said, "That girl needs a caning. You spoil her shamelessly."

"I did the same to you," his father said defensively. "And you seem to have turned out all right."

"I don't know. I suppose that will be tested when I see a little action at sea."

Christopher studied his tall, sturdy son. "You're anxious for it, aren't you? Well, you come by it honestly." He sat down in the leather chair, folded his hands, and began to speak softly. "My father's uncle, Thomas Wakefield, was a fine sailor."

"He died in the fight against the Armada, didn't he?"

"Yes, he did. Everyone who knew him admired him. The men on his ship practically worshiped him. It's unusual for men to love a captain. It was so with Drake and Hawkins, but few others. Somehow, they, like Thomas, had the ability to inspire men."

"Hard to do." Amos shook his head. "Common sailors have pretty bad lives: poor food, low pay, and the chance of getting their legs and arms blown off. I don't know why they do it."

"I suppose they hunger for glory." He studied his son's face. "Just like you do."

Amos flushed. He hated to be reminded of this streak within himself, but he could not deny it. "I suppose you're right. You shared a similar inclination, didn't you, when you were young?"

Christopher nodded. "Yes, I did. Like many in England, the sea seemed to have a hold on me. Maybe it's because we live on this little island surrounded by it. Our whole lives are controlled by the sea, really. It saved us from the Spanish; it's saving us now from the French. There's something about standing on a ship out in the middle of the ocean with nothing in sight that stirs a man deeply. He realizes how small he is. I'd like to do that again," he said wistfully. "But it will be your job now." He gave Amos a sudden glance. "It's not as glamorous as some think. It's hard, dirty, dangerous work—boring, too, at times."

"I know." Amos nodded. "Yet I still can't help looking forward to it."

Christopher's tone was somber as he said, "You might get killed, you know. I pray not, for that would be hard indeed on me, Amos. I've loved seeing you and Gavin grow up, become men. Indeed, it's been my life in many ways." He sighed and fell silent for a few moments.

Amos came to stand beside his father, laying his hand on his shoulder. Christopher nodded, understanding and accepting the love his son had for him, the regret he felt at possibly causing him pain, but his need to follow this path. "Aye," he said quietly. "And so it goes. Well, what does Gavin have to say about this adventure of yours?"

"He'd like to go, too, I think, but he's married and Susanne just won't let him. That's one good thing about not being married," he said with a laugh. "I can do as I please."

"I suppose that's true, but I'd be lost without a wife. I've been blessed with two remarkable women: your mother and now Angharad. Most men don't even get one."

The two sat there talking until Angharad came in and told them that their meal was ready. As Christopher rose, Amos said with a wry grin, "This birthday party of Hope's is going to cost enough to outfit a ship. Almost."

"Yes, it will be expensive," Christopher agreed. He was thinner now and slightly stooped. His hair was streaked with gray. Still, there was an inner strength about him and he went over to hug Angharad, smiling faintly. "But you can't spend too much money on a good wife or a good daughter!"

Portsmouth was crowded with ships, transforming the harbor into a forest of masts. The four people who made their way down to the shore had to struggle to get through the crowd. All about, people were shouting and men were jostling for position to load the small boats.

"It's not fair!" Gavin growled. "You two are getting to go out on an adventure and I've got to go home and plant potatoes."

Amos laughed at his brother. "You should have thought of that before you got married. A family man can't go out on adventures."

Gavin reached out and punched his younger brother lightly on the shoulder. "You dog!" he groaned. "Go on, then, and come back covered with glory while the rest of us have to grub around and do the work." He turned around to Evan. "I'm depending on you to watch out for this scoundrel, Mr. Morgan."

Evan grinned. He had decided to make the voyage with Amos and had had no difficulty persuading the young man to take him. "I'll do that, sir, and he'll come back a gentleman and a scholar."

Hope threw her arms about Amos, hugging him. "You be careful, you hear me? I don't want anything to happen to you."

Amos hugged her and then stepped back. "Aye, and you be good till I get back. We'll probably take a Dutch ship or two and I'll bring you back some dresses that'll make that old ball dress of yours look like a rag."

"As much as Father has spent on that ball," Gavin said quickly, "you'd better bring the whole Dutch fleet back!"

The four stood there, waiting for an opening in one of the skiffs transporting people to and from the ships. Finally Evan said, "Sir, there are two places here. We'd better take them."

Amos shook hands with Gavin. "Thanks for bringing us to Portsmouth, Brother. I wish you were going with us but I'll bring you back the sword of an admiral." He turned then to Hope, who was beginning to get teary-eyed, and laughed. "Don't you begin squalling, you hear? See your men off with a smile! Come on now, let's see it!" She obliged him, making herself smile.

Amos stepped back from his family. "Good bye, all. Come on, Evan, let's get in that boat."

Gavin and Hope watched the two as they were ferried out to the ship. Hope said mournfully, "I wish he wasn't going. It all sounded so wonderful at first, but now it doesn't."

"I guess that's what happens in every war." Gavin nodded slowly. "There are the speeches and the flags waving and the trumpets blowing. Everything is fun and exciting and noble—and then the men go off and we begin to see that war is a little bit more than just a flag. Come along, Hope. Let's go back to Wakefield."

Both Amos and Evan discovered that the glory of warfare did not take place the minute they boarded a ship. Within days they had learned that life on board the small fighting ship, the *Renown,* was crowded and uncomfortable. Evan was found to have whatever mental attributes are necessary to aim and fire a gun, and so his place of action was below deck on the port side. Amos, serving as second lieutenant, worked night and day for weeks to learn more of his trade.

In June of 1665, the English fleet of more than one hundred and fifty ships, manned by twenty-five thousand men and carrying five thousand guns, met the Dutch off Lowestoft. The action occurred so quickly that the two young men from Wakefield scarcely had time to feel any qualms. Actually, Evan had been asleep when the first lieutenant shouted almost in his ear, "Get to your gun, Morgan! The Dutch are right on top of us!"

As Evan tumbled out of bed and scrambled his way to the dark gun deck, Amos was being thrown into the middle of the battle. He had gotten the word *"Clear for action!"* and had driven the deckhands in a frenzy until now they were ready. He held his glass on the leading ship and said, "She handles badly, sir."

Captain Thomas nodded. "That will be a help," he said, and the first lieutenant agreed.

The Dutch ship closed on the *Renown,* and then the earsplitting roar of a broadside struck Amos's eardrums. He saw the great bank of choking smoke as it was blown toward the enemy. Looking up, he saw the enemy sails were pockmarked with shot holes. He opened his mouth to give an order when suddenly the world seemed to dissolve. He was vaguely aware of being thrown through the air, then striking the bulkhead with such force that he felt it in every fiber of his being. Even as he fell, he saw the captain fall back on the deck, his chest a bloody mess.

There was a strange, metallic taste in Amos's mouth. He heard the guns roar again and struggled to his feet. The first lieutenant was standing over him, his right arm hanging limply. "Are you all right, Lieutenant Wakefield?"

"Yes, sir." Amos shook his head and said, "Just stunned a little." He looked out over the sea and saw action everywhere. The enemy ship was pulling alongside their vessel and the first lieutenant said in a shaken voice, "I'm not going to be able to take much. I've lost too much blood." He motioned to his ruined arm. "You'll have to direct the battle."

Amos wanted to run, but there was no place to hide in a battle like this. He drew a steadying breath, then looked at the wounded officer. "Yes, sir, I'll handle it. Get down to the surgeons. You're going to lose that arm if you're not careful."

"I'll come back if I can."

Amos nodded and began to give orders. "Reload!" he shouted. "I want three rounds every two minutes!" He turned to the boatswain, who had come to stand beside him. "Gunnery's all we have now."

There was a ragged crash of cannonfire from larboard, and Amos realized that another Dutch ship had swung around on the other side. "Larboard battery!" he yelled. "As you bear, men!"

Down below, Evan was directing his small crew. "Come on! Sponge out!" He wiped his streaming face as men quickly hurled themselves on the tackles and handspikes. They reached blindly for charges and fresh shots, retching as smoke funneled downward into the gun deck.

Evan listened for the command—and it came quickly: *"Fire as you bear!"* At once he stepped behind the cannon and lined it up with his eye. He saw the enemy ship passing by and waited until the last minute, crying out, "Fire!"

The starboard guns hurled themselves inboard on the tackle. The orange-tinged smoke rolled downward across the ship, which now seemed to lie diagonally across the starboard bow. Evan's shot struck the Dutch ship and he cried, "Fine, lads, now load! Stop your vents! Sponge out! Load!"

He never knew how long it lasted down there. The thunder of cannonfire, the squeal and rumble of guns being run out, the endless mad chorus of yells and cheers that seemed to be reaching out from another world—or from the depths of hell.

Up on deck, Amos found himself in a mad world as well. The rigging twisted like snakes on the protective nets and the gun crews stooped and heaved, their naked bodies running with sweat and powder until they looked black-skinned.

"Fire!"

More shots slammed through the smoke.

"We can't keep on like this, sir! We're taking too much shot!"

Amos glared at the boatswain. "We'll fight as long as we're afloat," he roared.

The battle raged on and man after man fell down until no more than a handful were left to man the guns. The quartermaster came running to Amos shouting, "We're taking water, sir! If we don't man the pumps, we'll go down!"

But there were no men to send to this task. All were engaged in the battle. Amos stared at the quartermaster, then said quietly, "See if some of the wounded can help. That's all I can spare."

The quartermaster stared at the young lieutenant and then said quietly, "Yes, sir, I'll do the best I can."

The climax of the battle came two hours later. Amos's ship was low in the water. The guns were still firing, those that were able to do so. Looking across the water, he saw a huge Dutch ship bearing down on him, and he knew it was the end. Nevertheless, he cried out cheerfully, "Here she comes! Give her the best we've got!"

A ragged cheer went up, and down below, Evan saw the bulk of the huge ship come into his aim. He knew it was unlikely that his shot would even pierce the side of the monster. Nevertheless, he cried out, "Fire!" As soon as he had, he felt the *Renown* shaken with shot that seemed to tear the world apart. Water was rushing in belowdecks; he could hear it sloshing and knew it might well be the end of their ship.

There was no chance of getting off another shot and he heard the command from above, "All right, men! Everyone man the pumps! We'll see if we can keep her afloat!"

Evan turned at once and went to the pumps. It seemed hopeless, but he took his place. He was working hard when he heard a voice, "All right, Evan?"

He looked up to see Amos, his face black with soot, blood on his left thigh. "I think the battle's over," Wakefield said quietly. "If we can stay afloat, we can make it back to England."

Evan tugged at the pump and grinned at Amos. "Yes, sir!" he said. "We'll do it! You get some sail up, point us right, and I guarantee we won't get flooded."

Amos grinned back. "I'm glad you're here, Evan," he said. "You did a great job! They were just too big for us. But we won the battle. The Dutch are driven off."

"Are they now?" Evan sighed, relieved. "Well, all we have to do now is get this ship home without drowning, if the Good Lord will be with us. That's what your father would say."

"Yes," Amos said. "That's what he would say." He turned and went back on deck to direct the operations.

It was a long, hard trip back to England. The men had to work the pumps around the clock. The surgeon did the best he could, but many men died before reaching land.

When the coast of England came into view, Amos heaved a great sigh of relief. "We made it," he said under his breath. "Thank God, we made it!" He went down at once and gave the good news to Evan saying, "We're all right! England's right off the bow."

The two friends stood wearily, staring at each other. Finally Evan said, "Well, we know what it's like, don't we, sir?"

"Yes, we do." Amos looked around at the wounded men and the canvas-wrapped bodies and shook his head. "I hope we don't have to do it again soon."

The *Renown* was put in for repairs. Evan and Amos stood looking at the battered hulk and it was Amos who shook his head. "It's a wonder we got back. But the admiral was pleased with us. He said he wouldn't forget our efforts or our struggle."

"Well, it'll be good to be back home again."

"Yes, but first we're going to London to celebrate." Amos grinned. "I think we deserve it."

The two men reached London the next day. Amos found a room at an inn, saying, "It's all on me, Evan. We're going to have a good time here. One thing I want to do is go see Jenny. It's been a long time."

Evan nodded eagerly. "Yes, I'd like to do that, too."

It was not difficult to find her. She was now the star of her own play, since Nell Gwyn had been promoted to the king's mistress.

The two men went to the Red Bull Theatre, where Jenny was appearing. Upon arriving, they were taken aback by the size of the audience.

And by Jenny herself.

Evan had seen Jenny in these circumstances, but Amos had not. "She's beautiful," he gasped. "I didn't realize how beautiful she really was."

Evan shot him a diffident glance. "Yes, she is. I wish she wasn't in this business, though."

The two of them went backstage and, as before, Jenny was very happy to see friends from Wakefield. The three of them went out after the play and Jenny dimpled with pleasure, saying, "Everyone will envy me, being with two handsome sailors."

Amos was exhilarated over the battle. It quickly got out that he had commanded one of the king's ships and had received accolades from the admiral himself. This brought him swarms of well-wishers as well as those curious to hear of the battle. For the next week he was out every night and became the center of attention wherever he went.

Evan, merely a common sailor, received no such notice. He soon refused Amos's offer to go with him, remaining at the hotel. Alone.

Amos enjoyed every second of the week. And he made a point of going every night to Jenny's play. She laughed at him, saying, "You've come so often you know the lines better than some of the actors do."

Amos grinned at her. "Well, maybe I'll become an actor myself," he said. "Maybe I could be the one that gets to kiss your hand all the time, who's so crazy in love with you."

Jenny laughed at his impudence. "I'd like to see you on the stage, Amos. It's not as easy as it looks."

They were seated in Jenny's large sitting room. He had brought her home after supper and now it was growing very late. Nevertheless he said, "Well, give me an acting lesson."

Jenny shook her head. "No. Everyone will tell you it's a low occupation. Bad enough for actors, much less for actresses."

"Oh, come on! I know the lines." Amos came over, took her hand, and began to recite a line: "'Ah, my dear, the stars above are not more faithful in their rounds than I to pursue your love.'" He reached over and kissed her hand and pulled her to her feet. "'And I am more in love with you than all the poets could say.'"

He had pulled her close, as the character in the play had done, when he suddenly realized that she was looking up at him with a strange expression. He broke off his speech, unable to say more, overwhelmed with—and somewhat stunned by—an intense feeling of attraction for her.

"Jenny—," he said and pulled her to him, enfolding her in his arms and touching his lips to hers. She did not draw back but remained still in his arms. Amos's arms closed more tightly about her when he realized suddenly that she was leaning against him, returning his kiss.

For her part, Jenny had been attracted to Amos for days. His dark good looks and courageous spirit had drawn her from the first. And he had treated her as though she were a lady. Indeed, most of the men who sought her company were crude in their manners, assuming that any actress was theirs for the asking. Amos was so different. Until now he had done no more than kiss her hand and he always showed her the courtesy that he showed to all women. Now, as she was held in his arms, she felt that here was a gentleness and gentility that she had sought all of her life. Nevertheless, she did not remain in his arms for long. Too soon to Amos's way of thinking, she drew back.

Taking a deep breath, she looked up at him with a strange expression in her eyes. "I shouldn't have let you do that," she said quietly. "Men think actresses are common."

Amos was shocked. "Why, I would never think that, Jenny!" he protested.

His quick denial touched her and she smiled at him, the dimple appearing in her cheek. "I don't believe you would," she said. "Thank you, Amos." And then, when she saw the fire in his eyes, she said quickly, "I think you'd better go now."

Regretfully, he nodded. "As you say. Tomorrow, though, I'll be back. If that lout says his lines wrong, I'll jump up and take his place."

She laughed as he kissed her hand and disappeared through the door. With a deep sigh, she called her maid, Louise, to help her prepare for bed.

As the woman slipped Jenny's nightdress over her raised arms, she said, "You like that lieutenant, don't you, Mistress Jenny?"

"He's very nice."

"Yes. And he's different from the others." Louise nodded. She had been a maid for several years and had served many actresses—but she saw something different in this young woman. At first she could not believe that Jenny Clairmont was as virtuous as she made out, but now, after several months, she knew that it was the simple truth. She stroked Jenny's long, lustrous, strawberry blonde hair gently and said with affection, "When you marry, choose a man like that. He's far better than those blokes who follow you around like dogs with their tongues hanging out." It was a crude manner of speaking, but she had come up in a hard world. "That Lieutenant Wakefield, he has good in his eyes."

Jenny looked at her in surprise, then nodded slowly. "Yes," she said thoughtfully. "You're right. He does have good in his eyes."

Later that night, she lay awake thinking of Amos—and a smile played on her face when she finally drifted off to sleep.

Thirteen

A TASTE OF DEATH

The New Conventicle Act, which was enacted in 1664, declared that anyone found at an informal religious meeting would be sent to prison for three months and had the undesired effect of filling the prisons almost to overflowing. Then, in 1665, the Five Mile Act was established. This law made it illegal for any independent preacher who would not take an oath of nonresistance to come within five miles of his former places of ministry or of corporate towns. This act ensured that the prisons become even more crowded.

While all of this was a hardship on many ministers, it actually proved to be a blessing to John Bunyan. Bedford Jail, similar to prisons all over the country, became a scene of extreme confusion and overcrowding. As a result, Thomas Cobb, the jailer—who had been converted under Bunyan's ministry—allowed the longtime prisoner to visit home occasionally.

So it was, in 1666, that a small book with the title *Grace Abounding to the Chief of Sinners* was printed in London. This book, John Bunyan's record of his own spiritual odyssey, was received with great favor. Through this book, many were brought to a saving knowledge of Christ, which caused a great joy in the life of the Bunyans.

Now John sat in the midst of his family in his small cottage. In his hands he held a small book that had been delivered to him by post, an arrangement made through the kindness of Gavin Wakefield. Bunyan held the book almost reverently.

"I never thought I would see the day when I would be thankful for being in prison," he said to his family, "but if I had not been, I would never have taken the opportunity to write this book." He looked up at those gathered around the table. The room seemed crowded. Mary, now seventeen and a comely young woman, sat at his right hand. Beside her was John's younger daughter, Elizabeth, age thirteen. Across from John were his two sons, John and Thomas, who were twelve and eight.

The elder Bunyan's eyes grew damp with grateful tears and he said huskily, "Praise be to God who has allowed me to be back with you this day."

Elizabeth, his wife, was now only twenty-six. Despite years of hard living, she was still very attractive, her blonde hair undimmed by age, her blue eyes bright. Her heart was full and she had to clear her throat before she could speak. "Yes, God is good and he will do great things. Now ask the blessing, Husband, so we can eat."

John Bunyan did as she requested, and while they ate the simple meal, he asked for news about the parish. He had been released several times by Cobb for short visits. During those times he had gone about the county preaching with great success. He listened as Elizabeth and Mary gave him the news of the neighbors, the births and deaths, the occasions for rejoicing or for grief. Finally, he asked, "And what about our friends the Wakefields? What's the news of them?"

Mary said at once, "Evan was by about a month ago. He seemed downhearted, not like himself at all."

"What was wrong with him?"

"He wouldn't say much. I asked him if the family was all well and he said yes, but then, when I asked about Jenny, he said hardly a word."

Bunyan nodded slowly. "I'm worried about that young woman. The last time Gavin was by he told me she was a great success on the stage and that's a bad thing. That's no life for a young girl."

"Evan was rather odd about it," Mary said. "You know what good friends he always was with Amos—the two of them went off to the Dutch War together—but he seemed to be angry at Amos for some reason. He wouldn't say why."

Bunyan listened with concern. "We must pray much for Sir Christopher and all of his family," he said, "especially for the young people. Have you had no word at all about Jenny except that she's on the stage?"

Elizabeth shook her head. "It's a bad time to be in London, John," she remarked. "The plague has struck there again."

Her words sent a chill down her husband's back. Even the word *plague* was a frightful thing. After the terrible epidemic of 1349, which had claimed about a third of the English people, there had been many similar visitations of the Black Death. In fact, there had been few years in which London was wholly free from this dreaded disease. In 1603 and again in 1625, thousands of Londoners had died.

Now the blight was returning.

"I fear that this country is under the visitation of God," John Bunyan said slowly. "Since the days of Cromwell, England seems to have descended, most willingly indeed, into a hellish immorality."

Mary at once agreed. "Evan said he was going back to London to try to get Jenny to leave. I hope he will. The king and the royal house have already fled and so have many others."

"You can flee London, but you can't flee the justice of God. If this is a punishment of God because of the immorality of our people, there's no place on earth a man will be safe," Bunyan said. Then he grew more cheerful and looked around his family. "Come now, eat up. Let us remember God's goodness to us this day. Your father is home again with you and glad indeed for the blessing."

"Will you ever have to leave us, Father?" Thomas piped up.

Bunyan put his hand out and ruffled the lad's blonde locks. "We never know what tomorrow brings. Whatever it is, as long as God is at the center of it, all will be well."

Amos was never quite sure what had triggered the quarrel that flared up between him and Evan Morgan. Ever since their visit to London after the battle at Lowestoft, Evan had been standoffish. It was Hope who finally told him the truth.

"Evan is jealous of you, Amos," she said when her brother asked her why Evan was behaving so peculiarly.

Amos stared at her. "You mean—over Jenny?"

"Of course. You've been running off to London every other week, it seems, and everyone knows it's to see her."

Amos flushed but did not deny it. "All right, it's true. But there's nothing between the two of them. Jenny would have told me."

Hope was very fond of Amos, but she had a soft spot in her heart for Evan, too. "Mother knows," she said. "You know how she sees everything. She's worried to death about Evan. Why don't you ask her?"

"All right, I will."

Amos found his stepmother sewing and sat down beside her. He plunged at once into his concerns. "Hope's just told me that Evan's behaving so badly because he's jealous of me. Is that right?"

Angharad looked up at him. "No, it's not *right,*" she said quickly, "but it's true." She gave Amos a disgusted look. "Is it blind you are, boy? Didn't you see what was going on before you blundered in?"

Amos stared at her in bewilderment. He pondered the question, racking his mind for any sign he had missed. Perhaps he had been careless. He was so infatuated with Jenny that he had not once thought of Evan or how he might feel about the situation. And yet, try as he might, he could think of nothing Evan had said or done to hint that Amos *should* think about his feelings.

"No, I didn't see anything going on. I didn't even think of checking with Evan," he said. "Why should I? Jenny never talks about him and he never says anything about her. I think you and Hope are wrong."

"There is blind you are," Angharad said quietly. She put her sewing down. "You don't know the Welsh very well. Evan is like Owen and I. He's hurting now deep inside, but he would never breathe a word of it to a living soul."

"Has he said anything to you?"

"Enough to know that that's his problem."

Amos's lips grew into a tight line and his jaw grew tense. "Well, I'll talk to him," he said. "I'll have to have this straightened out, Mother. We can't go around like we have been. He's drinking a lot, you know. I didn't know it was because of this, though."

"Be careful what you say," Angharad said quickly. "He's got a bad temper. Not unlike yourself."

Amos stood up, reached over, and pressed her shoulder reassuringly. "Don't worry. I'll be very gentle with him."

Amos intended to do what he said, but he caught Evan at a bad time. He didn't see him that day. The next night one of the workers told him that Evan had come in from the village. "You asked me to tell you," he said. "But I must warn you, sir. He's drunk."

"Thanks, Carl. I'll have a word with him."

He left the house and went at once to the small house Evan

shared with his cousin, Will. When he knocked on the door, Will answered. "Why, Mr. Amos," he said. "Is there trouble?" At sixty-seven, Will Morgan had grown rather frail. He was thin and had not been well for some time.

"I'd like to see Evan, if you don't mind, please?" Amos said.

"I'll get him."

Amos waited and soon Will was back. He had had a difficult time awaking Evan. "It's likely not a good time to talk to him, Mr. Amos. Mayhap tomorrow?"

"This won't take long," Amos said, then met Evan's groggy, bloodshot eyes. "You mind stepping outside, Evan?"

Evan didn't say a word but marched through the door, his chin held out pugnaciously.

"Let's walk away from the house a little," Amos said.

"This is far enough for me," Evan said stubbornly.

Amos could tell it would be a good idea to postpone the talk, but he was a rather strong-minded young man himself. And Evan's cavalier attitude fired his frustration.

"All right, this suits me as well." He stared at Evan for a moment, then said, "You're behaving badly, Evan. I've come to talk with you about it."

Evan's eyes flashed. "Is that so, now? Well, if my behavior's bad, you're no saint to preach to me about it!"

Amos's face flushed. He was not accustomed to such talk and his temper flared. "Well, *someone* needs to talk to you about it and I'm here to do it! What's this foolishness I hear about you being in love with Jenny?"

Instantly the deep-seated anger and jealousy that had been building up in Evan boiled to the surface. He well knew that Amos was in love with Jenny. And while he had had no way of knowing her feelings for certain, it made sense that she would never look at a working man when the son of a noble family was courting her. All the violence of his youth, which he had thought was gone for good, suddenly flooded him. Without thinking, he cursed Amos and told him to mind his own business.

Amos reached out to grab Evan by the shirt. "You can't talk to me like that!" he roared.

Without warning, Evan drove his fist into Amos's face. It knocked Amos backward on his heel. He stood for one moment, staring incredulously at Evan, then let out a wild cry and surged forward, fists flailing. He caught Evan high on the head with a blow that sent pain shooting down his own arm and knew he had broken a finger. But he had no time to worry about that. Evan had turned into a wild man. He threw himself toward Amos, silent, yet with all the ferocity of a wild beast gone mad. Amos suddenly found himself lying in the dirt, straddled by Evan, who proceeded to pummel his face with punishing blows.

Evan was in a blind rage, aware only that he had to strike out. He gave no thought to the fact that he might well be doing Amos serious—perhaps fatal—injury. Through the red haze filling his mind, he heard a voice speaking to him. He ignored it. Then a crashing pain filled his head and he slipped to the ground.

Amos lay panting, filled with pain, then rolled over and pushed himself shakily to his feet. Through eyes already beginning to swell he saw Will standing there, a stool in his hand. He had struck Evan over the head with it and now tossed it to one side. He pinned Amos with his eyes.

"I think you'd better go now, Mr. Amos," he said quietly.

Amos held his injured right hand carefully and stared down at Evan's still form. "Will," he said, "he's a crazy man. I just wanted to talk to him."

Will Morgan knew well what was going on in the mind and heart of his young relative. He had grieved with him and seen this coming. "I'm sorry it's come to this, Mr. Amos," he said. "There's nothing to be done for it. He's in love with the girl and so are you, I suppose. You can't both have her. So there it is. Go along now."

Will waited until Amos had left, then picked up the stool and set it on the ground. His heart was fluttering rapidly and he took deep breaths trying to get his strength back. He sat there, his gaze fixed on the still figure of his relative, and knew that something had come to an end.

After a long while, Evan stirred. Will waited until he struggled to his feet, then said quietly, "Go to bed now, boy. We'll talk about it later, in the morning."

Evan stared at him blankly, then staggered inside the house and went to fall across his bed.

Will turned and walked slowly toward the big house. He knocked at the door and asked to see Angharad. The servant who let him in knew him well and was startled by his pallor.

"What is it, Will? You don't look well."

"Tell Lady Wakefield I need to see her at once. I'll wait in the library."

He made his way to the large room, then sat down heavily in a leather chair. Almost at once Angharad came in, her face troubled. "What is it, Will?"

"It's Evan," he said briefly. He related what had taken place and then said heavily, "Evan will not stay on this place now. You know he won't."

"No, he's too proud for that and the sight of Amos would be gall to him. Where will he go, do you think?"

"To London. That's where she is."

"I hope not." Angharad took a deep breath. "The plague is so bad there, people are leaving in droves."

"Those are sensible people in their right minds," Will said sadly. "But Evan's not sensible. A man in love rarely is." He summoned up a smile and said, "Why couldn't he have fallen in love with

Jenny when she was here? They could have gotten married and lived happily. Now, instead, we've got a bit of a tragedy."

Angharad went over to her brother and put her arm around him. "You don't need all this trouble, Will. Come along, spend the night here."

"No, I'll need to be there to talk to Evan when he wakes up. But I know he'll be gone by midday."

Will's words were prophetic. The next day, Evan rose and refused breakfast. He gathered his few belongings and said, "I'm leaving now. I'll write you when I get to London." A strange sort of premonition came to him as he looked at his cousin. He had never seen Will Morgan look so fragile and the thought came to him, *You'll never see him alive again.* Under other circumstances he would have stayed, but now he could not. Sorrow struck him, sharp and deep. "Take care of yourself, Cousin Will."

Will also felt the touch of mortality—he knew he was living on borrowed time. "My boy, it's love I have for you. You're my own blood and I will only say this: learn to follow God. I know you're in a turmoil now over this young woman, but God is your greatest need. Put him first, the Lord Jesus, and everything else will come." He spoke quietly, almost in a whisper, and then reached up and embraced the boy.

Love for his cousin washed over Evan and when he felt the man's frail form he nearly changed his mind. But he could not stay. "Tell Angharad I'll write her and I'll come back as soon as I can."

He turned and left. As Wakefield passed out of his sight, he cursed himself for being a fool but could do nothing other than follow the path he was on.

All along the way to London, Evan found people fleeing the city. When he stopped to eat his lunch, he talked to one man who told him he was a fool for going there. "Don't you know?" the old man said. "A blazing star appeared for six months before this plague. Plain enough that God is saying that he's going to send his wrath upon England. Don't be a fool, young man. Flee from the wrath to come."

Evan, of course, did not listen.

As soon as he arrived in London, however, he found that the populace was behaving like crazy people. The streets were filled with self-appointed prophets who ran about the streets with their predictions, preaching their "gospel" to the city. On Evan's first day in the city, one such man ran down the street almost naked, screaming, "Yet forty days and London shall be destroyed!"

Evan found no trouble in obtaining a room. It was mid-September, a time when the city normally was bustling with activity and the inns were filled. Now, however, so many houses and inns had been vacated that, in one sense, the city was like a ghost town. As he walked down the street, he saw that many of the houses had strange signs written outside. Some of them were the signs of the zodiac, but the most common was an upside-down triangle made from the word *Abracadabra.* Evan studied this sign with interest. At the top, the full word was written. Below that, the word was written again, but this time the first and last letters were left off. And so it continued to the bottom line, which was nothing but *a.*

May it protect them, Evan thought, though he doubted it would. He moved on, talking along the way with several people who were walking the streets, selling charms, philters, exorcisms, and amulets—each of which, the vendors guaranteed, would keep the plague away.

After finding a room at a very low price, Evan set out to find Jenny. He discovered quickly that most of the actors had fled, as had the royal family. He hunted for three days but found no trace of Jenny. He finally found a man who had worked in the theatre. Evan interrogated him closely about Jenny's whereabouts.

"Why, she ain't a fool, is she?" the old man, Silas, slurred. He was drunk and apparently intended to stay that way until the plague took him off. "Only a fool would stay in this place. Have you seen the dead cart?"

Indeed, he had. He had been shocked the first time he had seen it. The bodies of those who died were collected early each morning and tossed into a huge cart. Most of the bodies appeared to be naked and their arms were raised in strangely eloquent gestures—but their faces, covered with sores and grotesque stains, were terrible to see.

"Yes, I've seen the dead cart, but *where* did Mistress Clairmont go? Can you tell me that?"

But Silas just sat there in a stupor as though he either hadn't heard the question or merely didn't care to respond.

Evan desperately shook him back to awareness for one moment. "Where can I go to find her? Tell me!"

The old man blinked owlishly at him. "Go down in Holburn, the Bird and Baby Tavern. Her maid's people run the place. I think the woman's name's Louise. 'At's all I know."

Evan found his way to the Bird and Baby Tavern. The sign outside showed an eagle carrying a child away, hence the name. Entering, he informed the innkeeper, a tall, cadaverous man, "I'm looking for Mistress Jenny Clairmont. I was told I might gain word of her here."

"Aye, my daughter was her maid," the innkeeper replied. "If you'll sit there, I'll fetch her."

Evan sat down at once and soon the woman came out and approached him. He rose, bowing slightly. "Good day, miss. My name's Evan Morgan and I'm trying to find Mistress Clairmont. Do you know if she's still in the city?"

"Aye. Last I heard she'd taken a room," she said and gave the address. "There's not much acting going on now, but she wouldn't leave," she added with a shrug.

Evan thanked the woman and set off to search for the place. He found it with little trouble—it was a frame-and-timber building with a thatched roof—and knocked on the door eagerly.

As soon as it opened, he saw Jenny and his heart gave a leap of relief. "Jenny!" he said quickly. "Are you all right?"

She looked at him, stunned. She stepped back to allow him entry. "Why, Evan! Come in. What are you doing in London?"

Stepping inside, he explained. "I wanted to find out if you were all right." He would not tell her of his fight with Amos; she would discover it soon enough.

"You shouldn't have come to London. It's too dangerous. All the houses are quarantined where there's been any sign of the plague. Where are you staying?"

"At the Blue Hawk Inn."

She asked at once, "Are you sure there's been no plague there?"

Evan stared at her blankly. "Why, I don't know. I never thought—"

"You'd better make sure. It's terrible, this plague. You can wake up well in the morning and be dead before nightfall."

But Evan was more concerned about her. "Why didn't you go with the rest when they left London?"

Jenny seemed very tired and she turned from him, walking listlessly to stare out a small window at the bleak street. "I don't know why. I just didn't." The truth was she had grown tired of the theatrical life. The continual pressures to join in the immoral practices had worn her down until she had found herself almost giving way to them. She did not deny the plague had been a curse, yet it had given her time to think. She had taken the small house, which cost only a small portion of her abundant funds, and for weeks now had been living quietly, thinking of her life. She turned back to Evan, lifting her eyes to study his face.

"Did you come just for me?" She hadn't meant to ask the question, but suddenly it had come forth, as though her heart needed to hear the response.

He stared at her wordlessly. He could not answer her. He didn't even try. "I'm concerned for you," he said instead. "So is everyone at home. Won't you come to Wakefield until this is over?" The plea cost him greatly. He knew her return—and her reunion with Amos—would bring him great pain.

Disappointed in his response, though not quite certain why, she shook her head. "Why, no, I won't do that," she said gently, her eyes on his. The bleakness in his expression troubled her greatly. She came toward him, laying her hand softly on his arm. "What is bothering you so?" she asked. "Can you tell me?"

Her nearness was almost more than he could bear. The touch of her hand on his arm seemed to sear him, so that he wanted to jerk away—or pull her to him. The desire to blurt out his trouble—that he loved her, completely, hopelessly—surged within him, but he felt that would not help. So he simply said, "I've decided to stay in London a while. I may go out to sea again."

The surprise was clear on her face. "You're leaving Wakefield?"

"Yes, I think it's time."

Intuitively, Jenny understood. While she and Amos had not discussed Evan, she had heard from Angharad twice. The letters had hinted that Evan had feelings for Jenny. Now as she studied him, saw the bleakness and sorrow on his face, she knew it was true. But what could she say? She was strongly attracted to Amos Wakefield.

And yet . . . for all that she was drawn to Amos, she had never felt she loved him enough to spend her life with him.

"Come and sit down, Evan," she said at last. "You look tired."

He stayed for an hour and they talked of many things—though not of the thing uppermost in both their minds. When he left to go back to the inn, he was almost undone by the grief that welled up within him. Perhaps it was caused by the joy he had felt on seeing Jenny mixed with the devastating knowledge that she would never be his. At the inn he went to bed at once, hoping the oblivion of sleep would bring relief.

For the next two days he wandered the streets of London, seeing horrible sights everywhere he went. He shouldn't have been out—he knew that. He was risking exposure to the plague, but he could not stand the confines of his small room. He saw Jenny once during that time but did not wish, if he had contracted the disease, to expose her.

One night he went walking the streets and encountered a huge pit that had been dug in the churchyard in Allgate. He stared at it. It was forty feet in length, about fifteen or sixteen feet broad, and almost twenty feet deep.

And it was filled with bodies.

Each day the corpses were laid in a row, then a thin layer of dirt was laid over them. Staring at this horrendous sight, fear came upon Evan. This was nothing a man could fight! Evan had proven that he had need only of a sword in his hand and he would stand against any danger . . . but this! No man could battle this.

He went back to his room, shut the door, and sank down on his bed. He grew warm and opened the window, then stripped off most of his clothes. An hour later, he knew the truth. He had the fever. He lay down on the bed and tried to think, but the fever rose rapidly. He drifted off to fitful sleep, and when he woke, the fever was raging through him. He reached to feel his armpit and what he found there almost caused his heart to stop beating. He had heard that a sure sign of the plague was growths—lumps—in the armpit and in the groin. He made a quick exam, dread washing over him as he found them in both places.

He was a dead man.

All day he lay there, knowing that when the innkeeper came,

he would be cut off from everyone. This was the way it was with those who had the plague.

The innkeeper did come, took one look at him, and hurried from the room. When he returned a short while later, he held a cloth over his mouth and nose with one hand and carried a pitcher of water in the other.

"Make your peace with God," he said solemnly. "I'll leave water here, at least, and food. But you can't go out of this room." He hesitated, then said, "My wife has it, too, and my two children."

Evan had never experienced a serious sickness. He had led a healthy existence—but now he was racked with pain. The lumps grew so agonizingly sensitive that he had to bite his lip to keep from screaming every time he moved or accidentally touched them. The fever continued to rage until, after several days, he went into delirium. From time to time he would come out of the fog that filled his mind, but only for brief periods. It was during one such time that he thought someone had come and was bathing his face.

Or was it a dream?

Time ceased to exist. As far as Evan was concerned, the pyramids could have been built during the time of his unconsciousness or it could have been only a split second. He had no way of knowing. Life beat in his body and yet he knew himself to be dying. Many times he tried to pray. There was one moment in particular, when the pain seemed to be ebbing away, and as he lay there feeling the cool cloth on his forehead, he opened his cracked lips and said, "God, be merciful to me, a sinner."

He recognized somewhere deep in his being that the prayer had been in him for many years, but he had never uttered it. Now he despised himself for coming to God when all was lost. A voice seemed to come straight from the pit, saying, *Why do you think*

God would hear you? You who denied him all your life? No! It's hell and the pit for you, Evan Morgan. Forever!

He had no energy to fight these words and yet he felt no fear because of them. It was as though he were sheltered somehow, protected from them. He did not understand it, but he felt a flash of gratitude before he again succumbed to unconsciousness. But this time was different. He seemed to float in space—and the pain was gone. Slowly he grew more aware, until one day he opened his eyes to see a slanting bar of sunlight coming through the window. His licked his parched lips and tried to swallow, but his throat was drier still. Then he caught a hint of movement to his left.

Turning his head carefully, he saw a face. But his eyes could not focus and the image seemed to swim and change. He tried to speak, but only a croak came out. He shut his eyes, then opened them again. This time the face was clearer.

"Jenny," he said, his voice a cracked parody of itself.

"Yes, Evan." She was leaning over him, bathing his face.

He stared at her disbelievingly. "You can't be here," he whispered. "You'll catch the plague."

"You're going to get well," Jenny said calmly. "The doctor was here. The lumps have broken and he says when that happens, the sick almost always get well."

"Get . . . get well?" He couldn't take it in. His head swam and he could say no more.

He lay there quietly, thinking, and then drifted off to sleep. When he awakened again, Jenny was there, this time with food. "You must eat," she said. "To get strong again." She was wearing a dark brown dress and her face was drawn with fatigue.

"How long have you been here?" he asked between sips of the broth she fed him.

"Over a week." She looked at him strangely. "I thought you were going to die."

"Why did you come?" he asked, his voice filled with anguish. "How could you put yourself at such risk?"

Jenny put the spoon down and then the plate. She gave him a drink of water, then sat back, her eyes steady on his face. "I sent for you and they told me you were sick." She hesitated, then went on in a low voice, "I remembered that night, so long ago, when I came to you from the woods. You took me in. You fed me—" Her voice broke with emotion, and she drew a steadying breath. "You saved my life, Evan."

He stared at her for a long time, then raised his hand to brush his fingers softly against her arm. "That was a long time ago," he whispered.

She took his hand, holding it for a moment between both of hers as though she would not let it go, then laid it back on his chest. "We're even now," she said.

Evan looked at her and nodded. "Aye," he said in a thin whisper, his eyes never leaving her face. She was lovely, even wreathed in fatigue.

He knew he would die loving her.

But he only said, "Aye, we're even now."

END OF PART TWO

Part THREE

The Merry Monarch

1666–1669

Fourteen

Hope Meets a Man

The plague had reached its height in August and September of 1665. By the end of the year it seemed to have passed, and by early 1666 London again became a bustling town. This was good news to many, particularly those involved in theatre. Jenny's company was one of the first to return and it wasn't long before they were once again in full swing, putting on plays and attracting huge audiences.

Despite her feelings and uncertainty, Jenny went back to acting because she wasn't sure what else to do. Life fell once again into the old predictable pattern, which meant she once again had to exercise an ability she had gained from her profession: showing considerable discernment and resistance concerning men. She had discovered early on as she had gained acclaim that most men felt she was little more than a prostitute and treated her accordingly. She had learned to keep the disgust she felt for such creatures from showing on her face. More important, she had developed a defensive strategy to avoid finding herself in any proximity to these men. Most actresses, after their performances, were quick to accept invitations from wealthy men for dinner—and other involvements. Jenny Clairmont rarely did so.

One evening, however, a young man who came backstage

caught her attention. Or rather, the introduction she was given by one of the regular attendants did.

"This is Mr. Darcy Wingate," the man said. "A fledgling lawyer on his way to becoming rich and famous."

Wingate protested this. "I'm hardly likely to become that in a small village such as Bedford, am I now?"

At the mention of Bedford, Jenny's attention was stirred. "Are you going to Bedford quite soon?"

"Why, yes," the young man answered, surprised. "As a matter of fact, I'll be leaving first thing in the morning."

Jenny took a quick survey of Darcy Wingate. She found him to be a young man of about twenty-five, six feet tall, and very lean, though he appeared strong. He had chestnut hair, gray eyes, and a fair complexion. As she studied his face, she saw none of the dissipation that she so frequently found in men of his age. He had a long face with a strong nose and a stubborn mouth and chin. On the whole, he was not handsome but was healthy looking and quite virile.

"Mr. Wingate, would you care to have a small supper with me?" she asked quietly, aware that her question had shocked others. "I have friends in the vicinity of Bedford and you might encounter some of them."

"Why, the pleasure would be all mine, Mistress Clairmont."

In less than thirty minutes, the two of them were sitting at an inn, where Jenny allowed him to order her meal. Until it came, she listened as her companion gave her a brief sketch of his past. He was from a good family in the north of England and had just finished his studies at the university. He was now going to study for a time with his uncle. "Mr. Francis Wingate," he told her. "Do you know him?"

"I know *of* him, Mr. Wingate, but I've never met him."

The two talked easily and Wingate was quite impressed by the beauty of the woman who sat with him. Her green eyes matched the shade of her dress, which outlined her shapely form. Her strawberry blonde hair was of a tint that he had never seen before.

A stunning woman, indeed! he thought. *And yet she is quite different from most of the actresses I've met.*

After the meal, they sipped tea and talked more. Wingate asked abruptly, "Do you usually ask your admirers out for supper, Mistress Clairmont?"

She met his inquiring eyes calmly. "No, sir, I do not. As a matter of fact, you are the first."

He smiled, his broad mouth turning up slightly in a strange twist on the right side. "I must be more charming than I thought to receive such an honor. Was it my good looks that enticed you into this invitation?"

"No," Jenny said, her voice suddenly cool. "It was not your appearance at all."

Wingate laughed aloud. "Now that's coming right out with it!" He took a sip of tea, then cocked his head to one side. "I know it couldn't have been my fortune you're after, as I don't have one." He leaned forward, resting his chin in his hand, his eyes filled with curious interest. "So please enlighten me, Mistress Clairmont. What prompted you to invite me to supper?"

"I'll be honest with you, sir," she replied. "I have a favor to ask." She smiled at him over the rim of her teacup, her eyes sparkling with a wry humor. "And now you know the worst of me. I am a woman who asks favors of strange men."

Wingate leaned back, impressed by her honesty. Most actresses were rather coarse and generally quite a bit older. This girl was in her early twenties at the most, he guessed, and had an air of unmistakable dignity. "I'd be honored to be of service to you, Mistress Clairmont," he assured her sincerely.

"I hope you believe me when I say this is not a habit of mine. However, my need forces me to unusual measures. I have a friend who has been very ill—"

"The plague?" Wingate demanded.

She nodded, her eyes not wavering from his. "Yes. However, he's recovered now to the point that there is no danger of contagion." She leaned forward and the lanterns bathed her face and shoulders with a warm, golden glow. She had a beautiful complexion and now her cheeks were slightly flushed in her intensity. "His name is Evan Morgan. He needs to leave London, but he's very weak. If you could see him back to Wakefield, sir, I would be most grateful to you."

Darcy watched her expressions as he thought rapidly. "You're certain he's not contagious?"

"You could check with a doctor," she said firmly, "but I can assure you, sir, that he is completely healthy now. Only weakened."

"Then I see no reason why I couldn't do as you ask." Darcy nodded. "I've rented a carriage that I drive myself. There will be plenty of room." He hesitated, then asked curiously, "Is this one of your admirers, Mistress Clairmont?"

"Oh no, nothing like that," Jenny protested, the slight color in her cheeks growing much deeper.

Darcy found it most intriguing that this young woman, who was in such a worldly profession, would blush at a simple question.

She went on hastily, "He's a very old friend of mine. We grew up together. Both of us were servants of Sir Christopher Wakefield."

Darcy's estimation of Jenny rose yet again. "Not many actresses would admit to having been a servant." His crooked smile flashed. "Most of them 'admit' instead to being an illegitimate child of the dauphine of France or to being a member of the Austrian noble house."

Jenny smiled, a dimple appearing in her cheek. "Nothing like that, sir, for me. I was a maid for Lady Wakefield's daughter for many years. Evan worked in the stables, with the horses. We both come from Wales."

"Well, I'll be happy to do you this service, Mistress Clairmont," Wingate declared. He was an openhanded young fellow and when he saw the grateful smile on the actress's face he felt well rewarded. "I'll be leaving in the morning. If you'll inform me as to where I can pick up this man, I'll be glad to do so."

"His family will be very grateful to you. Both Sir Christopher and Lady Wakefield hold him in great affection. As a matter of fact, Evan is a relative of Lady Wakefield's. She, too, is from Wales." She rose then and held out her hand, which was an unusual gesture for Jenny.

Darcy took it, brought it to his lips for a gallant kiss, then released it. "I must say," he remarked, his eyes shining with admiration and his voice low, "that your Evan Morgan is fortunate to have so fair a protector." As a flush once again rose in her cheeks, he smiled. "You may inform your friend that I will pick him up early in the morning."

"Well, Mr. Morgan, shall we be on our way?"

Evan had been informed by Jenny that a gentleman would call to take him back to Wakefield. Now as he settled into Wingate's carriage, he replied quickly, "Yes, Mr. Wingate. But 'Evan' is what I'm usually called." As the carriage started up he went on, "It's grateful to you I am, sir." He cast a disparaging glance over his shoulder. "Faith, it's sick I've been of that room for a week now."

"This sunshine will do you good," Wingate said empathetically. "We've a good day for traveling."

Darcy drove the carriage through the crowded streets of London. There were still signs of the plague: Many buildings were boarded up, several of which still had warning signs posted on them. Wingate glanced at his companion.

"Indeed, sir, you must have a hearty constitution." He noted that Evan appeared thin, almost emaciated, but that there was some fairly healthy color in his cheeks. "Many do not survive this sickness."

Evan considered the words. "I'm convinced, sir, that it was God who brought me through it. There's no other answer."

Darcy nodded but made no reply.

When they came to the London Bridge, Wingate looked up at the heads of those unfortunates who had been beheaded for various crimes. Their severed heads were stuck high on pikes. Darcy remarked with distaste, "I don't see the necessity for such as this."

"Nor do I, sir," Evan agreed. "When a man's dead, he's no longer an enemy to anyone. An emperor and a beggar are on the same ground when they pass through those final gates."

"I agree. My family were Royalists, but I thought the treatment given to the bodies of the leaders of the revolutionaries was abysmal." Wingate referred to strange and bizarre revenge wrought by those who came to power after Cromwell's death. These men had dug up the bodies of Cromwell, Ireton, and other leaders so that they could hang them. Then, as a final humiliation, they cut off the corpses' heads and put them on pikes. "Cromwell and the others were good and honorable men," Darcy muttered. "They did not deserve such treatment."

As they traveled that day, Wingate managed to elicit most of Evan Morgan's story. As a lawyer, he was quite adept at getting people to reveal things. He was particularly interested in this young man's relationship with Jenny Clairmont. By the time they had reached an inn late that afternoon, Wingate knew the story of how the two had come from Wales and served Sir Christopher Wakefield. He also had sharply deduced that Evan Morgan felt more than a brotherly concern for the famous actress. He said nothing about it, but as they completed their journey the next day, he further discovered that there was a son of the house named Amos who also was interested in Mistress Clairmont.

Well, wheels within wheels, Wingate thought. *I wonder what Mistress Jenny thinks of these two young men?*

They reached Wakefield at three o'clock and were met at the door by Angharad, who embraced Evan warmly. "Why, look at you! Nothing but skin and bones!" she exclaimed. She hugged him again. "Wait you now and see if I don't fix that!"

"Lady Wakefield, this gentleman is Mr. Darcy Wingate," Evan said. "He's been so kind as to see me home."

"It's welcome you are, sir," Angharad said graciously. "I insist that you stay the night. It's too late to travel any farther."

Darcy hesitated, then smiled. He liked this tall, well-shaped woman with the warm brown eyes. He had learned that she was in her middle fifties, though neither her form nor her hair gave any evidence of aging. "If it won't be a difficulty," he assented.

"And how could it be that? Come now, I'll take you to your room. Evan, will you be at your house?"

"Yes, I will. I'm rather tired."

"Good, you!" Angharad declared. "I'll be down with some food very soon. Get yourself into bed now."

Darcy found himself in a very pleasant room with tall windows that admitted plenty of fresh air. Angharad turned to him with a smile. "Perhaps you'd like to lie down and rest a while. But you must have supper with us tonight. It's grateful we are for your attention to Evan."

She left the room and Darcy went at once to the washstand to pour out some fresh water. After stripping off his garments, he washed slowly, luxuriating in the bath. He lay down on the bed and dozed, awakening when a voice summoned him to supper.

He dressed quickly, and when he reached the foot of the stairs, found Lady Wakefield with a tall man whose hair had gone white.

Lady Wakefield smiled at him. "And this is my husband, Sir Christopher Wakefield. Sir Christopher, Mr. Darcy Wingate."

"Ah! A relative of Sir Francis Wingate, I understand," Christopher said.

"Yes, sir. My uncle." Wingate had heard a little of the Wakefield family. He was impressed with Sir Christopher Wakefield, who Evan had said was now in his middle seventies. Though there seemed to be a lack of physical strength about Wakefield, his eyes were sharp and he had a genial air about him.

"Come, sit down," Sir Christopher said. "I'm nigh famished, as I'm sure you must be."

As they entered the room, Darcy saw a young woman standing by the fireplace. She turned as they came in and Sir Christopher said, "This is my daughter, Hope. My dear, this is Mr. Darcy Wingate."

"I'm happy to meet you, Mistress Wakefield," Darcy said, bowing from the waist. The young woman regarded him and he took in her lovely features. Though not tall, she was well formed, and the same dark hair as her mother had flowed over her shoulders down to her waist. Her eyes were the darkest brown he'd ever seen. She had an oval face with broad, mobile lips—and she seemed . . . watchful.

"Welcome to Wakefield, Mr. Wingate," she said. "I hope you're hungry."

"I hope you are, too," Angharad said, smiling fondly at Hope. "I left the dinner up to Hope and she's known for overdoing such things."

Wakefield chuckled and put his arm around the young girl, who Wingate guessed was no more than eighteen. "She thinks she's cooking for King Charles and the royal host." He smiled at her fondly, and Darcy could see the closeness of the two.

They all sat down at the table and servants began bringing in the meal. Darcy was much impressed with the variety of food. First there was a plate of hot fish, followed by a shoulder of mutton, and then a fried rabbit, sweet and spiced in a way he'd never tasted. After this came pumpkin, sliced and baked with candied apples. Accompanying all this were salads and vegetables of various ilk.

"I believe the royal family would be satisfied with this, Mistress Wakefield," Wingate said admiringly. His crooked grin suddenly appeared. "Your husband will have the gout and a big stomach if you feed him in this manner!"

Hope smiled her appreciation, but there was a slightly calculating look in her eyes. The young man's ease in conversation had impressed her.

He must be a good lawyer, she thought. *He has quite a gift of getting along with people.* Now she said, "What about yourself, Mr. Wingate? Where is your home?"

"In the north part of England," he answered. When she pressured him to tell more, he shrugged and went on, "We're not a very exciting family. We survived the revolution and now that the king is back, we breathe a little bit easier."

"You were opposed to the revolution then?"

"My family felt it was not the best for the country." Darcy saw that this answer didn't satisfy Hope and instantly realized she was politically opposed to the royal scheme of things as it now stood.

Christopher took mercy on the poor man, sitting as he was in a rather uncomfortable silence. "Please do not let our girl dismay you. We were quite active under Mr. Cromwell."

"So I understand." Darcy admired the man's simple honesty. "This makes it difficult for you now, does it?"

"So far there has been little difficulty," Chris answered readily. "But my eldest son has a friend, Mr. John Bunyan, who's come into great misfortune." He related the history of Bunyan's arrest and imprisonment. "Your uncle is the magistrate who had Bunyan arrested."

Wingate shifted uncomfortably. He knew that there were many areas in which his uncle and this good man probably differed, but he did not want to become involved. He was aware that Hope Wakefield watched him carefully. "I'm sorry to hear of it," he ventured. "The king has been opposed to this. Had he been free to do so, he would have allowed complete freedom of worship."

"If he's the king," Hope asked sharply, "why can't he simply command that it be done?"

Darcy's crooked smile flashed briefly. "That, my dear Mistress Wakefield, was what the revolution was all about. When the king did what he wanted without accountability to the people, a revolution was the result. No, the king is now responsible to parliament, which is as it should be. It is they who passed the laws concerning preachers."

Angharad recognized the stubborn light that came into her daughter's face and broke in. "Mr. Wingate, I trust that you will have time tomorrow to look over our little estate."

Christopher put in, "I won't be able to go myself." A mischievous light flashed in his shrewd eyes. "Still, I'm sure my daughter will be pleased to stand in for me. Won't you, Daughter?"

Hope's eyes slid to her father's face. She knew he was teasing her, and could not resist a smile. "Certainly, Father," she said effusively. Turning back to Wingate, she added, "Perhaps we can discuss politics some more, Mr. Wingate."

"Anything you desire, Mistress Wakefield," Wingate said, his eyes gleaming. "The meal was delicious. My compliments."

Angharad left shortly after to make a quick trip down to the house where she herself had lived with her father until he had passed on. There she found Evan sitting at the table, his face haggard. "What is it?" she asked anxiously. "Don't you feel well?"

"I didn't know that Cousin Will had died," he said.

"I thought I would be the one to tell you," Angharad sighed. She went to put her hands on his shoulders. "He went quickly, Evan. Almost his last words were of you. He loved you very much. He was praying that God would be with you."

"I—I'll miss him. He was like a father to me, and patient beyond what I deserved."

Angharad sat close by him and they talked of Will Morgan for some time. "Owen, my father, is gone now—and we've lost Will." She took his hands in hers. "It's just you and me from the old country. We must stick very close together, we two."

"Cousin," Evan murmured, "I've been thinking a lot of what my life has been. When I almost died, I thought of God—for the first time, really."

Angharad's eyes filled with tears. She was a woman of deep, rich emotion and had prayed long for this young relative of hers. "I'm glad, Nephew," she whispered. "It must have been a terrible time for you. But if it brings you to God, it was a blessing indeed."

Evan bowed his head but clung to Angharad's hands, and they sat in silence for a while. Then she asked softly, "What about Jenny?"

"I owe my life to her. If it hadn't been for Jenny, I would have died," he said simply.

"She's determined to stay in London then?"

"Yes. I think so." He took a deep breath. "I'll have to tell Amos I was wrong. I've been wrong about so many things, but somehow I feel that things will be different now."

Angharad leaned over and kissed him. "You rest now and we'll see what the good Lord will do."

"I trust you slept well, Mr. Wingate."

Darcy Wingate nodded. He and Hope had just finished breakfast and the sun was barely peeping over the eastern hills. "Yes, and after that fine breakfast, I'm ready for anything."

"Then come! Perhaps you'd like to see the mews. We're very proud of our hawks here."

Hope led the way to the mews and Wingate was amazed to find how much this young girl knew about the ancient sport of hawking.

"I learned a great deal from my brother Gavin," she told him. "He began teaching me when I was just a little girl." She showed him the peregrines and the goshawks, adding, "Do you know, by law, who is allowed to fly a peregrine falcon?"

"Why, no," Wingate said, mystified. "I supposed anyone can."

Hope's dimple peeked out. "And you call yourself a lawyer, sir? No, indeed. Legally, you must be of at least an earl's rank to fly a peregrine." She turned to the birds and pointed to one. "You can fly this one. I'll take this female."

They donned heavy leather gauntlets, hooded the birds, and mounting fine steeds, they rode to an open field. The falcons were quiet during the ride. "I love this little hawk," Hope said simply. "I had a hard time training her. She's very strong. Why, last week, she took a full-grown hare." Leaning over, she held the small raptor high and made small clucking noises. "Your bird, there, his name is Pluto. He loves to swoop out of the sky like lightning. Mostly he takes crows."

"Not very good eating," Wingate commented.

"Not for us, maybe." Hope smiled. "But they are for him."

They moved across the open field and soon sighted game. Pulling the hoods from the birds' heads, they tossed both the falcons into the air. It was no more than a flight of blackbirds, but it was obviously exciting to Hope.

Darcy watched her eyes brighten and listened to her laughter as the birds descended from the heights to make their kills. "I'm surprised to see a young woman who likes hawking so much."

"Why should you be surprised?"

"Why—I'm blessed if I know," he admitted, "except that most of the young women I've known are more interested in dresses, dancing, balls, and things of similar nature."

"And can't a woman be interested in those things," Hope retorted, "and still be a flyer of hawks?"

"I suppose so." Darcy smiled at his companion. She was charming as she sat easily astride her great horse. She wore a plum-colored riding dress, with her hair tucked under a velvet hat of the same rich color and trimmed in silver. He wondered what the cause could be for the sharp tone she had been using with him. He could not imagine it was characteristic of her.

As the hawks returned to the gauntlets and the two falconers were hooding them, he asked her curiously, "You seem to be a bit upset with me, Mistress Wakefield. Or perhaps it is my family with which you are not enamored. Are you mayhap still fighting the battles of the revolution?"

"I think you know some of the injustices that have taken place," she answered, gazing directly into his eyes. There was something very strong, almost aggressive, in the way she watched him. There could be nothing more enticing than her features, which contained a delicate beauty. And yet he knew without a doubt that this was someone who could make a fierce foe.

"I prefer to put the past away," he said quietly.

"As do I," she said flatly. "So it is unfortunate indeed that some of your friends in high places are still out to punish those who were against them."

Her manner aggravated him slightly. "When Cromwell was in power, these 'friends of mine,' as you call them, were driven from their homes," he asserted. "Some of them still haven't been restored to their family estates."

Hope made no response. She merely turned her horse back

toward the mews. They rode on in an uncomfortable silence until Darcy relented.

"I must apologize, Mistress Wakefield. Come, let us not quarrel."

"Very well," Hope said, somewhat grudgingly. "Are you interested in dogs?"

"Hunting dogs? I know very little of them."

"Then come with me and I'll show you some fine ones." They made their way to the kennels and for some time Wingate was lectured on the quality of the Wakefield dogs.

"These are Scottish deerhounds," she explained. Reaching down, she picked up a puppy and held it close to her face. He licked her cheek and she laughed. "You're a darling," she whispered.

And so are you, Mistress Hope Wakefield, Darcy answered in his mind. *When you're not filled with indignation and righteous fury!*

"They say these dogs have been in Scotland for hundreds of years," she told him. "They breed good animals there." There were foxhounds and a group that she called harriers, all of which were used for tracking hares. She introduced him to a small, sparsely haired dog, which she called a terrier.

"They're rather ugly," she admitted, ruffling the dog's rough, sand-colored fur. "But they're good for chasing vermin, such as foxes and rats. They're from the border country."

"Well, the border abounds in vermin," Darcy remarked. "Some of them are even two legged. It's not surprising they've developed a special breed of dog to hunt them."

After they left the kennels, Hope gave him a sly grin. "Now, let's give the horses a workout." She had noticed that Darcy Wingate was not an expert horseman and thought—somewhat perversely, though she would never have admitted it—to embarrass him. They mounted again and she leaned over to mutter a few words to her own mare, which promptly dashed away.

"Blast that woman!" Darcy muttered through clenched teeth. "She knows I'm not much of a rider!" Even so, he would not be bested easily. He did the best he could, slapping the horse with his heels and hanging on for dear life. Unfortunately, when he had gone fifty yards, the horse shied at a rabbit that hopped up directly into his path. The sudden movement put Darcy off balance and he fell headlong over the horse's withers. He landed on his feet, but one foot went in a hole and he went down with a sharp cry of pain.

Hope looked back to see Wingate struggling to get back to his feet. Immediately she reined in her mare, turned, and hurried back to him. "Are you all right, Mr. Wingate?"

"Yes—that is—no." Wingate tried to put his weight on his foot and the agonizing pain made him gasp. "I—think—I've hurt my—ankle."

"Let me get your horse," she ordered. "You can't walk on that ankle." Hope retrieved his horse, which had stopped his bolt a short distance away, and brought him back to where Wingate was struggling to stay on his feet. "Here, let me help you, Mr. Wingate."

It was difficult for Wingate to mount. His right ankle felt as if it had been set on fire. With Hope's help, he finally managed to scramble up. Gritting his teeth, he muttered, "I'm afraid it's going to have to be seen to."

"Mother is an expert at injuries such as this," Hope said reassuringly. She mounted her mare and turned back to him, her face stricken. "I'm sorry. I—I shouldn't have done that. I was just showing off."

When Hope had raced away, Wingate had decided that he definitely did not like this arrogant, challenging young woman. But now her face was open and her concern for him was plain.

He shook his head. "You're not to blame for my poor horsemanship." He shrugged. "Don't trouble yourself about it."

In the end, the injury was more serious than either of them realized. Angharad insisted that Darcy be helped into the house by two of the servants. Then she stripped off his boot and felt his ankle with sensitive fingers.

"It's not broken," she said with relief. "But it is twisted badly. You'll not be going anywhere for a while, Mr. Wingate."

"I need to get to Bedford," he insisted. "My uncle is expecting me."

Angharad shook her head firmly. "No, I think not. We'll send word to your uncle. We need to put compresses on that ankle immediately and you must stay off of it for at least two or three days."

Hope stood by, watching and listening as Angharad treated Darcy's injured ankle. Finally she spoke up, her voice filled with remorse. "It was my fault, Mother. I was showing off again."

"Well, devil fly off!" Angharad said with exasperation. "What are you about, to treat a guest like this?"

Hope felt terrible about the accident. While she believed Darcy Wingate deserved less than admiration for his politics, she was nonetheless a kindly girl at heart and was truly distressed at his misfortune. "I'm so sorry, Mr. Wingate. But I'll make it up to you. See if I don't."

When Hope had left the room, Darcy asked Angharad, "Does she often do things like this?" The pain was lessening now; the compresses had eased it quite a bit. In addition, Angharad had given him something to take for the pain—a bitter-tasting substance—and he was growing drowsy.

Angharad suddenly smiled and stood to her feet. "More than I like to confess," she maintained. "You rest now, Mr. Wingate. You'll be our guest for a few days."

Fifteen

A Call From God

Darcy Wingate stood carefully to his feet, tested his right ankle, and found that the sharpest of the pains were gone. Picking up the walking stick carved from a piece of blackthorn, he limped out of his room. Navigating the steps proved to be somewhat difficult, but he arrived safely at the lower landing and made his way through the hall. The three days of relative inactivity had been difficult for him; he could not stand that sort of thing for long.

"Oh, you're walking well, Mr. Wingate!" Angharad had been passing through the large hall, which was used for the dining of large groups, and smiled as she came to him. "And how is the ankle this morning?"

"Much better." He smiled cheerfully, his gray eyes friendly. Darcy had learned to appreciate Angharad Wakefield. "If you'd set up a medical practice in London, you'd put some of the leeches out of business, Lady Wakefield."

Angharad shook her head. "Not for me, I assure you, Mr. Wingate. Come, sit down with me in the kitchen. I'll have Alice fix you some breakfast." She led him to the large kitchen, where a fire burned cheerfully in the huge fireplace, and endeavored to make him comfortable. Seating him at the high table, she busied herself helping the cook. Soon Darcy was enjoying a fine breakfast.

Angharad sat and talked to him as he ate. She seemed genuinely interested in him and he responded by speaking openly to her. "I'm looking forward to doing something more than read books," he told her. "I feel I'm covered with dust from all those ancient tomes and parchments I've had to try to jam into my head over the past few years."

"I'm really surprised that you chose law as your field, sir," Angharad remarked. "'Tis a dry, dusty business. To me, at least. You seem more fitted for an active life."

"It was my father's desire. And I've agreed to give it a try." Secretly Darcy agreed with Lady Wakefield. He had been reluctant to enter the study of law, but his father had insisted, and he had given in. "Perhaps I won't stay in it forever. Though, upon my word, I can't say what else I should like to do with myself. I'm not fit—obviously—to be a horseman of any kind!" The crooked grin flashed. "I think Mistress Hope thinks ill of me for being such a poor cavalier."

"If she weren't full grown," Angharad said, a frown on her face, "I'd give that girl a switching! She's too forward." Searching Darcy's face, she added, "I trust you'll not let her talk about politics offend you, Mr. Wingate. Hope is too outspoken. As for me and my husband, we have no complaint with the manner in which the king has governed since his return. Nor has my son Gavin, who served actively under Cromwell. Indeed, we were afraid there would be severe penalties for the Wakefields. However, the king seems to be fairly successful at restraining the cavaliers from wreaking vengeance."

"I'm happy to hear it."

Angharad chatted with him until he finished his meal. Then she suggested, "Why don't you go out into the garden? I believe Hope is out tending the roses." At his quizzical look she smiled faintly. "Perhaps you'll find her in a better mood. At least you won't injure yourself smelling flowers."

Darcy rose, picked up his stick, and bowed clumsily. "I believe I will do that. Thank you for the fine meal, Lady Wakefield."

Making his way through the house, he went out into the fresh morning sunshine and inhaled deeply. Dew had fallen in the night and the grass that covered the rolling hills surrounding Wakefield glittered as if strewn with fine diamonds. "This is a beautiful place," he murmured to himself as he made his way carefully down a cobblestone walk. He passed through a gate into an enclosure formed by a stone wall and was pleased by what he saw.

The flower garden glittered in the fresh morning sunshine. The garden was awash in roses of all varieties and colors: reds, yellows, whites, and pinks adorned the geometrical layout of the beds. Seeing Hope with a basket on her arm, clipping some of the roses, he hobbled over and said cheerfully, "Good morrow, Mistress Wakefield."

Hope turned swiftly, somewhat startled, for she had not heard his approach. She carried a flat basket by a strap and held a deep crimson rosebud. Although she could not have known it, she made a breathtaking picture; the deep tint of the red roses about her brought out the red of her lips as the white roses accentuated the ivory skin of her cheeks. "Good morning, Mr. Wingate. I see you're mobile again."

"Yes, but no more horseback riding for me. I've proven my ineptness in that area well enough, I think," he said wryly.

Hope had proven to be more friendly to him in the past days. Now she smiled warmly at him. "You have other talents, I'm sure."

"Not yours for gardening. I've never seen such a lush flower garden!"

This pleased Hope, for the rose garden was her pride. "Come, let me show you," she said delightedly. They moved through the beds where the roses bloomed heavily on their stems. "Look!

These are my trophies!" She waved toward the back wall, which was an almost solid mass of climbing roses.

"It looks like a wall built of roses," he ventured. "How sweet they smell!"

"Yes, I love the fragrance. There are so many bad smells in the world that when I get out here and breathe this perfume, I never want to leave."

Reaching out, Wingate touched the stem of a delicate pink rose. His finger was pierced by a thorn and he jerked his hand back, automatically popping his finger into his mouth in a boyish gesture. "Well," he admitted, "the thorns seem to be quite as healthy as the blossoms." Examining the wound, he added lightly, "I wonder why God made thorns for roses? It would be better for us if they didn't have any."

"I can't say, since I don't know the mind of God," Hope said with a shrug. She wore a heavy glove on one hand and carried a pair of scissors in the other. "I understand Henry VIII instructed his gardener to develop a rose without thorns."

"I didn't know that," Wingate said with interest. "And what was the result?"

"Unsuccessful, I believe."

"It might be worthwhile for you to try, Mistress Wakefield. A rose without thorns!" Darcy slowly made his way closer to her and saw that she watched him cautiously as he neared. "Why do you always stare at me so?" he asked abruptly. "You're always on your guard as though I'm a highway bandit or some such dastardly sort!"

Hope flushed. She was aware that she became very defensive around Darcy Wingate, but she had no satisfactory explanation for her behavior. "I'm sorry," she said rather lamely. "I suppose I'm just too . . . sensitive or something." She held up the crimson rose, looked at its stem, and murmured, "I suppose, in one sense, that I'm like this rose. I have thorns." She looked at him, resignation in her eyes. "At least, that's what Mother says."

"You're like the rose in far more pleasant ways than that," Darcy said in a low voice, noting the color rise high on her cheeks. He deliberately lightened his tone. "I've enjoyed my stay with your family. I suppose I'll have to be going soon."

"Evan left this morning," Hope said. "He was going to stop and tell your uncle of your progress."

The two walked slowly around the rose garden, Darcy asking polite questions about the flowers and listening closely to Hope's replies. After a while she said, "I wonder if I may speak freely with you, Mr. Wingate."

"Why, of course. Say what you will."

"My brother Gavin is very concerned over his friend Mr. Bunyan," she said with a little difficulty. "We think it is unjust that he's kept in prison. Forgive me if I go too far . . . but—if you could look into this case—"

Wingate at once felt a twinge of apprehension. "I will, of course, inquire, if you wish it. But you realize it does place me in a rather embarrassing situation?"

"How so?"

"If what your brother says is accurate," Wingate said heavily, "and I have no doubt that it is, then it was my uncle who brought Mr. Bunyan to trial. It would be awkward if I were to arrive—a newcomer, young and inexperienced—questioning his judgment."

"But if the man is innocent, what matter that you feel a little uncomfortable?" Hope demanded.

Her insistence irritated Wingate. "You have no understanding of matters of the law, I fear. Justice must be done."

Hope gave him a sharp look, then tossed the rose into the basket with an impatient gesture. "Yes, justice must be done! But it is *not* being done, for John Bunyan has never legally been tried!

These six years he has been in jail, leaving a wife and family to suffer! But I know it might be *awkward* for you, so I could hardly expect you to put yourself out!"

Darcy watched her wordlessly as she whirled around and left the garden. Then he muttered under his breath, "Blast! That young woman is irritating! She's pretty as a rose, all right, but I'm hanged if she hasn't got thorns enough to prick a man's hands bloody! I'll have no more of her!"

That determination made, he went back into the house.

Elizabeth was startled by the knock at the door, for her mind was far away. She turned as Mary scurried across the room to open it.

"Good morning, Mary."

Mary recognized Evan's voice and put out her hand to him. Pulling him inside, she said excitedly, "Evan! You've been gone so long! Mother! Evan's here!" At seventeen, Mary had grown into an attractive young woman with dark brown hair and a neat figure. She wore a simple gray dress and her face was flushed with excitement as she clung to Evan's arm. "Come! I must hear what you've been doing!"

Elizabeth crossed the room to greet their visitor, noting that he was very thin and his face showed unmistakable signs of a recent illness. "You are welcome here, Evan. Come, please sit down. Have you just come from Wakefield?"

Evan nodded as he seated himself at the wooden table. "Yes. I'm glad to see you both. Where are the rest of the children?"

"Outside playing. I'm surprised you didn't see them," Elizabeth answered. "Why don't you go get them, Mary? But give Evan and me a little time to talk."

As soon as the girl left, Elizabeth continued, "I heard about your illness, Evan. Your cousin wrote me. It must have been terrible."

Evan was looking about the interior of the small cabin, thinking of the times he had spent here. "Yes, terrible indeed," he said slowly. "And not just in London, but everywhere."

"Yes, we've lost about forty people, even here in Bedford." Elizabeth observed Evan with anxious eyes. Not only was he thin and drawn, but there was a sad lack of vitality about him. "How was it that you recovered?" she asked gently. "You must have had good attention."

"Yes, I did." Evan nodded. "It was Jenny. She heard I was sick and came to me at once." He halted and his lips drew together in a thin line. "I don't see, to this day, how she did it—or why. Everyone locked themselves away from those who were even suspected of having the plague. But I woke up at the height of my fever and there she was. She acted as if I had no more than a bad cold."

Angharad's letter had told Elizabeth part of this story, but now, seeing Evan, the horror of the disease became much more real to her. "She must be a very courageous young woman," she said.

"Aye, that she is."

The conversation began to lag and soon Elizabeth found herself more concerned about Evan's emotional state than the condition of his weakened body. "You don't seem at all well," she said with difficulty. "You shouldn't be out running around like this."

"I've had enough of bed," Evan said roughly. "Being cooped up in that room in London almost drove me crazy. But Lady Wakefield has been feeding me and fussing at me—and I'm much better now."

"But you seem . . . troubled somehow," Elizabeth persisted. "What's the matter?" Deep down, she suspected that it was some sort of disappointed love. She had heard of Jenny's rise as an actress and longed to ask Evan about this, but she decided to keep silent on that matter. "Are you worried about something?"

"Worried about something?" Evan asked wearily. "I suppose I am." He managed a small smile. "I don't want to bring any more trouble to this house. You have enough to bear."

"You could never be a trouble, Evan."

He waved his hand almost listlessly, then let it fall. "What about your husband?"

"Lately," Elizabeth answered, "he's been paroled. He's out right now, preaching near Danforth. But it's only temporary."

Evan's eyebrows shot up. "I'm surprised that the authorities would release him! I understood they were very adamant about refusing to let him go."

"About his general sentence, they are," Elizabeth explained. "It's Mr. Cobb, the jailer, who arranges it. The jail's so full that he lets some of the local men go to take some of the strain of overcrowding from the jail. The authorities know about it, of course, and they rail all the time, but there is no other answer."

"I'd hoped to see him while I was here," Evan said thoughtfully. "I need to speak to him."

"He'll be home by dark. That's one of the conditions Mr. Cobb insists on. He must be here and I must know where he is at all times."

Evan said hesitantly, "Then, if I may, I'd like to stay over."

"Of course you may," Elizabeth assured him. "The children haven't gotten to see you for such a long time. Now, I'll fix something for you to eat."

"I brought a wagonload of supplies from Wakefield," Evan said eagerly.

Elizabeth's gentle blue eyes softened. "Lady Wakefield . . . she's been our strong support all these years. How many times have you or someone else from Wakefield driven over here to bring us something wonderful? Just when it seems we've reached the bottom of the barrel, someone from Wakefield arrives with a wagon full! God bless Lady Wakefield for her kindness!"

At that moment the door burst open and the room was filled with children. The younger Elizabeth was fourteen and growing to be a beauty. John and Thomas, aged twelve and eight respectively, had always been fond of Evan. For the rest of the afternoon Evan found himself busy entertaining them and in turn being entertained by all the children.

When Bunyan came home just before dark, he was very glad to see Evan. Shaking the young man's hand warmly, he grinned. "Look what's come to Bedford! How are you, Mr. Morgan?"

"Well enough," Evan replied, smiling. "You're looking well, Mr. Bunyan." Actually, he was rather surprised by Bunyan's appearance. At thirty-eight, some of the effects of his lengthy prison sentence showed in his pallor. Still, aside from that, Bunyan seemed to be strong and vigorous. He was leaner than when he had gone into prison, certainly, but his mood seemed optimistic and hopeful.

Before long, the two men managed to disengage themselves from all the children and sit down at the table. As the rest of the family found their seats, Bunyan asked Evan the details of his illness and of his return from London. Evan found himself talking easily to the older man. He enjoyed the discourse greatly, for he found great pleasure in the Bunyan family. There was no time to speak privately to Bunyan that day, but after supper he took a long walk alone with Mary, with whom he had always shared a special bond.

Birds were murmuring softly in the falling darkness and Evan listened with pleasure as Mary spoke, her voice ringing clear in the quiet evening, her face alight. He loved to watch her as she spoke, for her face was delightfully expressive and animated

"It's getting dark," he said after a while. "We'll have to go home soon."

Mary turned toward him and smiled. "Getting dark? But that's not a problem for me."

Evan was taken aback. The girl seemed not at all bothered by her blindness. He was certain he could never deal so gracefully with such a challenge. "No," he said gently, a smile tipping his mouth, "but it is for me. Still, we can go a bit farther."

"Tell me more about London," she beseeched him. Mary had an active imagination and demanded full details from everyone about everything. She had an ability to take these details and in her mind create images so vivid that it was almost as if she had actually seen the people and places she was hearing about. She seldom forgot even the smallest detail. Evan found himself feeling as though it were *his* eyes that did not see as he struggled to remember the sights of London.

Finally they turned back toward the Bunyan home and Evan mentioned Darcy Wingate. "He was very kind to bring me back from London," he told Mary. He described the young lawyer's accident, then went on. "Mr. Wingate will be coming to Bedford soon."

"He's a lawyer?" Mary asked.

"Yes, he is."

"Do you think he could help my father get his case heard by the magistrates?" she said eagerly.

"I don't know, Mary." Doubtfully he added, "He comes from a Royalist family. His uncle is Francis Wingate—and you know all about him."

"Yes," she sighed. "He arrested my father. I remember that. But Father says he's not an evil man and that he can't help himself. Maybe this Mr. Darcy Wingate could speak to him." Her sightless eyes seemed to beseech Evan. "I'll ask him, if you'll bring him by."

"You would, wouldn't you?" Evan laughed softly. He said no more about Darcy Wingate, but her question had planted a seed in his mind. That night, as he went to bed, he whispered, "Maybe

Darcy could say something to his uncle. There must be some way to get John free from prison."

Early the next day, Bunyan invited Evan to go with him on a trip to Elstow. Bunyan felt obliged to visit a man, one of the small congregation, who was very ill. Evan agreed to go.

They made their way to the small village and found the man's home. After Bunyan had made his visit, they stopped to sit beneath a spreading oak tree close to the moot hall.

"Now," Bunyan said sturdily, taking off his hat and placing it on the ground beside him, "tell me what's bothering you."

Evan knew that he had fooled neither Bunyan nor Elizabeth. "I've been having a great deal of difficulty, Mr. Bunyan," he said slowly. "When I nearly died of the plague, it was like nothing that's ever happened to me before." He struggled for a few moments, trying to describe the terrible sickness, then he blurted out desperately, "It was as if hell itself opened up under my feet—and I was about to be plunged in!" He shuddered at the memory. "That was worse than the illness itself!"

Bunyan examined the young man shrewdly, noting his cheeks, which still had not filled out with the customary Morgan robustness, and his pale complexion. Finally he said evenly, "Death lies before all of us, Evan. 'As it is appointed unto man once to die—'"

"'—but after this the judgment,'" Evan breathed. "I know that much. I saw a play once, one of Mr. Shakespeare's. There was a line in it that I could never escape from."

"What was it, Evan?"

"One of the characters said: 'That fell sergeant Death is strict in his arrest.'"

"A good line." Bunyan nodded. "Mr. Shakespeare has many such." It was the kind of line that Bunyan liked very much. He himself had written several things in this manner. "'That fell sergeant Death is strict in his arrest,'" he repeated to himself. "That's interesting, to make a military sergeant, like an officer of the law, into a deathlike figure." He looked back up at Evan sternly. "And he *is* strict in his arrest, Evan. We can't turn him away, can we, when he comes?"

Evan swallowed hard and looked away. Bunyan continued, not unkindly, "You were afraid?"

"Afraid?" Evan retorted. "Certainly I was afraid! What man in his right mind wouldn't be afraid of going to hell?"

"You'd be surprised how many men show no fear at all."

"They're fools then!" Evan exclaimed bitterly. "I've not been a man to think of God much, but I've got sense enough to know that this life is not all there is." Now he looked at Bunyan directly. "I've heard you preach many times, Mr. Bunyan. We had some fine preachers back in Wales, too. But I ignored them, as I ignored you. Oh, the words went into my ears, but—that's all."

"Like the seed that was sown in the parable Jesus told," Bunyan said. "Some fell by the wayside and never took root. Others the fowls of the air gobbled up. Many men and women hear the gospel with their ears, but it's not a matter of hearing."

"What then?" Evan demanded almost violently. "I've been praying ever since I nearly died! And it's as if God—well—almost as if God were dead!"

"You know better than that!" Bunyan rapped out sharply. "You had many chances, Evan. Now I think God is waiting for you to seek him. So many Scriptures have to do with seeking God," he mused. "'Seek the Lord early, while he may be found.' It's too late for you to go back to your childhood and find God. But the Lord Jesus said, 'They that seek will find.'" He smiled at the younger man. "You and I will seek him together."

Evan gave him a look of relief. "That's kind of you, sir. That's really why I came to Bedford."

Bunyan had his Bible with him and for over two hours he

moved forward and back, through the Old Testament, then over to the New Testament. It seemed to Evan that the tinker-preacher hardly needed to glance down at the book, for the words flowed easily and strongly from him in a powerful river. His voice was muted, somber and quiet. When Bunyan preached, he could raise that same voice like a trumpet, but now he spoke gently, quoting Scripture after Scripture, patiently answering the questions that Evan raised.

Soon it was time to return home, and the whole way there Evan and Bunyan spoke of the Scriptures and of the Lord. Likewise, for the next two days they were together almost constantly.

On the third day of Evan's visit Mary asked, "Where's Evan? Why isn't he here for breakfast?"

Elizabeth glanced at her husband with a worried expression. She had noted, too, that their young visitor was not in the house. "He did say he'd come, John," she said, concern tinging her voice. "You don't suppose he's gone back to Wakefield, do you?"

"No, I don't think so," Bunyan said. "We talked until late last night and prayed long. God is laying heavily now upon Evan's spirit. Never fear. He'll be back."

But Evan did not return to the Bunyans' home all that day—or that night. The following day, as Bunyan was digging for potatoes in the backyard, he looked up to see Evan coming around the side of the cottage.

"Evan, you're back—" Bunyan halted and let his spade fall unnoticed to the earth. Something in Evan Morgan's face caught his attention. "What is it, my boy? Something has happened—!"

Evan came to stand close by Bunyan. His eyes were alive in a way that they had not been during his visit. He licked his lips and seemed to have difficulty speaking. His voice was husky when he finally formed the words. "Mr. Bunyan—" Then he could go no farther, for tears welled up in his dark eyes.

John Bunyan put his arms around the young man, overwhelmed with a sense of gladness. "You have found God, haven't you?"

Evan hugged the older man for a moment, then stepped back. "No, sir . . . he has found me," he whispered. "That is what has happened."

"Sit down! Tell me! Then we must go tell Elizabeth and the children!" The two sat down. Or rather Bunyan did. Evan could not be still—he paced back and forth, gesturing with excitement. He described the restless hours he had spent walking in the woods, unable to sleep or eat.

"Early this morning, at dawn," he said, "I was exhausted. I had given up on ever hearing from God. And that's when he came." He cleared his throat and took a step closer to Bunyan, his face shining. "It was incredible. Wonderful. Terrifying! I'd been calling on him for days—but this time when I called, I *knew* he was there! I asked him to forgive me, and I heard, in my spirit, the Lord Jesus say, 'Your sins are forgiven.'"

"Glory to God!" Bunyan breathed, his own eyes misty with tears. "I'm so happy for you!"

Evan met his eyes and said slowly, "But there's more, Mr. Bunyan."

"Aye? What else did the Lord say to you?"

"He said . . . that I would preach his gospel. The gospel of the Lord Jesus Christ. For the rest of my life."

John Bunyan stared at the young man. For one moment, fear washed over him; how well he knew what lay ahead for a young preacher who was not in the established church. But he pushed the doubts from his mind and stood to clasp Evan's hand between his own. "God will be with you!" he exclaimed. "You will see the hand of the Lord on your life!"

The two went into Bunyan's home to share the good news with the rest of the family.

Sixteen

A Time for Hope

Darcy Wingate's decision to leave Wakefield was set aside by the arrival of Gavin and Susanne Wakefield. They were accompanied by Amos, who had been engaged in the naval war against the Dutch and now had arrived back home bursting with exciting tales of the war.

Wingate was cordially received by Gavin and his wife, Susanne. The couple demanded the admiration of all the family for their two children: Lucy, a girl of six, and Alfred, a toddler of two. Both children had blonde hair and dark blue eyes like their mother, with the same heart-shaped face.

At their first dinner together, Darcy said little. He listened as Amos related the details of a sea battle.

"It was a near thing," Amos said thoughtfully. "Even greater than Lowestoft, back in June."

"I heard that the French were in the battle," Christopher said. "What were they doing there?"

Amos shrugged. "Louis XIV promised to aid Holland if she was attacked."

"But she wasn't attacked," Gavin snorted angrily. "The Dutch were the aggressors! Nevertheless, France declared war on England."

"It was a close thing," Amos said again. "Their admiral De Ruyter is a fine sailor. This time their ships had heavier cannon."

Susanne was holding Lucy in her lap and looked up to say, "I could hear the sound of the cannon in London. We were afraid the next thing would be the Dutch fleet sailing up the Thames."

"It might have been," Amos sighed, "for we lost on the second day. Completely outmatched we were. Then Rupert arrived and restored the balance. But the fourth day," he went on sadly, "Monk and Rupert had heavy losses. De Ruyter won. That didn't stop us though." Amos's eyes glittered. "Our ship was refitted and we put to sea even stronger than before. That was the last battle, just last week, on August the fourth. We beat them that time!"

But Gavin was not so exultant. "Yes, but not for good. The Dutch will be back and the French are still in the Channel. England is isolated now—cut off from all friends."

Talk of the war went on for some time and finally Hope left the table with the two children. Darcy began to feel a little out of place when the Wakefield men began to speak of family matters, so he excused himself and went to where Hope and the children were playing a game in the library.

"Do you like children, Mr. Wingate?" Hope asked politely.

"I don't know," Darcy replied in some confusion. "I haven't really been around them much. I was the youngest in my family, so I haven't had any opportunity to find out."

"Come here, then," Hope ordered him. "You can join us in our game."

It was some sort of game with counters and a ball that rolled, so simple that even little Alfred could play. Wingate found himself enjoying his time with the children. After Susanne came to take the children to bed, Darcy and Hope were left alone in the library.

"I suppose I could become very fond of children," Wingate admitted.

"There's a little more to it than playing games," Hope warned. "I don't know of any job more taxing than bringing up youngsters."

"You'd be very good at it, from what I see."

They talked amiably for a bit, and then Hope took a deep breath. "Mr. Wingate," she said with determination, "I fear I have been unkind to you since you came. I'm a sharp-tongued young woman and should know better. My parents have certainly tried to tame me." She smiled ruefully and shook her head, which made her dark hair shimmer in the candlelight. "I wish I were more gentle. No man likes a sharp-tongued woman."

Wingate was charmed by her apparent remorse. "I know that you're concerned about political things," he said. "I wish I could do more about it. Perhaps you'll be a good influence upon me."

Two days later, Wingate and Hope were walking down the streets of Wakefield. The village was crowded, for it was Fair Day. Vendors of all sorts cried out their wares as the two strolled down the street, which was flanked by tables filled with all sorts of merchandise.

"Your ankle seems fully recovered," Hope observed. "You hardly favor it at all."

"Indeed it is, and I'm sorry of it."

Hope gave him a mystified glance. "Sorry? Why should you be sorry for that?"

"Because," Wingate said with a smile, "I will be forced to leave Wakefield now. I can't use this ankle as an excuse to stay any longer."

"I'm sure my father and my brothers would be glad for you to stay," Hope said lightly "And my mother, too."

He waited for her to say that she wanted him to stay, too, but she made no other comment. "I really must go," he said evenly. "But it's not too far from here to Bedford. I hope I shall be seeing you again from time to time."

"I don't attend the court sessions too often, Mr. Wingate," she said, mischief edging her voice.

"For heaven's sake, call me Darcy," he said with exasperation.

"Very well. First names then."

"Hope," he said in reverie. "I have always favored that name. The Puritans knew how to name their children, didn't they? Charity, Humility, Hope . . ."

She laughed aloud. "I knew one that was named Praise God. His parents must have had a time. It would be hard to be strict with a boy, all the time saying, 'Praise God,' wouldn't it?"

He grinned, quite delighted with her good humor. And all that afternoon he found their conversation most pleasant.

"I must make one more call," Hope told him later. "I need to visit a poor woman, a member of the local church. Perhaps you'd rather go on back to Wakefield."

"Unless I would be in the way, I'll stay with you," he demurred.

"Of course you won't be in the way. Please come along."

She led him to a shabby cottage on the outskirts of the village. As they approached, they were greeted by an elderly woman. She looked to be in her seventies, Darcy thought as he watched her greet Hope warmly and invite them in for a cup of tea. It was the lowest sort of place, comprised of a mere two rooms—yet it was neat as a pin.

"I'm sorry to hear of your trouble, Addie," Hope was saying. She turned to Darcy. "Mrs. Smithfield has come upon great troubles, Mr. Wingate."

"What sort of troubles?" Darcy inquired, studying the elderly woman. Despite her advanced age, she seemed hale and hearty and alert. "Not a sickness, I trust?"

"No, it's legal troubles," Mrs. Smithfield said.

Wingate glanced suspiciously at Hope, who met his gaze without expression. "It's very serious, I'm afraid," she said calmly. "Addie is about to lose her home, which is all she has."

Wingate said hesitantly, "I'd like to hear about the problem."

For the next ten minutes Addie Smithfield sat at the table relating the fact that she had borrowed a sum of money to help a daughter who was in trouble and that the creditor was now foreclosing on her home.

"I hate to lose this place," she moaned. "But I must go, it seems. Well, the good Lord will be with me."

The color rose in Hope's face and she looked almost accusingly at Wingate. "It's such a shame! And it's not just a matter of money. My father offered to pay the loan, but Mr. Darrow wants the place."

"Darrow is his name?"

"Yes, Ralph Darrow." Mrs. Smithfield nodded. "My children were born here. My husband died in that room. It's all the home I've known for these many years."

Wingate thought quickly, then asked a few more questions but said nothing more than that.

As they left, Hope's eyes filled with tears. "I'm so sorry for her," she murmured. "I'm going to see if Father will find a place for her. She's too old to work, but surely we can find a place where she may lay her head."

"It is a shame. There's too much of this sort of thing going on." Wingate's face was solemn and he fell silent, saying little all the way back to Wakefield.

Hope had entertained some notion that he might offer a legal opinion, but when Darcy said nothing, she did not press him.

The next morning Darcy was gone for some time. He returned about noon and came to find Hope in the garden. He was waving a sheet of paper triumphantly. "I have something here you'll like to see."

She looked at him curiously, a small smile on her face. "Oh? What is it?"

He handed her the paper and she scanned it, then shrugged. "I could never understand these legal documents. What does it mean?"

"It means that your friend, Mrs. Smithfield, will be able to keep her home," Wingate said quietly.

Hope's eyes widened with surprised pleasure and she reached out to grasp his arm in her excitement. "Darcy! Do you mean it?"

The young lawyer was pleased with himself and quite enjoyed the light of excitement in the girl's dark brown eyes. "Yes! I wasn't happy with what Mrs. Smithfield told me about these business arrangements, so I took it upon myself to look into it."

"You did?" Hope asked breathlessly. "And what did you find out? Tell me!"

"I found out that our friend Ralph Darrow had shorted the law a bit," Darcy said nonchalantly.

Hope tightened her grip on his sleeve and pulled him down to sit on one of the stone benches. "All right, now, out with it. I want to know everything!" She kept her hand on his arm; he could feel the warmth of her palm through the material.

His lopsided smile was wide and his eyes gleamed. "It was a bit of fun, actually. I gathered some evidence, which wasn't hard to do. Mr. Darrow is not a very popular man—"

"Everyone hates him," Hope grumbled. "He's an old miser!"

"Yes, well—I don't fool myself that I can change his character," Darcy said. "But he certainly had to change his tune about Mrs. Smithfield."

"You went to see him?"

"Indeed I did," Darcy replied, finding an even greater pleasure in Hope's sparkling eyes than in telling his story. "He wasn't very happy after I told him why I'd come. He ordered me out of the place."

"Oh! The old rat! What did you say?" Her lips were parted with anticipation and he could see a faint line of freckles across her nose.

"Why, I told him that that would be fine," Darcy declared. "And that if he would rather settle in court, I should be happy to oblige him. Then I proceeded to relate to him that before this fight was over he would not only *not* gain the widow Smithfield's house, he would be liable for court costs. And perhaps be prosecuted for dishonest practices."

"Good!" Hope cried. "Oh, I'm so happy I could scream!"

Wingate related the rest of the tale, making it much longer than was strictly necessary. He could not deny, however, that he had reveled in rescuing Mrs. Smithfield. Ralph Darrow was a beady-eyed, sly old miser who had been squeezing his creditors until his hands met in their throats.

"I don't really think I could have done as much as I threatened," he admitted. "But I must be a pretty good actor, for he certainly believed it."

"So then, what about the house?" she said insistently.

"The loan will have to be paid, but I believe you said your father will be willing to do that."

"Oh yes! That's nothing at all!" she said joyously. "Come, Darcy, we must go tell them!" She seized his hand, pulled him to his feet, and hauled him imperiously down the path. They found Christopher and Angharad sitting in the study. They looked up with surprise when Hope burst into the room, yanking on Darcy Wingate's hand as he followed more decorously behind her. Hope poured out the story.

"Isn't it wonderful!" she exclaimed. "And Darcy did it all!"

"I'll be most happy to do anything that will cause Ralph Darrow some discomfort," Christopher maintained stoutly. "He's a miserable old skinflint!"

Angharad laughed at Hope. "Well, look for me on the floor if you're not a manipulator, girl! You said you could do it but I didn't think you could!"

Frowning slightly, Darcy turned to look at Hope, who suddenly seemed quite embarrassed. "Oh?" he said rather coolly. "Did you plan all this?"

Hope realized she was still holding his hand, as she had been ever since they entered the room. She dropped it guiltily, her face reddening. But she met his eyes and nodded. "Yes, I planned it all. I thought you might be clever enough to help Addie, so I took you there in hopes that you would help her. Now you know what a conniver I am! Despise me if you dare!"

But Darcy Wingate, looking into the clear blue eyes of the defiant young woman before him, could only smile. "Indeed," he said quietly, "I do not dare. If you have any more brave deeds that a poor legal scribe might do, then lead on."

She grinned cheekily at him, a pleased flush on her cheeks. "No, that's all for now. Come, we must go to Addie! I must see her." She grabbed his arm and tugged until he followed her obediently out of the room.

Angharad shook her head. "Faith, I don't know who that girl takes after. . . ."

Christopher smiled, his fond gaze resting on his wife. "Indeed? I daresay I think I do."

Angharad looked at him, mystified, then she caught the hint of his smile and said, very sweetly, "Go and scratch, Lord Wakefield."

The supper that night at Wakefield was excellent and Wingate felt as though he were drawn into the family as a much favored member. He was especially drawn to Sir Christopher, and said as much after the meal as he and Hope stood outside the house, looking at the bright stars that spangled the sky.

"Your father is one of the most unusual men I've ever known," he said thoughtfully.

"I think he's the most wonderful man who ever lived," Hope responded simply. "He spoiled me abominably, but that's not why I love him so much."

Wingate watched her as she spoke of her father, her musical voice soft and filled with affection. The moonlight played across her features, making her beauty seem remote and cool. She was wearing a simple dress of pearl gray that fit both her and the moonlight. There was a classic quality to her features, the sort that he particularly admired in women. When she finished speaking he said, "You are fortunate in your parents. Your mother is a beautiful woman and very fine. I've always admired the Welsh. They seem to have so many good qualities."

"Do you think so?"

"Why, yes." He was surprised at the question. "Your father apparently thinks so, too. Enough to marry her."

"He's far older than she is." A worried look marred her smooth face and she turned away from him to lift her eyes to the moon. "I worry sometimes. He's not getting younger."

"He seems very well, though. How old is he?"

"Seventy-seven."

"I hope he has good health and many more years of the life that seems to suit him so very well," Wingate said quietly.

They were silent for long moments, then Hope turned to look up into his face. "I can't tell you, really, how much I appreciate what you did for Addie. I think it was marvelous, Darcy. Especially considering the way I treated you when you first came here."

"It was nothing."

"Maybe not to *you,* but to Addie it was everything," Hope countered. "Wasn't she happy when we talked to her?"

Darcy studied his companion thoughtfully. She was wearing a fragrance that Darcy couldn't quite identify. It was light, but at the same time rather heady. He tried to decide whether it smelled more like magnolia, violets, or the roses that Hope loved so much. In any case, it made him intensely aware of her femininity. The moonlight outlined the smooth curves of her figure in the plain dress, and a necklace with a single red stone hung round her neck. Her hair was done somewhat differently this night, with curls at each side of her face and the rest of the heavy strands flowing down her back.

Abruptly he said what was in his mind. "Hope, you are a most attractive young woman."

His words caught her off guard and she blinked her eyes rapidly. "You really shouldn't say such things to me."

"Perhaps it's not good for you to hear," he said reluctantly, "but we lawyers have such devious ways of speaking—sometimes maybe it's better for us to say just what's on our hearts without worrying about what will be made of it in court."

Again, silence fell between them, but this time it was a little uncomfortable in spite of Wingate's light words. Hope did not really know what to say. She had actually disliked this man at first—or fancied she did. Now, as she looked up at him, she was suddenly aware of the strength of his features. He was a most masculine man—not handsome, really, but strong. She was searching his face when she suddenly realized he was going to kiss her.

Of course, she had been kissed a few times before, but none of those occurrences had been significant. Now, as Darcy leaned forward and gently cupped her face in his hands, one clear thought came to her: *I must not let him do this!*

But she did.

He bent his head and his lips touched hers firmly. A shock ran through her. There was such strength in him as he encircled her with his arms and pulled her close. Her thoughts grew confused and she thought she might drown in the pleasure washing over her. Slowly her arms slid behind his neck and her lips returned the pressure of his.

A vague warning seemed to be sounding deep in her spirit, but she ignored it and took the moment for what it was.

Darcy Wingate felt as though his head were spinning. Hope filled his awareness and there was a freshness and innocence about her lips that he had not encountered in other women. She was warm, soft, and yielding—yet he could sense that she held part of herself back from him.

The kiss lasted for another moment, then Hope put her hands on his chest and stepped back. Her eyes seemed enormous in the moonlight. "I should not have let you do that," she whispered.

He felt her hands trembling against his chest. "I'm glad that sometimes you do things you shouldn't," he answered hoarsely. "As we all do." He saw a troubled light in her eyes. "I didn't mean to offend you, Hope. It wasn't that kind of a kiss."

She felt terribly vulnerable and wondered what sort of a young woman she was to accept a virtual stranger's kiss. "It must not happen again."

But Darcy, after holding her gaze for a moment, said firmly, "It probably will." She started slightly, but he continued in a matter-of-fact tone. "I'll be leaving in the morning, so I'll say good-bye now."

They parted and Hope went to her room. Disquieted by the kiss—and by Darcy Wingate's words—she knew as she slipped into her bed that she would not sleep. The memory of that kiss would not let her.

Gauzy clouds passed over the silver crescent of the moon as Hope stared out her bedroom window. She thought long, deep thoughts and finally, restlessly, turned over on her side, away from the moonlight, and tried to sleep.

Seventeen

THE GREAT FIRE

Jenny had been in several houses of the great and powerful English aristocracy during her relatively brief stay in London. Always she had managed to go with a group, so that there would be no mistaking her intentions and agreements. However, she had never seen anything like the palace where King Charles II lived out his dissipated life.

"Come along, Jenny," Nell Gwyn had insisted. "It's like nothing you've ever seen before!" Nell, of course, was a constant visitor to the palace—and more than a visitor, if the rumors that connected her to the king had any truth. She had invited Jenny to accompany her one evening after the play was done. After some resistance, Jenny had agreed.

The next day she accompanied Nell to the palace, where they were admitted at once. The guards spoke familiarly to Nell, who answered them in like fashion. As she and Jenny went through the ornamented gateway into the forecourt of the palace, Jenny was stunned by the size and opulence of it all. Mullioned windows of the best glass bulged from the great bays high up on the upper stories. Groupings of slender, round chimneys were situated so as to resemble the columns that held up the interior ceilings.

Although it was still early in the afternoon, the outer court was filled with attendants and guests of all sorts. The blazing colors of satins, velvets, laces, taffetas, and silks formed a kaleidoscope of hues that almost dazzled the young actress.

"Come along, Jenny," Nell whispered. "I want you to see what a banquet is really like!"

The two entered a large dining room where spritely music overlaid a low hum of conversation. The king ate on a table on the dais, and as Jenny took her seat, she looked down at a solid gold plate—the first she had ever seen.

"Look at that fork," Nell whispered as proudly as if it were her own. "It's made of solid silver! The king imported it all the way from Italy!"

The courses began to appear, and truly Jenny was stunned by the variety. The wine itself came in so many varieties that she could hardly keep up with it. One of these drinks, recommended to her by Nell, had a rich raspberry taste. She sipped lightly at it while others seemed to guzzle down several different glasses of wine as if they were water. The food was of an amazing variety as well: mutton, cold meats, spiced and sweetened sparrows on toast. There was a fat hen, boiled with leeks and mushrooms. Seafood was abundant: lobster, crayfish, boiled shrimp, assorted fish. Afterward they were brought fruits of different sorts and pies decorated with royal symbols, filled with meats and seasoned with the finest of fresh herbs and spices. Finally, cherries with cream were set before them—a dish Jenny could not eat because it was so rich.

Jenny noticed that others, including the king, were cramming their mouths full with grapes, apricots, and translucent jellies that quivered in shapes of different animals. All in all, Jenny thought that it was simply too much. She thought of all the hungry people in the country—especially with the effects of the plague not yet over—and wished that some of this could be distributed back in Wakefield or Bedford.

After dinner there was dancing and entertainment, but after an hour of that, Jenny was surprised by a voice behind her. "Ah! You are Mistress Gwyn's companion!"

Jenny turned and was stunned to see the king himself standing behind her. She was standing away from the crowd, at the side of the large room, slightly behind one of the large pillars. She curtsied hurriedly, then murmured, "Yes, Your Majesty, I did come with Mistress Gwyn."

Charles smiled. He had a loose, sensuous mouth that spoiled his fine looks. He was wearing, as usual, rich, ornate clothing, including a plum-colored doublet spangled with pearls and precious stones of red and green. He was a very tall man and there was something overwhelming in his presence. He studied her with his large brown eyes and nodded. "Yes, Nellie tells me that you may be one of the great stars of the stage in days to come. I did enjoy your performance, I assure you."

"Thank you, Your Majesty." Jenny could do no more than whisper. She had heard so much about this man that, in her mind, he was almost like a figure in a storybook. But here he was—flesh and blood—trying to carry on a simple conversation with her. And she could not think of a single word to say.

The king sensed her fear and confusion. "You must let me show you a little of the palace." Without waiting for her agreement, he took her arm and led her on a tour. They went through courtyards with fountains bubbling. There were suites of rooms and chambers leading from one to the other, seemingly creating a labyrinth of rooms. Everywhere the walls were either covered with heavy tapestries, velvet curtains, and hanging pictures, or had painted on them the most magnificent murals, each one brilliant and detailed.

He led her to a long gallery and she was impressed with all that she saw there. Finally he took her out onto a portico. "The gardens are almost gone, of course," he said. It was late August and the flowers had long since vanished. Still, there were fountains and paths and benches among the evergreens and manicured hedges.

They walked slowly down one of the myriad paths, and Charles stopped in front of one of the larger fountains. Some sort of pump drove the water high into the air. The falling drops caught the reflection of the many lanterns that illuminated this part of the garden. "They look like falling diamonds, don't they?" Charles murmured.

Jenny dared to search his profile for a moment. It was handsome and undeniably regal. "Yes, Your Majesty."

He turned to her and again she dropped her eyes. "Tell me about yourself," he said abruptly. "Here, the air is turning cool. Take my cloak." Again without waiting for her to give him permission, he whipped off the rich ermine cloak and put it around her shoulders. Then he led her to one of the stone benches and pressed her down. "That's better, is it not? Now, proceed."

Jenny never felt less like telling her story. But once she began she discovered that Charles was not only a sympathetic listener, he was quite adept at drawing people out. She was not the first to discover this. Others had found that Charles might be weak in the flesh, indulgent and sensual, but he had a sharp, alert mind that enabled him to outthink most people.

Jenny ended her brief recitation by saying, "So Mistress Gwyn kept me as her maid and then let me appear in a few plays."

"Do you like the theatre?" Charles asked with interest. He was sitting rather close to her. As he spoke, he shifted in a way that seemed casual and yet brought his knee into firm contact with hers.

Jenny's heart thundered. She had no notion how to treat a king's advances! If she moved away, she might insult him. If she remained as she was, it might give him an entirely wrong impression. Quickly she said, "I do like some of it, Your Majesty. But it's very hard for a woman."

"Why, men follow you everywhere!" The dark eyes gleamed in the semidarkness. "Many women would wish to have that sort of attention!"

"Not I, Your Majesty," Jenny replied simply.

Charles blinked in surprise. He had known many actresses and as was the opinion of many people, found that none of them had any virtue to speak of. Now as he studied the clear, youthful features of the young lady beside him, he saw none of the signs of looseness that were characteristic of others in her profession. He was fascinated by her apparent innocence, which drove him to go even further than he had intended. Pressing closer to her, he reached over to cover her hand with his. In a voice that was low and exciting he said, "A beautiful woman like you could do very well, my dear. Very well indeed."

Again Jenny was uncertain. His hand pressed upon her and the invitation he extended, though unspoken, was nonetheless quite clear. She well knew of the many mistresses that this man had. She had heard often enough that immorality was of no significance to him. As king, he was a law unto himself. Now he was simply proposing that she join him.

Difficult as the situation was, Jenny's hesitation was brief. Turning her face to his, she met his gaze squarely. "I suppose most women would be tempted by what you have just said, Your Majesty. However, my only interest is in learning how to be an actress."

Again Charles was stunned and amazed by her reply. "You do not misunderstand me?" Her innocence was such that he thought perhaps she mistook his meaning.

"No, Your Majesty, I think not." Then she took a deep breath. "I think I should like to go back inside. Perhaps you would be so kind as to escort me?"

Charles laughed aloud and slapped his thigh. Rising to his feet, he put his hands on his hips and looked down at her with imperious amusement. "By heaven! You make a man feel bigger by your refusal than most women do by their acceptance!" He grew solemn then. "I have never pressured any woman and certainly have no inclination to begin now. Come, I will take you back inside as you so charmingly requested."

He took his cloak from her shoulders as they reentered the large room where the crowd still danced and watched jugglers and magicians. With one last mocking bow, he slipped away.

After he left, Jenny found that she was trembling. She passed the remainder of the evening quietly, watching and listening, seeing nothing that would entice her to change her own position with those who pursued this kind of frivolity.

When they were on their way home, Nell shocked her. "And did the king invite you to become part of his household?" She laughed, seeing Jenny's startled look. "Oh, I could see he was taken with you. He came to me and told me everything, Jenny." Suddenly Nell reached out to hug her. "You made the right decision, Jenny. This kind of life isn't for you! It's for the likes of me."

"And are you happy, Nell?" Jenny asked quietly.

The older woman shook her head slightly. "No, but I'm as happy as my sort can be upon this earth. I was born to be low, and if one must be low, she might as well take the best that comes along."

Jenny felt a great sorrow for this woman. Nell had risen from nothing and now had given herself over to immorality and debauched living, as was evidenced by the lines in her smooth face and around her eyes. Watching her, Jenny knew that despite the gaiety that shone from Nell Gwyn, inside she was a deeply disturbed woman.

As much as she wished she could help her friend, Jenny realized that she was certainly in no position to help. As she pondered this, she had one fleeting thought: *I wish I knew more about God. Maybe I could talk to Nell . . . but there's no help for it.*

As September of 1666 came in, Jenny thought much about her visit to the court of Charles II. Not once did she regret refusing his invitation. She knew Nell was right—such a life was not for her.

Still, she was grateful that she could spend time with her mentor and friend. She and Nell were in the process of rehearsing for a new play and they had stayed late one night at the theatre along with the rest of the cast. They were in the middle of a scene that involved Jenny when they were interrupted by the manager of the company, Thomas Benton, who burst through the front door and began shouting.

"The city's on fire!"

All of the actors and actresses stared at him. Nell demanded, "What do you mean, Thomas? Is there a house close by here that's caught fire?"

Benton's eyes were wide with fear. "I'm not talking about a house! The whole city's about to burn up! Hurry and see!"

Instantly Jenny joined the rest of the troupe as they rushed out of the theatre. Benton led them around the corner where they could see the entire horizon glowing beneath the night sky. Jenny was stunned by the enormity of the fire.

"The whole city can't burn!" she cried.

"It will if they don't stop it!" Benton cried. "There's already been three hundred houses burned!"

"Three hundred!" Nell exclaimed. "How did it start?"

"There's all manner of rumors," Benton explained. "But it seems it started in the king's baker's house in Pudding Lane. It's already burned Saint Magnus's Church and almost all of Fish Street is gone."

There was consternation on every face, but some of the bolder souls decided to go get a closer look. Jenny hurried inside to get her cloak and joined them. They made their way through the streets and got as far as the Steelyard. Everyone was endeavoring to remove their goods, flinging them into the river or loading them onto boats. The poor stayed in their houses until the fire actually licked at their walls, then they fled, carrying what they could.

Jenny and Nell finally decided to go home, but they had little sleep that night. When they arose the next morning, the entire city was aware of the enormity of the conflagration. After eating a light breakfast, Jenny decided to visit a friend, a dressmaker who lived in one of the areas nearest the fire.

Nell pleaded, "Don't go, Jenny. It's too dangerous."

"I just want to be sure she is safe. I'll stay away from the fire," Jenny promised. "Don't worry about me."

Leaving their house, she made her way back through the lanes until she was close enough to feel the heat of the blaze. Once she looked up and saw a group of pigeons whose loft had been on top of one of the burning houses. They hovered about the windows and balconies until some of them suffered burned wings and fell. Jenny felt sorry for them—but there were far worse things to see.

She saw the fire jumping almost in a single instant from one house to another. One house would be blazing, until the inside glowed white-hot, and suddenly the house next to it, which had seemed untouched, would explode into flame. The heat crackled against her cheeks as she made her way through the crowds. Finally she found her friend, Mistress Hampton.

"Are you all right, Mistress Hampton?" she asked anxiously.

"Yes, but my poor house, my poor house!" the dressmaker cried piteously. "All is lost!"

"You're alive and that's what's important," Jenny said soothingly. "Here, we'll get a wagon and save as many of your things as we can."

All that day she helped her friend as well as two other ladies who were in much the same trouble as Mistress Hampton.

Late that night, though darkness had fallen long ago, it was almost as light as midday. The flames of the burning city illuminated the darkness for miles. Jenny hardly noticed, though, for they were removing the last of the goods from the dressmaker's house. As she carried a load to the wagon, Jenny saw the king and his brother, the duke of York. They did not see her, but she was standing close enough to hear the king shouting orders.

"Look there! We must raze that whole line of houses! If we don't, the fire will jump it!"

The duke of York nodded and shouted to be heard above the roaring flames. "Yes! And if we do the same on the north, I believe we can confine it!"

Jenny had no time to linger, but she was impressed at the king's demeanor and determination. He was there, in the middle of the devastation, doing all he could to save the town. It made her think better of the king to see him acting so heroically.

Another night passed, and another day. The fire spread inexorably. The king's plan had not worked and the fire moved farther and farther through the city. The only hope was to break the fire line, but many refused to let the workers and soldiers do this. Their selfishness assured that many of their homes would burn—and much of the city, too.

Jenny saw terrible sights during that fire. It was a horrid, malicious, bloody flame—nothing like the fine flame of an ordinary fire. At night the city was covered by an arch of firelight that stretched a mile across the sky. Churches, houses, and places of business succumbed to the flames. The horrific roar of the blaze and the crackling of houses as they were consumed filled the air.

The cries of the homeless mixed with the hoarse shouts of the soldiers and magistrates trying to restore order.

Jenny grew very weary, for she slept hardly at all. Once she saw a shower of fire drops as the flames seemed to wing toward the sky and then fall like burning pitch. The enormity and intensity of the blaze was greatest in Thames Street, where there were warehouses full of oil and wines and brandies—as combustible materials as one might find.

It was on the third night of the fire that Jenny found herself cut off from safety. Somehow she had ended up where the fire raged on every side, or so it seemed. Bewildered, she looked around, her skin scorched, her eyes gritty from lack of sleep and the cinders that permeated the air. The very street under her feet was so hot that she felt as though she were walking on hot coals.

To this point, Jenny had not worried about the danger of the fire. She had been concerned about her friends' losing their houses and possessions, but never felt any threat. Now she looked around and realized she was trapped. Her back was against a wall of a church that even now was growing heated. Ahead of her and on both sides flames were shooting out of the windows of the buildings. Near panic washed over her. She threw her shawl over her face to shield her from the fierce heat and pushed away from the wall of the church.

To her left she saw what appeared to be an alleyway leading out of the inferno. Running down it, she suddenly stumbled and twisted her ankle. As she struggled to her feet she heard a grinding sound behind her. Whirling, she saw that the steeple of the burning church was collapsing. It was blazing as if it had been soaked in pitch—and it was falling straight toward her!

Jenny felt death coming and knew there was little she could do to avoid it. Her only coherent thought was, *I've left God out of my life and now I've come to this!*

The steeple toppled toward her, crackling and hissing ominously. With a last desperate lunge, Jenny threw herself into an opening of the wall that was surrounded by stone. Even as she pulled her foot out of the alleyway, the steeple crashed with a tremendous thunder. The flames leaped at her skirt, which quickly caught fire. Crying out sharply she dropped to the ground instinctively and rolled, almost losing consciousness from the fierce heat. With every gasp she felt her lungs were searing.

The world seemed to be made of fire.

She was barely conscious of struggling to get away. Ahead of her was darkness and she threw herself into it. It turned out to be some sort of large pipe and she huddled in the relative cool as the fire outside blazed. Shaking helplessly, she shut her eyes like a child who refuses to see the monster—and waited to see if she would live or die.

The Great Fire of London was said by some to be God's judgment on a licentious and sinful nation. Others saw it as a cleansing. The blaze burned almost one-fourth of the entire city, utterly consuming some of the worst areas—areas overrun with rats and filth.

In many ways, the fire produced a new city. Sir Christopher Wren, an accomplished and successful architect, became a very busy man. He designed more than one hundred churches to replace those that had been destroyed. Streets were laid out anew. New buildings were constructed. The old passed away and that which was new was better.

Jenny escaped, although she never knew how. And yet it was as though somehow she died in that fire. Badly shaken, she could not go back to her old life. She went to Nell Gwyn and told her she was leaving. Nell tried to dissuade her, but something had touched Jenny in that moment close to death. Now she knew how Evan must have felt when he thought he was dying.

For a few weeks she stayed in a room outside London, trying to decide what to do. She had saved every penny she had made during her acting career, except what she had spent during the plague and used for living expenses. For the first time in her life, she had no fear of poverty and could do whatever she desired.

And what she desired was to go back to Wales.

It proved to be a good decision. In her native land she found a small cottage where she adopted a simple and uneventful life. The days turned to weeks, the weeks to months, and Jenny found that a peace had come to her. She never knew exactly how or why, but there was a stillness in her spirit that she had never known before. As she walked the quiet ways around the small Welsh village, God spoke to her—and soon she gave herself to Christ.

Now there was a new and exciting aspect to life. She began attending the local church, which had a fine pastor. With every sermon, she soaked in the teachings of the Word. All of the passion she had poured into her acting she now poured into studying the Scripture and drawing closer to her Lord.

After a year she grew aware, deep within, that it was time to leave. She packed her few things together, said good-bye to the pastor and to the few close friends she had made within the church, and left.

As the carriage rolled along over the gentle hills, Jenny thought about what lay ahead. She did not know where God was leading her. All she knew was that she had to return to Wakefield.

Eighteen

RETURN TO WAKEFIELD

The weather was raw and gusty as the stage rolled across London Bridge. Jenny wondered how much she had changed during her year in Wales. She wore a lighter cloak than she needed and shivered at the cold. It had been a difficult trip for her, but as she looked out the window she suddenly thought of how she and Evan had first come to England so long ago.

With this memory, she wondered yet again at the urgency she felt to return to Wakefield. She shook her head slightly, still unable to explain it—even to herself.

She had decided to stop overnight in London and was glad when the carriage pulled to a stop. The sky was dark with the smoke from thousands of chimneys and a fog was rolling in along the Thames.

She found an inn where she might spend the night and inquired about departure times so she could complete her journey to Wakefield as quickly as possible. After changing clothes and resting for an hour she went out for a walk.

She could see that the city had been rebuilt to a large extent. Much construction was still taking place, with scaffolding everywhere and church spires, new and gleaming, rising above the city. Curious as to how she would react, she moved through the streets until she arrived at what she thought was the place where she had nearly died. It was impossible to recognize it at first, and she merely stood watching as workmen scurried around busily, erecting what seemed to be a large inn.

For months she had dreamed about her near fatal experience. Now, however, though she had not forgotten it, the memory brought no fear to her. She had settled all that in Wales. With a grateful smile she turned and made her way back to the inn.

She slept well that night and the next morning arose and made the decision to seek out Nell Gwyn. Though she held little fondness now for her overall experience on the stage, she did at least owe Nell a visit. Leaving the inn, she made her way to the theatre section of town. She was warmly received by several actors and actresses, all demanding to know if she had come back to resume her profession. The manager of one troupe offered her a role on the spot in a new play by Mr. Wycherly.

"No, I'm not going to do anything for a time, Mr. Hobbs." She smiled. "I'm just in town to visit. Is Nell in a play at present?"

"Ho! You *have* been out of the country!" Hobbs stared at her wonderingly. "You haven't heard, then?"

"Heard what?"

"Why, Nell's gone up in the world!" He winked broadly. "Her new address is the palace. She's the mistress of the king now. One of them, at least."

The news did not surprise Jenny, for she had seen it coming. "I suppose I won't see her then," she sighed. "It would be impossible."

"Not a bit of it," Hobbs countered with jollity. "She does as she pleases, our Nellie. Go right in and send your name. She'll be glad to see you. She was always fond of you, Jenny."

This proved to be accurate information. After some uncertainty, Jenny finally decided she would make one attempt to see her friend. She went to the palace and sent her name in. Almost at once the guard came back smiling. "Right this way, miss."

She followed him through the labyrinthine pathways of the palace and was greeted by Nell, who came to embrace her warmly. "I can't believe it! Come in now! Tell me everything!"

Jenny allowed herself to be entertained royally. Nell seemed to delight in having as many servants as possible standing by and sent them on various errands. Some went for chocolate, some for cake, some for this, and some for that. At length she dismissed all of them and turned to Jenny. "Now, what do you think of your Nellie?"

Jenny hesitated. "I just hope you're happy," she finally said.

Nell stared at her. "Of course I'm happy! I have everything a woman could want! What more could I ask for?" Her voice sounded too vehement, even to her own ears, so Nell laughed loudly and went on. "Where have you been hiding? I've tried everywhere to hear of you!"

"I've been in Wales for the last year."

"In Wales? Why would anyone go there? Truly, I don't understand you, Jenny."

For some time Jenny tried to explain. She knew that it was fairly useless, for Nell Gwyn was a woman who lived from day to day, from pleasure to pleasure. The idea of death apparently never occurred to her. When Jenny had finished her tale, Nell responded carelessly and finally tired of the subject.

"So what are you going to do now? A play, I suppose."

Jenny shook her head. "No. I'm not sure I'll ever go on the stage again."

This brought on a long conversation in which Nell attempted to persuade Jenny that she was making a big mistake in leaving the theatre. Finally Nell threw her hands up in capitulation. "Well, it seems your mind is made up and there is nothing more I can say. Where will you live?"

Jenny outlined her plans and Nell listened impatiently. When Jenny finished, Nell said breezily, "Come. I have something to do."

Jenny waited while Nell allowed her maids to dress her in finery. Then they left Nell's quarters.

"Where are we going?" Jenny asked.

"The king is touching this morning," Nell replied. "He likes for me to be there."

"Touching?" Jenny repeated, mystified. "Touching—what?"

"Why, touching for the King's Evil! You've never heard of this?"

"No. What does it mean?"

A smile lifted Nell's lips. "It's believed that the sovereign has been given the ability to heal people of scrofula—what they call the King's Evil. It's a disease."

Jenny stared at her friend. "The king has the gift of healing?"

Nell's smile widened. "He thinks so. It goes all the way back to Queen Elizabeth—or maybe Henry VIII. Oh, I don't know when it started. Come, you shall see."

Jenny never forgot the scene that followed. The two women arrived at an enormous room that seemed to be filled with people, most of whom were poor and clothed in pitiful rags. Some, however, wore ermine and expensive jewels. Jenny watched with interest the way they mingled together without apparent uneasiness.

Charles was seated on a low platform, wearing a scarlet doublet. An ornate golden chain hung around his neck, his dark hair flowed down his back in thick clusters of curls, and his thin mustache was carefully trimmed. As Jenny watched, an elderly woman hobbled forward and knelt before him. Charles reached out, touched her head, whispered a few words, then leaned back.

The woman struggled to her feet, curtsied to the king, and then left the room.

She was instantly replaced by a tall man wearing expensive dress, who knelt and bowed his head just as the woman had. Again, the king touched him, spoke a few words in a barely audible tone, and then released him.

For twenty minutes Jenny watched the king as he performed the ceremony repeatedly. She was confused, for she knew of the immoral life Charles led. When Nell motioned to Jenny and the two women made their way back to Nell's quarters, Jenny asked, "Do any of them ever get healed?"

"I don't know," Nell admitted. "Charles thinks they do." A puzzled look twisted her still pretty face. "He's not really a good man. I know that—and so does he. But somehow this is very real to him." Her voice deepened. "I suppose it's as close to God as he ever gets."

"Is he a Christian man at all, do you think?" Jenny wondered.

"I think he'd like to be a Catholic," Nell replied. "But he can't. His brother, the duke of York, is an outspoken Catholic. But Charles is too good a politician to allow himself to fall into that. He values his head too much. And his comfort, I suppose."

"He's a strange man," Jenny said slowly. "It must be very odd to have so much power—even the power of life and death—in your hands. He could do so much good!"

"Yes, he could. But Charles never will." Though Nell seldom seemed given to deep thought, Jenny could tell she had long considered this subject. The woman continued matter-of-factly, "Charles would never give himself to any cause except his own gratification. He had a bad upbringing, and then, as you say, great power was put in his hands. He lives for pleasure, although he's a very intelligent man. He'll never put himself out." With an impatient toss of her head, Nell changed the subject. She tried again to persuade Jenny to stay but soon gave it up.

As they said good-bye, she hugged Jenny. "You'll get tired of the country. Come back and see me. We'll have you perform at the Queen of London Theatre!"

As Jenny returned to the inn, she was filled with sorrow and pity for her friend. *Her beauty will soon be gone,* she sighed to herself, *and Charles will cast her aside, as he has so many others. Nell could have been—different—if she'd had the chance.*

Jenny had intended to leave London at once, but a chance remark by a friend she encountered caused her to postpone her journey for at least a day.

She was joined at breakfast by an older actor named Reginald Simmons. They spent an hour talking of old times, for Simmons often had shown Jenny kindness and friendship. He'd been one of the more genteel men among actors; he was in his middle fifties and had not pursued her as so many younger men had. They enjoyed their meal together, and Simmons spoke of the Wakefields. He had known Gavin and had met Sir Christopher once.

"Fine family," he said. "And you're going to visit them, are you?"

"Yes, for a while."

"Give my greetings to them." He leaned back on the bench and studied her from across the table. "There's another old friend that Sir Christopher would like to see. I suppose Sir Christopher's unable to travel much now. He's getting on, isn't he?"

Jenny replied, "I don't imagine he gets about much, but I haven't seen him for several years."

"Have you ever heard of John Milton?" Simmons inquired.

"No."

"Well, he was a very famous man back in Cromwell's day. He wrote tracts supporting the Puritan cause and then he became part of Cromwell's government. He was appointed the secretary of foreign languages. He and Sir Christopher were quite close, as I recall," Simmons mused.

"I never heard of him," Jenny said with curiosity.

"After Charles regained the throne, he suffered somewhat," Simmons sighed. "He had gone blind—too much study, I suppose—and was put in jail for his political activities. However, he continued to write. Now he's come out with a book that everyone is talking about. He lives here in London, you know. He married a young woman who takes care of him."

Jenny thought for a moment. "Do you suppose I might visit him? I would like to carry word back to Sir Christopher. Perhaps I might even attain a copy of Mr. Milton's book."

"Nothing easier!" Simmons exclaimed. "Come along with me. I'll take you and introduce you myself. I was a budding writer myself once—a poet, you know. John Milton and I talked about poetry a lot in those days." He smiled slightly. "Not that I'm in his class, of course."

Simmons took Jenny in a carriage to a small house on the outskirts of London. At his quiet knock on the door, a young woman promptly answered. "Ah, Mrs. Milton," Simmons said. "I come unannounced, but I have a young visitor here who would like to meet your husband."

Elizabeth Milton seemed a pleasant young woman. She smiled and stood aside. "Please come in. My husband is in the study. If you will give me a moment, I'll see if he will receive you."

She disappeared, leaving Simmons and Jenny in a tiny sitting room. "Milton's fortunate indeed to have such a woman to care for him. It's a mystery to me how he writes, considering his blindness. Surely his wife is his secretary."

Mrs. Milton came back into the sitting room. "Come in, Mr. Simmons. John will be glad to see you."

When they entered the small study, Simmons apologized for their intrusion. He spoke to an elderly man with gray hair and the telltale blank stare of the blind. "Mr. Milton, I apologize for coming unannounced, but I have a young visitor who wants to meet you."

John Milton turned toward Simmons's voice and replied courteously, "Quite all right, Mr. Simmons. Won't you be seated?"

Simmons and Jenny sat down close to their host and the older actor made the introductions. "This is Mistress Jenny Clairmont. And this, of course, is Mr. John Milton. Mistress Clairmont is on her way to visit Sir Christopher Wakefield. I told her that the two of you had been good friends, and she hopes to purchase your new book."

Milton smiled. "I'm happy to meet you, Mistress Clairmont. Please convey my kindest regards to my dear friend Sir Christopher. Is he well?"

"I haven't seen him in several years. I've been away," Jenny explained. "But I trust that he is. He and his wife both have been very kind to me."

Milton leaned back in his chair and told Jenny of the days of the rebellion, when he and Sir Christopher Wakefield had served Cromwell. "Those were hard times," he said, "but good times. I miss them." The three were quiet for a few moments and then Milton said wistfully, "I wish I could see Sir Christopher again. But that is not possible. I don't travel anymore. However, I will send him a copy of my little book."

"Little book!" Simmons echoed, laughing. "I shouldn't call it that! It's the longest poem I ever heard of." He turned to Jenny. "The name of the book is *Paradise Lost,* and there's nothing like it, Jenny! Absolutely nothing like it! It makes all the little chatterings of the preening poets today seem like the screeching of jackdaws!"

Jenny turned to John Milton with a smile. "I know Sir Christopher will be glad to receive your book and to hear of your interest in him."

"And you, Mistress Clairmont?" Milton said cordially. "Please tell me a little about yourself."

Jenny hesitated, then gave Milton a brief sketch of her life.

When she finished he asked, "So you are finished with the stage?"

"Yes, sir. It's not a good life."

"It is not," Milton agreed firmly. "I'm glad to hear of your decision. I feel you've made a wise one, Mistress Clairmont. May the Lord bless you in your new way and your new life."

The visitors did not stay long. Milton refused to take money for his book. He dictated to his wife a warm greeting to Sir Christopher, which she inscribed on the first page. Then Simmons and Jenny took their leave.

"Is the book really that good?" Jenny asked as they were on their way back to her rooms. "I'm afraid I am woefully uninformed where poetry is concerned."

Simmons gave her an odd look. "My dear, we poets are given to exaggeration, I know. Yet that book that you hold in your hand . . . it is astounding. I must admit that some of it is over my head. But for a man to write such a book through dictation! Unable to see what he's written! Why, it's a miracle! And I know that it will be blessed by God."

A snowflake floated down and touched Jenny's cheek as she walked slowly toward the entrance of Wakefield Castle. The coldness of the snow seemed to burn her cheek, and she looked up to the sky, which was as gray as gunmetal. It was the first day of December and a cold wind had rocked the coach all the way from London.

Jenny stood hesitantly for a moment before nearing the doors, sorely tempted to turn and hail the driver who had brought her from the stage station. Her eyes swept the high parapets of

Wakefield and she was flooded with a thousand memories of the days—years—that she had spent in this place. Back in Wales she had felt such a strong impetus to come here. But now she wavered.

Even as she stood undecided, feeling the grasp of the sharp wind, the door opened and a voice carried clearly across the forecourt.

"Jenny! Why are you standing out there? Come in the house!"

The sound of Angharad Wakefield's voice was welcome to Jenny's ears. She hurried forward and found herself embraced in a tight hug, then drawn quickly out of the cold. Angharad slammed the door behind them and turned to her. "Well! It's glad I am to see you! Come in, come in. Thaw out by the fire!" She practically dragged Jenny into a small study where a fire crackled cheerfully in the grate. "Here, give me that cloak! Come here and warm yourself, girl!" Angharad commanded.

Jenny studied Angharad, noting that her black hair now had an inch-wide band of pure white at one temple. With a start, Jenny realized Angharad was fifty-six. Though she'd been gone for several years, Jenny had never once pictured this gracious and loving woman growing any older.

Noting the girl's gaze at the white streak, Angharad touched it and laughed. "An old woman, I am now, you see! But it's of no matter. Sit you down and I'll have something hot brought in to warm us."

Twenty minutes later Angharad and Jenny cautiously sipped scalding tea, and Angharad was forcing bits of food onto the girl. "Eat now!" she scolded. "While you do, I'll tell you what's happening here at Wakefield."

Jenny, her mouth obediently full, nodded, her eyes wide.

"Amos is off on one of his voyages," Angharad told her. "And Gavin and Susanne are here with the children for an extended visit. Hope comes and goes. Restless as the wind, she is."

"She's not married yet?" Jenny asked in surprise. "I was sure she would be."

Angharad smiled briefly. "She's had chances enough, but I think her tongue's a little sharp for most men's taste."

"I truly thought she would be settled with a husband by now," Jenny murmured.

"And she's probably thinking the same of you, Jenny," Angharad countered. "But for naught, I suppose . . . ?"

She shook her head and smiled. "No, nothing like that."

"Ah, well, you're young yet." Angharad waited for a moment, but Jenny merely dropped her eyes and ate another bite. Angharad went on smoothly, "And have you heard from Evan?"

"Not a word. But of course I haven't written him, either." Jenny felt some explanation was necessary, so she went on, "I wrote you from Wales once, Lady Wakefield. But it's been a difficult time for me."

"I've thought and prayed much about you," Angharad said warmly. "And how is it with you now?"

"I don't know," Jenny sighed. "I don't know what to do. I don't even quite know why I'm here. I just felt I needed to see someone from my old life. The theatre is not . . . real—and the people are so—so—" She was unable to finish the thought, so she went on hastily. "I hope I'm not a bother. I won't stay long."

"Ah, you'll be staying as long as the good Lord lets you," Angharad insisted. "We have plenty of room in this drafty old place. How would you like to have the Green Room?"

"Oh, that's too much for me!" Jenny protested. "That's for important guests!"

"And what are you? A rat with green teeth?" Angharad retorted. "Come now, we'll get you settled in."

She took the indecisive girl up to her room and settled her in. "Would you be wanting to see Sir Christopher now, Jenny?"

"Oh yes," Jenny exclaimed. "I've thought about him so much—and I've brought a gift for him."

"Come along then. It's glad he'll be to see you."

They left the Green Room, went down the hall, and entered the large bedroom the elder Wakefields shared. "A visitor for you," Angharad announced. "Look what the December wind's blown in!"

Christopher was sitting in a chair, a book on his knees. When he looked up and saw Jenny, he brightened at once. "My dear!" Rising to his feet slowly, he put his book down and came to put his hands on her shoulders. "What a fine surprise on this gloomy day! Let me look at you!"

Jenny was shocked at how Sir Christopher had aged. His hair was completely white now and his cheeks were sunken. She noted the age spots on his hands and the careful manner with which he moved. She had heard from Evan at one point that Sir Christopher was experiencing improved health. Apparently that was no longer the case. A pang of sorrow went through her, though she did her best not to let her feelings show. "I'm glad to see you, Sir Christopher," she said with a smile. "I've thought about you so many times over the past years."

"Sit down, sit down," Christopher said. "I must have a full report. What have you been doing with yourself? Amos is driving me crazy wondering when you were coming back!"

"I—I've been doing very little," Jenny said lamely. She was hesitant to go into the story of her past, so said quickly, "I met an old friend of yours in London. Mr. John Milton."

"Did you indeed!" Sir Christopher's eyes brightened even more. "How is John? I haven't seen him in years, but he's a dear fellow."

"He's doing well," Jenny said cautiously. "And he sent you a gift."

She handed him the book and watched as Christopher took it,

slowly opened it to the first page, and read the inscription: *To my dear friend Christopher Wakefield, in memory of the good days that we had together. John Milton.*

He looked back up at Jenny and said quietly, "Bless his heart. He still remembers."

"A friend of mine tells me that this is the most important book ever written, next to the Bible," Jenny remarked.

"*Paradise Lost.* Yes, I've heard of it." Christopher nodded. "But this is the first I've seen a copy." He turned the pages slowly, looking at the lines, and then smiled at Jenny. "Thank you, child. How did you happen to meet Mr. Milton?"

Jenny related her acquaintance with Reginald Simmons and told Christopher in detail of their visit to Milton.

He listened avidly, then told her, "I hope you can stay here with us, Jenny. This is a gloomy old place, except for my grandchildren."

Angharad watched and listened as her husband and Jenny visited, noting how Christopher brightened up in the presence of the young woman.

Later, when she and Jenny left Sir Christopher, Angharad said, "It's good for you to be here, Jenny. Good for all of us, it is—but especially for Christopher. He always held a deep fondness for you."

During the days that followed, Jenny discovered that she could be a great help to Angharad. She had worried about being a burden, but she realized that being company for Christopher Wakefield more than paid for her keep.

When Jenny expressed her relief, Angharad scoffed, "My soul, you eat no more than a baby bird! And you more than make up for that little in your kindness to Christopher!"

The days passed and Christmas drew near. Several times Jenny mentioned to Christopher that she needed to find work—to get on with her life—but he waved the idea aside. "There's time enough for that," he argued. He enjoyed her company immensely, but most of all he enjoyed reading to her from the book she had brought him.

And for Jenny, the book was a revelation. She had read plays and novels but never poetry to any extent. Now, as the great, ringing words rolled forth from Sir Christopher's lips, she began to sense some of the beauty of the work that John Milton had done. It was a majestic book, one that dealt with the greatest subject of all: man's fall from God—and his redemption.

One morning, when the snow was falling, turning the ground white, she listened closely as Christopher read from the book. The fire blazed in the fireplace, and her eyes were fixed on Christopher's worn face. She worried about him, for she could plainly see that he was not at all well. There was a shadow in his eyes and despite his attempts to be always cheerful, she knew that he was sometimes in pain. It would come sometimes so suddenly that he would gasp.

When he read from Milton's book, however, he seemed to be happiest of all. "Now, here are some lines that I'd like to memorize. I have a hard time with that these days. But you might be able to do it, Jenny."

"Yes? What are they about?"

"It's the part where Jesus agrees to go down and die for man, to be his substitute," Christopher explained, his voice reverent. "Listen to this:

On me let thine anger fall;
Account me man: I for his sake will leave
Thy bosom, and this glory next to thee
Freely put off, and for him lastly die
Well please'd, on me let Death wreck all his rage;
Under his gloomy power I shall not long
Lie vanquished; thou hast given me to possess
Life in myself forever.

Christopher read with excitement and finally concluded with the victorious line: " 'But I shall rise victorious and subdue my vanquisher!' " He looked at Angharad and the two of them shared a thought that Jenny could not quite interpret. "We shall rise with him, won't we, Wife?"

"Yes, praise his name forever!"

Christopher closed the book and clasped his frail hands over it. He said nothing for a few moments, his eyes faraway. Jenny listened to the green wood popping loudly in the fire, the great words echoing in her ears. She saw that two tears rolled down Christopher Wakefield's cheeks. "Is it sad for you, sir?" she murmured.

Sir Christopher shook his head. "Oh no, not sad. Joyous! Joyous to think that Jesus would leave the Father, from whom he had never been separated, to come here and die for a man like me! Great is God's mercy, child! Great is his mercy!"

Jenny felt her own eyes grow misty. As she pondered the truth of Sir Christopher's words, she wondered yet again where her life would take her and what God wanted from her.

Christopher took a handkerchief from his pocket, wiped his tears away, and smiled at her. "I've had a long life and a blessed good one. But it's all through the mercy of God. Now the thing I desire most is to see my children and grandchildren—and young friends like you—follow after Jesus. Only in him is there peace, and happiness, and contentment!"

Nineteen

A KING GOES FORTH

Francis Wingate stared at his nephew and when he spoke, his voice was harsh. "What's this about John Bunyan? How is it that you're taking an interest in his affairs?"

Darcy Wingate had found his uncle to generally be a charitable man and had learned to respect him during his time in Bedford. However, he was well aware that John Bunyan and other independents were a sore spot with the judge. "I'm interested in the case," he replied mildly.

"So I hear," Wingate snapped. "You've been asking questions of everyone. And I also hear that you've visited Bunyan in jail several times."

"Yes. Does this disturb you, Uncle?"

"No good will come of it. If you don't have enough to do, that's your problem, Darcy."

"You're probably right, Uncle." Darcy shrugged. "I don't see how I'll ever make a living in a small town like Bedford."

This was true enough. Darcy had learned a great deal from his uncle, who was a scholar of the law. But Bedford was a small village. There was one lawyer already there who had staked out his claim on most of the legal work in the county. Darcy had applied himself to his studies under Francis Wingate's care but had done little actual work.

He had visited John Bunyan and had been carrying on a correspondence with Hope Wakefield concerning the possibility of helping the man. As he watched and listened to his uncle now, he realized that there would be little gain in having an argument with the judge over a prisoner that he held, on the surface at least, in disfavor.

Nevertheless, he couldn't keep himself from remarking casually, "I don't think Bunyan's a dangerous man."

"He refuses to keep the law," Francis countered. "That is quite enough to keep him in jail. All the fellow has to do is to agree to stop preaching and he can come out any time he likes!" Wingate slammed shut the book that lay open on the desk before him. "He's out right now, as I understand it!" he went on angrily. "I've warned that jailer, Cobb, about this, but the jails are so full there is hardly standing room."

Darcy gave his uncle a curious glance. "I have the feeling that you admire Bunyan, deep down." With a careless shrug he continued, "A man has to have a deep faith to endure Bedford Jail. It's a pretty foul place. From what I've seen, Bunyan is quite a man, Uncle Francis."

Francis Wingate thought back to the time when he had offered Bunyan his freedom. Since then, he had been tempted several times to again use his influence to do something for the man. But the pressures against the tinker were strong—though he could not admit this to his young nephew. He had grown fond of Darcy and foresaw great things for him, so he felt constrained to give him a stern warning. "You'd best be careful about things such as this, Darcy. There's a great deal of ill feeling, even now, against men like Bunyan. I don't expect you to stay in Bedford. You have much too bright a future for that." Now he gave his nephew a curious glance. "You're seeing the Wakefield girl from time to time. Are your intentions serious?"

Laughing shortly, Darcy shook his head. "I really can't say. She's a beautiful young woman, smart, witty—but sometimes she frightens me a little. I don't know quite how it would be to live with a woman who is that intelligent." With a few more casual words, Darcy left his uncle's office and walked to the Bunyan home. He wasn't quite certain if he was doing it because his uncle advised against it or simply because he had learned to enjoy John Bunyan's company.

When he arrived at the small cottage, he found Bunyan and Evan Morgan sitting before the fire, studying the Scripture. Mrs. Bunyan greeted him and he took a seat near the two men. "I can't stay long. I've just left my uncle."

Bunyan held the big Bible loosely in his hands. "And what did Judge Wingate say?" he asked with a shrewd glance at Darcy's closed expression. "I'll warrant he didn't send you here to study the Bible with an outcast such as me."

The corners of Darcy's mouth twitched. "No, Uncle Francis didn't do that! As a matter of fact, he warned me against coming here. I suppose I'm just a rebel at heart. When someone tells me not to do a thing, I do seem inclined to immediately throw myself into it."

Evan Morgan laughed aloud. "Sounds like a description of myself! At least, until lately." He had gained back the weight he'd lost during his illness and looked strong again. His recovery from his deadly bout with the plague seemed complete. The firelight caught the gleam in his dark eyes as he regarded Darcy. "So you came to join our Bible study, Mr. Wingate, in the sure knowledge that your uncle would tell you not to?"

Darcy's crooked smile flashed. "Suppose it would do me no harm. But I'll have to be a spectator. You two are beyond me. I haven't read the Bible as I should. Truth to tell, some of it completely baffles me."

Bunyan held his Bible out to Darcy. "Show me the part."

Taking the Bible, Darcy thumbed through it, found the place, and said, "Here, what about this?" In his fine, clear tenor voice he read: "'Behold, thou art fair, my love; behold, thou art fair; thou hast doves' eyes within thy locks: thy hair is as a flock of goats, that appear from mount Gilead.'" Darcy looked up and smiled, though his gray eyes were puzzled. "What in the world does *that* have to do with a man's salvation, Mr. Bunyan?"

Bunyan leaned forward and clasped his big workman's hands. His blue eyes glowed, his reddish brown hair was long and slightly rumpled, as if he'd just run his hands through it. His face was full fleshed and had regained much of its strong appearance, and he had gained weight during these latter days of limited imprisonment. "Well asked, Mr. Wingate," he said with approval. "This is from the Song of Solomon and it puzzles many people. Actually, it's poetry—a love poem about a wedding, a bride and a groom, and their love for one another."

Evan added, "That's not too far from Saint Paul, when he likens the church to the bride of Christ, is it, John?"

"Exactly, Evan!" Bunyan said enthusiastically. "You're learning your Bible!" He turned back to Darcy and took back his Bible. "It is rather rich language: 'Let him kiss me with the kisses of his mouth: for thy love is better than wine.'" Bunyan read several more passages from the Song of Solomon and then for half an hour spoke of how the love of God had been illustrated in this unusual form for a purpose. "I do not claim to know all of God's mind, naturally. But it seems to me that the one kind of love that most men and women know something about is that between husband and wife. I think, in this book, God uses this rich language to show us that God's love is even greater. Jesus often did that. He used earthly things to show heavenly truth." He turned to Darcy. "Can you give me an example?"

Darcy was startled. "Why, I'm not a scholar, certainly not of the Bible. But I've often thought of the parables that Jesus used. The parable of the sower, for example. I've always thought that that was a masterpiece of a story used to illustrate truth." He shrugged his sinewy shoulders. "However, I came to learn. You'll have to do the instruction."

It was over two hours before Wingate left the small cottage. As he returned to his room in his uncle's house, he thought how strange it was that he found greater richness and depth in the teaching of a simple tinker than ever he had found in the educated men of the high church he attended.

He makes it come alive, the Bible, Darcy mused to himself. *And that's what people are seeking: life. No wonder they're willing to take the chance of being arrested to hear something so unlike the dead sermons being preached in the cathedrals!*

When he reached home, he found the housekeeper holding out a letter for him. He glanced at the seal and opened it at once. It was from Sir Christopher Wakefield, but the handwriting was Hope's. Quickly he scanned the brief note:

> December 18, 1667
> My dear Mr. Wingate,
>
> I realize you are a busy young man, but you would do us all an honor if you would come for a visit. It would be most gracious of you if you could come quickly, for I have one item of business that I hope you will handle for me. Come for part of our Christmas celebration if you can. My daughter Hope adds her voice to mine in this invitation.
>
> Your obedient servant,
> Sir Christopher Wakefield

The letter puzzled Darcy, but at once he made up his mind to go. He informed his uncle and rode out of Bedford that same afternoon.

The weather was cold and the snow was deep, but he enjoyed the briskness of the wind. He was filled with the thought of spending time with Hope at Wakefield. She had caught his fancy as no young woman ever had before or since, and he spurred his horse into a gallop as he left the small village.

Amos arrived home a week before Christmas and was greeted by his parents with great joy. Angharad whispered to him, "I'm so glad you got here in time for Christmas. Christopher has been looking forward to it so much."

He searched her face carefully. "How is Father?"

Angharad hesitated for long moments. "He's very weak, Amos," she finally replied. "He eats hardly at all. I know he's in pain most of the time, though he never complains."

"Has the doctor been in?"

"Yes, but he knows nothing." She took Amos's hands in hers. "We must be prepared for losing him, Amos."

He blinked with shock. He knew Angharad was a woman of deep faith and had great spiritual insight. Often she had seemed to know things that could not be known. Now he asked her quietly, "Has the Lord told you this?"

She took a deep breath. "Yes, I think so. It's hard to turn loose of the things we love so dearly. But the time does come, you know, for all of us."

"Does he know, do you think?" Amos asked with difficulty.

"I'm sure he does. He may speak of it to you, Amos, but then again he may not. I'm glad you are here, though. I want the whole family to be together this Christmas."

Amos was deeply disturbed by Angharad's words but was determined not to let his father see his distress. He spent time with him every day, joining him and Hope and Jenny for the reading of Milton's book.

He had been shocked to find Jenny there, for he had not expected to see her at all. Their greetings were subdued, but he found time to spend with her every day as well. She spoke little of her time in Wales, so finally he asked her directly, "What went on all that time you were gone? Why didn't you write?"

Jenny was prepared for this question. "I was troubled, Amos, and I was unhappy. I didn't like the theatre—you were right about that, it's no life for a woman. So I had to go away, be by myself. I suppose I was seeking God."

Amos looked at Jenny's calm face, her steady eyes, and reflected upon her serene voice. "I would say you found him, did you not? I feel a certain . . . spirit about you that I've never encountered in you before."

"I am finding him—more every day," she said calmly. "It's something that a person does every day, you know. Not just once."

Amos was glad that Jenny was back and he smiled. "I've missed you, Jenny. We'll have a fine time this Christmas." His eyes narrowed slightly as he asked, "Have you seen Evan?"

"No. He's been gone to Mr. Bunyan's ever since I've been back. I hear he's doing well, though."

"We made a couple of fools out of ourselves, fighting the way we did," Amos grunted. "I hope I've grown up a little since then. Did you know Evan's setting out to be a minister?"

"Yes." Jenny nodded. "Angharad and your father are very proud of him." Her eyes grew farseeing. "It's hard for me to see Evan as a preacher. But I know he will do well if he lets God have his way."

As Christmas drew closer, Wakefield was filled with happy voices. Lucy and Alfred added the childish joy that Christmas always brings, and Susanne was glad she and Gavin were there so that the family was one. Evan came four days before Christmas. He arrived unexpectedly and it was Jenny who happened to respond to the knock at the door.

"Oh," she said in confusion. "Well—well—don't just stand out there in the snow! You'll freeze! Come in the house, Evan."

He had known Jenny was at Wakefield and had prepared himself for seeing her. As he took off his cloak and watched her shake off the snow crusted on the shoulders, he said, "It's good to see you, Jenny. It's been a long time."

Jenny hung his coat on a peg next to the door and turned to look him over. "And great things have been happening with you, I hear. I'd like to hear all about it." There was no time for that, however, as the two soon found themselves in the center of the Wakefield family activities.

The days passed quickly. For Jenny there was a strange tension between herself and Evan. She spoke of it once to Angharad. "I thought when I came back that Evan and I would be close again. But he seems so different! I can't explain it."

Angharad was knitting. Without looking up she said, "He has a great deal on his mind. You know what a dangerous thing it is to be a preacher these days. At least, a nonconformist preacher. He could very well end up in jail, like his friend John Bunyan."

Jenny thought about this, then said wistfully, "I wish we could go back to the way we were. But that isn't possible, is it?"

"No, and I'm not certain you'd want to, now would you?" She looked up briefly, her fingers busy. "You are who you are *now,* Jenny, and it wouldn't be the same. You're thinking, I suppose, of when you and Evan first came: both of you young and everything in life seemed bright and shiny, as it does to very young people."

"Can it ever be like that for older people?"

"Not in the same way," Angharad sighed. "There's something about youth that is simply . . . different. Of course, as we grow older, we find other things that are good. But I truly don't think you'd wish to go back and be again that girl that you were."

While she did agree, Jenny couldn't help but long for one part of that onetime Jenny . . . the part that knew a sweet closeness with Evan.

All the family was aware that Christopher was failing, but they did not speak of it among themselves. He himself said little but obviously enjoyed the companionship of his family, perhaps more than he ever had in his life. He said as much once to Angharad. "This is a fine time. I'm glad to see all of the children and all the grandchildren." His voice was weak and he saw a glimmer of sorrow on his wife's face. Usually she hid it from him well, but this time he could tell it struck too deeply for her to hide. "Angharad," he went on quietly, "you have been my life."

Startled, she came to sit close beside him and looked into his worn face. They joined hands and sat quietly for a long time. Christopher smiled faintly at her as he went on, "God has been so good to me to let me have you during my last years." It was as close as he had ever come to mentioning that he might be near death. He went on to speak all that he had been wanting to say to his wife. Quietly, without fear, he spoke of the fact that he had not much more time on earth. He mentioned a few things he wished to have done and once again told her of his love for her.

Angharad held his thin hands and listened quietly. When his voice stopped, she kissed him, tears glimmering in her beautiful eyes.

"Aye, God has given us to one another." She rested her cheek against the palm of his hand as emotion swept over her. In a voice choked with gratitude mixed with sorrow, she told him, "You've been the best husband a woman could ever have, Chris."

The house was decorated top to bottom. The most beautiful room by far, however, was the great hall. Holly and ivy had been brought in from the woods near the river and the apple trees had been stripped of the mistletoe that grew on them. The servants had found bay leaves, and rosettes made of yarn were strung across the hall.

In a moment's weakness, Angharad—who had never been wont to observe Christmas in this fashion—had ordered some of the windowpanes painted crimson and vivid green. During the day the light streaming in was tinted with Christmas colors and at night the light shining out on the snow was of red and green rectangles. Oranges and lemons were tied together in bunches and bits of colored cloth were hung upon the walls to hide some of the duller paintings.

On Christmas Eve the family had a fine supper, and the Yule log was dragged in and laid across the hearth.

"It'll burn for at least four days," Gavin said with satisfaction. He looked over as Christopher came in and sat down, pulling a heavy blanket over his knees. "I remember once I brought in a Yule log so big I hoped it would last a week! I never got enough of Christmas, did I, Father?"

"Nor did I," Christopher said with enthusiasm, though his voice was faint. "Now, let's have some singing."

Jenny knew she would always remember this Christmas—and this night. Some of the servants who had good voices were summoned and the great hall rang with madrigals and carols. At midnight they had a Bible reading.

During all of this, Darcy Wingate was quiet and unobtrusive. He had intended to stay only for a brief visit, but his time with Sir Christopher had stretched out and he had finally decided to stay over Christmas.

He glanced now toward his host, remembering his interview with Sir Christopher when he had arrived at Wakefield. Sir Christopher had told him, with little preamble or fanfare, "I want you to do all you can to help John Bunyan. I understand that your uncle is opposed to this, but I wish to retain you specifically to aid this man."

Now, looking at Christopher Wakefield's wan features and wasted body, Darcy thought, *He knows he won't be here long and he wants to serve Bunyan while he can.*

Hope was sitting beside Darcy and leaned close to his ear. "I didn't know you were such a fine singer!"

"Oh, just fair," Darcy said modestly. "I like madrigals, though. We did a lot of them at Oxford." He studied her unobtrusively. Hope had been different. Perhaps the shadow of her father's illness lay on her more heavily than he knew. In any case, her tongue had not been sharp and the two had spent considerable time together in the days of Darcy's visit. Now he leaned toward her and murmured, "This is such a fine Christmas! It's always been like this here?"

"No, it hasn't. When Cromwell was alive, it wasn't popular to have anything like traditional Christmas festivities," she told him. "But we've changed. I think for the better."

On Christmas Day they all went to church. Except, of course, for Sir Christopher—and Angharad, who stayed with him. The group came back to a great dinner, where there were meat pies of all sorts, mincemeat pies, plum porridge, and saddles of mutton. Afterward there were little gifts; nothing large, mostly very personal things.

Darcy was pleased to receive a pair of fine gloves from Hope. "You will have to expect a late present from me," he told her in some embarrassment. "I'm afraid I didn't bring you a thing."

"That's all right," she assured him. "Father told me that you've agreed to help Mr. Bunyan." Her eyes glowed as she smiled brilliantly up at him. "That is present enough for me! I am so pleased." She dropped her eyes and muttered, "I thought that you were the most selfish young man I'd ever met."

"Probably was. Maybe I still am." Darcy shrugged. "But I think you've been a good influence on me."

The two went to visit the mews, where Hope again taught him about the finer points of the hawks. Then they went to the kennels and took the dogs out for a run. Darcy thought he had never seen anything more beautiful than Hope's face. She had knelt down to hug one of the dogs, then looked up at him, her eyes shining and her cheeks glowing.

"This has been a good time," he told her in a low voice. "I hope there will be many more like it."

Hope's smile and suddenly pink cheeks were all the answer he required.

Later Hope sought out Jenny, who seemed depressed. "What's the matter?" she asked anxiously. "I thought you were enjoying Christmas."

Jenny smiled faintly. "Oh, I am. I'm just worried about your father. He seems to grow weaker every day. And Angharad is worried, too."

In truth, there was an underlying air of anxiety at Wakefield. Three days after Christmas, that which they had all been secretly dreading, but also expecting, came to pass. Hope was sitting with Darcy as he was explaining some of the difficulties of the legal problems with John Bunyan's case. He broke off abruptly when Angharad came in.

With one look at her mother's face, Hope burst out, "It's Father, isn't it?"

"Yes," Angharad said calmly. "He's had some sort of attack. Go find Amos and Gavin and have them bring the children."

Soon all the family was gathered in the master bedroom. Jenny had not intended to come, thinking herself an outsider. But Angharad had told her, "He wants you, Jenny. Come now." So Jenny had joined the Wakefield family at Christopher's bedside.

Christopher opened his eyes. His voice was a whisper, but it seemed to grow stronger as he spoke. "It's been a fine Christmas," he said with satisfaction. "I have seen many Christmases. I think back to the time in Plymouth, with John Bradford, and Miles Standish, and Patience. . . ." He reached out and his sons took his hands. "Your mother, boys, was a fine woman. I've never forgotten her."

Angharad was close beside him and now Christopher released Gavin's hand to take hers. "You must watch the children now, my love." He smiled. "You've been a good wife. All that any man could want."

Jenny could not keep the tears from her eyes. She stayed back, hidden, trying desperately not to intrude. But soon she heard the thin voice from the great bed calling her name. She went to him and bent over to catch his whispered words.

"God has a work for you, my daughter. Be faithful to Jesus. You have been good to me and God is going to use you." She leaned over to kiss his cheek, then stepped back.

Christopher hovered for a while between life and death. Finally, one hour later, he took a deep breath, then settled more deeply in his pillow with the finality that death brings.

Angharad leaned over to push a lock of his white hair away from his forehead, then kissed his face softly. Straightening, she looked around at the Wakefields with shimmering eyes. "A king goes forth!" she said with pride in her voice. "He is in the presence of another King now—and we shall all, one day, meet him there!"

END OF PART THREE

Part FOUR

The Calling

1670 – 1672

Twenty

Amos Takes the Plunge

"Come in, Amos."

"You're not busy, Gavin?"

"No, not at all." Gavin waved his hand toward the chair that sat opposite the large walnut desk on which he leaned his elbows. The top was covered with assorted papers and books. "I've just been going over some of Father's papers." He sat back and looked around the spacious study, then shook his head. "It's been five months now, yet I can't believe he's gone."

Amos noted the sadness in the eyes of his brother, then sighed heavily. He sat down in a chair. "I know what you mean. In a way it's like the sun has gone out."

"An odd way to put it, but not at all amiss." Gavin's eyes swept the tall bookcases bulging with leather-covered volumes and loose manuscripts, noted the carefully drawn maps that hung on the walls. Then he rose and walked to the globe beside a small rosewood table. Giving it a spin, he gazed at it until it slowly came to a halt. He turned to face Amos. "He was a great man, all in all. I will not look on his like again."

"Angharad is taking it better than I'd expected. He was her life."

"I've been thankful that Father married her, Amos. She made this house a home."

"Yes. I'm glad Father had this last Christmas, too. It was a good time for him."

Gavin took a gold watch out of his pocket and stared at it fondly. "This was his last gift to me. I'll think about him every time I look at it. Did you know it has a minute hand on it?"

"A what?"

"A hand that measures off the minutes. Don't know why watchmakers didn't think of it years ago! A man needs to know a little more than what hour it is."

"Why, that's so!" Amos exclaimed. He studied the watch as Gavin passed it over, then returned it, observing with a smile, "Someday they may even make a watch that measures seconds—or even one that gives the day of the month."

"No, that's too much to ask of them." Gavin shook his head positively.

"I suppose so." Amos studied the room for a moment, then turned back to ask, "How does it feel to be *Sir* Gavin Wakefield?"

Gavin went to sit in his chair. He stared at the clutter on the desk for what seemed like a long time and when he looked across at Amos, he seemed disturbed. "Just exactly as it felt to be *Mr.* Gavin Wakefield," he said evenly.

"Why, that's odd," Amos remarked.

"What's odd about it?"

"Oh, I don't know, Gavin. It's just such a big change—or I think it is. To be a peer of the realm isn't a thing to take lightly."

Gavin shrugged his broad shoulders, seeming to be slightly disturbed by the subject. Like his father and grandfather, he had never sought after honors for their own sake. The things he treasured were home, fireside, the sounds of his children's voices, neighbors.

"Let others run the kingdom, Amos," he said abruptly. "As long as the good Lord lets me have Wakefield, that's empire enough for me!" He waved the subject of empires away, asking, "Now, what about you, Brother? Ready to go to sea again?"

The question made Amos twist restlessly in his chair as though it were something he didn't like to hear. His dark auburn hair fell over his shoulders in rich curls, and he reached up and pulled at a strand nervously—a sure sign to any who knew him that he was struggling with some sort of inner problem.

"Gavin . . . I want to marry Jenny."

"That's no surprise to anyone," Gavin answered. "You've been walking around in a daze for a long time. I've been wondering when you'd make up your mind. When will it be?"

"Why—I haven't asked her yet." Amos got up and paced the floor nervously. "It's a momentous decision, taking a wife, isn't it, Gavin? I mean, a man can back off when he makes a mistake in some things, such as when he buys a horse. If the animal doesn't work out, why, he can sell the beast and get another one."

Gavin laughed aloud. "I hope you don't let Jenny hear you talking such nonsense—or Angharad!" He rose and came to clap his brother on the shoulder. "Comparing getting a wife to buying a horse! Amos, you're impossible!"

Amos grinned, not embarrassed in the least. He was very close to this older brother of his, having learned long ago that Gavin was a man of great insight. "You're right, it's a bad way of putting it—but you know what I mean."

"Yes, I do. And you've touched on a great truth. Next to getting his life right with God, nothing in a man's life is as important as finding a good wife."

"Jenny would be a good one!"

"Aye, but for who?" A sober light touched Gavin's eyes and he said thoughtfully, "God is in these things, Amos. If he notes the sparrow's fall, he cares for our lives infinitely more. I believe God planned for me to have Susanne for my wife before I was born."

It was a novel concept for Amos. In his world marriages were the affairs of men. Nobility married their daughters off to men who could bring wealth and influence into the family. Poorer classes had no romantic notions along this line. Now as Amos stood there, he thought hard about what Gavin had said. Finally he said slowly, "You mean that there's only one *right* woman for a man—and if he misses her, he's out of God's will?"

"Sounds ominous, doesn't it?" Gavin had thought much about this and now expounded on it. "I heard an old story once, can't remember where. It was a story about a creature that God created, a creature that got torn in half and the two pieces were scattered. Well, these two pieces sought for a mate—but the only one that would fit was the one that had been torn from it." He hesitated, noting the puzzled look on the face of his brother. "God wants the best for all of us, Amos, but we often don't take the best way. Man is a disobedient creature, isn't he? Adam and Eve went wrong and we've been going wrong ever since. We're selfish to the bone, most of us, and we reach out to grab whatever will gratify us. We can't see God's hand plainly—mostly because we don't seek it—so we plunge into our own devices, taking whatever we want."

Amos tugged at his hair, then shot a glance at his brother. "I think God gives us common sense, Gavin. We don't need to hear a voice from heaven telling us what to eat for breakfast or what suit to wear for the day."

"Right enough, dear Brother," Gavin said, nodding. "The Scripture says, 'The prudent man looketh well to his going,' and that means we have to make wise decisions. Every day we move in the world and God has given us a compass to show us the way." His ash blonde hair caught the beams of the yellow sun that filtered through the high window behind him. He seemed to think deeply, then said quietly, "Amos, every morning I pray for two things."

Amos waited for his brother to speak, then when Gavin remained silent, he asked, "What two things?"

"I pray for wisdom. God says, 'Wisdom is the principal thing'—the most important thing, that is. Study the book of Proverbs and you'll see how God has given us that wisdom to help us make our choices. When you're at sea, how do you know which way to go?"

"Why, I look at the compass!"

"Right! And God has given us his Book and wisdom to know which choice before us is *his* will."

Amos considered that, then asked abruptly, "That's one thing. What's the other thing you pray for?"

Gavin smiled, his high cheekbones and long face breaking up into planes as the sun touched him. "It's one thing to *know* the will of God, Amos—but it's quite another thing to *do* it."

"Why, that's so, isn't it?" Amos murmured. "As dull as I am, I can remember quite a few times when I knew full well what God wanted but did just the other thing!"

"Just as your grandsire Adam?"

"Yes, I suppose so." Amos took a few nervous steps toward the window, stared down at the scene below him, then turned to say, "You're telling me to be sure Jenny's the woman God wants me to have for a wife?"

"It would be wise, Amos."

"Well, I'll have to think about all this. I never thought about it much before." Amos nodded, then walked from the room, leaving Gavin to stare after him. Finally he sat down at the desk, studied the grain of the fine wood, then said aloud, "Why does it always have to be so hard to grow up?"

For three days Amos thought about what Gavin had said, struggling with the strange concept. He lay awake at night, staring at the stars that glittered in the sky, his mind whirling with confusion. His life had been simple enough, but his thinking was rather shallow. He had been a Christian for years, yet because he had been confronted with no great trials, he had not done more than observe the ordinances of the church. Now he was suddenly confronted with what seemed to be a far more profound decision than he had ever considered.

Finally he sought out Angharad. He found her in the room she used for sewing and planning her activities. It was a small room, illuminated by a single window that allowed the afternoon sun to fall in a long slanting bar of gold over the floor. Amos knew she used this as her special place, where she read her Bible and sought God in prayer.

"Are you busy, Mother?" Both he and Gavin had called her by that name since she had married their father. Neither of them had ever known one moment's jealousy for their real mother, for Angharad had made it plain that she could never take the place of Patience. But she had made her own place in the hearts of the two young boys, filling some of the loss they had felt at their own mother's death.

"Come in." Angharad smiled, looking up from the Bible she held. "What are you up to this morning?"

Amos sat down and stared at his hands—then pulled at his hair. "Well—I need to know what to do with my life, Mother."

"Do you now? Well, *that's* a big order!" Angharad knew at once what was troubling the young man who was so precious to her, but she merely asked, "What particular part of your life needs attention?"

"I—I'm thinking of marrying Jenny," he blurted out.

"Are you now?"

Amos glanced up at her quickly. "You've known all about it, haven't you?"

"Do I have eyes, boy?" Angharad could not have loved this

dark-eyed young man more if she had borne him in her own body. She studied him thoughtfully. "Do you love her, Amos?"

Amos blinked at the question. "I *want* her—she's so beautiful!"

"And will you love her when she's no longer beautiful?"

The question caught Amos off guard. "Why—I never thought of it!"

"Most young people don't think of such things." Angharad smiled softly, her warm brown eyes on his face. "I want to read you something," she said.

"From the Bible?"

"No, it's a poem. I'm not as much a one for poetry as your father was, but I like this one." She rose and moved to the rosewood cabinet against the wall. Removing a small sheet of paper, she came back and resumed her seat. A slight twinkle touched her eyes as she said, "Jenny gave this to me." She saw his interest increase as she read the poem slowly:

Let me not to the marriage of true minds
Admit impediments. Love is not love
Which alters when it alteration finds,
Or bends with the remover to remove:
Oh, no! it is an ever-fixèd mark,
That looks on tempests and is never shaken;
It is the star to every wandering barque,
Whose worth's unknown, although his height be taken.
Love's not Time's fool, though rosy lips and cheeks
Within his bending sickle's compass come;
Love alters not with his brief hours and weeks,
But bears it out even to the edge of doom.
If this be error and upon me proved,
I never writ, nor no man ever loved.

Angharad read the lines in the cadences of the Welsh blood that lay in her, her voice rich and deep, tingling with the power of the language. She handed the paper to Amos, saying quietly, "I think you might do well to study it."

He stared at the lines, then looked up at her. "I don't understand poetry very well. What does it mean?"

"I don't understand it all myself, but I'll share what I do." Closing her eyes, she lifted her head and recited, "'Love is not love which alters when it alteration finds.'" She opened her eyes. "That means love doesn't change when its object of desire changes. It stays the same." When she saw that he was still struggling with the meaning, she took the paper and pointed out some lines, reading them aloud. "'Love's not Time's fool, though rosy lips and cheeks within his bending sickle's compass come.'" She smiled at him. "I thought of that for a long time before I understood it. Think of Father Time, with his sickle, Amos. He comes like one who cuts down the grain—but it isn't grain he cuts down. No, it's our youth—our rosy lips and cheeks."

His eyes brightened and he nodded. "Why, I see it now! When time takes away youth and beauty, if we really love a person, that won't matter!"

"There is clever you are!" Angharad's face was illuminated with a glow that came from deep within. "Your father was a man who knew this. If he'd lived and I'd have grown ugly, he'd have loved me the same! Just as I loved him when he lost his fine looks. It wasn't his handsome face I loved, Amos, but the man *within.*"

Amos stared at Angharad, for she had never spoken so of the love she'd had for his father. Finally he looked down at the lines and studied them closely. "'Love is not love which alters when it alteration finds,'" he read, his face sober. He looked up to say, "Is it wrong to love a woman for her beauty?"

"Of course not, Amos! It's part of Jenny—her good looks. But you must love more than that or you'll never know what love is!

Remember, 'Favour is deceitful, and beauty is vain, but a woman that feareth the Lord, she shall be praised.'"

Amos sat beside Angharad for some time, listening as she spoke of love and marriage. As he listened, he began to understand what it meant to let God into his life. Finally he rose, thanked her for her time with a kiss on the cheek, and left. For the rest of the afternoon he wandered in the woods, enjoying the crisp air. It was some time later when he finally turned and made his way back home.

Jenny was in the rose garden, replacing an older plant with a fresh one. She was wearing an old dress and a pair of heavy gloves and her hair caught the last rays of the setting sun as she looked up to see Amos striding toward her. He looked so serious she rose at once, asking, "Amos—is something wrong?"

Amos ignored her startled look. "Jenny, I love you," he said and then he put his arms around her and kissed her.

Jenny was too astounded to speak. Somehow she had always known that she would hear this, but now that it had come she was confused.

"Why, Amos . . . ," she whispered. He was holding her tightly and she tried to pull away. "Someone might see us!"

"I don't care," Amos said. "I want you to marry me." He saw the shock of this sweep across her face and said quickly, "You're so beautiful, Jenny—but it's more than that. You're the sweetest woman I've ever known!"

Jenny swallowed, trying to collect her thoughts. She was very conscious of his arms around her. *If I marry him, life will be so easy!* She had known so little security, for her childhood had been terrible. She had found love and acceptance at Wakefield, but that was not a home. The stage had offered her money and adulation, but she knew full well that she would never be happy with that. Now as he held her, his dark blue eyes fixed on her, she wanted to surrender, to give herself to him.

But she could not say the words he wanted to hear. "I—can't give you an answer," she said and drew back from him. "I like you so much, Amos . . . but that's not love, is it?"

"I'll make you love me!"

"No, that's not possible," Jenny said firmly. "Love can't be forced."

Amos stared at her for a moment, then insisted, "I think you do love me—a little."

"You don't want that, Amos—a *little* love. You want a woman who will love you with her whole heart."

Amos nodded. "All right, Jenny, but you *will* marry me!" He looked very stubborn, his youthful face set in determination. "I'm going to court you until you can't say no." He took her hand, removed the heavy glove, and kissed her trembling fingers. "I love you so much that when your rosy lips and cheeks lose their color, I'll love you still."

Jenny was startled, recognizing the line. She laughed and her color rose. "You're going to win me with poetry? Angharad's been coaching you!"

"She read me the poem," Amos admitted. "And it's true, I don't know much about love, Jenny. But I'm going to learn and you're going to get poems and flowers and—and all the things a lover is supposed to give to his sweetheart."

He looked so young and handsome that Jenny could not help feeling the force of his words. She removed her other glove, tossed it aside, and took his arm. Smiling up at him, she said, "It'll take more than a poem and a flower to convince me you'll love me when I'm old and homely, Amos Wakefield! Now come on and let's go for a walk. You can start convincing me now!"

Evan arrived at Wakefield early one morning. He had been warmly greeted by everyone—except Jenny. She had been stiff and rather formal with him and he had sensed at once that something was wrong.

After breakfast, Angharad had taken him to her sitting room and said, "Now then, boy, let me hear about this preaching of the gospel you've been doing." She sat quietly, her face fixed on his, and when he had finished telling her of his efforts to become a minister, she put her arms around him, whispering, "There's proud of you I am! I wish Will and your father could have seen this day!"

"I knew you'd be glad, Angharad." He held her hand for a moment, deep in thought, then shook his head. "It's not going to be easy, you know. Mr. Bunyan thinks there'll be more persecution."

"Gavin is hopeful. He thinks Mr. Bunyan may be released soon. And Mr. Wingate—he comes to see Hope, you know? I asked him if his uncle might not relent, and he's promised to try to secure Mr. Bunyan's release."

"Yes, I've talked to Mr. Wingate—but he has no authority and neither does Judge Wingate, his uncle. If the enemies of the Independents have their way, all freedom will be removed."

The two spoke of the dangers that lay ahead and finally Angharad said, "Does Darcy ever speak to you of Hope?"

"He's fascinated by her—but thinks she's very headstrong."

"He's right about that. If the two of them married, I don't know what would come of it!"

Evan left shortly and spent the rest of the day with the servants. Some of them teased him about becoming a minister—especially the young women. Betty Longbow, a buxom maid, dug her elbow into his ribs and winked lewdly, whispering loudly, "I suppose now that you're a minister, you won't be after me to go walking to the river with you tonight?"

Evan flushed at the laughter that went up and could only say, "I'll preach you a sermon instead, Betty." He said it lightly enough, but at once they all began to urge him to follow through and on the next Sunday, Evan found himself preaching at the local church. The pastor was a fine man and took pride in Evan's new vocation. When Evan rose to preach, he faced a church packed to overflowing. He had been a popular young man and his old drinking friends were there, grinning broadly, as well as many of the young women he'd courted in the moonlight.

In the very front of the church sat the Wakefields: Angharad, Gavin and Susanne, Hope and Amos, and—between these last two—Jenny!

Evan stood up and for one moment was confounded. He swallowed, saying, "I see many of you who know me well." He waited until the wave of laughter died down, then lifted his head, and his voice rose like a trumpet. "But if any man be in Christ Jesus, he is a new creature! I hope to prove to you that I am not the man I was, but that Christ Jesus has made me into a new man!"

"Amen!" Angharad had punctuated this with her strong voice, and several of his old friends said, "Let's have the sermon, Reverend!"

Evan preached a simple sermon—but though it was not long or concerned with deep doctrinal truths, he held up Jesus Christ with such force that the Spirit of God moved with great power over the congregation. He spoke of the Lord Jesus with such warmth and obvious love that those who listened knew that this was a new Evan Morgan!

After the service, he was surrounded by many who shook his hand, but Angharad put her arms around him, her eyes filled with tears. "And there is a man of God you are!" she whispered.

Jenny came to stand before him and he waited, his heart beating rapidly, for her reaction. But she said only, "It was a fine sermon, Evan."

Disappointment shot through him, but he nodded, his eyes on her face. "Thank you, Jenny."

That night Evan joined the Wakefields for supper, and the talk turned to Bunyan's book. Gavin said, "This book, *Grace Abounding . . .*, everyone's reading it. The booksellers in London are sold out. Mr. Bunyan must be very happy."

"I think he sees it as another way of getting the gospel before people," Evan answered.

Angharad spoke up. "It's the best book ever written—after the Bible, of course."

Jenny listened as the others spoke of the book, but it was Hope who said, "Evan, Mr. Wingate writes me that the book has stirred up some of Mr. Bunyan's enemies. He says they are going to pass a new act to stop the Independents from preaching."

"I fear he speaks the truth," Evan said grimly.

"Is Mr. Bunyan in jail now?" Amos inquired.

"No, he's been allowed his freedom—but under this act he could be sent back to jail."

"But—what about you, Evan?"

Evan gave a startled look at Jenny. She had not said a word at dinner, but now everyone saw that her face was strained. Amos turned to look at her and something in her face disturbed him.

Evan answered her calmly, "I will be arrested if I preach, the same as the other ministers, Jenny."

A silence fell on the table, and it was Susanne who said quietly, "I know God will be with you, Evan, no matter what happens."

Afterward, when the dinner was over, Evan was startled when Jenny came to say, "I—wish you didn't have to go to Bedford."

"I have to follow my calling."

She looked up at him and the two of them seemed to be caught back to the time when they had been so close. Jenny was about to speak, but at that moment Amos came to stand beside her.

Slipping an arm about Jenny, he said, "Have you told Evan about our engagement?"

Evan gave the two of them a startled look, then his mouth settled into a thin line. "No, she hasn't. I congratulate both of you."

Jenny was about to say that they were not really engaged, but Evan turned and walked away abruptly. Jenny shot Amos a glare and said reproachfully, "Amos, you mustn't say we're engaged!"

"Well, I suppose not," Amos said quickly. "But you'll agree soon."

Jenny hoped to have some time with Evan to explain more clearly what Amos had said—but she had no opportunity. The next morning when she asked Angharad about Evan, she discovered that he was gone. "He felt he had to return to help Mr. Bunyan," Angharad said.

"Oh, I thought he'd stay for a time," Jenny murmured. She was disturbed by the misunderstanding and kept to herself for the next few days.

The old enemy of John Bunyan, Dr. William Foster, had lost none of his venom since becoming commissary of the Archdeacon's Court. As soon as parliament reenacted the Conventicle Act, he threw all his energies into a violent repression of the Nonconformists of Bedford.

On Sunday, May 15, 1670, Foster struck. His forces invaded a small group that was worshiping at the home of John Fenn, a haberdasher. All who attended were fined and the ministers committed to prison. On the following Friday, Mr. Battison, a churchwarden, made his rounds to levy the fines but met with some resistance. Foster grew livid and sent soldiers to collect the fines. They smashed down doors, seizing plunder of all sorts—

much of which was retained by the grinning officials—and arrested many hapless Christians.

Foster made it a point to arrest John Bunyan in person. Taking four stout soldiers with him, he made his way to the Bunyan cottage and struck the door with his fist, shouting, "Come out, Bunyan!"

The door opened at once and John Bunyan appeared. "Dr. Foster," he said quietly. "I assume you've come to collect the fine."

"Yes!" Foster snapped. "And I'm authorized to take all of your household goods if you don't pay up!" A sly grin touched his lips, for he was certain that Bunyan would not be able to pay. "Now, just stand aside—"

"I have the fine, sir," Bunyan said immediately. He had foreseen this and so had sold some of his household goods to make up the sum. Evan Morgan, who came to stand behind his friend and mentor, had contributed to the total. As John handed over the money, both he and Evan could see that Foster was angered.

"Very well!" Foster snapped, grabbing the purse. "But you're not getting off so easily! I have a warrant for your arrest—and this time Cobb won't let you wander off!"

Evan said at once, "Is there a warrant for Evan Morgan?"

"Why—yes," Foster blinked with surprise. "Are you he?"

"I am."

"Then you can rot in jail along with the rest of the rebels!"

Bunyan turned to his family, embracing them one by one. He smiled at them just before he was led away. "God will not desert us—be of good cheer."

"Take them, Sergeant!" Foster cried. He marched along with the two prisoners and when they reached the jail, gave Cobb a warning. "If you let these men go—or any of the prisoners, for that matter—I'll see you in their place!" He turned to John and gave a final triumphant sneer. "Now, Bunyan, we'll see how your God gets you out of this!"

Cobb had a troubled look on his face and as soon as Foster left, he said, "Mr. Bunyan, you heard what he said."

"Yes, I did." Bunyan put his hand on the jailer's shoulder. "Don't grieve, Cobb. You must keep the law—but God will be with us."

Cobb shook his head dolefully and turned to lead the two men to the cell. "I don't know, sir. That's what you said back ten years ago—but you're still here." He opened the heavy door and stepped back. "Makes a man wonder. I mean, here's Dr. Foster and Judge Wingate outside, and you and others like you in jail." He scratched his head furiously, then spread his arms wide in an eloquent gesture of despair. "Sometimes it makes me think God don't care much what happens to poor people."

"Never think that, Cobb!" Bunyan had stepped inside the cell but turned at the jailer's words. His dark eyes glowed with the fire that lay deep inside his breast. "Jesus is the friend of sinners! A friend that sticketh closer than a brother!" He waved his hand at the dank cell. "'Tis better to be with Jesus in here than to be without him in the palace!"

Cobb stared at the preacher, his face a study of doubt. He could not boast either intellect or moral force, yet he had seen John Bunyan endure more than ten years of unjust imprisonment without losing faith. He nodded slowly.

"I'll see you get some fresh straw, you and this young man." He closed the door and walked back into the room that served him for an office. Sitting down in his chair, he stared at the wall blankly for some time, then finally whispered, "He's a fearsome man, this John Bunyan!"

One evening at Wakefield, Gavin came to say at dinner, "Bad news—Mr. Bunyan is back in Bedford Jail. He was taken three days ago."

Jenny asked at once, "What about Evan?"

"He's in jail, too." Gavin shook his head morosely. "They're out for blood this time!" he said angrily. "Both of them might be transported for life!"

Jenny felt a cold hand close around her heart and Angharad saw her face grow pale. Later she said to Jenny, "God will take care of him." But she saw that Jenny was greatly troubled, and there was no more she could say. Later she and Hope spoke of it and Hope said, "She's very concerned about Evan, isn't she, Mother?"

"Aye, and I fear for him myself. He's really a new believer, Hope, and I can't help but wonder if it isn't too soon for him to go through the fire."

Twenty-One

DOUBTING CASTLE

Any man would have found Bedford Jail a frightful place, but for Evan Morgan, being cooped up in the fetid den was pure torture!

He had visited Bunyan in the common cell, of course, but those had been only brief times. After a week Evan knew that it would take all his faith to endure the prison. He had been a man of the out-of-doors all his life, but now to be deprived of fresh air, of the grass and trees and the open sky! Even on the second day he was driven to spend most of his waking hours at the iron-grated window, staring at the world outside.

Mary and Elizabeth came in the afternoon, bringing food and encouragement. While John and his wife talked, Mary sat down beside Evan, who was at the window. "I hope you like the food we brought," she said, turning her sightless eyes toward him. Feeling the slight breeze, she asked, "Do you spend a great deal of time here, looking outside?"

"Yes, I do." Evan came to sit down and began to eat, listening as Mary spoke about things that filled her life. He was always amazed at the joy that flowed out of this young woman. "I'm a little depressed today, Mary. I spent a few days in jail when I was a young man, but this is different." The thought of the future loomed grimly in front of him and his food was tasteless. "I know your father's been here for years, but I fear my faith's not as strong as his."

"God will be with you, Evan," Mary responded quickly. "You're in here because you're faithful to his Word, and one day you'll see the fruit of all this."

"In heaven?" Evan asked and made a wry face. "That seems a long way off." He laughed shortly, a little ashamed of himself. "Forgive me. Here I am, in jail *one day,* and already complaining. I won't do it again."

After Mary and Elizabeth left, Evan moved away from the window and came to sit beside Bunyan, who looked up from the Bible he was reading. "That Bible of yours is falling apart, Mr. Bunyan," he remarked.

A twinkle lit Bunyan's large eyes. "I think if you see a man whose Bible is falling apart, you'll find a man who *isn't!* It's the Bible that keeps me from breaking, Evan."

"Teach me some more," Evan said, then smiled, his face half hidden in the darkness of the cell. "Lots of young ministers would like to have Bishop Bunyan for a teacher. If I can't learn like this, with ample time and a good teacher, why, I'm a dunce!"

Bunyan smiled broadly. "We'll both learn, Evan. The trick is to take it one day at a time."

Looking around the cell, which was crowded with more than sixty prisoners, Evan remarked wryly, "I don't see how we can do other than that."

"Most wisdom is simple." Bunyan nodded. "Today we've got food, we've got a roof over our head. Neither of us is sick and we're not under sentence of death. We've got each other to share the Lord Jesus." He looked around at the prisoners and smiled. "And we've got a congregation who won't walk out on our sermons, no matter how much they disagree with our doctrine!"

Evan was warmed by Bunyan's cheerful spirit. "I see what you mean, Mr. Bunyan. But—don't you *ever* get discouraged or afraid?"

"Afraid? Certainly I fear. When I was threatened with hanging, I thought I'd make a scrabbling shift of it when I had to climb the ladder—pale face and tottering knees! And I grieve being cut off from my ministry." Bunyan's round face grew solemn and he nodded sadly. "And of course, being cut off from my family—that's very hard!"

The voices of the prisoners made a humming noise almost like bees, and the bars of yellow sunshine that fell across the floor of the cell illuminated their faces. Bunyan studied the other men with compassion, then turned to face Evan. "When I first came here, I nearly lost my mind worrying about my family. I thought I was pulling the house down on their heads! But finally I prayed, 'O God, I must venture all for you!' And that's my prayer to this day—to venture all for Jesus Christ!"

The two men sat together and Evan listened as the older man poured his wisdom out. *As long as I have John Bunyan beside me,* he thought, *I'll be able to bear this place!*

Evan stared morosely out of the window, gripping the steel bars until his hands ached. He had never grown accustomed to the vermin that swarmed in the foul straw covering the floor, and he released his grip to claw at his sides. There was no way to keep the fleas from biting, and though he knew that scratching only made the thing worse, he could not refrain.

"Blast you to the pit!" he muttered, clawing at his beard, which was also infested. Shaving was a torture, for he had only cold water and a dull razor, so he had let his beard grow for the first time. Now he wished he had not, for he fancied he could feel tiny feet moving under the tangled whiskers.

Outside, the moon was sullenly hidden behind thin skeins of

dark clouds. He peered vainly at the sky but saw no sign of stars. Slumping down, he rested his face against his forearms, trying to ignore the dark cloud of depression that seemed more concrete than the clouds in the sky. The weeks and months had passed and he tried to feel that his confinement had been a good thing. But at times like this he could almost hear the laughter of demons, and in dreams he heard sly, persuasive voices whisper, *Give up, Evan Morgan! What good are you doing? How can rotting in this place make God happy? If you could only get outside, you could be of some use. But if you die here, who will be the better for it?*

Evan heard them now and with a mighty effort to shut them out, bit the flesh of his forearm until the pain grew unendurable. "Fine!" he muttered. "I'm biting myself like a mad dog!" He lifted his head, stared into the ebony sky, then went back to sit down, slumping wearily beside Bunyan, who was writing carefully by the dim light of a candle.

The *scratch-scratch* of the quill raked across Evan's nerves and finally he broke the silence. "I've been thinking about something," he said. His voice was rusty with disuse and he leaned over and took a sip of tepid water from the bucket the two of them shared. He had not slept for several nights, no more than a few fitful naps, and his mind seemed almost paralyzed. But he had been thinking and now said doggedly, "We are missing souls, it seems to me."

"Missing souls?"

"I mean, we preach to the other prisoners, of course, but they're mostly saved men."

At once Bunyan's eyes narrowed and he carefully laid down his quill and leaned back against the damp stone wall. "And you think if we were free, we'd be able to preach to more people. Is that it, Evan?"

"Why, it makes sense, doesn't it?"

"God's ways rarely make sense," Bunyan replied, a sharpness in his tone. "You know your Bible better than to say such a thing! It didn't make sense for Jesus to die on a cross!"

Evan squinted in the dim light, noting that Bunyan's face was etched with fatigue. The bad food and lack of exercise had worn him down, but his eyes were steady. Still Evan argued his point. "No, of course it didn't—but he *had* to die. It was the Father's will."

"As it is God's will for some to suffer. The blood of the martyrs is the seed of the church. If William Tyndale had used common sense, he'd never have given his life to get the Scriptures into the hands of the English people."

Evan was half angry, not at Bunyan so much as at himself. He knew that Bunyan suffered worse than he himself did, for Bunyan had a family as a burden. He lowered his head and stared at the dirty floor

He sat thus for so long that Bunyan looked up and studied his young friend. Despite his own hardships, he felt a sharp pity toward Evan Morgan. For some time he sat in the murky darkness of the cell, the flickering candle making the planes of his face seem craggy, his eyes shadowed in deep sockets. Bunyan had learned to seek God for all things and now prayed silently for some words that might bring comfort to his young companion.

"Evan," he said finally, "I've been working on my Pilgrim book. I'd like to read you some of it."

For months Bunyan had been working on a book that was different from anything he had ever written. He'd read parts of it to Mary and Elizabeth. They had listened eagerly, seemingly fascinated by the story. It concerned a man called Christian, who was a symbol for all men. In the beginning of the story, Christian appeared with a huge burden on his back—a burden that represented his sins—and set out to flee from the City of Destruction. He had heard of a Celestial City and determined to find it but almost at once fell into a Slough of Despond where he almost perished.

"Let me read you again how Christian loses his burden," Bunyan said. Leafing through the sheaf of papers to the beginning, he began to read:

> "Now I saw in my dream that the highway up which Christian had to go was fenced on either side with a wall that was called Salvation. Up this way, therefore, did burdened Christian run, but not without difficulty, because of the load on his back.
>
> "He ran thus till he came to a place somewhat ascending; and upon that place stood a cross, and a little below, in the bottom, a sepulcher. So I saw in my dream, that just as Christian came up with the cross, his burden loosed from off his shoulders, and fell from off his back, and began to tumble, and so continued to do till it came to the mouth of the sepulcher, where it fell in, and I saw it no more."

Evan looked at Bunyan and managed a smile. "I remember when the burden fell from my own back," he whispered. "What a glorious day that was!"

"For all of us," Bunyan agreed. "But God does more than forgive us of our sins. That's the first work and no man can go to heaven unless he's found the cross of Jesus. But do you remember those most wonderful verses in the fifth chapter of Romans, verses eight through ten?"

"I can't call them to mind."

Bunyan quoted, "'But God commendeth his love toward us, in that, while we were yet sinners, Christ died for us. Much more then, being now justified by his blood, we shall be saved from wrath through him. For if, when we were enemies, we were reconciled to God by the death of his Son, much more, being reconciled, we shall be saved by his life.'" Bunyan let the words linger in the air, then said softly, "Do you understand, Evan? We are *reconciled* to God by the death of Jesus on the cross—but we are *saved* by his life."

"I don't grasp it, Mr. Bunyan."

"Why, the Christian life is in two parts for us all. The first part is the new birth, and that takes place when the blood of Jesus washes us from our sins. It takes but a moment of faith, as my hero Christian knew when he looked at the cross. Anyone who repents and calls on God claiming the blood of Jesus—why, he's born into the kingdom of God!"

"I see that. But the second part?"

"Evan, *after* a person is saved, he has to live—either until death takes him or the Lord Jesus comes to reign on the earth. And how are we to bear our trials until one of those things happens?" Bunyan's face glowed, the amber light of the candle reflected in his eyes. "Why, as the verse says, we are *saved by his life.* That's why we must have God's Holy Spirit every hour and day of our lives, brother! No man can live for God without the Spirit!"

The two whispered for some time, Bunyan encouraging Evan to let God have his total being. Finally Evan closed his eyes and leaned his head back against the cold stones. "I feel—as though I've missed my way, Mr. Bunyan," he whispered. "At first, I felt close to God. Jesus was so *real* to me! But now—I can't think and God seems so far away."

"Don't despair, my friend," Bunyan urged. He hesitated, then went on, "God is more pleased when we trust him at those times when we have little or no sense of his presence than when we trust because we sense a great manifestation of his presence."

"But I long for the sense of his presence!"

"Certainly! But think of David. How many times in the Psalms does he cry out, asking, 'Where are you God? Why have you forsaken me?'" Bunyan let the question hang in the silence of the cell, then said, "I think, Evan, God whispers to us in our prosperity—but he shouts to us in our trials."

"Then why can't I *hear* him?"

"There is a thing called the dark night of the soul," Bunyan answered slowly. "I know a little about it, though others have gone through it for much longer than I."

"The dark night of the soul? What does it mean?"

"Simply that God separates himself from a person so that the believer has no sense at all of the presence of God. And when we *still* trust him, even when we have no joy nor sense that God is with us—why, that's when our Father is most pleased with us!"

Evan stared at Bunyan. "It's the worst of all this, isn't it?"

"Yes, but remember, it's not our *sense* of God that's important. Oh, he gives that sometimes in a marvelous way. But there are other times when he lets us know loneliness even from him." Bunyan spoke of the need of trusting God in dark times and finally said, "Let me read you another episode of my hero, the stout Christian." He thumbed through the sheaf of papers and found his place. "Now, you may remember that Christian had a friend named Hopeful, who joined him on his way to the Celestial City?"

"Yes, I remember."

"Well, let me read you about an experience that the two pilgrims encountered." He began to read, his voice low, but intent:

> "Now the way was rough, and their feet tender because of their travels, and the souls of the pilgrims were much discouraged because of the way. Wherefore still as they went on, they wished for a better way. Now a little before them there was, on the left hand of the road, a meadow, and a stile to go over into it, and that meadow's called By-path

Meadow. 'Here is the easiest going,' said Christian. 'Let us go over.'

"'But now if this path lead us out of the way?'

"'That is not likely,' Christian said, so persuaded Hopeful to leave the road. At first the way was easy, but before long they came to a deep pit which was on purpose to catch fools who left the way. They floundered along the way, at last lighting under a little shelter where they fell asleep, being very weary.

"They were awakened by a rude voice, and were alarmed to see a fearful giant who said with a grim and surly voice, 'You have trespassed on my grounds and must come with me.'

"He took them to a castle, which was called Doubting Castle, and put them into a dark dungeon, nasty and stinking. Here they lay from Wednesday morning until Saturday night, without one drop of drink or bit of bread or any light."

"I think I can guess where you got that scene from," Evan interrupted. He gestured at the cell where they lay. "It's Bedford Jail, I doubt not."

"Yes, it is." Bunyan nodded. "I put in my little book that which I know." He continued to read and Evan paid close heed.

"Now Giant Despair was the name of the giant, and he had a wife named Diffidence. She told her husband to beat his prisoners, and he arose in the morning and got him a grievous crab-tree cudgel, and going into the dungeon, beat them fearfully. He left them to mourn under their distress, and they spent their time in nothing but sighs and bitter lamentations."

"As I've been doing," Evan said with some shame.

"As we *all* do at times," Bunyan replied. "But hear the rest of my tale."

> "The next day Giant Despair came to the two pilgrims, telling them that their only way out of Doubting Castle was to make an end of themselves. He beat them again so that indeed they had no hope. When he went back to bed, he said to his wife, 'They are sturdy rogues!'
>
> "And she said, 'Take them tomorrow and show them the skulls of those thou hast dispatched.'
>
> "So when the morning came, Giant Despair took the two into the Castle Yard and showed them the skulls. 'These wee pilgrims were as you are once, and they trespassed in my grounds as you have done. And when I thought fit, I tore them to pieces; and so within ten days I will do to you.'
>
> "With that he thrust Christian and Hopeful into their foul dungeon, where they at once began to pray."

"And does that sound somewhat like you and me, brother Evan?" Bunyan looked up to ask.

"Yes, very much. My bones are sore from the beating I have taken. I have been wallowing in doubt—and somehow I've gotten off my road—just as your pilgrims."

"Then hear the end of this adventure."

> "A little before day, good Christian, as one half amazed, brake out into this passionate speech: 'What a fool am I to lie in a stinking dungeon, when I may as well walk at liberty! I have a key in my bosom called Promise, that will, I am persuaded, open any lock in Doubting Castle!' He pulled a key from his bosom, and at once tried the dungeon door,

> whose bolt, as he turned the key, gave back and the door flew open with ease—and Christian and Hopeful came out!"

Bunyan put his arm around Evan. "We will read the Word of God together, until we find a key—and then we will unlock the gates of Bedford Jail, even as Christian unlocked the iron gates of Doubting Castle!"

Twenty-Two

"Come and Help Us!"

As the weeks drew on, Evan had to force himself to keep the goal of finding a promise in the Scripture foremost in his mind. The winter of 1671 was fierce, with snow drifting two feet high around the jail. Bunyan and Morgan wrapped themselves in blankets, but their lips grew blue with cold and their fingers became so numb that they could not feel the pages of the Bibles they tried to read.

Had it not been for the help they received from Bunyan's family and from the Wakefields, they might not have survived. They shared their food with those who had less help, but several men died as the winter ground on through December.

Angharad came to see them once, bringing warm garments and nourishing food. She appeared without warning, and Evan thought for one brief moment he was seeing an apparition as she came to stand over him.

"Well, how's the old man?" She smiled down at him, using the fond name she'd given him long ago. "Still in the world, are you now?"

Despite the stiffness of his joints, Evan got to his feet with alacrity. "Angharad!" he whispered and then she came to his arms. "I can't believe it's you!"

He held her at arm's length to stare into her face. She was

wearing a blue wool cloak with a hood but now pushed the hood down so that her thick black hair caught the gleam of pale sunlight that filtered through the barred window.

"Sit you down and eat," Angharad prompted as she took a seat on a stool beside him. "Good hot beef broth and fresh bread. And plenty to share with Mr. Bunyan and some of the others—so fill yourself." She watched with a slight smile as he ate, giving him news from Wakefield. He asked about everyone. Except for one person. "And aren't you going to ask about Jenny?" Angharad finally asked, her dark eyes fixed on him.

"Why—yes," Evan said. "Is she married?"

"No, not married."

"I thought she might be." Evan looked down at the remains of the food, then glanced up. "I could never fool you, could I? You know how I feel about her."

"Yes, *I* know how you feel, but does Jenny?"

Evan shrugged his shoulders in a restless manner. "What good to tell her? She's in love with Amos."

"I don't know that she is—and neither do you." Angharad studied Evan's lean face and said forcefully, "If she loved him, she'd marry him, isn't it so?"

Slowly Evan shook his head. "No matter. I can't marry, Angharad. Who'd want a husband who is in jail?" When she attempted to say more, he changed the subject so abruptly that she knew better than to force the matter.

"I didn't come just to bring food, Evan," Angharad said, her countenance growing serious. "God has spoken to me about you."

Evan looked startled, but listened intently. "Oh, Angharad, I *need* to hear from God! What did he say?"

She shook her head slowly. "'It is the glory of God to conceal a thing: but the honour of kings is to search out a matter.'" She saw a puzzled look on Evan's face. "That's the second verse of

Proverbs, chapter twenty-five. I woke up in the middle of the night and it was in my mind. I prayed and God assured me that it was the verse for you." She saw disappointment on his face. "I don't know what it means—except that God wants you to search for him."

"But—I *have* been searching."

"Perhaps you're tempted to give up, then, and God sent me to encourage you to keep at it. God is going to use you mightily, Evan! I know that in my spirit. But some people give up just before God is ready to reveal himself to them. Let us pray that you'll find your honor by searching until you find the thing that God wants for you."

Angharad stayed for some time, speaking with Bunyan and distributing the food and blankets she had brought. When she left, Bunyan said thoughtfully, "A woman of God, Evan! Why, a man can *feel* the Spirit of God flowing out of her!" He listened carefully as Evan shared what Angharad had told him, then said forcefully, "Hang on to that, man! It's clear that God is going to do something!"

A sense of excitement and hope came to Evan Morgan from that moment. He had become a man of prayer, but now he poured out his heart to God with a faith that had been missing. December passed and 1672 came. On the surface all seemed the same—but Evan knew that he was about to hear from God.

The word of the Lord came to him very simply. He had been reading the book of Acts, the sixteenth chapter. When he read the ninth verse, something seemed to flash into his mind. He read the verse aloud: "'And a vision appeared to Paul in the night; there stood a man of Macedonia, and prayed him, saying, Come over into Macedonia, and help us.'"

Closing his eyes, Evan sat quietly, letting the verse sink into his spirit. Bunyan had taught him that meditation was the only way to grasp the spiritual sense of the Bible. "Anyone can learn what the verse *says,*" he had remarked. "But only the Spirit can teach us what the Father *means* by the words."

For several days Evan pondered the verse, saying nothing to Bunyan or his other companions. He knew that God was preparing his heart to receive something that would change his life.

He was prepared to pray for as long as it took, and when the answer came after Angharad's visit, it was as clear as if it had been printed on a page. Evan was standing at the window, staring out at the frozen ground, thinking about the Scripture, and into his mind leaped a part of the verse—with one small change: *Come over to Wales and help us.*

So forcefully did the thought come that Evan spoke aloud, as if someone had whispered in his ear.

"What?" Then he realized that the words had not been audibly spoken. He stood very still, waiting, and again the words came: *Come over to Wales and help us.*

There had been a time when Evan Morgan would have shouted his experience aloud to any who would hear, but prison had tempered him. He kept the event in his heart for two days and at the end of that time, he was as certain of God's will as he was of his own name.

"Mr. Bunyan," he said quietly as the two had finished their devotional early in the morning, "God has given me the key."

Bunyan gave him a startled look. "The key to get your freedom? What is it?"

"God has called me to preach his gospel in Wales."

At once the force of the thing struck Bunyan. "Of course! You can leave at once!"

"Yes, and with no shame." The officials had long said that any of the dissenters who would leave Bedford and give their word not to preach in the area would be released. Until now, Evan had refused. Now he was overwhelmed with the wonder of the way in which God Almighty worked his will. He turned to Bunyan.

"It's hard to leave you here, sir, but I must be obedient to the call of God!" Tears came into his eyes as he gazed on his mentor and friend. "I do hate to leave you in this place, Mr. Bunyan!"

Bunyan put his arm around the young man's shoulders. "We are both the servants of the Most High God. He will deliver me in his good timing. I only thank him that you will soon be preaching Jesus Christ to your people!"

Charles II had never wished to punish the supporters of Oliver Cromwell. From the time he came to the throne he had attempted to modify the harsh measures that the Cavalier parliament imposed on dissenters, but without much success. All of his efforts were frustrated by the reinstated bishops or by others in power who sought vengeance.

Despite all of this, at the beginning of 1672 Charles ran a great risk. He issued a second Declaration of Indulgence. Two years earlier he had made a secret treaty with France in which he had agreed to declare himself a Catholic and restore Catholicism in England in return for secret subsidies from Louis XIV. Perhaps the Declaration of Indulgence was an attempt on the part of the king to prepare the people of England for freedom of worship for Catholics. Whatever the reason, this declaration resulted in the release of hundreds of prisoners.

Judge Francis Wingate entered Bedford jail unannounced. Cobb looked at him, startled. Well he knew it was not the judge's custom to visit prisoners.

"Why—Your Honor, I'm surprised to see you!"

Wingate nodded. "Cobb, bring Mr. Bunyan out. I want to speak with him in private."

"Right away, Your Honor!"

Wingate entered the small room Cobb used for an office, but

did not sit down. There was a tense expression on his face. When the door opened, he said, "Mr. Bunyan, it's been a long time."

"Good day to you, Judge." Bunyan nodded. He was wearing a dark suit of heavy wool and looked rather tired. "It has been a long time."

A silence fell on the room and Wingate suddenly exclaimed, "You are the most stubborn man I've ever known!"

Amusement touched Bunyan's eyes. "I prefer to think of myself as *firm,* Judge. I am *firm*—other men are *stubborn.*"

In spite of himself Wingate had to smile. "You still have your rather waspish humor, I see."

"'A merry heart doeth good like a medicine.'"

"Yes, I suppose." He looked at Bunyan curiously. "Twelve years you've been in this foul place?"

"Yes, Judge."

"And at any time you could have left to be with your family!"

"But I could not have kept my honor."

Wingate seemed to flinch. He had spent sleepless nights thinking about this man. More than once he had asked himself who had the more honor, the judge or the tinker—and the answer had not been pleasant to contemplate.

"And suppose you are forced to stay here for another twelve years?"

"I would be grieved, but God knows my life, sir. If I can serve him better in this place than outside, I will stay."

Wingate didn't move. He seemed fixed to the floor, almost paralyzed. A sense of shame came to him—not for the first time—and he shook his head. When he spoke, his tone was thin and weary. "I regret my part in your confinement."

Surprised, Bunyan studied the countenance of the other man. "Why, sir, you are not at fault. It is the system."

"I'm glad you think so, but I cannot be so kind to myself." Wingate pulled himself upright and a lighter expression came to his face. "I am a harbinger of good news, Mr. Bunyan." Reaching into the pocket of his coat, he drew forth a roll, which he then spread out. "This has just come from London, fresh from the king." He moved to stand beside Bunyan, holding the paper before him. "Read it, sir. I daresay you will find it good news indeed."

Bunyan read the words, then started. "Why—it's a Declaration of Indulgence!"

"Yes, and from this moment, John Bunyan, you are a free man. And thank God for it!"

Bunyan began to tremble. His eyes grew dim with tears, which he hastily wiped away. "Are you certain? Could it not be just another false political trick?"

"No! And to show you how real it is, you can walk out of this jail right now!" Wingate's voice was strong. "Go man! Go to your family!"

It took only a few minutes for Bunyan to collect his few belongings; thirty minutes later he was standing in front of his house. He bit his lip, his spirit filled with joy—and with apprehension. "Lord, is it true? Am I to be free of that place?" A sense of peace filled him, and he ran at once toward the door. Opening it, he saw Elizabeth turn from where she stood. She began to tremble and he moved to take her in his arms. She wept and clung to him, asking, "John—what is it? How long can you stay?"

Bunyan held his wife tightly, whispering, "I can stay with you for the rest of my life, dear heart!"

"Evan! Is it yourself?" Angharad had answered the knock at the door, expecting to find a carpenter she'd sent for to mend a door. Instead, she'd been shocked to see her nephew.

"Yes, Angharad. I'm free."

"Come you inside! Come now, old man, let me hear it!"

Evan allowed Angharad to fuss over him. When the two of them were having hot tea in the kitchen, he finally was able to tell of his calling. Angharad listened with wide eyes and when he finished, tears came to her eyes. "Glory to God! A minister to Wales, is it? I would that your good father and your cousin were alive this day. There is proud of you, they'd be!"

"If you hadn't come to me, Angharad, I'd have given up, I think."

The two of them talked for an hour about Evan's plans. Finally Angharad leaned back and scrutinized her nephew. The strain of his stay in jail was evident on his face. "Wales will wait! You'll stay here for a few days and give your family a share of yourself!" She hesitated and added, "Jenny's not here. She's gone to London with Hope and Susanne. You'll want to see all three of them."

Evan agreed and for the next two days he enjoyed visiting with Gavin. The two of them spent much time speaking of Bunyan and his family. Gavin had heard rumors of the new law that might set Bunyan free and Angharad had insisted, "God will set him free."

Knowing that he would be gone from England for a long time, perhaps for good, Evan filled himself with the things he treasured at Wakefield. He renewed his friendships with the servants and on the third day, he took a bow and went hunting. The spring had not quite arrived, but tiny shoots of green had pierced the frozen earth and golden buds were awaiting the touch of the summer sun to explode into blossoms.

Leaving at dawn, he roamed the hills all morning, killing a large buck shortly after two o'clock. He tied it to his horse and made his way back to Wakefield, tired but happy. As he reached the outskirts of the estate, leading the animal, he was startled to hear his name. "Hello, Evan." He turned quickly to see Jenny standing beside the path. "I'm glad to see you," she said quietly.

"Jenny!" Evan tied the horse to a sapling and went to her at once. She was wearing a thick fur coat with a hood that framed her face, and as he came close, she put out her gloved hands. Evan took them, pressed them, then stared at her. "I've missed you," he managed to say.

"Have you?"

"Yes." Evan had forgotten how smooth her skin was and how beautiful her green eyes. Her lips were full and red, and he forced himself to say, "There were times in the jail I'd have given ten years of my life just to see you like this."

Jenny studied Evan's face, noting the marks of suffering. He was lean and as fine looking as ever, but now there was a maturity and a strength in him. "Come," she said quickly. "I want to hear everything!"

Evan went to his horse and hoisted the deer to his shoulders. Jenny walked beside Evan to the house, where he surrendered the buck to one of the servants, who set about dressing it at once.

"Come on," Jenny said, touching Evan's arm. "Let's go to the tower. We can be alone there." She led him to the tallest tower of the castle. When they stood looking out over the rolling countryside, she suddenly turned and smiled at him. "Do you remember the times we came here?"

"Yes." Evan gave a smile that made him look much younger. "I remember once I found you here crying."

"Yes. Thomas Matthews had teased me about my red hair and my heart was broken."

"You were going to cut it off as I remember."

Jenny laughed, her eyes suddenly merry and a dimple breaking the smoothness of her cheek. "Yes, and you called me a fool."

"And you slapped me." Evan grinned. "I think you took it out on me that Thomas teased you. I wanted to spank you, but I didn't."

"You should have. I was a beast to you!"

"I thought of that day once, when I was very downhearted. I think it was just before this Christmas." Evan grew thoughtful and his dark eyes came to rest on her face. "I thought of you as a little girl, of your ragged face and haunted eyes the day you came out of the woods. And then I thought of you as you are now . . . a lovely woman."

Jenny blinked with surprise, for Evan had rarely commented on her beauty. "I—I thought of you, too, Evan," she said. She found that she was stirred by his presence and this disturbed her. With a sigh, she turned to look out the window again. "We had some good times, didn't we—when I was growing up?"

"Aye, we did indeed."

The two of them stood quietly, watching the cows as they moved across the fields. The air was still and the setting sun shed crimson gleams over the landscape. The small pond in the pasture became a scarlet mirror, reflecting the dying sun.

The quietness of the hour sank into Evan. He leaned on the parapet stones, letting the peace sink into his soul. He was intensely aware of Jenny, who stood so close that he could feel the pressure of her arm on his.

"Now come on," she said. "Tell me everything."

He began to speak, detailing his stay in jail and his lessons with Bunyan. He found her as ready a listener as always. Soon they went to sit down on a bench, and she kept her eyes fixed on him as he spoke of his trials. When he related how Angharad had come to encourage him, she said, "I wish I'd come to visit you. I should have."

"It's not a nice place to visit."

"I know . . . but you'd have come to me if I'd been there." She turned to him and he saw that her eyes were glimmering with tears. Her full lips were trembling and she put her hand on his arm. "Wouldn't you have come, Evan?"

"I'd come to you anytime!"

She reached up and touched his cheek, her voice more gentle than the cooing of the doves. "You were always good to me, Evan! I'll never forget how you took care of me when I was a little girl!"

Evan knew at that moment that this was the only woman in the world for him. He reached out and took her in his arms and felt the quickening of her heartbeat. He looked deep into her eyes, aware that he could no longer hide his love from her. He fully expected her to pull away from him, but she did not. He struggled with himself, then gave up all his fine resistance and lowered his head—slowly, tenderly—to savor his first kiss with the woman who owned his heart.

Her lips were soft and warm under his, her body soft and pliant. Holding her was like nothing he'd ever known, for she was an endless softness. And yet . . . the rapture that swept him was bittersweet, for he knew he could never have her. Her hand rested on the back of his neck and she gave him her lips with a eagerness that surprised him.

And then her lips slid away from him and she moved away. The scent of her hair seemed to envelop him, and he swallowed painfully, leaning back against the wall. He closed his eyes, willing his pounding heart to slow and his ragged breathing to even. After a moment he opened his eyes, drinking in the picture she made as she stood near the window. His heart was awash with a poignant ache, and he whispered, "I'm sorry, Jenny. I—shouldn't have done that."

She looked at him quickly, as though displeased. "Why offer regrets, Evan? Surely you've kissed other women." Her cold tones struck him as though with a physical force.

"You're not like other women," he protested. "Not to me!"

Jenny stood looking at him. She had been deeply shaken by his kiss. She knew she could have turned away, could have disallowed the encounter. But when she'd realized he planned to kiss her, something in her had cried out to surrender—and she had done so without hesitation. She could not deny that she had found a wild sweetness in his embrace . . . a sweetness that apparently, considering his apology and the troubled expression on his face, he had not shared.

"What's the matter, Evan?" she asked quietly.

He wanted desperately to say so much to her, to tell her of the love for her that had grown within him—but he could not.

What have you got to offer a woman? he thought bitterly. *No money, no home. You'll always be poor. No woman in her right mind would turn down a rich man like Amos for one such as I.*

"Nothing's wrong," he said, a heaviness in his tone that brought a frown to Jenny's face. Again he studied her, mentally saying good-bye to his hopes, then went on. "I'll be leaving for Wales tomorrow . . . so we'd best say good-bye now, Jenny."

Hurt shot through her that he could so callously dismiss what they had just shared. Indeed, if he could bid her farewell with so little emotion, he could not have been as affected by their embrace as was she. So be it, then. She would bid him good-bye with equal distance and never let him know how his kiss had moved her. Straightening, she responded in even tones, "We'll miss you, Evan."

There was an equanimity—and a finality—in her voice that struck Evan deeply. He could not face the idea of never seeing her again . . . any more than he could face the hurt he saw in her eyes. He wanted to go to her, to draw her into an embrace that would leave her breathless, to inform her that he would never let her go.

But he could do none of that. Getting to his feet, he held out his arm. She moved forward stiffly and slipped her hand through it, and he turned to lead her down the steps.

The next day, when the time for his departure came, his family bid him a warm farewell. With Jenny, however, the parting was formal. She waited until he was gone, then walked slowly to the tower. She watched him ride away, and as he disappeared in the distance, she whispered, "Why did you kiss me like that, Evan?" She felt the sting of tears in her eyes but dashed them fiercely away as she turned and ran down the steps.

Twenty-Three

The Last Temptation

George Fairchild looked more like a butcher than a successful theatre manager. He stuffed his bulging muscles into fine clothes, but his hands, thick and raw, could not be concealed. He had donned a fine plum-colored velvet suit for his visit to the palace, but the attendants had given him suspicious looks when he asked to see Mistress Nell Gwyn.

"Just let Mistress Gwyn know that Georgie Fairchild wants to see her," Fairchild said with a confident nod. The guard snorted, but he knew that Nell was fond of her old friends, so he moved to forward the request. He was back almost at once with a more polite air. "Mistress Gwyn will see you, sir."

Fairchild chuckled and nudged the tall guard in the ribs. "Told you, didn't I? Nellie's not like some who forget their old friends!" He walked beside the guard, adding confidentially, "Why, it was me that found her, man! She wasn't no more than fifteen, but she had what it takes to be an actress. I poured myself into that girl, I tell you! And it was a sorry day for George Fairchild when the king seen her!" He sighed heavily, his thick lips pouting. "I needed Nellie for my plays, but—" Fairchild winked lewdly and nudged the guard in the ribs again—"but I reckon the king needed her worse, eh?"

"I suppose so, sir." The guard smiled noncommittally. He came to a huge oak door and nodded at it. "Mistress Nell says you're to go in."

"Right!" Fairchild shouldered his way through the door and looked around curiously at the enormous room that was flooded with sunlight from the dozen windows set symmetrically along the walls. Four of these windows were bay windows with covered seats and cushions. Four large fireplaces sent colored smokes that were highly scented through the air. The floor was a chessboard of gleaming marble and was lightly covered with matting and several rich Turkish carpets. The ceiling was composed of plaster work, measured with spaces for ornate designs worked in gleaming gold and silver.

"Watch out you don't swallow your tongue, Georgie!"

Fairchild pulled his attention from the opulence of the room and turned it to the woman who sat with her feet pulled under her on a couch covered with yellow silk. Nell smiled, revealing a set of gleaming white teeth—a minor miracle in a day when even royalty endured rotten, discolored teeth.

"Nellie, you're more beautiful than ever. Blast me if you're not!"

Nell laughed with delight. "You must want something, Georgie," she said, a knowing look in her eyes. "That's the only time you speak so sweet to me."

"Now, Nellie, be fair!" Fairchild came to kiss her hand, then plopped himself down beside her with a familiar air. "I was the first to spot you, wasn't I? Who was it but me who seen what a gell you'd be if you was cleaned up and had a little help?"

"Yes, I give you that, Georgie." Nell smiled, for her memories of Fairchild, who had brought her into the world of the theatre after the Restoration, were fond. She well knew that if it had not been for the man sitting beside her, she'd be no more than one of the prostitutes that swarmed the streets of London. "I haven't forgotten, Georgie—and I never will."

"That's me, Nellie!" Fairchild nodded with his chops set in a wide grin. He looked around, studying the richness of the gleaming furniture and the glow of silver and gold in the room. "A long way from the old days, eh, Nellie! Never thought you'd be in a place like this, did you now?"

"No, I never did," Nell admitted. Her full lips turned up in a smile and she leaped up from the couch. "Come here, Georgie, let me show you something." She moved across the vast room, pausing before what seemed to be a tent made of highly embroidered green silk. Pulling the panel back, she giggled, "Look at this. Did you ever see such a jordan in all your life?"

Fairchild peered into what was the most ornate privy closet he'd ever seen. Inside was a great thronelike chair, all padded with velvet. It was studded with gems and padded with goose down, and he could see that the chamber pot beneath it was made of what seemed to be solid gold!

"Well, I never seen nothing like it," he admitted. A grin tugged at his meaty lips. "Did the king have it made just for you?"

"Oh no." Nell shrugged. "It belonged to Henry VIII."

"Is that a fact?" Fairchild stared at the privy, then shook his head. "Just think, Nellie, King Henry sat on that very spot!"

"And planned how to get rid of one of his wives, I suppose," Nell said with a laugh. She pulled him away and sent the servants for tea and cakes. After they'd enjoyed their tea, Nell made George talk of the theatre. She listened avidly, for her heart was still with the stage. "I'd love to do a play, Georgie," she admitted.

"Why don't you? You'd pack the biggest theatre in London!"

"Charles wouldn't like it. He wants me all to himself."

"Selfish, that's what he is! A woman like you needs to be seen!"

Nell gave Fairchild a careful glance. She had a great deal of intelligence, for she had had her wits sharpened in a hard school. "You want something, don't you, George?"

Fairchild shifted nervously. "Well, not to put too fine a point on it, Nellie—I do."

"What is it?"

"Why, I need a new actress. I come to ask you to do a play—but that won't do. I sees that plain enough. But I got me an idea and you can help me."

"I don't see how I can help. You know the stage better than any man alive."

Fairchild hunched his shoulders and leaned forward. "Mr. Wycherly's going to do a new play—just for me. You know what that means. People will flock to any play he writes."

"Why, that's fine, Georgie!"

"It is—and it ain't. He's a very particular man, Mr. Wycherly, and he won't let me do the play if I don't get the actors and actresses to please him."

"That should be easy enough," Nell observed. "Every actor will want to do it."

"That's what I thought at first and I got a good cast—but Mr. Wycherly, he's got his head set on the actress who'll play the lead. Says I've got to get her or he'll take his play to Tom Broadhurst."

"Who does he want?"

"He seen Jenny Clairmont back when she was on the stage—and he ain't never forgot her. Says she's born to play this here role." Disgust crossed Fairchild's thick face and he shook his head. "Ain't that something? Fifty actresses crying for the part and Wycherly wants Jenny!"

Nell was surprised, but not too much. "She had something that most of us lacked, Georgie. Kind of an innocence, I think. It came across, you remember?"

"I know it," Fairchild said grudgingly; then despair crept into his voice. "Nellie, I ain't done well lately. I needs another success to set me up and this would do it. You was Jenny's friend. What I want is for you to get her to do the play."

Nell had seen this coming and she considered it carefully. They talked for some time about strategy, and finally Nell summed up her thoughts. "Georgie, Jenny never really loved the stage. Oh, she liked the acting, but she was always disgusted with the men who came after her. At first I thought she was just waiting for her best chance, but I was wrong. She's really a good woman."

"Can't you put it to her, Nellie?"

"I can write to her. She's staying with Sir Gavin Wakefield still. But you'll have to take the letter, Georgie. I'll ask her to do it, but you'll have to persuade her."

"All right, Nellie. You write the letter and I'll do my best!"

Shortly afterward, Fairchild left the palace, Nell's letter in his pocket. He returned to his house and told his wife, "Blanche, I got to be gone for a time." He explained his mission, then sighed heavily. "I wish we was praying people! Because if I can't get Jenny to come and do this play, we're likely to wind up in the workhouse!"

Darcy Wingate lolled back on the oak bench, admiring Jenny and Hope as they tended the roses. He had arrived unexpectedly, which had become his custom over the past few months. His life at Bedford had grown increasingly boring, so he came to Wakefield, drawn by his friendship with Gavin—and his feelings for Hope.

He and the two young women had breakfasted; then he had followed them to the garden, his tablet on his knees, his quill held lightly. But he had not been able to keep his mind on the dry legal script before him.

"You're not getting any work done," Hope chided him. She

paused long enough to give him a critical look. "You're only loafing."

"Now there's where you're wrong!" Wingate put an indignant tone in his voice and lifted his tablet. "I've written a beautiful piece of work. Want to hear it?"

Hope sniffed diffidently. "I hate legal things."

"You'll like this," Wingate insisted. He held the tablet up and began to speak in a pleasant baritone voice:

"Go, lovely Rose,
Tell her that wastes her time and me,
That now she knows,
When I resemble her to thee,
How sweet and fair she seems to be.

"Tell her that's young,
And shuns to have her graces spied,
That hadst thou sprung
In deserts where no men abide,
Thou must have uncommended died.

"Small is the worth
Of beauty from the light retir'd:
Bid her come forth,
Suffer herself to be desir'd,
And not blush so to be admir'd.

"Then die, that she
The common fate of all things rare
May read in thee,
How small a part of time they share,
That are so wondrous sweet and fair."

Hope turned to Jenny, hiding her smile from Wingate. "What's your opinion of a man who sits around writing foolish poetry instead of working?"

Jenny had just cut a crimson rose and handed it to Hope. "I think he's lazy and shiftless . . . and that any girl would fair die to have a beautiful poem like that written about her."

"Hear! Hear!" Wingate applauded. "Now *there's* a woman with astute judgment!"

Hope looked at him doubtfully. She had grown very fond of Darcy Wingate, so much so that she distrusted herself. "What does it mean?" she asked. "I don't understand poetry very well. Why don't poets just come out and say things plainly?"

"Because some things can't be put in ordinary words," Wingate answered immediately. "Just to tell a lady 'You're very pretty'—why, that's *nothing!* But in a poem like this, I've said that you're as lovely as that rose you're holding."

"Meaning I'm skinny and have sharp thorns?"

"Oh for pity's sake!" Wingate groaned. "Don't you have any—any *soul,* woman?" He rose and came to look down at her. "Here I've labored to bring forth a magnificent poem—one that the Bard himself might have penned—and you miss the whole point!"

"What *is* the point?" Hope prodded him. She could not help but admire his striking features and knew that his gray eyes were laughing at her. It was this witty streak in Wingate that made her welcome his visits. Compared to him, other men seemed rather dull. "I'm like a rose—is that it?"

"It means more than that, Hope," Jenny spoke up, a smile tugging at her lips. "It means that your beauty should be seen by man, that you shouldn't hide it. A rose in the desert isn't enjoyed, so what good is its beauty there? Likewise, a beautiful woman should be seen and appreciated."

"Vanity!" Hope scoffed. "You'd have me put myself on display?"

"Nay, fair one. Hardly that," Wingate laughed. "No, what I'd do is keep you in a garden, like this one." He waved his hand at the flowers that moved in the breeze, then went on. "And I'd come here and enjoy your beauty at my leisure."

Hope's dark blue eyes flashed. "Oh? I'm to be some sort of slave? Just a pretty flower to be enjoyed when *you* have time? Is that it?"

"Zounds!" Wingate exclaimed. "You *do* have thorns! Can't you just accept my poem as a compliment and let it go? Must you be so blasted cantankerous? It isn't fitting in a woman, Hope!"

Jenny smiled and went on trimming the roses. She had seen the attraction between these two grow stronger and took pleasure in Wingate's visit. He was an honest man, and though she did not find him particularly handsome, she admired his strength and keen sense of honor. *I wouldn't be surprised to see them marry,* she thought, and then the arrival of a servant drew her attention. "What is it, Betty?"

"A gentleman to see you, Mistress Jenny," the maid replied. "His name is Mr. George Fairchild."

Jenny hesitated, then nodded. "Show him to the small sitting room, Betty. I'll be there straightaway." When the maid left, Jenny took off her gloves. Hope glanced at her friend, and something in her eyes seemed to indicate the visitor was not expected. Or welcome.

"You don't want to see him?" Hope asked.

"Oh, I don't mind." She turned to Hope with a shrug. "He's a man I knew when I was on the stage."

"I've heard of him." Wingate nodded. "He's an important man in the drama, I believe." He saw the troubled frown that creased her forehead and asked, "Like me to go with you, Jenny?"

"No, it's all right, Darcy." Jenny turned to him and said with a gleam in her eye, "The poem—it's very fine."

"Why, thank you!"

"I met Mr. Waller once."

Jenny's statement caused a flush to appear in Darcy's cheeks. Hope asked curiously, "Who is Mr. Waller?"

"I'll let Darcy explain him to you," Jenny said, then left.

Darcy at once met Hope's inquiring gaze. "Well . . . actually, he's a poet," he said carefully.

Hope's eyebrows rose in understanding. "I see. And did he write the poem about the rose?"

Darcy coughed, then straightened his back. He came to stand before her and put his hands on her shoulders. "As a matter of fact, he did."

"And you took credit for it?"

Darcy tried to look lofty. "When an artist creates a work, it belongs to the world." Seeing that she was unimpressed, he pressed on. "I think Mr. Waller should be proud that I applied his poem to you, Hope. It's almost worthy of you!"

Hope laughed aloud. "It's clear to see why you're a lawyer, Darcy! You use words to get what you want—and to get yourself out of trouble."

Darcy's expression grew somber and his eyes held her gaze. "Indeed, I am in trouble, Hope. Most serious trouble. I'm in love with you."

Hope stared at him in stunned silence. He was not joking! "And it's trouble to be in love with me?" she hedged.

"Yes, because I'm a lawyer without firm prospects and you're a member of a dynasty, a Wakefield through and through." He slipped his arms about her and gently pulled her forward. "But I'm a stubborn fellow, Hope, and sooner or later, you're going to be mine!"

Hope was stirred by the strength of the arms that held her

captive and the broad chest upon which she rested her hands. In a voice that she willed to be steady, she retorted, "And you're going to keep me in a garden?"

"Yes! That's what I want to do. A garden that is mine and mine alone." Darcy lowered his head and kissed her, and Hope found herself clinging to him. When he lifted his lips, he whispered, "Hope, I love you! Do you feel anything at all for me?"

At that moment, Hope knew of a certainty that she had found something wondrous—something she had longed for all her life. She met his eyes and, in a voice filled with tender amazement, murmured, "Yes, Darcy . . . dear Darcy. I care!"

She pulled his head down for another kiss.

Gavin Wakefield found Mr. George Fairchild quite fascinating as a dinner guest. He had been surprised when Jenny introduced her guest and had insisted that he stay for dinner. Now as the family gathered for the meal, he found that Fairchild was not only knowledgeable about the world of the theatre but also an astute observer of the political scene.

"And what about the Dutch, Mr. Fairchild?" Gavin asked, watching with some amusement as his guest devastated the huge slab of mutton that he'd severed from the joint and transferred to his plate. "Will there be another war, do you think?"

"Bound to be, Sir Gavin!" Fairchild deposited a huge chunk of meat from his knife into his mouth, then appeared to swallow it without chewing. It was, Gavin thought, like a snake swallowing his prey—for the morsel went down Fairchild's throat, which moved convulsively. Fairchild washed it down with the contents of a silver goblet, then nodded vigorously. "The Treaty of Dover settled that!"

Amos was sitting beside Jenny and looked up sharply at that. "I thought that was a secret treaty, sir?"

"Ah, some of it is. No telling what our monarch promised Louis. I suspect, though, that a goodly part of his pledge was that he would become a Catholic—or at least to lend his support to that church. Everyone knows that he leans that way—his mother was a staunch Catholic, and James, his brother, is the same. Scratch the surface of our king and you'll find a papist, sir!"

"You speak boldly, Mr. Fairchild," Wingate observed. He sat between Hope and Susanne and had kept his sharp gray eyes on the visitor. "There are those who would be afraid to speak so of Charles. But what of the Dutch?"

"Why, Louis of France paid Charles to come to his aid when he attacks Holland, and most of those inside the government think the time is near."

"Let's hope it won't happen," Gavin said, glancing at Amos. "Well, enough of politics. What of the stage, Mr. Fairchild? Tell us the latest."

Fairchild hesitated, then seemed to make a decision. "Why, Sir Gavin, that's what brought me to your house." He turned to smile at Jenny. "I've come to persuade Mistress Clairmont to return to London with me."

Amos looked up instantly, a frown on his face. He turned to Jenny, demanding, "You're not going, are you?"

Jenny flushed as they all turned to her. She had listened to Fairchild's pleas for her return. Indeed, he made a good case. Jenny liked the man, for he was one of the few who had been decent to her. In fact, he had done what he could to shield her from much of the raw aspects of the profession. When she had finally refused, he had said, "Jenny, I don't know your reasons, but this is your chance to make enough money to be secure. Just one run of this play by Mr. Wycherly and you can retire!"

Now Jenny looked at Amos. "I've got to earn my living, Amos."

"That's not a factor," Angharad spoke up at once. "You can stay with us as long as you like."

"Of course," Gavin agreed. "You more than earn your lodging with all you do around here."

But Jenny had long been concerned about her position. She knew the hospitality of the Wakefields was boundless, but it troubled her to feel she was taking advantage of them. "I haven't given Mr. Fairchild a final answer," she said quietly.

That gentleman spoke up at once, painting a fabulous picture of the success that would come if Jenny would only return to the stage. In the end, the group broke up and Amos laid his hand on Jenny's arm.

"I need to talk to you," he said and led her to a quiet place. "Now, this is the time, Jenny. I want you to marry me. The stage is no place for decent women, a fact you should know better than anyone."

Amos meant well, but his harsh words succeeded only in putting him at odds with Jenny. Had he thought more carefully about the situation, he would have realized she needed gentle words, not demands.

Now she shook her head stubbornly. "Amos, I've got to make my own way."

"Not if you marry me," he urged. "I'll take care of you. You know you love me!"

Jenny hesitated. As she considered Amos, an image of Evan came to her. She had thought of his kiss many times and now wondered what kind of woman she was to accept such a kiss when she was almost engaged to another. A thought came to her and she said, "Amos, you're going with the naval forces if war comes, aren't you?"

"Why, of course!"

"Then we don't need to think of marriage." She hesitated, then said, "When you come back, I'll give you your answer. I promise."

Amos smiled and reached out to take her in his arms. "I take that as a solemn pledge, Jenny!" He kissed her, then turned to leave the room.

Jenny watched him leave, uneasy over her commitment to Amos. The next day she went to Angharad. She found the older woman sewing and sat down to say, "Lady Wakefield, I'm confused."

"About going back to the stage?"

"Well . . . yes."

"What does your heart tell you?"

Jenny faced Angharad. "I feel it would be dangerous. It's a very hard profession and I hated most of it. The plays promulgate immoral behavior, and I felt shamed and degraded to act in them."

"What about this new play?"

"George says it's not as bad as some of the others, but it probably is bad enough." Jenny twisted her hands together, then gave a deep sigh. "Oh, I've been so—so *sheltered* here, Lady Wakefield! To go back to the stage would be like going into the fire!"

"Then don't do it, child," Angharad said instantly. She had grown to love this girl and longed to have her as a daughter-in-law. With this in mind, she asked cautiously, "How is it with you and Amos? Will you have him?"

Jenny lowered her eyes, unable to answer. Finally she met Angharad's gaze. "I've promised him I'd give him an answer after he gets back from the Dutch war. But I don't know what I'll say." She bit her lip. "Is growing up always so hard, Lady Wakefield?"

"Always," Angharad said with a smile.

Jenny left her then and went at once to find George—who took one look at her face and groaned. "You're turning me down!" he wailed.

Jenny comforted Fairchild as best she could, then sent him on his way. As she watched the coach leave the grounds, she took a deep breath. The future was not clear, but she knew that she had escaped a great snare. To have gone back on the stage would have been the easy way, and now she knew that she had burned her bridges. Slowly she turned from the window, wondering what Evan was doing. She missed him dreadfully, but there was no way she could share this part of herself with Angharad.

I wish things weren't so complicated, she thought with a sigh. She went to her room, picked up her Bible, and turned the pages almost absentmindedly until she came to the Song of Solomon. Once again the image of Evan Morgan flitted through her mind as she read: *Let him kiss me with the kisses of his mouth. . . .*

Twenty-Four

In the Cannon's Mouth

Mayor Ian Watson looked at the tall young minister with satisfaction. The church had been full, the sermon bold, and the offering overflowing. Watson, who served as the leading elder in the church, said to Rev. Ianto Ellis, "Now we've had a fine revival, Reverend, have we not?"

"Indeed we have, sir. It was a blessing when God sent Evan Morgan to Wales!"

The mayor swelled with satisfaction, then after a few more words with the pastor, moved to intercept the preacher. "A fine sermon, Reverend!" he said effusively. "Now, you must come home with me for a good dinner."

"I'll be glad to sample your good wife's cooking, Mr. Watson," Evan said, smiling. He accompanied Watson to a carriage and listened quietly as the mayor spoke enthusiastically about the healthy state of the church. "I wish your da could have lived to see it, my boy," he said as they pulled up in front of his house. "It's fair proud of you he'd be."

"I wish it, too, Mayor," Evan said at once. "I gave him much sorrow when I was younger. That grieves me now."

"Well, well, that's past, Evan," Watson said quickly as he pulled the rig up to his house. The two of them entered the house and the fragrances of food drifted around them. Mrs. Watson had arrived earlier, and now the three of them sat down to a good dinner. Once during the meal, Watson said, pointing with his fork at Evan, "I knew you'd grow up to be a fine man, Evan Morgan."

Evan resisted the smile that leaped to his lips. He had vivid memories of the clashes he'd had with the mayor but said only, "I was nothing to buy a stamp for in those days—but the Lord uses what he has to work with."

Mrs. Watson was a thin woman with fine blue eyes and a wealth of silver hair. "It's a blessing you've been to our people, Rev. Morgan. I'm hoping that you'll not leave soon."

"Leave? Why should he leave?" Watson demanded. "The pastor is getting on and when he steps down, what better man to fill his place than Evan Morgan, eh?"

Evan toyed with his teacup for a moment, then looked directly at his host. "I've been happy here, Mr. Watson. But as for the future, I'm not certain. If God wants me to stay, I'd count myself honored." He changed the subject and after visiting with the couple for a brief time, he left the house and started the walk back to his residence.

On the following Tuesday, he received a visit from Watson, who caught him just as he was leaving the house where he lived in a small room. "Ah, I was that afraid I'd miss you," Watson puffed. He pulled a letter from his coat pocket and extended it toward Evan. His eyes crinkled as he attempted to read the fine writing and he informed Evan, "It's from England. I thought it might be important." He was incurably curious and stood as close to Evan as possible, attempting to read the letter. "Not bad news, I hope?"

Evan looked up, smiled at the little man, then shook his head. "No. At least nobody's sick or dead."

"From Sir Gavin Wakefield, is it? I couldn't help seeing the seal."

"It's from an old friend of mine who lives with the Wakefields," Evan said calmly. He folded the letter, put it in his pocket, then said, "I'll have to be making my calls now, sir." The mayor was miffed, for he'd longed to hear what the noble family might have to say, but he said no more.

Evan went about his duties, which meant calling on the sick and infirm. The pastor was too frail to do much of this sort of thing, and as assistant pastor, Evan had taken the task on himself. He was a favorite with the members of the church—especially with those parents who had marriageable daughters! Trying to keep free from the snares that were set for him by mothers who wanted their girls to marry the pastor took considerable skill. However, he had managed to keep his marital status as a bachelor.

Only when he got home that afternoon did he pull the letter out and read it carefully. It was from Angharad and was brief:

My dear Evan,

We are well here, no plague and little sickness. Timothy Boggs went to be with God last week. He was very fond of you, and I know you will miss him.

Mr. Bunyan is becoming most popular as a preacher. He was elected as pastor of Bedford church, and the place is always overflowing. He gets invitations even from the big churches in London and elsewhere. His books have made him famous, and everyone wants to hear Bishop Bunyan!

My heart is heavy over this war with the Dutch. Amos must go to sea, of course. As must Gavin. The king issued an edict that all able-bodied must go into military service. And with Gavin's experience, they were especially insistent that he go to sea. I hate to see him leave, as does Susanne. But I feel certain God will return him to us safely. I only wish I felt the same about Amos. I have a burden, a heaviness, over Amos. I feel that he's going into some terrible danger, and never have I had such a shadow in my spirit! Amos laughs at me, of course, but I know that God is warning me.

Amos has done all he could to get Jenny to marry him before he leaves, but she says no. Hope and Darcy are engaged and will be married in the spring. They will be happy, I know.

I bless God for the mighty way he is using you, Evan. I pray that you will be used to bring many souls into God's kingdom.

Write when you can, and come if possible.

Angharad Wakefield

Evan found the letter disturbing. He read it many times, wondering why this should be. He prayed but got no clear answer. Finally he came to the conclusion that it was Angharad's fear for Amos that troubled him. He had never known her to be far wrong about things like this. She seemed to be so close to God that she just *knew* things that were hidden from others. The deeply mystic side of the Welsh character was highly developed in Angharad, and he could not get away from the uneasiness her fears had raised within him.

For several days he struggled with contradictory feelings. He was pleased with his ministry to his own people—yet there had never been a sense of permanence about his future. Many were urging him to stay, and that was tempting. Still, a nagging sense of concern for Amos would not leave him.

Finally he came to a decision. "I'm probably being a fool," he muttered after making up his mind, "but somehow I *have* to go with Amos to the war!" This made no sense and he knew that Amos would be difficult. Angharad had informed him that Amos was jealous of Evan's closeness to Jenny, and now to put himself forward would not be something Amos would welcome.

Leaving the village proved to be difficult, for Watson and the other elders pressed him to stay. "God is using you, Evan Morgan," they all said, and the pastor was so distressed he offered to step down and let Evan take his place. To all this Evan gently gave the same answer.

"God is speaking to me and I must obey his voice." He promised to return as soon as possible and left on an April morning.

As he rode out of the village on a fine horse—the gift of the congregation—he felt a stab of regret. However, he determined to follow what he thought was the will of God. He came to the same place where Jenny had come to him so long ago and, on a whim, spent the night there.

After building a fire and cooking his supper, he leaned against a thick oak and thought back to the night he met Jenny. The memory was clear and distinct in his mind, and he seemed to see her thin, youthful face as it had been that night. A smile touched his wide lips as he remembered her fright—such a birdlike thinness! He'd never forgotten how she'd pleaded with him, "Please, take me with you, sir!"

He poked the fire with a stick, sending myriad red, glowing sparks up toward the star-spangled sky. They died out quickly, but overhead the gleaming stars did their great dance. He traced the constellations absently, thinking of the events that had passed. He seemed to see Jenny as she grew from a thin, leggy girl of twelve into a young beauty of fifteen, then into the fullness of womanhood, with all its mystery. He could almost hear her laughter and smell the fragrance that she wore. Finally he recalled the kiss they'd shared—and the memory brought a pang to his heart.

He stared into the glowing coals for a long time, then sighed deeply and wrapped himself in his blanket. He rose the next morning, and there was a set in his jaw as he nudged his horse forward. *I have to let Jenny go. She'll never be mine and it's high time I accept it.*

For days Gavin labored to get affairs at Wakefield in order. He had spent much time and effort training his servants so that, in his absence, the many activities of the estate would go on efficiently. Now he sat with Angharad in the large study, the two of them going over a long list of necessary duties. They had worked on it for over two hours, and finally Gavin sighed and shoved his chair back. "Well, that's the lot, Mother."

Angharad looked tired, which was unusual for her. She was a strong woman with a store of energy that could not be matched by many younger women. Now she looked at Gavin, her dark eyes troubled. "I wish you didn't have to go, Gavin."

"Why, so do I, Mother. But I have no choice. The king has made it clear that Amos and I must serve." He noted the lines of fatigue in her face and was concerned. Rising from his chair, he came around the desk and put his hands on her shoulders. "Don't worry. Amos and I will be all right. We'll be very careful."

"How can you be careful in a battle? When you're in the cannon's mouth, anything can happen."

Knowing that she was right—and that she was too wise a woman to fool—Gavin shook his head. "There's no guarantee for any man who goes into battle. You'll just have to pray harder for us." Not wanting to prolong the scene, he said, "Amos isn't as keen to go this time. He's got his mind on romance. In a way, I wish Jenny had married him."

"So do I, Gavin."

"Why didn't she, I wonder?"

Angharad had thoughts about that, but she didn't want to

burden Gavin with them. "I suppose she just wants to be sure he's the right man to be her husband."

"Well, he tells me she'll marry him when he comes back."

"She hasn't promised, Gavin. She only said she'd give him an answer."

Gavin was puzzled by this. "I gave up a long time ago trying to understand women." He grinned, then rose and patted her shoulder. "Well, the place should run pretty well until we get back." He hesitated, then said quietly, "I expect to come back, Angharad—but just in case something happens, I want you to know how much you've meant to me all these years. No woman could have been a better mother than you." He lifted her up and embraced her warmly, then kissed her cheek. "Father got a gem when he got Angharad Morgan!"

Angharad was moved by his words. She loved her stepsons fervently, and now that they were going into battle, she needed all her faith to keep a smile on her face. "I have no fear for you, Gavin. God has given me perfect peace about your safety."

Gavin was surprised by this but was accustomed to Angharad's ways. However, he noted that there was something missing from her statement. "What about Amos?"

"I—I'm troubled about him," she said slowly. "Watch over him as close as you can. As captain you can't be everywhere—but pray much and do whatever you can."

"We'll be on different ships, Mother, but I'll do what I can." He was disturbed by her words, and after leaving her, he went at once to the stables where he found Amos unsaddling his horse. "I've been talking to Mother," he said abruptly. "She's worried about you."

"About me? What about you?" Amos was flushed after his ride and the sun of May had given his skin a slight burn. His dark blue eyes were curious as he turned to Gavin.

"She says she's not worried about me, that God's given her peace. But she's got some sort of fear for you."

"Mothers are like that."

"You know her better than that," Gavin said almost sternly. "She's the strongest person at Wakefield, Amos. And she's closer to God than any of us. If she's troubled, we've got to pay attention to her." He hesitated, then said, "I think you'd better stay home. I can get another officer to serve in your place."

"And I stay home like a baby?" Amos's sunburned face stiffened and a stubbornness came to his lips. "What would Father say if I did that? He never ducked a fight in his life."

Gavin knew that argument was useless, but for some time he tried to persuade Amos. Finally he gave up. "Very well, I suppose you'll have your way. But I'm glad you didn't marry Jenny."

"Well, I'm *not!"* Amos snapped. As soon as Gavin left, he gave his horse to a groom and went to find Jenny. She was not in the house and after questioning the servants, he finally discovered that she had gone with Corwin Mattox, who tended the sheep. He left at once, walking through the meadows until he saw the fleecy spots that moved across the fresh green grass. Scanning the field, he caught a glimpse of light blue and went at once to where Jenny was sitting with a tiny lamb in her lap.

"Oh, Amos," she spoke as he approached. "Look, he's brand new!" Her eyes were bright with excitement and she stroked the small animal, laughing as he uttered small sounds. "Isn't he sweet?"

"Yes, I suppose so," Amos said, then threw himself down beside her. "I've got to talk to you, Jenny," he said. "We're leaving day after tomorrow—and I want you to marry me before we go."

At once the smile left Jenny's face. She pushed the lamb off her lap and as he wobbled off, they stood. Turning to face Amos, she said quietly, "Please, let's not go into that. I've told you I'll give you an answer when you get back."

"What if I don't get back?" he demanded.

"Why—then I'll grieve for you," she said simply.

"Jenny, if I did get killed, if you were my wife, you'd have a place here always. You'd be a Wakefield. Wouldn't you like that?"

"It's . . . not that simple." Jenny struggled to explain how she felt, ending by saying, "Marriage is forever—at least, for as long as we live. I've watched so many couples who married unwisely. I think that most of our troubles in this life come because of marrying the wrong person." She put her hand on his chest, pleading, "Don't press me on this, Amos. It's for your sake as much as mine that I want us to wait."

Amos was frustrated and in his confusion made a rash assumption. "I think you won't marry me because of Evan."

The words struck with force against Jenny, so much so that her cheeks flushed. "You shouldn't think that," she whispered.

But Amos had seen her flush and noted that her hands trembled. He stared at her, anger rising in him. "He's not the man for you!" he protested. "He'll never be anything but a poor preacher. You'd have a terrible life, always struggling to get by! But as my wife, you'd have everything you wanted."

It was the wrong argument; Amos knew that as soon as he had spoken. Jenny lifted her head and said flatly, "And is marriage nothing more than pounds and pence, then? I tell you, Amos Wakefield, I'll not marry any man to be rich! If I loved a man, I'd wear rags and be proud!" She whirled and walked away, crying, "Let me alone, Amos!"

Amos felt anger and shame. He knew he was wrong but would not admit it. He turned and went back to the house, his mood black and gloomy. He said nothing to Gavin or Angharad about the quarrel, but when the two men left for Portsmouth, both Gavin and his stepmother noticed that the parting between Jenny and Amos was stiff and uncomfortable. As the two men rode out,

Angharad asked Jenny, "You two had words? Well, he's young, Jenny. Try to forgive him."

Jenny's eyes were tragic as she turned them to Angharad. "I'd never forgive myself if something happened to him, Lady Wakefield!" She turned away and for days was pale and quiet. Angharad was troubled as she had rarely been. She prayed more than ever, and finally, late one night, she found peace.

She was on her knees, almost in agony over Amos, and then, like a sudden ray of sun that dispels darkness, a peace swept over her. The worry and fear and anguish eased, and she slumped to the floor, weeping. Somehow she knew that God had answered and that Amos would be safe.

The next morning she went at once to Jenny, her face radiant. "It's all right, Jenny. God has told me that he will take care of Amos!"

"Oh, how wonderful!" Jenny felt a load lift from her spirit, for she sensed the victory that was in Angharad. "How will he do it?"

"I don't know—but God is faithful, Jenny. We will pray, but the victory is won. God will make a way!"

Captain Amos Wakefield of the *Intrepid* sat looking down at the list of able-bodied hands, noting that most of them had made a mark rather than sign their names. He nodded briefly at the gap-toothed sailor who looked more like a pirate than a sailor on a king's ship, saying, "Good to have you aboard, Simpson." As the man nodded and stepped aside, Amos blinked and picked up his quill, preparing to sign up the next man. He sat on the quarterdeck at a small desk, and the sun over the port side was brilliant.

"Next!" he rapped out, and against the sun, the man who stepped up was a mere blur. "Name?" he asked.

"Evan Morgan, sir. Gunner and foretopman."

Amos stiffened in surprise, recognizing Evan's voice. His mind seemed to go blank for a moment and he was aware that the bosun at his side, a lanky man named Swan, was surprised at his hesitation. "We need experienced gunners, Captain Wakefield," Swan offered. "Some of our men ain't never heard a cannon fire."

Amos nodded slowly and rose to move around the desk. He regarded Morgan unsmilingly. "I didn't expect to see you here."

Evan saw the animosity in Amos's eyes. It was no more than he'd been expecting. "I'd like to sail with you, sir," he said carefully. He'd reached Portsmouth two days earlier and had waited until word came that the *Intrepid* was signing hands for the action to come. He felt more than ever that God had led him to this duty and now waited for Amos to speak.

"You're a minister, Morgan," Amos said. "How do you feel about killing men? Is that in your gospel?"

"A man must fight or let him put skirts around his knees." Evan allowed a small smile to touch his lips. "I heard your father say that many a time, Captain Wakefield."

Swan stood watching the two, aware that some sort of tension had risen that he could not grasp. Obviously the captain knew this man—and he was not happy to see him. *Don't rightly know what's bothering the captain—maybe he don't like preachers. I don't care too much for 'em myself. But if he can lay a gun, I don't care if he's the pope; I'm glad to have 'im!*

Amos knew he had no choice. "All right, you'll do, Morgan." He sat down and had Evan sign his name, then said in the briefest of tones, "See you behave yourself."

Evan moved away and found a place to stow his gear. He was approached shortly by the first lieutenant, a stocky man named Croft with a cast eye. He said without preamble, "Captain Wakefield tells me you've had some experience on the guns."

"Yes, sir. I served under Captain Wakefield at Lowestoft in '65. He was a lieutenant then."

Lieutenant Croft considered Evan, then nodded. "You're a

preacher of some sort, I understand. Well, you're here to fight, not to preach. Do your duty and there'll be no problem." He shifted his weight, then added, "We're going up against Admiral De Ruyter again, Morgan. He's got a fine fleet and he's probably the best sailor alive." He studied the tall form of Morgan, then said, "Our men are green. I'll depend on you to get them trained. Can you do it?"

"I'll do my best, Lieutenant."

The fleet sailed three days later, and for Evan, life became frantic. Lieutenant Croft had not been wrong—the crew was as green as gourds. Only a handful of the men had even *heard* a cannon fired, and soon Evan was working fifteen hours a day training the raw crews. He was resented by some, for word got out that he was a minister. It was only after he had thrashed a hulking sailor that he got the full respect of the gun crews—a respect that only increased when he showed them that he was the hardest working man on the ship.

Amos saw Evan only briefly and had no conversation with him. He resented him more every day. Croft once said, "Thank God we've got Morgan! He's got the gun crews hopping, Captain!"

"He's doing his duty, Lieutenant," was his only remark, which made the lieutenant say to Swan, "Captain don't like Morgan. Bad blood somewhere."

"I'm sorry for that, but we need 'im, Lieutenant." Swan looked across at the fleet, which was bobbing up and down as they fought a headwind. "We've got ninety-eight ships—and God knows how many the Dutch have!"

The two fleets came together at Sole Bay on June 6. It was too late for battle, but action was certain the next day. Amos walked the deck, staring into the distance, trying to catch a glimpse of the enemy. He turned suddenly, aware that a sailor was at the rail. He recognized Evan and said roughly, "Get below, Morgan. We'll be in a fight tomorrow."

"Aye, sir."

But when Evan turned to leave, Amos could not stand the silence. "Why in God's name did you sign up on my ship?"

Evan halted and turned to face him. "I felt it was what God wanted me to do," he said simply.

Amos stared at him, and the question that had gnawed at him for weeks erupted. "Are you in love with Jenny?" he demanded.

"Yes, sir, but it will come to nothing."

The answer was not what Amos expected. He stared at Evan, then asked, "Is she in love with you?"

"That's not likely, sir," Evan answered. "We've been good friends, but I don't think I'll marry. The ministry is too hard a life for most women." He waited, then when Amos made no reply, he said, "Be careful in the battle, Amos."

Then he was gone and Amos stood alone at the rail. He was still dissatisfied with himself, but he knew that a man should not carry such thoughts into battle. He turned and went to his cabin, but no matter how hard he tried, he could not get the picture of Jenny out of his mind.

The battle of Sole Bay on June 7, 1672, was a hard-fought battle. Admiral De Ruyter surprised the English by his audacious tactics. He attacked though he had fewer ships, and the battle was hot and furious. The French squadron was prevented from coming to the aid of their English allies. The duke of York, brother to the king, was the English admiral. His flagship, the *Prince,* was beset on every side. She was practically destroyed and the duke shifted his flag to the *St. Michael.* When this vessel was also demolished, he shifted again to the *London.*

Captain Wakefield drove the *Intrepid* into the fiery center of action. He stood on deck with shot and shell ripping his canvas to shreds. Lieutenant Croft was killed in the battle, and finally the weight of the Dutch fire shot away most of the guns.

Below deck, Evan had fought until the last. The gun deck was littered with bodies and the sides of the ship were practically shot away. As the ship began to settle, the call came: "Abandon ship!"

Evan made his way to the main deck just in time to see one of the Dutch ships swing alongside, her guns run out. *They'll be loaded with grapeshot,* he thought. Such fire would kill every man on the deck of the *Intrepid,* for the range was no more than one hundred feet.

The ships were closing, and it was then that Evan saw Amos Wakefield. He was working with the steersman, trying to bring the ship about. His back was to the Dutch ship, and the hail of deadly metal that was about to sweep the decks would not miss.

"Amos!" Evan cried out, but the booming of cannons from the ships around them drowned out his voice. He raced desperately across the deck, which was slippery with blood and cluttered with wreckage. He had one thought: to get to Wakefield and pull him down to the deck.

He arrived just as he heard the booming of the Dutch guns. He managed to throw himself at Amos, clutching his friend's shoulders and dragging him down—but a fiery fist seemed to strike him in the back. He was driven to the deck, and the last thing he heard before he slipped into unconsciousness was Amos's voice crying out his name.

Twenty-Five

Love is Forever

Evan struggled to pull himself out of the dark currents that seemed to suck him deeper and deeper into darkness, but pain swept him like a flood. It was easier to slip back into the restful oblivion than to fight, so time after time he allowed himself to drop away into the warm ebony pool.

He was aware at times of voices. They seemed to be coming from far away, and he could only make out a few words such as his name. Hands touched him—sometimes roughly, so that he escaped the agony they brought by dropping away into the place of darkness where he knew nothing.

Sometimes, though, the hands were gentle, bringing a soothing sensation to his body. He came to recognize that touch and allowed himself to emerge, sometimes almost coming to the light, to where the voices were, somewhere above him. He was like a swimmer held far down in dark depths, aware that above there was light and warmth and cheer. But every time he tried to rise to those things, the pain came, stabbing and slashing with keen, burning blades.

Once, when the touch of the soft hands had soothed him greatly, he emerged far enough to hear a voice calling his name, begging him to wake and come out of his dark cavern.

"Evan! Evan! Please, come back to me!"

He knew that voice! Out of all the voices that had floated to him, that one touched a chord of memory and he struggled to reach out and answer. He seemed to be paralyzed, his body dead—except for the pain—but as the voice pleaded, he found that he could move his lips. He tried to speak and finally managed a parody of a word that sounded even to his own ears like a feeble croak.

"Jenny—!"

At once he heard the voice again, this time coming clearly, calling his name. He felt the pull to fall away, to leave the light and the world of pain, but he was aware that if he did, he might well never return. Wrestling with all his might, he managed to open his eyes. The light hurt them, but he peered out of mere slits. Everything seemed to swarm—colors swirled madly for a moment so that he was forced to shut his eyes. He swallowed, then opened them cautiously—and there was a face!

The features were blurred at first, then they sharpened and came into focus. It was a kind face, but with sorrow in the deep green eyes. It was a woman with reddish blonde hair—and out of the past, Evan's memories came, first in bits and fragments, then finally all together.

"Jenny—is it you?"

"Yes, Evan, it's Jenny."

He felt a drop touch his face and looked up to see that tears were running down her cheeks. He tried to reach up and wipe them away, but found he was very weak. Licking his lips, which seemed to be dry as paper, he whispered, "Don't cry. . . ." He looked around the room and after a moment spoke slowly. "This is—my old room, isn't it?"

"Yes, Evan." Jenny wiped her eyes with a handkerchief and then bent over him. "Don't try to talk for a little while. Are you thirsty?"

"Yes!"

Jenny quickly poured water into a cup, then held his head up as he drank noisily. "Not so much, Evan. You can have more a little later."

He struggled to put things together and finally said, "I was in a battle—on the *Intrepid*. And I got shot."

"Yes, you've been very sick."

He looked at her curiously. "How long have I been here?"

"Nearly two weeks. You were shot in the back and the doctors were afraid you'd die." She took a pitcher, filled a basin, then came to bathe his face. Her touch was light and he smelled the fragrance of lilac. He studied her face as she bathed him, marveling at the smoothness of her skin and the freshness of her features. He tried to move and pain shot along his back. He winced.

"Don't move! You've still got some bad wounds." She finished bathing his face, then asked doubtfully, "I need to change the dressings on your back. But I don't want you to—to fall away." She bit her lip. "Can you stand it, Evan?"

"Yes."

He gritted his teeth at the hot pain that seared him, but managed to sit up while she changed the dressings on his back. He lay back with a gusty release of his breath. "How bad am I?"

"You were struck with four shells, small balls. Three of them weren't serious, but one of them was very deep. It got infected and you've been in a coma. Your fever was so high you almost died. I—I think the only thing that saved you was when we wrapped you in cold, wet sheets."

He listened intently, but then hunger struck him like a mailed fist. "May I have something to eat?" he asked abruptly—and was surprised to see her smile.

"You must be better if you're thinking about food! Yes, I'll go get some broth. You lie still now!"

Jenny left and Evan lay still, avoiding the pain that movement sent along the nerves of his back. He tried to remember the fight, and flashes of it came to him. He was very weak—weaker than he'd ever been in his life. When he tried to lift both hands, he could barely manage it. He snorted and whispered, "There's an old weakling you are, Evan Morgan!"

The door opened and Angharad came in, her face alight with a smile. "It's awake you are," she said, coming to kiss his cheek. "You gave us quite a fright." She stood over him, soothing his hair back from his forehead, a strange look in her dark eyes. "God used you well, Evan," she whispered.

"All I did was get shot," he protested wryly.

Angharad stared at him with surprise. "You don't remember how you were wounded?"

"Why, the Dutch ship raked us with grape."

"That it did, but don't you remember running to Amos?" She saw that he did not and reached down and took his hand. It seemed frail and weak, and she held it tightly. "Amos had his back to the enemy and didn't know they were about to rake the deck. You saw it and ran to him. The bosun, Mr. Swan, saw the whole thing."

"I don't remember it."

"You came and threw yourself between the guns and Amos. When they fired, you took the balls that would have killed him." Angharad squeezed his hand and her eyes grew warm. "Now we know why you had to go to sea, don't we, Evan? If you hadn't been there, Amos would have been killed!"

Somehow Angharad's words made Evan uncomfortable. "I'm glad he's all right," he said finally. "What about Gavin?"

"Not a scratch. Both of them are home now. They'll be wanting to talk to you—" She broke off as Jenny came in bearing a silver tureen. "Aye," she remarked, smiling down at her nephew. "Now, this is what you need. It's sick we both are of having to ladle soup down your gullet!"

Evan felt like a fool as the two women made over him. He

protested that he was able to feed himself, but after spilling a spoonful of the hot broth on his bare chest, Jenny said firmly, "It's a big baby you are, Evan Morgan! Now open your mouth and let me feed you like one!"

As soon as Evan finished the broth, he fell asleep so suddenly that Jenny was alarmed. But Angharad assured her, "It's all right, Jenny. He's begun to heal. In a few days it'll take both of us to hold him in that bed."

Jenny looked down at the thin face on the pillow, and the sight of him so weak and helpless pulled at her. Angharad said gently, "Now, you've missed enough sleep. Get you to bed. He'll be fine now."

Jenny made her way out of the room and started to her own. She was groggy with lack of sleep, for she had nursed Evan night and day since he'd been brought by Gavin and Amos back to Wakefield. As she passed the entrance to Gavin's study, she glanced in and saw the two men engaged in some sort of work on the desk.

"Evan's all right," she stopped to announce. Her face was drawn and thin, and there were shadows under her eyes. "He woke up a little while ago, and Lady Wakefield says he's going to be well."

"Fine! Fine!" Gavin exclaimed. He came to Jenny asking questions but then noticed that she was almost trembling with fatigue. "Go get some rest, my dear," he said gently. When she turned and continued down the hallway, he turned to Amos, relief on his features. "That's good news!" he said fervently.

"Yes, it is," Amos said briefly. He shook his head and added, "I don't think I could have stood it if he'd died—for me."

"It was a noble thing to do, wasn't it?

"More than you know, Gavin," Amos confessed. "I—gave Evan a hard time on the ship. I was jealous and treated him badly."

Gavin had not been blind to Amos's jealousy, but now said, "Well, he's going to be all right. You can make it up to him."

"Yes, I'll do that."

Amos walked out of the room and Gavin stared after him. *He's not happy—but I guess I'd be the same. To have your rival save your life, that would be pretty hard to take!* He thought suddenly of Jenny and how she'd practically worked around the clock taking care of Evan—and his brow creased with concern. *One of them's going to get her—which means that the other one's going to be a miserable wretch!*

"Hope's going to make a beautiful bride, isn't she?"

Evan had been walking along the pathway that led to the woods that banked Wakefield. He was making his first effort at managing without his cane and moved very carefully. Glancing at Jenny, who was matching his slow pace, he nodded. "Yes, she is." He studied the wealth of tiny flowers that carpeted the ground, then added, "She's going to be a handful for Mr. Wingate."

Jenny stopped and stared at him, her green eyes indignant. "Well, I like that! I think it's the other way around—she's going to have *her* hands full with Darcy!"

Evan took a deep breath of the fresh, warm air. It was late June and every tree was laden with bright leaves, and the flowers almost burned the earth with their brilliant colors. "I don't think I've ever seen a more beautiful summer," he murmured. "Maybe because I came close to not seeing it at all."

Jenny shook her head, sending her strawberry blonde hair into shimmering waves. "Don't change the subject," she insisted. A smile touched her red lips and she tossed her head in a saucy gesture. "Why will Hope be a handful?" she demanded.

Evan could not keep the smile from his lips. "Because she's strong willed," he commented. "Her father spoiled her and she'll expect a husband to do the same."

"She's very sweet!"

"That she is, when she gets her own way. I suppose all of us are like that, though." He walked slowly down the pathway, studying the arabesque pattern made by the bricks, then added thoughtfully, "And he's a poor man, Jenny. Hope's been used to the finest things all her life. Now she'll be married to a man who can't give her all those things."

"Those things don't matter."

"You know better," Evan admonished her. "When you grow up with nothing, it's not so hard to do without. But once a person has wealth and the things money will buy, it's hard for them to go back."

Jenny said nothing to that and kept silent so long that he finally stopped and looked down at her. "You don't agree with me, do you?"

"No, I don't." Jenny was wearing an emerald green dress with white lace on the cuffs and bodice. It fit her snugly, setting off her figure to the best advantage. "When I was on the stage in London, I saw people doing everything for money—but Hope's not like them."

Evan nodded. "I think you're right. She's a fine young woman. She'll be satisfied with whatever comes. It's Mr. Wingate who'll have trouble."

"Why—he's very much in love with her!"

"Yes, and he'll grieve because he can't give her all the things she's always had," Evan countered. "He may not say so, but he can't help but wish he could provide for her."

They came to a bridge that spanned the small stream that fed into the river. They paused to stand on the structure. As they watched the clear water bubbling underneath, Jenny once again fell silent. Ever since Evan had come to recover at Wakefield, she'd thrown herself into bringing him back to health. Amos had watched her carefully and to her surprise had said nothing about marriage. She'd been expecting him to pressure her for the answer she'd promised, but he had yet to mention it. With Hope's marriage approaching, she thought surely he'd ask her, but he had not.

"Look!" Evan said, grasping her arm. "I'd like to catch that fellow!" He pointed with his free hand to the shadow of a large pike that lay under a lily pad.

Jenny glanced at the fish but was intensely conscious of Evan's touch on her arm. She felt a strange stirring in her breast and pulled away. Evan turned to her at once, a flush on his cheeks. "I'm sorry," he said quietly. "I didn't mean to grab you like that."

"It's—it's all right," she answered. She felt awkward and ill at ease. While he'd been helpless she'd tended him with something like a strong maternal instinct—but what was in her now was far different. Ashamed that she held so little control over her emotions, she turned away. "I have to get back. I promised to help Hope with her dress."

Evan watched her walk back toward the house, aware that he'd made a mistake. He hobbled along the pathway alone, thinking of the days that had passed. He had made fine progress physically, but there was an odd sense of frustration that surfaced in him from time to time. He felt it strongly as he walked for an hour. Finally he returned to the house.

He was sitting in his room an hour later, staring at the wall, when a knock at the door startled him. "Come in," he called and was surprised when Amos entered.

"Sorry to bother you," Amos said at once. "But Mr. Bunyan is here."

"Is he now?" Evan rose and would have left the room, but Amos stopped him.

"Evan, I've tried to thank you for saving my life . . . but how does a man do that?"

"Why, it's done, sir," Evan said instantly. Amos had tried to speak of the thing once, but Evan had been embarrassed and made light of what he had done. "Don't think of it."

"That might be easy for you, but it's hard for me." Amos had steeled himself for this meeting and now faced Evan squarely. "I was riding this morning, and it came to me that I'd be dead and buried if you hadn't taken the shot in my place." His eyes grew cloudy and he shook his head slowly. "I can't make that up to you, Evan."

"No need to," Evan protested. "Your family's done so much for me, I'd not be much of a man if I didn't do all I could to return the kindness."

Amos stared directly into Evan's eyes. "You know what makes it worse, don't you?"

Evan did not pretend he didn't understand. Slowly he nodded. "Aye. Jenny."

"Yes. I've always been jealous of what she feels for you. You've known about that for a long time." Amos dropped his eyes and stared at the pattern in the carpet for a long moment, then lifted his head. "I can't pretend I'm happy that it was *you* who saved my life. I'd rather it were any other man!"

Evan nodded again. "It's honest of you to say so. But I wish you'd put it out of your mind." He sought for words and finally said simply, "I want you to know, Amos, I'll never ask Jenny to share my life. It's too hard for a woman. Can you trust me with that?"

"I've never known you to lie," Amos said. He was still nervous and unsatisfied, but he put his hand out. "I take you at your word."

Evan managed a smile. "I'll be leaving after the wedding. But now, let's go down and greet Bishop Bunyan."

The two men descended the stairs and found Bunyan engaged in an animated conversation with Angharad and Gavin. Susanne and Hope came in at the same time, and Darcy Wingate, who had come with Bunyan, went to greet his fiancée.

"Ah, here's the hero, home from the war." Bunyan beamed, coming to shake Evan's hand. He was heavier and his face was sunburned so that he looked the picture of health. "Now then, tell me about your adventures, Evan."

"No, tell us about what's happened to *you,*" Evan countered. He had no wish to discuss the war, but he was intensely glad to learn of Bunyan's status.

"Why, I'm a free man!" Bunyan exclaimed. He turned to Darcy, smiling broadly. "Tell them the legal end of the thing, Mr. Wingate."

Darcy turned from Hope, saying, "Why, the thing is done! The king has issued a full pardon to Mr. Bunyan."

"And you can come back to Bedford, Evan," Bunyan added. "This time we won't have to hide in barns to do our preaching."

Every eye turned to Evan, and he said at once, "That's an enticing offer, Mr. Bunyan, but I'm obliged to go back to Wales."

He saw that Jenny had entered the room and when he said this, she seemed startled. He had neither the time nor the inclination to say more. He joined the group that moved into the dining room, where Angharad had the servants bring refreshments. As the group ate, Bunyan gave the details of the pardon. When he was ready to leave, he pulled Evan aside for a private word outside.

"Well, my boy, you're looking well," Bunyan said as he took the reins in his hand. He examined the younger man carefully. "Must it be Wales, then? We need you in England. Now that Charles has opened the door, I'm expecting a great revival."

"For now, God is telling me to go back. But I can't say what will be in the future."

Bunyan stepped forward and embraced Evan. "I'll never forget you," he said huskily. "We found God in that foul cell—so we'll find him now wherever he puts us!"

"Amen!" Evan said. He watched as Bunyan mounted and then rode off. As he turned away, he was aware that he'd never meet a man with more of God in him than John Bunyan. When he entered the house, all the talk was about the wedding. He sat quietly, saying little, and tried to put his mind on Wales—but he found that the thought of going back was a heavy one. It didn't help that Jenny and Amos were drawn apart from the group, speaking in a rather animated fashion. At once he averted his eyes and walked to his room. For a long time he sat staring out the window, struggling with his thoughts, then said heavily, "This is no good! I'll have to stay for the wedding, but then it's back to Wales for me!"

"You two are now husband and wife, for as long as you both shall live."

As the minister pronounced the final words of the ceremony, Darcy squeezed Hope's hand. She turned her radiant face to him and took his kiss.

"Now—you can't ever get away from me," he whispered. The two of them turned and moved out of the church and as soon as they were outside in the bright sunlight, they were besieged by family and friends. For a long time Evan stood in the doorway of the church, watching as the festivities continued. He was slightly startled when a voice interrupted his thoughts.

"They'll be very happy, I think."

Evan had stayed in the background during all the activities that had made Wakefield hum for days. Now he turned to find Angharad standing beside him. She was watching him with a contented light in her eyes, and he'd rarely seen her looking so well.

"Yes, I think they will. They love each other very much." Evan's voice was low and Angharad looked at him. He seemed dispirited.

Noting her intent gaze, he stirred himself with an effort, adding, "They'll probably have their troubles, but that's part of marriage, isn't it?"

Angharad nodded. "That it is." She hesitated, then said, "I wish you'd stay on here, Evan. Mr. Bunyan wants you to help him with the church in Bedford. And Rev. Symes would help you find a church close to Wakefield. I'd like to have you close."

Evan was touched by the woman's words. She was the closest relative he had in the world and the thought of leaving her pained him. He shook his head, however, saying, "I couldn't stay here, Angharad."

His simple statement, she knew, covered more than he would ever speak of. Angharad nodded slowly. "Never give up on what is real," she said abruptly. When he gave her a puzzled look, she said, "You love Jenny, but you've given up on having her."

"I've promised Amos I'd not ask her to marry me."

"That was a foolish promise!"

"Angharad, I can't give her anything. All I have is the clothes on my back."

"Don't be a fool!" Angharad's voice was sharp and her eyes were fixed on the young man with something like anger. "You remember that fool Jephthah in the book of Judges?"

"Why, yes—"

"He made a foolish vow to give as a sacrifice the first thing that met him after a battle. What should that end up being but his own daughter! He made a bad vow, but it was worse to *keep* it!"

Evan considered Angharad with surprise. "You love Jenny, and Amos is your son. Why are you speaking like this?"

"Because if she doesn't love him the way a woman should love a man, she'll not be a good daughter-in-law, any more than she'll be a good wife!"

Evan dropped his head, thinking hard. When he lifted his eyes to her, he said, "I think she does love him, Angharad . . . but in any case, I can't come to her. I can't break my word to Amos." He suddenly reached out and hugged her, saying huskily, "I'll be leaving right away. But I'll come back to visit, though it may be a long time."

Angharad held him close, then watched as he strode toward the house. She saw that Jenny was standing alone, watching Evan go. At once she moved toward her. "Jenny, come with me," she said abruptly. "We must talk."

Evan didn't notice the two women, for he was sick at heart. He went at once to his house and gathered up his belongings. In the stables, as he was saddling his horse, one of the stable hands came to ask, "Why, you ain't leavin' are you, Evan?"

"Yes, Dick." He cinched the saddle, then turned to slap Dick on the shoulder. "Going back to Wales."

Foster stared at him with surprise. "Why, you might as well wait and get a good start in the morning. Not more'n an hour or so of daylight left."

"I'll camp out by the big bend in the river where we caught the big pike, remember?" Evan swung into the saddle and rode out with a wave of his hand. The sun was falling behind the castle, and the battlements were outlined against a crimson sky. He turned away and spurred the horse, putting as much distance as he could between himself and all that the place held for him.

By the time he reached the river, darkness was falling, and he quickly dismounted and built a small fire. He unsaddled his horse, fed him part of the grain he'd brought, then went to sit beside the river. It was a quiet night with only a whisper of a breeze. The water purled at his feet, making a sibilant whisper. Overhead the stars began to appear. For over an hour he sat there, thinking of many things. Finally a restlessness took him and he moved away from the river.

The fire was burned down to glowing ashes and he carefully tended it by feeding small twigs into it until it blazed up again.

He didn't need the fire but had always liked the cheerful sound of crackling wood. He watched as the red-and-yellow flames swayed in the slight breeze, and he tried to think about the future.

Finally he gave up and stretched out beside the fire. The warmth of the earth came to him, and after a time he seemed to hear the earth roll under him. It was a fancy of his—one that amused him—to think that he could feel the motion of the rolling ball of planet Earth. He put his hands under his head and stared up at the glittering stars. "You're bigger than I am, but you can't do the things a man can do!"

He lay there quietly, his mind going over the past, and time after time he had to pull it away from thoughts of what might have been. Once, he rose and built up the fire, then lay back. He finally dozed, but came awake with a start when a sound broke the silence of the night. Quickly he came to his feet, stepping back from the glowing coals.

"Who's there?" he called out as a horse cast a black shadow to his right. His own horse nickered, and Evan put his hand on the dagger at his belt. Traveling was a dangerous business at times, and he stepped back to the shelter of the trees, his eyes alert.

"Evan? Is that you?"

Shock ran along Evan's nerves. "Jenny!" Moving forward, he came to catch the bridle of the horse and stare up at her. "What are you doing here?"

Jenny slipped from the horse but said nothing. Evan tried to catch a glimpse of her face but could see little, for she had the cowl of her cloak over her head. "Well, let me tie your horse," he said and soon had that chore accomplished. He moved to bend over the fire, tossing on several dry sticks. As it flamed up, he turned to her. "Now, what's all this?"

Jenny loosed the tie of the hood and it fell back over her shoulders. Her hair was down and the flickering light of the fire made reddish glints in it. Her face, Evan saw, was pale and there was an intense soberness in her features. "Is somebody sick?" Evan demanded. "What *is* it, girl?"

Jenny turned to put her hands out to the fire. "The stable hand, Dick, told me you'd be here," she said finally, keeping her face averted. Now that she was in this place, the urgency that had driven her to follow him seemed foolhardy. All the way from Wakefield she had tried to think what she could say to Evan, but now it all sounded strange and forced even to her. "I . . . had to talk to you," she said finally. Then she turned to face him, her eyes enormous. "Why did you leave without saying good-bye?"

Evan shrugged his shoulders. He tried to think of how to explain his abrupt departure, but finally said honestly, "Jenny, I just couldn't face it. I'm sorry. But you shouldn't have come out here all alone. It's dangerous."

Jenny's lips curved slightly. "I came to you out of the night once before," she said. "You treated me pretty roughly, Evan. Do you remember?"

"Aye." Evan's mind went back to that time, and he said gently, "That was a long time ago, Jenny. You were just a little girl then, with no place to go." The sight of her stirred him more than he had thought possible, and he shut his mind firmly to the power of his feelings for her. "You're not a little girl now . . . and you've got a place to go."

"Have I, Evan?"

"Why, of course you have!"

Jenny moved closer to him, her face turned upward. There was a vulnerability about her as she reached up and touched his chest. "Do you remember what I asked you that night we met?"

He gazed down at her, feeling as though he were falling into her emerald eyes. His pulse pounded and he struggled to keep himself from touching her face. "I've never forgotten." His voice was low and husky. "You said, 'Take me with you.'"

Jenny hesitated, then put her other hand on Evan's arm. Her

voice was quiet, yet it seemed to vibrate with a quality he had never heard before.

"Take me with you, Evan!"

Evan Morgan was struck dumb. Her words seemed to echo in the silence of the night air—and in his heart. For one brief moment he was overwhelmed with the desire to crush her to him, to bury his face in her hair and let the wonder of her surround him. Then reason returned and he swallowed painfully.

"I can't do that, Jenny!" he said finally.

"Why not? Don't you love me?" Jenny whispered.

It was more than he could bear. He reached out and put his hands on her shoulders. "Yes!" His voice was hoarse with emotion. "Yes, I love you! But I've promised Amos . . . I told him I would never ask you to marry me. That I could never take you from all you have at Wakefield and ask you to share a life of hardship with me. You deserve better."

Jenny's eyes shimmered with unshed tears and she slowly reached up, slid her hands to rest at the back of his neck, and pulled his head down. He knew he should resist, should stop her from such a foolhardy action . . . but he didn't. Her lips were soft, yet somehow demanding under his, and he could no more help putting his arms around her than he could help breathing. She nestled in his embrace, offering him, with a shattering sweetness, all that she was.

After a long moment, Evan raised his head and stared into her face, his eyes searching as though to find an answer. "Jenny . . . sweet, sweet Jenny. I do love you. I have for a long time." He closed his eyes in despair and leaned his forehead against hers, forcing the words that threatened to destroy him through his lips. "But I can't marry you."

"Because of Amos?"

"Aye, in part. I gave my word."

"But you're not asking me to marry you. I'm asking *you!*"

Jenny smiled at the look on Evan's face. "I know women aren't supposed to do that, but Angharad suggested it and you know how wise she is. I felt it was only prudent to follow her counsel."

"Angharad!"

"Yes, Evan. She came to me and helped me see that I'd never be a good wife to Amos." Jenny stirred slightly in Evan's embrace, her eyes thoughtful. "She truly is wise, Evan! She said she'd known for a long time I didn't love Amos enough to be his wife. And she told me—" She broke off abruptly, as though she had said more than she had intended.

"Told you what?" Evan demanded.

"She said that I loved you."

Evan stared at her, dumbfounded. "What about Amos?"

"I talked to him, Evan. He was angry, but he'll get over it. Even he understood that I would be doing us all an injustice to marry one man while loving another."

An owl floated overhead, his shadow dancing across the two who stood so close, holding each other.

Evan wanted desperately to give in to Jenny, to take what she offered and claim her as his wife, his love. But his troubled heart would not let him off so easily. "Jenny, I love you, but—"

Jenny put her hand over his lips, cutting his words short. "Evan, I'm not afraid of poverty. I'm only afraid of one thing. All my life I've been afraid of it."

He turned his face into her palm, kissing the soft skin that restrained his words. Then he took her hand in his own and held it. "What are you afraid of, Jenny?"

She was very still, then turned her face toward him. "All my life I've been afraid I'd never find someone to love me. When I was on the stage, men came to me offering me all sorts of things. Faith, even the king made an offer! But I knew that none of them loved *me.* It was always something else." Her body grew tense and she asked, "Evan . . . do you love me? Will you love me always?"

He held her gaze as emotions washed over him. Eyes shining with confidence, he nodded. "Aye, love. Forever. For always. I will love you until this life is ended . . . and then, when we are with our Lord, I will love you for eternity."

He drew her close and kissed her gently. She leaned against him, savoring the tenderness and strength of the arms that held her. And, as he kissed her, she knew that she had come into harbor. She finally drew back to look at him, tears in her eyes. When she spoke, her voice was a broken whisper. "I thought—I thought I'd lost you, my dear!"

"Never!" he pledged, filled with the knowledge that he held the world in his arms. "I know now that God has brought us together, and you will never lose me." He buried his hands in her luxurious hair. "Don't you know, my Jenny, when I have you, I have the world! That's what you'll always be: my world!"

Jenny's tears ran down her cheeks, and she touched Evan's face. "We'll go back to Wakefield, and then God will tell us what to do."

The full moon broke from behind a cloud and washed the world with silver, but the two who stood beside the dying fire were not aware of it. From far away a bell sounded, making a faint melody, but they did not hear it. They saw and heard only each other.

Finally Evan stepped back from Jenny, reaching down to take her hand in his own. "Aye, Jenny. Let's go home."

They broke camp, doused the fire, then mounted their horses and left the clearing. As the sound of their horses' hooves faded, silence fell on the small spot. A tiny mouse emerged from a burrow, stared at the scene with silver eyes, then scratched his ear. Finally he picked up a seed and nibbled nonchalantly as the clouds veiled the moon.

THE END

In addition to this series . . .

THE WAKEFIELD DYNASTY

#1 The Sword of Truth 0-8423-6228-2
#2 The Winds of God 0-8423-7953-3
#3 The Shield of Honor 0-8423-5930-3

. . . look for more captivating historical fiction from Gilbert Morris!

THE APPOMATTOX SAGA

Intriguing, realistic stories capture the emotional and spiritual strife of the tragic Civil War era.

#1 A Covenant of Love 0-8423-5497-2
#2 Gate of His Enemies 0-8423-1069-X
#3 Where Honor Dwells 0-8423-6799-X
#4 Land of the Shadow 0-8423-5742-4
#5 Out of the Whirlwind 0-8423-1658-2
#6 The Shadow of His Wings 0-8423-5987-7
#7 Wall of Fire 0-8423-8126-0
#8 Stars in Their Courses 0-8423-1674-4

RENO WESTERN SAGA

A Civil War drifter faces the challenges of the frontier, searching for a deeper sense of meaning in his life.

#1 Reno 0-8423-1058-4
#2 Rimrock 0-8423-1059-2
#3 Ride the Wild River 0-8423-5795-5
#4 Boomtown 0-8423-7789-1
#5 Valley Justice 0-8423-7756-5
#6 Lone Wolf 0-8423-1997-2

Just for kids

THE OZARK ADVENTURES

Barney Buck and his brothers learn about spiritual values and faith in God through outrageous capers in the back hills of the Ozarks.

#1 The Bucks of Goober Holler 0-8423-4392-X
#2 The Rustlers of Panther Gap 0-8423-4393-8
#3 The Phantom of the Circus 0-8423-5097-7